Dandy Gilver and an Unsuitable Day for a Murder

CATRIONA McPHERSON

Dandy Gilver and an Unsuitable Day for a Murder

HODDER &
STOUGHTON

First published in Great Britain in 2010 by Hodder & Stoughton
An Hachette UK company

I

Copyright © Catriona McPherson 2010

A CIP catalogue record for this title is available from the British Library.

Hardback ISBN 978 0 340 99297 5

Typeset in Plantin Light by Palimpsest Book Production Limited,
Falkirk, Stirlingshire

Printed and bound in the UK by Clays Ltd, St Ives plc

Hodder & Stoughton policy is to use papers that are natural, renewable and
recyclable products and made from wood grown in sustainable forests.
The logging and manufacturing processes are expected to conform
to the environmental regulations of the country of origin.

Hodder & Stoughton Ltd
338 Euston Road
London NW1 3BH

www.hodder.co.uk

For Louise Kelly, with love.

Thanks to

Lisa Moylett, Suzie Doore, Francine Toon, Imogen Olsen, Alice Laurent, Jessica Hische and Katie Davison.

Bronwen Salter-Murison, for designing and maintaining the Dandy Gilver website.

Sharron McColl, Dorothy Hall and Jeanette MacMillan of the Local History Dept in the Carnegie Library, Dunfermline and library user James Fraser, for information about old Dunfermline.

Louise Kelly, for unflagging support and unsettling craftwork.

And Neil.

One of the differences between academia and fiction-writing that I cherish most is no longer having to record and then cite all my sources, but I must mention the insanely detailed and unexpectedly riveting Lee E Gray, (2002), *From Ascending Rooms to Express Elevators: A History of the Passenger Elevator in the Nineteenth Century* (Mobile, Ala: Elevator World, Inc.), without which Aitkens' lift would still be a mystery to me.

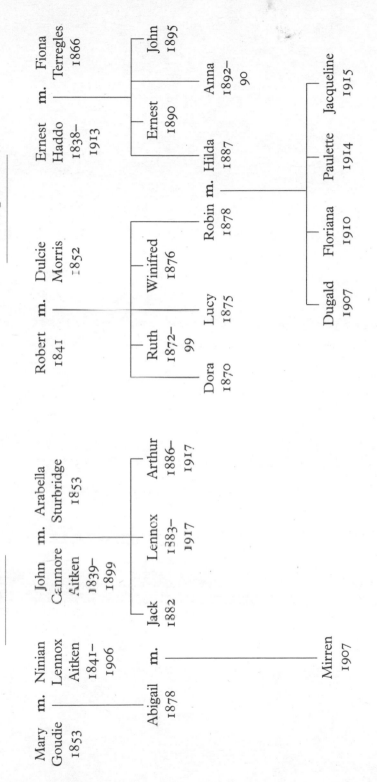

The Aitkens

Mary Goudie 1853 **m.** Ninian Lennox Aitken 1841–1906

John Canmore Aitken 1839–1899 **m.** Arabella Sturbridge 1853

Abigail 1878

Jack 1882 — Lennox 1883–1917 — Arthur 1886–1917

Mirren 1907

The Hepburns

Robert 1841 **m.** Dulcie Morris 1852

Ernest Haddo 1838–1913 **m.** Fiona Terregles 1866

Dora 1870 — Ruth 1872–99 — Lucy 1875 — Winifred 1876

Ernest 1890 — Anna 1892–90 — John 1895

Robin 1878 **m.** Hilda 1887

Dugald 1907 — Floriana 1910 — Paulette 1914 — Jacqueline 1915

Prologue

15th May 1927

Darling,

I wish you would tell me what is wrong. I cannot imagine what it is I have done to make you angry with me or what someone might have said to turn you against me so. If you refuse to meet me or speak to me when I ring you up how can I make it right again? I know that you love me as I love you and I am going to trust that whatever has happened to upset you it will pass and you will be my same old darling again soon.

Your Dearest xxx

17th May 1927

Dearest,

We have had more happy times this spring than some people get in their lifetimes and must count ourselves fortunate for them. I will treasure the memory of your love as long as I live. I am not what you thought I was and not what I myself thought I was either. I cannot explain and I must not see you again but you surely know that my heart is yours for ever.

Your Darling xxx

I

Whatever I was expecting when I decided to take a turn around Dunfermline – I was early for my appointment and it was a particularly pleasant day – it was not this air of jubilance. Indeed, if one were taxed with naming five jubilant towns and ran out of inspiration after Paris, Barcelona, New Orleans and Rio one would not search for the fifth in Scotland's Gazetteer. (And if one were taxed with naming five jubilant towns in Scotland and did not, for some reason, face the facts and pay the forfeit right away, I daresay Dunfermline would still not spring to mind.)

Yet I could not help but notice that, today at least, the whole town effervesced in the most remarkable way. The whole city, I should properly say, for – as Hugh never tires of reminding me with much retelling of the glories of King Robert and the shenanigans of Malcolm Canmore – Dunfermline *is* a city and one groaning with history too: the birthplace of Charles I and more lately (not to mention more beneficially to the world at large) Andrew Carnegie. Indeed I was passing the Carnegie Library now, thinking how generous it was of him to endow it, since here was one place he might have been sure to get a library named after him anyway.

As for the present mood, the weather had to be responsible for some of it, but soft spring sunshine and the kind of gentle breeze that teases at hat ribbons and turns the new leaves over to show their silvery undersides only go so far and further explanation was needed for the exuberance of the window displays in all the small shops along Abbot Street and up the Kirkgate, the newly planted flower beds glimpsed through the park gates, as neat as samplers with their white pansies and pink tulips stitched into the smooth brown backing, and the giddy high spirits of the girls who flitted about in giggling pairs and threesomes, all decked out in their new spring costumes and with their shingles glistening.

There was plenty for them to see: behind the plate-glass windows of a department store called – rather splendidly – House of Hepburn (Hosiers, Glovers, Clothiers and Milliners), instead of the expected outcrops of sensible hats and pyramids of sturdy china there was a series of tableaux showing a beautiful mannequin girl accompanied by a broad-shouldered mannequin admirer, the pair set before a succession of lurid backdrops and dressed in the height of fashion for golf, tennis, the seaside, and – against the most improbable backcloth of all – yachting, complete with ice buckets and open picnic hampers. In the seaside window, I was almost sure, they stood on real sand.

I walked on. At another department store further up on the High Street – Aitkens' Emporium (Tailors, Mantle Makers, Silk Merchants, Domestic Bazaar): no less splendid, with just as many enormous windows *and* a revolving door – one could hardly see the sensible hats and sturdy china for exotic arrangements of ostrich and peacock feathers in urns, silver-sprayed fans of seaweed and gold-sprayed shoals of little fishes sprouting out of conch shells (also gold), with billows of sequined silk on the floor for waves, and around the top of each window . . . bunting. Actual bunting, in the dark mauve and gold livery of the store and hanging from golden rope with tasselled ends like the cords which used to hold back dining-room curtains.

There was, however, no time to penetrate the revolving door in search of whatever unheard-of delights the fish and feathers were there to advertise: I had used up my store of time in hand and was in danger of being late unless I hurried along and struck the right street first time.

The right street – Abbey Park Place – was very easily found, since my amble around the town had taken me close to one end of it already although I was surprised to see how far I had since wandered, but number fifteen was not at all what I had been imagining. The postcard I had received was of good quality, thick and cream-coloured with the address deeply engraved in plain black, but I had not foreseen how one of at least fifteen houses in a street in Dunfermline could be anything except a sandstone villa, with a bay window above and one below, joined to its neighbour at the front door and inside stairway. In fact, 'No. 15' was merely the Post Office's designation of Abbey Park itself that presented stone gateposts and a lodge house to the street which I supposed had sprung up around it and taken its name. I glanced at my wristwatch and opened the small pedestrian gate set into one of the large ones.

There were limits, I soon saw, lodge or no lodge; the drive was only yards long – hardly a drive at all – and the house lay at hand just before me. Nevertheless, it was a solid chunk of good grey Georgian stone, sitting there as calm as a bull walrus on a sunny rock; one of those houses where the carriage circle reaches up to meet the front door but whose grounds drop away to lawns at the back so that the porch spans the basement area like a covered bridge (they always make me think, for some reason, of a sedan chair) and its size and solidity despite the deficiencies of the drive presented me with a problem.

For there was no name engraved on the card in my hand, just the address, and I had expected, after rapping on the door of the sandstone villa, to be greeted by whoever had sent it. Clearly, however, this smart black door would be answered by a servant – perhaps even a butler – and I did not know for whom to ask. I pulled the bell and squinted at the card again: *Please come at eleven o'clock on the morning of the twenty-fifth. I have an urgent commission to put to you*, and an unintelligible string of initials written in a wavery but deliberate woman's hand.

Butler indeed it was who answered, a portly sort in mauve and gold, and drawing myself up I conjured my grandest stare and my coolest voice to address him (taking a moment to note, with sadness, from how near at hand I conjured them these days).

'Mrs Gilver,' I said, 'to see the lady of the house.' And I waved the card in his direction. He recognised it, but continued frowning.

'To see . . . Mrs Jack?' he asked. I gave a nod that might have cracked a walnut under my chin; a gesture I had seen in a police superintendent of my acquaintance and had at once decided to add to my own repertoire. 'Step this way, madam,' said the butler and swept me inside.

As we clacked across the tiles of the porch, under a soaring arch, across an expanse of pillared hall and under a second soaring arch I peered at the signature, trying and failing to resolve that final initial into a J, then my attention was caught by the sudden blaze of light as we entered a library. The butler left me and I wandered over to the windows, the card – for the moment – forgotten.

The room faced due south and was bowed out at the far side, with the three tall windows of the bow looking over the lawns I had glimpsed while arriving. And the light simply poured in – warm, thick, honey-coloured light – rolling lazily in through the rippled old glass and washing the room in gold, making it pulse and gleam.

Perhaps it was not a library at all, I judged at a second glance around. To be sure, it was panelled from floor to ceiling and the ceiling itself was covered with panels too, but the wood was some species unknown to me – a rich glossy amber, smelling of wax and resin in the sunshine, and as far from the good dark oak of libraries as could be imagined. Add to this the fact that there were no bookshelves and it seemed less of a library still.

Then, lifting up the velvet cover from one of a number of shrouded tables, I saw that there *were* books after all. The cover had been guarding a glass-topped case, flattish but tilted a little for display, and in it was what looked to be a book of hours, open at a calendar page. I bent over this surprising item the better to study its decoration and marvel at its obvious antiquity and was still in that undignified position – stooped and snooping – when a gentle cough from the doorway caused me to drop the cover back again. The brass rod along its edge clattered onto the frame and, turning, I banged my ankle against one of the table legs.

'Mrs Gilver?' said a voice.

'Mrs Jack?' She had stopped in the doorway and stood there for a moment in a frame of that glowing, honeyed wood like a painted saint in an altar panel. It would have been a comely setting for ninety-nine women out of a hundred but it did not flatter this one, at least not today. She was about fifty, I guessed, but anxiety or exhaustion had further aged her; her face was tight, her skin pale and her long dark-red hair was bundled back into an inexpert knot from which great hanks of it were escaping. She wore a wool shawl over her dress and tugged it closer around herself as she moved towards me.

'Have you brought news?' she said, searching my face. Her eyes were drawn up into diamond shapes, red-rimmed.

'I—' I began, but she interrupted me.

'Have you discovered her? Has she been found?'

'I—' I said again and then mutely held out the postcard for her to see. She blinked at it and then looked back at me.

'From my mother,' she said. 'My goodness, my mother actually wrote to . . . Who are you?'

'I do apologise, Mrs Jack,' I answered. 'My name is Dandy Gilver. I asked for the lady of the house, you see. Perhaps someone might fetch your mother now?'

'But who are you?' she said again, all politeness, all decorum driven away by whatever suffering had caused the careless hairdressing and the shawl.

I hesitated. It would be monstrously unprofessional to discuss a case with anyone but my client in person and ordinarily I would not have dreamt of doing so, but surely her worry sprang from the same source as her mother's card.

'I'm a detective,' I said. 'Now, someone's missing?'

'A detective,' she echoed, going over to a chair against the wall and sinking into it. She nodded slowly. 'Yes, that would make a great deal of sense. That would be exactly what— My daughter.' She looked up at me with a new, clear look in her eyes. 'My daughter Mirren has been missing for five days. Since Saturday.'

'Well, Mrs Jack, your mother got her postcard off to me in admirable time.'

'It's not Mrs Jack,' she said, and for the first time a ghost of a smile passed across her. 'Trusslove has known me since I was a child, you see. It's Mrs Aitken.'

'Aitken?' I said, trying to remember where I had just come across that name.

'My husband is Jack Aitken and so, in the family, I am Mrs Jack.'

'I see,' I said. 'And your daughter went missing five days ago. Do you have any idea where she might have gone? Did you have any warning? Had you quarrelled? Or do you – forgive me, but your distress is only too clear and it leads me to wonder – do you fear that she might have come to harm?' I had not thought it possible for Mrs Aitken to increase her look of wretchedness but she did so now.

'The very gravest fear,' she whispered, sending shivers through me. 'Unspeakable harm.'

Before I could respond there came the sound of hurried footsteps across the marble floor of the hall and an elderly lady entered the room at some speed.

'Abigail? Is that Mirren? She's not back, is sh—' She stopped dead, seeing me, and pressed a hand to her heart, breathing hard. 'Sorry, dear,' she said to the other woman. 'I heard voices and thought she'd come back again. Phewf!' She eased herself down into another chair and sat panting, her feet set well apart and her hands braced on her knees.

'Do forgive me,' she said, cocking her head up in my direction. 'We're having quite a time of it here just now.' I smiled, uncertainly. Her mood did not at all match that of the younger woman's. If anything, she seemed diverted by the problem of the missing Mirren, nowhere near as distraught as the girl's mother.

'This is Mrs Gilver,' said Mrs Aitken. 'She's a detective. Mother sent for her.'

I frowned, because of course I had assumed that this new arrival was the grandmother in the case and the sender of my card. She was the right sort of age and she obviously lived here in the house; she was wearing bedroom slippers and still had

8

some pins keeping in place the curls across her forehead, while the rest of her ensemble – a voluminous day-dress cut for comfort and a long string of very white beads trying, although not hard, to look like pearls – was just conventional enough to persuade me that its wearer would not go a-visiting in slippers and pin curls. On the other hand, I thought, looking more closely at her, there was no family resemblance: Mrs Jack was a sweet, plump thing with a face like a little pansy and that extravagance of crinkly russet hair. The newcomer, in contrast, was very tall with large hands and feet and the kind of strong plain features which must have released her from all vanity at an early age and given her lots of time for other things.

'I'm Mrs Aitken,' she said. 'Bella. Widow of John. Jack's mother. You don't look much like a detective.' She fished in her dress pocket for her cigarette case, waving them at me before selecting one and lighting up.

'I was just beginning to ask your . . . daughter-in-law, whether she had any idea where Mirren might have gone,' I said.

'Good heavens!' said Mrs John Aitken, staring at me with the match still burning. 'You don't sound like a detective either.' And because a large proportion of my instinctive bristling took the form of trying to decide what *she* sounded like, her loud, easy voice with its good round vowels and its crisp, clear consonants, and concluding that she sounded like the wife of a very comfortable merchant, at last I made the connection.

'Aitken!' I said. 'As in House of Aitken?' It might have sounded insufferably rude and so I was lucky that Mrs John took no offence but said only:

'Emporium, my dear. House Of is – ahem – the other lot.'

Mrs Jack said nothing at all and registered no offence either; she had withdrawn from us entirely, returned to her inner woe like a horse with colic.

'So what do you do?' said her mother-in-law. 'Where do you start looking?'

'I'm not sure I do anything,' I replied. I turned to the other woman again. 'You mentioned "grave fears", Mrs Aitken. If you think your daughter's life is in danger you must summon the police.'

Again young Mrs Aitken said nothing, but I thought I could see that mention of the police had caused a slight shrinking. Her face looked more than ever like a little flower as her chin dipped and her eyes fluttered.

'No, no, no,' said the elder woman, shaking her head emphatically. I noticed that the row of curls did not budge; those pins had to be very firmly anchored. 'You've got the wrong end of the wrong stick, my dear.' She laughed. 'Abigail thinks she knows exactly what's in danger.'

Mrs Jack, hearing this, was roused at last.

'Aunt Bella, really!' she said, flushing.

'We think she's eloped,' the other went on. '*I'm* sure she has.'

I felt a flush blooming in *my* cheeks now, but not a flush of embarrassment at the woman's coarseness, rather one of anger.

'I see,' I said. 'In that case, I'm afraid I shan't be able to help you, ladies. I'm not that sort of a detective.'

Then all three of us jumped.

'I don't know *what* sort of detective you think you are,' said a voice. Someone had entered the room and come right up beside us without being heard. 'What are you doing here?' She was a woman in her seventies, I guessed, very small and neat, encased from neck to knee in a column of the stiffest, tightest, blackest imaginable bombazine, which made her look like a downpipe. Her white hair was arranged on her head in up-to-the minute style – a spiral of flat coils like seaweed at low tide – and on her breast, heaving hard against the restrictions of her costume, was a pair of spectacles on a black ribbon.

'Mother!' said Abigail. 'You *asked* Mrs Gilver to come. I saw the card you wrote out to her.'

'I asked Mrs Gilver to come tomorrow,' said the new arrival. 'When I would have been looking out for her, to greet her and enter the *private* discussion to which I thought my invitation would entitle me.' Her voice was icy, her vowels constricted by rage and refinement.

I took the – by now rather battered – little postcard back out of my bag and held it out to her.

'Eleven o'clock in the morning on the twenty-fifth of May,' I said. She flicked it a glance and drew herself up to her insignificant but somehow still very impressive height. Or perhaps it was just the bombazine; her dress was quite ludicrously tight, like a horse bandage.

'You're a whole day early,' she said.

I looked at the card again.

'It's quite clear, Mrs . . .'

'Aitken,' she said. 'Mrs Ninian Lennox Aitken.' I frowned and turned to look at her daughter. 'My husband was John Aitken's elder brother.' John Aitken's widow rolled her eyes; at the 'elder', I guessed, and since it seemed that both men were dead it *was* rather pointless still to mark precedence between them. 'I seem to have made a mistake with the date.' She coloured and her hand rose to the collar of her dress and fluttered there. 'Understandable at such an anxious time. I meant the twenty-sixth. And today is not suitable at all.'

'Anyway, you just said you wouldn't touch it with a pole,' said her sister-in-law, stubbing out her cigarette on the sole of her slipper. 'I don't blame you. Anyone can see you weren't brought up to go grubbing round guesthouses checking the register.'

'Mirren did not elope,' said the senior Mrs Aitken, Mrs Ninian I shall have to call her, following family tradition, if I am ever to keep them all in order. 'I can guarantee it.'

'As can I,' said Abigail very faintly. Her mother glanced at her but said nothing.

'Well then, time might well be of the essence, mightn't it?' I said, wondering at a grandmother who would send off a postcard to a detective so hastily that she made a mistake on it but delay the start of the searching.

'Yes, but today,' said Mrs John, then she lay back in her chair and twirled her string of beads like a propeller. 'Lord, it's like a comic operetta.'

'Today is our golden jubilee,' said Mrs Ninian, and she spat the words out as I am sure they have never been spat before, not being made for spitting. 'Aitkens' is fifty today, Mrs Gilver.' She gave me a smile so swift and unconvincing that it was more like the flick of a lizard's tongue to catch a fly than an expression of any human emotion. 'And we owe it to the memories of John and Ninian not to let that little minx spoil it for everyone.'

2

'Ah,' I said, nodding. 'A jubilee. I thought there was something in the air.'

'Festivities begin at one o'clock,' said Mrs Ninian. She threw a look towards her daughter. 'One sharp, Abigail.'

Again it took a moment for young Mrs Jack to grasp the fact that she was being spoken to and then another to comprehend the words. Eventually, though, she shook her head.

'I can't, Mother,' she said. 'Why don't you understand that? I can't go.'

'You must,' said Mrs Ninian, her words more clipped than ever. 'I will not thole this day being spoiled. We have gone to a great deal of trouble and expense, Abigail. The Provost is making a speech. Our very best customers have been invited. Lady Lawson is coming. And a photographer from the *Herald*— Oh, stop shaking your head that way, you stupid girl. And stop that idiotic moaning. You're like a lowing cow!'

'Mary!' Bella had risen from her chair and stepped in between the two women with one hand out towards her sister-in-law in the manner of a policeman holding up traffic and one hand reaching back towards her daughter-in-law as though to cup her cheek or stroke her shoulder.

In times gone by, I should not have known – as my maid Grant says – 'where to put myself'. Things being what they were these days, of course, I watched all three of them with my piercing detective's eye, wondering how the disappearance of a girl could produce three such very different reactions amongst a mother and two grandmothers, one fondly exasperated, one faint with terror and one so angry that I almost expected steam to hiss from her ears.

'Abby dear,' Bella went on, turning her back on the black pillar of fury and kneeling in front of Abigail, with some effort and some cracking at the knees, 'listen to me. Mirren will be fine. She'll turn up again. All will be well.'

Abigail lifted her head at these soothing words.

'There,' said Bella. 'That's better. Now, come along and get ready like a good girl. Mirren wouldn't want you to miss the frolics.' She sat back on her heels and smiled. 'We'll laugh about all this one day, you'll see. One of Mirren's children will ask how Mummy and Daddy met and we'll regale them with the scandalous tale. Abby!'

Abigail had surged to her feet and now pushed past her mother-in-law, knocking the old lady off balance and landing her on the hard floor with a thump. She stumbled towards the door and would have fled had not at that moment a man appeared there and gripped her firmly around the upper arms.

'What the devil?' he said.

'I can't do it,' said Abigail, burying her face against his chest. 'I can't go. I can't face everyone. Tell them. They can't make me.'

'This is my nephew, Jack,' said Mrs Ninian. I nodded, having guessed as much, but could not help feeling some surprise at her choice of words. Surely it was unseemly to advertise the very close connection quite so baldly, especially when the cousins were, as at the present moment, in one another's arms. Or perhaps it was unremarkable to the Aitkens by now.

Jack Aitken looked at me with some interest, clearly wondering who I was, pitched into the middle of the family drama this way, then turned his wife back towards the room and, with one arm around her shoulder and the other hand patting one of hers, brought her towards us again.

'Silly!' he said. 'No one knows yet. Of course you can "face them". We'll say Mirren has a cold.'

'I don't know why you say no one knows "yet", Jack,' said Mrs Ninian. 'There's no reason for anyone to find out at all. Ever.'

'We won't be able to hide a marriage,' said Bella. 'It'll get out in the end. And even if they never came back, people would put two and two together. Stands to reason.'

Mrs Ninian twitched her head at that, shaking off the notion as a horse would a fly, but it was Jack Aitken's reaction which interested me. He spoke to his mother in a light voice and with another of the fond smiles he had been bestowing on his trembling wife.

'You might have been that kind of girl in your day, Mother.' Bella Aitken gave a bark of laughter. 'But not my little Mirren. She would never do such a thing to her mother and me.'

And yet I found him not the least bit convincing. He sounded enough like the juvenile lead in a drawing-room comedy and, with his sleek hair and fine features, he even looked quite like one – a middle-aged sort of juvenile lead, as one finds in repertory companies of the second and third tier – but there was a slick of sweat on his upper lip and the hand gripping Abigail's shoulder was as tense as a claw. Also, like a third-rate actor, he had made a mistake with his delivery.

'But if you don't think Mirren has eloped, Mr Aitken,' I said, pouncing on the error, 'what do you think she *has* done?' He frowned. 'Or do you agree with your wife? That something has been done *to* her?'

I had the gratification of seeing Jack Aitken freeze.

'Allow me to introduce myself,' I said. 'My name is Dandy Gilver and I'm a private detective. Mrs Aitken engaged me but of course I shall be working on behalf of all of you who are hoping for Mirren's safe return.' Wicked of me – that 'Mrs Aitken'. The poor man's eyes rolled around the three women like billiard balls after a clumsy break.

At that moment, the butler, Trusslove, entered the room already drawing breath to speak. He hesitated upon seeing the tableau – the Jack Aitkens embracing, Mrs John still on the floor, Mrs Ninian glaring poison darts at me – but only for a second or two.

'Light refreshments in the garden room, madam,' he said. 'As ordered. I've set a place for Mrs Gilver, naturally.'

★ ★ ★

They could hardly get rid of me – they dared not even try – but their longing to and their hiding it hung over the garden room like a black rain cloud so that, of the four of them, only Bella, Mrs John, made a good meal, forking thick slices of ham onto her plate and demolishing ripe tomatoes in the most sensible way, by popping them whole into her mouth and munching. The other three picked and nibbled, sipped barley water and fiddled with their napkins. At least Mr and Mrs Jack did. Mary, Mrs Ninian, picked and nibbled and stared at me. For my part, I ate just enough to excite no attention (as Nanny Palmer had trained me to do) sitting in polite silence for just the proper length of time before I began speaking.

'The obvious first question,' I said, 'is who it is you're so sure she hasn't eloped with.'

'*I'm* not sure,' Bella said. 'I think she has.' Abigail picked up her barley water glass and her hand shook so badly as she did so that a little of it spilled onto the tablecloth. She stared at the blot, watching it spreading. Her mother tutted and I saw her push a hand up under the cloth, checking that the table protector was there.

'And who is the man?' I persisted.

'A mere boy,' said Jack. 'And Mirren such a child herself.'

'A most unsuitable family,' said Mary. 'Really quite unthinkable.'

'Oh?' I said and turned. 'You don't agree, Mrs Aitken?'

'I've nothing against any of them,' Bella said. 'And Dugald himself—'

'They have a shameful secret,' said Mary, drowning her out. 'Bad blood, Mrs Gilver. Weak blood. Not suitable talk for the dinner table. Luncheon, either.' She flushed and cleared her throat, hoping to hide the slip.

'Oh Mary,' said Bella again. 'There's nothing shameful about it. All families have their black sheep. Look at the Tsars of Russia! Look at Prince John! And you could say as much about the Aitkens if you had that turn of mind as you can about the Hepburns any day.'

'Hepburns?' I said. 'Hepburn as in—?'

16

'Drapers,' said Mary, as though she were saying 'vermin'. 'They've opened up a little shop at the bottom of the High Street. Opposite the police station.'

I said nothing to that. House of Hepburn was perhaps more modest than Aitkens' Emporium, but it was still a sizeable enterprise, and to my eyes it had looked as solidly established as the Emporium any day.

'It was getting on for twenty years ago, Mary,' Bella said, rolling her eyes at me and not troubling to hide the fact from her sister-in-law. 'And as for "drapers", let he who is without . . .'

'Ninian was a tailor,' said Mary. 'John was a businessman as much as any banker. And Aitkens' in case you have forgotten celebrates *fifty* years today.' She snapped round to face me and gave me the old on-and-off-again smile. 'I hope we can persuade you to join us for the celebrations, Mrs Gilver.'

'Mother,' said Abigail, speaking for the first time. 'Mrs Gilver isn't here to toast Aitkens'. The sooner she starts looking for Mirren . . .' Then, saying her daughter's name, she ran down like an unwound clock and returned to silence.

'I'd be delighted to come,' I said, for I had been plotting.

When we had finished our coffee I turned to Bella.

'Can you direct me to a telephone, Mrs Aitken?' I heard the creak of bombazine as Mrs Ninian stiffened beside me.

'Certainly,' Bella said. 'Nearest one's in the morning room.' She clicked her tongue and then went on: 'Easiest way is out into the garden, up to the drive, back in the front door and it's first left.'

I rose and made my purposeful way to the open french windows. (We were down on the basement floor in a room I guessed to be directly below the library, and I was grateful for the directions; I should never have found my way back through the passages of the house and might have had trouble getting rid of whoever volunteered to guide me.)

Before I was quite out of the room, Mary cleared her throat.

'Who are you—?' she began. 'That is, are you—? Are you going to ring the police?'

'I wasn't,' I said, 'but would you like me to?'

Various sounds emerged from all of them then and I made my escape.

You deserve to be spanked with your hairbrush, Dandelion, I told myself as I scrambled up the grassy slope to the gravel. The front door was open and I marched straight in.

Thankfully Alec was at home but I had a measure of listening to do before I got the chance to start talking.

'Hah!' he said. 'Well, then. See? What did I tell you? And so here you are, a matter of hours later, cap in hand, humbly begging.'

'Yes, yes, yes,' I agreed. 'Beg beg. But I *couldn't* have brought you. She wrote to me, just to me, and it would have looked dreadful to have pitched up with a burly sidekick.'

The 'burly' mollified him a little.

'Still, Dandy,' he said, 'we might like to put this thing on a proper footing someday. Or I'm always going to be ten steps behind you.'

'Hm,' I answered, thinking that if we did have cards made up or put ourselves in the Post Office Directory as Mrs Gilver and Mr Osborne, the world being what it was, Mr Osborne would have cases coming out of his pipe and Mrs Gilver would be reduced to making up invoices and filing. (Not that any of our cases had ever produced much to be filed. What is it that people who file file, I wonder?) 'You'll be ten steps ahead before today's out if you'll shut up and listen.'

'I'm all ears,' Alec said.

And so I told him about Mirren Aitken of Aitkens' Emporium and how she had fallen in love with Dugald Hepburn of House of Hepburn and how the Aitkens had refused to countenance such miscegenation, such soiling of the good name of Aitken with such upstarts, and such poor stock, with such shameful secrets they could not be spoken of, and how the Aitken obduracy had driven Mirren away from her home into the cold, cruel world.

Alec was silent when I finished.

'So she's run off with him,' he said. 'What are we supposed to do about it? It's her father's job to stand over the boy with a shotgun.'

'Yes, but listen,' I said. 'Of the four Aitkens I've met this morning only her paternal grandmother agrees with you. Her mother – Abigail – seems convinced that the girl is in some kind of peril – no, *not* that kind; stop snorting – and her father is, I am sure, just as rattled but he's trying to hide it and bungling the attempt so that nothing about his demeanour makes any sense at all.'

'How d'you mean?'

'The other grandmother,' I went on, ignoring him, 'the one who sent me the card, is furious. White with suppressed rage. And – here's the thing, Alec – she wanted me to come tomorrow. Not today. She was livid that I'd come today. Even livider that I spoke to her daughter and the other granny, as if some wonderful plan has got away from her and she can't get it back again.'

'Are you sure?'

'So I think it's pretty clear what we need to do. I'll go along to the jubilee and keep an eye on them all, and you come and do what I'd have done tomorrow, today. See if you can work out why Grandmama didn't want me to.'

'And what *would* you have done tomorrow?' said Alec. 'Or today if she hadn't stopped you.'

I noted that all thoughts of the equal partnership had withered and he was asking for instructions like an errand boy.

'Find these Hepburns, find out if Dugald has taken off too. See if anyone has an idea where they might have gone to. You might even find her, if they've taken her in. If they're all for it on his side.'

'Hepburn,' said Alec slowly, writing down the name. 'Did the girl's family say the boy's lot were keen then?'

'Well, Granny Mary hinted that they might be climbers,' I said. 'But apart from Granny Bella no one said much about them at all. They can hardly pronounce the name of Hepburn without choking.' I would have said more but I could hear footsteps approaching and so we rang off, with a plan in place to meet for tea and share our afternoon's gleanings.

'Ready, Mrs Gilver?' said Mary, stalking into the room and

looking just a little disappointed not to overhear the end of my conversation. She glared at the instrument as though she hoped to discern some fading echo of what had been spoken into it. 'You can come along in the first motor with Mrs John and myself.'

But Bella – Mrs John – coming in at her heels would have none of it.

'Nonsense, Mary,' she said. 'You and I are going together and Jack and Abby were to follow on with Mirren. So it makes sense for Mrs Gilver to go in Mirren's place.'

'Oh, yes, please do, Mrs Gilver,' said Abigail's voice from the doorway where she was hovering. 'Everyone will be expecting three of us, you see.'

I smiled uncertainly, not sure if she really meant to suggest that onlookers would mistake me for a twenty-year-old girl and let the awkward absence go unremarked.

'And if anyone else is going to be in the first car it should be Jack,' said Bella Aitken, *sotto voce* to her sister-in-law. She was not quite above all scrabbling for precedence then; she had an eye on her son's deserts as the Aitken heir.

'I'll be very happy to,' I said to Abigail, judging that more might be learned in a journey with her than with her mother. 'Good to see you've decided to go after all.' For she had substituted a short linen coat for the shawl and had most of the misrule which reigned in place of her crowning glory hidden with a straw hat, but it had to be admitted that these efforts seemed to have sapped her and she was paler than ever and wavering a little as she stood there.

'Good,' said Bella Aitken. 'Right then, Mary.' She too had tidied herself a little; the pins were gone, although the curls they had been holding were still in place in a row across her head under the brim of a hat which looked to be an old friend. The carpet slippers were gone too and she stumped away across the hall in a stout pair of gunmetal-grey shoes which managed to make her feet look bigger than ever.

A pair of liveried chauffeurs had brought around to the front door two large motorcars of some American provenance. They had their tops thrown back in that way that made me think of perambulators on a sunny day in the park and there were quantities of mauve and gold ribbon festooned around them in the manner of royal carriages. Mary Aitken gave another of her lizard smiles as she saw them and then she frowned.

'Those rosettes,' she said. 'They're covering the coats of arms. Couldn't we tuck them up somehow?' She began to shove some trailing ends of ribbon up away from the plaques on the motorcar doors – peacock feathers and shoals of little fishes, I saw.

'For the Lord's sake,' said her sister-in-law. 'You'll have the whole lot undone if you're not wary.'

'I don't think anyone will be wondering who we are, Aunt M,' said Jack, who was standing on the steps with his hat on the back of his head staring rather aghast at the motorcars. His eyebrows rose even further as one of the chauffeurs climbed down and began fixing little purple flags to the wing mirrors. I cleared my throat and pulled my mouth down hard at the corners, trying not to smile.

'And you'll go the right way,' said Mary Aitken to one of the chauffeurs. 'The way I told you.'

'Round and up the wynd, madam,' said the man.

'Nice and slow,' said Mary and turned to let Trusslove hand her in. Bella opened the other door and climbed in herself. Jack handed Abigail in, then me and then let himself in beside me. I shuffled over to the middle of the seat, nudging up against Abigail, an old chagrin smouldering in my bosom. At home, going visiting or to church in our landau, my mother and father always faced forward and the three of us sat with our backs to the driver, my younger brother and sister each with a side seat and a good view of what was passing – for my mother was as sentimental about early childhood as she was practical about travel-sickness – and me stuck in the middle with not enough room for my feet and nothing to look at except my mother looking back at me. It cannot have been for long, despite the fierce impression of injustice it had left upon me, because I was eight by the time my brother was old enough to sit up on his own and he went off to school when I was thirteen. After that, even in the holidays, there was no jostling, because my parents gave up the tradition of taking a footman with them and Edward instantly promoted himself to the seat beside the driver and a chance of holding the reins.

I blinked. It had been years since I had thought about that old feud over the carriage seats; these Aitkens, these fifty-year-old Aitkens still under their mothers' rule, were a bad influence on me.

'Clearly,' I began, as soon as we were under way, pulling out of the drive onto the shady quiet of Abbey Park Place, 'you have reservations about the alliance with the Hepburn family, but might I just ask, is the boy – this Dugald – is he himself unsatisfactory? Some kind of a wrong 'un?'

Abigail continued to stare glumly over the side of the motorcar door, as though she hadn't heard me, but Jack himself shook his head. He also recrossed his legs and wiped his hands one against the other and in all could hardly have done any more to shake my words away from him.

'Not at all,' he said. 'Not so far as I know.'

His tone did not invite further questioning and so I was quiet for a while. We were taking a most senseless route to the High Street, setting off in quite the wrong direction, and I had already toured Dunfermline once today. Still, it gave me some thinking time and this tour had been planned by one who knew the town's best side; the low, looping road which meandered past portions of ruined palace or cloister was extremely scenic, even with the Abbey glowering down from our other side as we skirted it, much to be preferred to the narrow streets of hat shops and cigar merchants I had found. All too soon, though, we turned and began to make our way hat-shop-ward once more. I tried again with Jack Aitken.

'The objections to his family must be weighty ones indeed, then,' I said. 'If it's not the boy himself.' I could not imagine the objections, truth be told. The hints at luncheon had been lurid but unhelpful and the couple seemed beautifully matched to me: the son of a merchant and the daughter of a merchant, of the same class, from the same town.

'Ha ha ha,' said Jack, although I had said nothing very clever or witty. 'My mother and aunt are pretty fierce about Aitkens'. Well, I mean, look at all this.' He flicked at a piece of the mauve and gold ribbon and shook his head again. 'Comes from being left to run it on their own, I suppose you'd say.'

We were turning into the High Street now and I could see that there were people collected along the pavement's edge. More of the mauve and gold flags had been handed out and the onlookers were waving them and cheering us as we swept by.

'And here we are,' I said, spying once more the frolicking mannequins in the shop window. 'Those tableaux are quite something, I must say. Your mother and aunt have excelled themselves.' I had gathered myself to alight but the motorcar slid past the last of the windows without stopping.

'That's Hepburns',' Jack Aitken said.

'Gosh,' I replied, craning back to look at the sand and hampers. 'Sorry.'

'Talk about upstaging,' he went on. 'Aunt Mary must be spitting if she noticed them, but no doubt she was looking the other way.'

'Quite right,' I said. 'Very provoking. So, is it professional rivalry that's the trouble?' I hoped that he would not suddenly shut like a clam under my probing. A bad liar who thinks he is a good one is treasure trove to an investigator and Jack Aitken had more baseless belief in the misleading power of his own charm than anyone I had met in recent memory.

'For my part, I just don't want my little girl to grow up so fast,' he said. He was wiping his hands on his trouser legs now. 'She's not ready for marriage. And marriage to a boy of just twenty who's no more ready for it than she . . .' He shook his head again, more slowly, and made a fond sort of laughing noise by breathing down his nose in short bursts. 'I was twenty-two and that was young enough.'

'When she comes home, then,' I said, 'when I find her, perhaps you could persuade them into a long engagement. A twenty-year-old boy is far too young, I agree.'

'No.' Abigail had spoken without turning, but she turned now. 'Mirren doesn't want to marry Dugald Hepburn any more. She changed her mind.'

'She told you that?' I said. Jack Aitken had craned forward to look past me at his wife.

'She doesn't want to marry him,' Abigail said again. 'She wouldn't marry him for a king's fortune. She'd rather—' She bit off her words, turned away and shifted even further round in her seat so that her husband and I could not see so much as the curve of her cheek.

Matters took on a positively surreal tinge halfway up the High Street (and, incidentally, about two minutes' drive from Abbey Park) when we pulled up at Aitkens'. The flag-wavers were four and five deep here and were held back by more gold rope, of which the Emporium seemed to have an endless supply. A pair of . . . one can only call them nymphs . . . in mauve togas with gold leaves in their hair were handing out sweets to children and paper tickets to adults, and a doorman whose finery would not have shamed the Dorchester stood ready to open the motorcar doors and help us down.

'God in heaven,' said Jack Aitken and, although I did not answer, privately I agreed.

Mary and Bella stood waiting on a piece of carpet which had been laid down beside the revolving door, Mary looking around the gathered crowd with fierce triumph in her eyes and Bella dealing with the horror of it all by gazing into the middle distance and pretending she was not really there. I stood watching the crowds clamouring for the paper tickets, waving them in triumph once they had secured one.

'They are fifty-shilling notes, Mrs Gilver,' Mary said, drawing up to me. I glanced sharply at the nearer of the two nymphs. 'Let Mrs Gilver see, Lynne.' The girl handed me one of the slips, on which had been embossed a large gilt *50* over a ground of the inevitable mauve feathers and little fish.

'And these are . . . ?' I said, turning the ticket over in my hands. 'These are currency?'

'Just for the day,' said Mary.

'Two pounds and ten shillings?' I said. 'That's extremely generous of you.'

Bella at my side gave a snort of laughter. 'Not currency exactly, Mrs Gilver. More like tokens. Redeemable against a—'

'—select range of specially chosen jubilee notions,' Mary finished in a hissing whisper. There was a very impressive closed motorcar drawing up now. Perhaps the Provost, I thought, or Lady Whatsername; in any case, Mary Aitken glided forward to offer a greeting. Bella leaned towards me.

'—job lot of pre-war overstock we'd never shift any other way,' she said. 'Some of it might be fifty years old, I daresay. Lord, here's the Provost too! Let's go in now and dodge them. Mary won't want me diluting her, anyway.'

Aitkens' Emporium had an inside to match its parade of windows and all the more so for being still and empty, poised for the show about to begin. The floor of the foyer was marble, or at any rate good enough linoleum well-laid over stone to look and feel like marble as one crossed it; the counters when we reached them were mahogany – or oak perhaps, stained with something treacly – and, as well as the vastness and splendour of the Haberdashery Department where we were standing with its scores and hundreds of little drawers and slides everywhere, there were archways leading away in three directions hinting at even more. In one back corner there was a staircase of some width and grandeur and in the other was what I came to understand as Aitkens' pride and joy, Aitkens' unanswerable poke in the eye to Hepburns': the lift.

It was a very impressive one. The metalwork of the shaft doors was as richly decorated and as glittering as a birdcage from a lady's boudoir and the way the shining polished lift carriage itself could just be glimpsed, nestled inside, put me in mind for some reason of an eye twinkling behind lowered lashes, especially when the light shifted, as it was doing now.

I glanced upwards to discover how the light could shift inside a building and saw that there was no upper floor above us, here at the centre of the store; only galleries around an atrium. Over our heads, at least three floors up, glass panes formed a roof, but a cat's cradle of ribbons and banners had been slung from gallery to gallery below, cutting out the sun which otherwise would have drenched us in warmth and light. It was, I supposed, these banners stirring in a draught which had sent shadows flitting and scattered the light.

As I brought my gaze back down again I saw that, despite the hush, Bella Aitken and I were no longer alone on the floor of the atrium. Behind each of the maybe mahogany counters, girls and women had come to stand silently to attention, as uniform as so many tin soldiers. That is, some of them were freshly minted and some battle-scarred but they were turned out of just one mould. They were dressed, encased is perhaps a better way of phrasing it, in the kind of simple black frocks easily run up at home from a paper pattern and I wondered if they were handed bolts of cloth and told to make their own uniforms like the housemaids in my mother's day. If so, then for the jubilee they had evidently been given extra rations. Some of them had run up ruffled collars, some had fashioned corsages, the less adept had plumped for sashes and bows in their hair, but one and all had touches of mauve and gold. I felt that I would see mauve and gold in my sleep that night, swimming and fluttering before my eyes in fish and feather form.

Little did I know what sight would indeed flash behind my closed eyelids that night and for many nights to come. In the first of my detecting adventures, one which I would hardly call a case since I slipped into it and was bobbing out of my depth before I had realised it had begun, I remember that there was an air of dread hanging around like the pall from a snuffed tallow candle, and it began long before the events which should have instigated it. I was almost tempted to call it a premonition once it had come true, but I resisted. For surely it is the mark of a fool to trumpet premonitions once they have been fulfilled. Surely, unless one has taken out a half-page announcement in advance, one really does have to keep one's lip firmly buttoned afterwards too.

I digress. Alec is wont to murmur, 'Yes, darling, you do rather,' in response to that comment and so I try not to give him an opening. My point is that while in the first case there was dread far in advance of anything dreadful, the beginning of the Aitken affair – a young girl missing, her mother awash with unspoken terrors and her father so well-hidden behind his own secrets that all one could really see was the hiding – found me no more than intrigued and diverted by the prospect before me. Mary and Bella Aitken were entertaining, the jubilee promised more entertainment still of one sort or another, Dunfermline's holiday mood was catching (and I was glad to know that flags and bunting still stirred a small corner of my girlish soul; of course, one must put away childish things as one is bidden, but I would not like to be quite beyond the reach of bunting).

Nor was I quite past being seduced by a wrapped and beribboned parcel, and the 'pre-war overstock' – I had been impressed by the way the term slipped from Bella's tongue – was heaped up in tantalising abundance like fruit outside a greengrocer's, except that instead of being in chip baskets at hip height – at Dalmatian's muzzle height as I had had brought home to me one day when Bunty snaffled a ripe pear in Dunkeld's High Street – the boxes were set out upon high circular stands, something like roulette wheels.

'Lord above us,' said Bella, 'where did she unearth these, I wonder.'

'What are they?' I asked.

'From the old food hall, I think,' Bella said. 'Repainted for the day. They must have been mouldering away up in the attics for twenty years at least.'

I tipped my head back to look at the ceiling again. I had never thought of a department store as a place which would have attics.

'From the old days when the clerks lived in,' said Bella. 'A warren of nasty little cells and now they're stuffed to the rafters with whatever Mary thinks she'll find a use for one day.' She stirred the heap of boxes in the roulette wheel and shook her head, laughing. They were, to be frank, a little battered-looking, slightly worn on the corners and slightly warped with damp or age. The ribbons tied around them, needless to say, were new. 'At a guess,' said Bella, 'I'd say these are probably braces, or collars, or possibly sock suspenders. Jubilee notions!'

'Mrs Aitken does seem to have a great deal of . . . um . . . zeal for . . . um . . .' I said, a new low even for me, who am often pressed into impromptu diplomacy and found wanting. Bella Aitken gave me a conspiratorial look and leaned in closer before speaking again.

'Forty-eight years since her ascension and she still can't believe her luck,' she said, in a murmur. I felt my eyes widen, but did not have time to pursue the hint, because Mary Aitken was crossing the shop floor towards us – the very shop floor from which I inferred she had been elevated to her current reign. She brought with her two groups of honoured guests. One group consisted of the Provost, red-faced, beaming, barrel-chested and in all his robes and chains, his good lady wife, equally red-faced, equally barrel-chested, in a costume and wearing a smile which put her husband's ceremonial garments and expression effortlessly in the shade, and two youths who must be their sons – plain, round, tricked out in boys' brigade uniforms for reasons best understood by their mama, and both with the same black hair as the Provost, flattened to their heads with such quantities of pomade that they appeared to be wearing little Bakelite skull-caps, with not a suggestion of individual strands of hair.

The other party were of quite a different order but were no less exemplars of their type; Lady Lawson and her three sons were very tall, very thin and had that worn, straggly look which comes either from avoiding any appearance of effort or from real hardship, gently being borne. I guessed that the Lawson specimens were probably impoverished rather than too grand to be seen trying; for why else would they be here if not for the buns?

There was a flurry of introductions and then a repetition of them all as Jack and Abigail arrived with yet more favoured guests. I nodded and smiled and was aware that all around us the haberdashery floor and the galleries above were filling with onlookers.

28

The flag-wavers, the bearers of fifty-shilling tokens, were jostling for a view with much respectful whispering and smothered giggles, but it was with some surprise I realised that what they were jostling for a view *of* was us, standing there in the middle of the floor. There did not seem to be any dais or other indication that this spot was one where a drama was to be played, or so I thought until I saw, wound around a brass hook screwed into the edge of one of the old food-hall wheels, the tasselled end of a cord. Its other end was lost amongst the banners high above us. Balloons, I thought, or possibly confetti; someone would pull it and the jubilee would begin.

As I stood there, squinting up, our number was swelled by two more; not exalted customers these but a middle-aged man of military bearing with a purple and gold handkerchief sprouting out of his breast pocket and a middle-aged woman dressed in Aitkens' black, most of her narrow bosom covered by a corsage which could have served as a table centrepiece for a large banquet. Mary Aitken welcomed these – they had to be the highest-ranking employees, surely – into the enclosure and introduced them around.

'Mr Muir is the manager of the gentlemen's side,' she said, 'and Miss Hutton for the ladies'.'

'Where's Mrs Lumsden?' said Bella. Mary Aitken treated Lady Lawson to one of her smiles before turning to her sister-in-law.

'The rest of our employees are watching from the upper gallery,' she said.

'Mrs Lumsden is in charge of Household,' Bella began to explain to me, but was interrupted.

'And what with curtains and upholstery being on the second and linens and housewares in the basement, I'm kept on my toes, eh?' She was a tiny woman, almost completely spherical, with her gold and mauve ribbon wrapped around her head and tied under her chin in a bow. 'Mrs, Mrs, Abigail dear, Jack son. Hello there, Netta.' This to the Provost's wife who at Mrs Lumsden's entrance had brightened back into smiles (the Lawsons had had a dampening effect upon her, as I imagine they had meant to).

29

'Mrs Lumsden is an institution at Aitkens',' said Mary tightly and the little woman, far from being offended at an apology being offered for her presence, chuckled and added more.

'In with the bricks, I am,' she said. 'And not a thing they can do about it.'

'Although they try,' Bella murmured, with a glance at Mary. 'They certainly do try. Too close to home by half, Mrs Gilver, if you know what I mean.'

I did. Mrs Lumsden was Mary's road not taken, by the grace of God, and she shuddered to be reminded of what might have been.

'And we are grateful for all your years of loyal service, Mrs Lumsden,' Mary was saying now, looking as though she had bitten down on a bad tooth. 'What would a department store be without its domestic wares? Nothing but a glorified draper's, no matter what they say.'

'Not today, Mary,' said Bella. 'Forget them for one day, can't you?'

'Mrs Ninian, dear,' said Mrs Lumsden. 'Don't upset yourself.' She dropped her voice and spoke to Bella. 'It's not true then? About the hatchet. Olive branch, I should say.'

'What's this? What?' said Mary Aitken.

'Nothing at all,' said Mrs Lumsden, but Mary was not to be fobbed off.

'What was that about an olive branch, Mrs Lumsden?' she said. 'I'm surprised at you, whispering that way.' The Provost's wife was shifting uneasily from foot to foot trying not to over-hear and Lady Lawson was looking fixedly up at the galleries.

'It's nothing, Mrs Ninian,' Mrs Lumsden said again, but the drilling stare was too much for her. 'I thought – that is, I hoped – I mean, my girls upstairs were talking about an *entente cordiale.*'

'What?' said Bella Aitken.

'You know, "them down by". I thought they might even come along.' Mrs Lumsden lowered her voice but jerked her head so theatrically that she attracted more attention than if she had spoken out loud. Lady Lawson and the Provost's wife had heard

30

something to overcome any polite scruples and were listening hard. 'All very ecumenical, I was thinking.'

'Mrs Lumsden,' said Mary, 'you should know better than to listen to those silly girls at your age.'

'But they said they saw Mr Hepburn right here in the—'

'Nonsense,' said Mary. And then under her breath: 'They wouldn't dare gatecrash. They wouldn't dare.'

'I don't know, Mary,' said Bella. 'They might think it was a "wheeze". You know what they're like when they—'

'Jack!' Mary swung round and skewered her son-in-law with a gimlet glare, then she softened it and spoke with a lightness and ease which fooled no one. 'Just you slip out and tell Ferguson to fasten the front doors. We've enough of a crowd to be going on with.'

Jack Aitken disentangled his arm from his wife's – she had been clinging on to him like a creeping vine – and set off for the front door at some speed. Abigail reached out her hand for some support to replace him but found nothing and took an unsteady step to the side.

'Need to sit, Mother,' she said vaguely.

'Not now,' Mary muttered through her teeth.

'Glass of water . . .'

'I'll fetch it. And a chair,' said Bella Aitken and strode off towards the back of the store. The Provost's boys stood as stolidly unremarking as ever, but every other one of the guests was showing signs of strain. The Provost himself made a great business of checking and winding a turnip-like pocket watch. The Lawson offspring were beginning to roll their eyes and murmur to one another, making my hand itch. They all looked to be in their twenties and therefore far too old for such rudeness. Lady Lawson, one of the old school, responded to the rising awkwardness as an engine responds to a crank handle: she turned to the Provost's lady and started talking about gardens. Mrs Provost, well-trained in the same game, took the baton and ran, describing some elaborate new scheme for a rockery at home. They had got as far as promising to swap some treasured specimens when Mary

31

gave a sigh which could have blown the crust off a sandwich (as Nanny Palmer used to say).

'This is getting ridiculous,' she announced and looked upwards. The crowds hanging over the balconies with flags in hand were quieter now, waiting for something to happen, hoping that it would happen soon. Looking around, I saw that not only had neither Bella nor Jack reappeared but Abigail had gone too.

Mary Aitken raised her hand and gave a signal to someone out of view and somewhere off to the side, but not far enough off for me, an uncertain bugler began a fanfare. A cheer went up from the balconies and Mary beamed and then nodded to the Provost.

'Ladies and gentlemen, boys and girls,' he said, sounding like a ringmaster. 'Welcome to Aitkens' Emporium. I know you are all *aching* to begin this afternoon of celebration and I hope you have made *provision* for plenty fun. We've all seen the advertisements in the *Herald* telling *what's in store* for us so without further ado I will render *the service* I offered.' Mary Aitken, still beaming despite the puns, pointed to the end of the cord wound round the little brass cleat. The Provost unwound it and stood hólding the end of the rope in one hand.

'Without further ado,' he repeated, 'it gives me great pleasure to say: happy fiftieth birthday, Aitkens', and many happy returns.'

A cheer rose, the Provost tugged on the rope and everyone looked up. There was a moment when all I could see was a kind of shimmering high above the web of banners and then came a sudden loud bang, almost an explosion.

'What—?' said Mary Aitken's voice.

The shimmering became clearer; a shower of little golden flakes drifting down through the ribbons.

'What was that noise?' said Mrs Lumsden.

The crowds on the balconies were silenced for a moment, waiting to see what had made the sound, but then a murmur started up again and they reached out to snatch at the specks of gold, whirling down like a shower of snow. I caught one in my palm and saw that it was a little *50*, stamped out of gilt foil. They were settling on our heads now and the Provost's boys began to chase them, holding out their caps.

'What made that noise?' said Bella. She had returned and was standing holding a glass of water, staring upwards. 'Where's Abby?'

'Perhaps when I released the . . .' said the Provost. 'Something up there . . .'

'What went wrong?' said Jack Aitken, reappearing. 'Oh! They've scattered all right, then.' He brushed one of the spangles from his shoulder and grinned at the Provost's boys. 'What was that banging noise? I thought for a moment the whole bag had come plummeting down in one! Where's Abby gone to?'

I sniffed the air, wondering if I were imagining it. I squinted up through the ribbons. They were swaying and rippling now as people on the balconies tried to shake free pieces of gold foil caught there. The noise had come from the back corner, I thought, but surely the gold 50s in their bag must have been in the middle of the roof; they had settled evenly all around the floor. I sniffed again.

'Mrs Aitken,' I said, turning to Mary, 'what *was* the trick to getting those spangles to fall?'

Mary Aitken was staring up, just as I had been. It was the manager, Mr Muir, who answered.

'Drawstrings,' he said. 'Just muslin bags, slung over the highest beams and drawstrings at the bottom.'

'So, nothing . . . automotive, then?' I said. 'Nothing like fireworks or anything?' I sniffed again and, because they saw me, the others began to sniff too. I took one last look at where I was sure the noise had come from and then made for the staircase in the corner. Halfway there, though, I caught sight of the lift again, winking from behind its golden grille. That might be quicker and I was sure the bang had come from that corner of the building.

'Who knows how to work this thing?' I called back to the little gathering in the middle of the floor. 'Mr Aitken?' Jack simply stared at me.

'There's a boy who works it,' Mary said, frowning at me.

33

'Good Lord, Mary, needs must,' said Bella. 'Jack, help Mrs Gilver, won't you?'

But Mary put her hand on his arm and gripped it tightly.

'Find Abigail,' she said. 'Keep her out of the way while we see what's happened.'

'Can you make it go?' I asked Bella, thinking that I could have been halfway up the stairs by now. She nodded, strode over the floor towards me, rattled open the door of the lift shaft and the door of the carriage itself and slammed both shut again behind us.

'It came from the top, don't you think?' she said. 'Above the galleries?'

'I think so,' I said.

'Good,' said Bella. 'I'm no expert with this contraption but the attics are as far as it can go.' She tugged hard on the rope and the lift groaned, slowly starting to rise. I would most definitely have been better on the stairs, I thought, listening to the creaks of the pulley winding.

'It was a gun, wasn't it?' said Bella. Her voice was under commendable control.

'Yes, I think so,' I said again. 'The noise and the smell of cordite together. I'm almost sure it must have been.'

The lift wheezed and slowed, then shuddered to a halt. Bella tugged the rope again, securing us up there, then she hauled back the carriage door and reached across the gap to the door of the lift shaft. It was solid up here, not the glittering concertina of the public floors, and when she had got it open I saw that *nothing* up here was the same. We were on a sort of landing or lobby of some kind open to the atrium at one side, but there were no polished railings; instead I saw a safety wall made of crude board painted brown and a ledge jutting in at the top so that no one could approach the edge and be seen by the customers below. It was curiously dark too, but then the ceiling was very low, the walls distempered a dull drab, the floor dark red linoleum of great age, worn to the weave from scrubbing. There was even a trace in the air of the strong floor soap used to scrub it; just a trace, and under it even fainter still there was gunpowder, catching the back of my throat and making me swallow, so that I tasted it too.

Bella Aitken was running her hands over the walls, searching for a light switch.

'I don't even know if there *is* electric light,' she said. 'It's been years since I was up here. Ah!' There was a snap as she threw the switch and revealed the landing in the cold plain light of an unshaded bulb near the ceiling.

Someone – a woman – was lying crumpled on the floor at the base of the opposite wall, with her head propped up at an awkward angle on the skirting board. She was looking at the open lift door, or so it seemed until I stepped closer and saw that her eyes were dull and blank, and then I noticed that her head, one side of her head, was wrong in a way I did not want to look at after the glance that made me flick my eyes away. They took in a dark stain blooming on the brown distempered wall above her and running in trickles down towards the floor.

Stupidly I thought to myself, if she fell against the wall and cut her head, what was that noise? For some reason I was creeping up to her on tiptoe and I was right beside her before I took in what was on the other side of her face. a round dark hole in her temple, and some strands of hair had fallen against it and were clinging there.

'Mirren,' said Bella's voice behind me, almost as quiet as breathing.

Both of the girl's hands were empty, lying there flung out with the fingers curled up. I knelt and felt under her skirt at the right side but there was nothing there.

'Is she . . . was she left-handed?' I asked. Bella Aitken said nothing. So, holding my breath, I reached under her body at the left side trying not to look at where drops of blood had fallen. I could feel her warmth through her clothes as I scrabbled around under her. She shifted a little, slumping further towards the floor, and I drew my hand away, knowing that the police would not want to hear that I had moved her.

'Mirren,' said Bella, just as quiet but with a high, strained note

35

as if she were very softly singing. I looked round at her and saw that she was swaying back and forward.

'Mrs Aitken,' I said, 'please don't faint. Please go back down and tell . . .' I ran over them all in my mind. '. . . Tell Mr Muir to telephone to the police, and see if you can stop anyone else coming up here. Do you understand?'

The firm voice, or perhaps just being given a job to do, rallied her and she tottered back to the lift, hauled the door closed and took the groaning old carriage on its way.

In the silence I made myself look at Mirren Aitken's face again. She was – or had been – very pretty, the sort of girl suited to the fashions of the day, with a heart-shaped face, softly waving hair and a slight, supple figure. Only now that figure was bent at ugly and impossible angles, the soft hair was matted with blood and worse than blood, and the face was a mask carved from bleached wood, unmoving.

'You poor child,' I said.

'Yes,' said a voice, very quietly. I leapt backwards, only just managing not to fall, and peered at where it had come from: a dark corner beyond the reach of the feeble light bulb.

'Mrs Jack?' I said.

'Yes,' said the voice again. I reached up to the bulb and swung it on its cord, trying to see her. She was sitting on the floor with her back against the wall and her legs splayed out like those of a rag doll.

'Mrs Aitken,' I said. 'What happened?'

Abigail Aitken lifted her hand and showed me a revolver, so heavy for her that it wagged from side to side in her grip. She looked at it as though seeing it for the first time.

'It's Jack's,' she said. 'I shot Mirren and now she is dead and they'll hang me and I shall be dead too.'

'Put it down, Mrs Aitken,' I said, concentrating on keeping my voice very gentle and steady. 'Put the gun down on the floor.'

'You don't need to worry,' she said, looking at the revolver again. 'I can't turn it on myself. I tried and I don't have the courage.'

36

'So can you put it down and just slide it away? I'll take care of it for you.'

'No, I want to hold on to it for now,' she said, but at least she put her hand back down into her lap and I thought I could see that her grip loosened. 'That would be the best thing.'

I kept my eyes on her, but I cocked my head up to the side and felt a warm rush of relief pass through me, leaving me tingling. Very faintly, in the distance, the piercing squeals of police whistles had begun.

3

Then followed an endless carnival of horrors, staged in three new galleried circles of hell and peopled by grotesques and ghouls too many to count. Or so it seemed as I lived through it and remembered it later. The Dunfermline City Police had turned out in their entirety and would not let anyone leave until all had been questioned, so the crowds continued to mill, weeping and shrieking, craning and muttering, some of them still trying to swap those tokens for jubilee prizes from the roulette wheels. Then as the afternoon wore on they grew restive, beginning to complain, beginning to make up their own stories since no one would tell them what had happened. Grimly, the constables wrote out names and addresses, double-checked who had been where and what they had heard and seen, until slowly, eventually, Aitkens' revolving door began to turn again, spitting out chagrined witnesses in weary ones and twos, to take the news and all the stories they had made out into the town and spread them there.

The family, exalted guests and staff were treated rather better but for all of that fared rather worse, corralled first in the haberdashery and then in the back office regions, with glasses of water and talk of tea, but with two constables watching them and deaf ears listening to their fading pleas and their growing anger.

The Provost, his lady and the boys were not kept long, to be sure; innocent youth, high office, and the fact that 'Netta' was the sister of a sergeant being sturdy claims to gentle treatment, it seemed.

'I told them what they asked me, Mrs Aitken dear,' said Mrs Provost – I never did learn her name, 'but not a word more.

38

They'll not get gossip from me.' Mary shrank under the assurances and I felt for her. That 'dear' spoke volumes; leather-bound, hand-tooled, gilt-edged volumes. The kind reference to 'gossip' did the same: Netta had a hold over Mary Aitken now upon which she would coast along for ever.

'Least said, soonest mended,' said the Provost. 'I'll bid you good day, Mrs Aitken, and thank you for all the civility you've shown me and mine.' This had a decided air of final summary about it and one inferred that whatever tradition of friendly warmth had culminated in the Provost's speech today the acquaintance was now over, finished off as rapidly and effectively as a new horseshoe plunged into the cold water of the smithy's pail.

'I'll jist see youse out,' said the constable.

He soon returned and it became clear that the Lawson family could expect no such favours. That is, Lady Lawson was handled with kid gloves and forelocks were tugged almost out at their roots around her; likewise the two younger sons, although I thought I could detect a more practical, a more instrumental, source for the swiftness with which they were ground through the mill and released from its workings. The police sergeant and constable concerned, I rather thought, spotted early on – or perhaps knew of old (Dunfermline is a smallish town) – that these two wilting, blinking objects did not have the brains to be sensible witnesses to a crime which did not involve them. When it came to the eldest son, though, the constable was a model of thoroughness, chewing surprisingly long and hard to see if there were any useful meat on the boy's spindly bones.

This was puzzling; young Mr Lawson had been in full view of scores of onlookers throughout the crucial time and he, no less than his brothers, had clearly been dragged along to the jubilee by his mother. Why anyone would think he was a named cast member with a speaking part in this tragedy was beyond me. And the mystery only deepened when I began to see the looks which flew around like shuttlecocks, batted from Mary Aitken to Lady Lawson, to the boy and back again.

When Roger Lawson, with stern glares and injunctions not to go on any journeys from home, was finally let go, the sergeant turned to the managerial staff: Mr Muir standing to attention with just his mouth trembling as he told all he knew; Miss Hutton weeping silently, the tears splashing onto her corsage; and Mrs Lumsden clasping her by her bony shoulders and shushing like a nursemaid, returning glare for glare until the sergeant relented and let all three of them leave.

Now we came to it; it was the family, of course, who interested me, the prospect of the family being questioned and having to give answers which had held me here all the long hours since I had stood watching Abigail Aitken cradling the gun in her lap, looking at her daughter, dry-eyed, expressionless, her chest rising and falling only a little and very slowly, as though she were enjoying a light sleep instead of waiting for her life to tumble down around her.

I shall never forget the moment when the heavy tramp of boots on the stairs stopped and the policeman joined us on the landing, for it is not often that one sees courage laid out with so little pomp, as though it were an everyday matter to be a hero. He was in his twenties, large and gangling, with a very new haircut and the aftermath of a very inexpert morning shave. He strode into the light, looked at me and then down at Mirren. He frowned and I saw his hand go for his truncheon but I nodded towards the corner where Abigail Aitken sat, where I was still training the light of the bulb, my arm aching from being held high above me. He turned, his boots squeaking against the lino, and she raised the gun again and pointed it towards him.

'Now, now, Mrs Aitken,' he said. 'Nane o' that. You dinnae want to be at that game.' And without hesitating he walked towards her, the same heavy, measured tread that I had heard ascending, squatted down, shook a handkerchief from his trouser pocket and took the gun from her hand. Behind his back, with marvellous dexterity, he wrapped the thing and laid it aside then, like a considerate beau helping his sweetheart to her feet at a picnic, he took her hands in his and rose gently until both were standing.

'I'm sorry aboot this noo, Mrs Aitken,' he said, and then he wrapped just one of his large hands around both of her small ones, unclasped a pair of handcuffs from his belt and, turning her away, fastened them behind her.

That was the end of tranquillity though. More feet were pounding up the stairs and I could hear the lift wheezing too and soon it seemed that the landing was full of constables and of shouting and more than one of them retched at the sight of Mirren and had to rush away and one of them grabbed me roughly around the upper arms and frog-marched me to the top of the stairway, until another stopped him and said he should wait and then the inspector came and the rushing, shouting men turned quiet and shuffled, looked for jobs to do and failed to find them, so only idled like cattle herded against a gate. And through it all Mirren lay with her eyes half-open and her neck bent so uncomfortably up against the skirting that one longed to move it and set a pillow under her head, but the inspector did not even touch her, only squatted and peered, and shouted at the herd of jostling constables to get out of the way, go downstairs and try not to step in any dust or handle the banisters on the way. Eventually he turned and looked over the four of us remaining.

'Take Mrs Aitken downstairs, McCann,' he said to the first young constable.

'Abigail,' I began, but the inspector interrupted me.

'Don't talk to the prisoner unless you want to say it again in the court,' he said.

'Sorry,' I said. 'Inspector, you should know, I think, that this young man of yours was quite splendid. Just terrific.'

'Naw, Mrs,' said the constable. 'No' really. Only jist Mrs Aitken wis ma Sunday school teacher and I ken her. She'd nivver harm a fly.'

'If you've finished your wee chat, then,' said the inspector and Abigail was led away. The inspector turned to look at the bloodstain on the wall and spoke over his shoulder to the constable who still had me in his grip.

'Escort Mrs Gilver to somewhere nearby and find her a seat. And for goodness' sake, boy, stop manhandling her. Don't you ever read the papers?' He looked at me again, unsmiling, and not I thought only because of Mirren lying there. He did not approve of my sort, I could tell.

'Is this why you're here?' he said. 'If I find out you knew this was coming and didn't say . . .'

'I knew nothing until two hours ago.'

'And what did you hear then?'

'That Mirren Aitken had gone missing. My first advice – the first words out of my mouth – were that the family should ring the police. Ask them and they'll tell you so.'

'Aye, well, *you're* all right then,' said the inspector and turned away.

'What a bloody nerve!' said Alec, staring at me unbelieving. I had withstood the inspector and then the hours of hell without a tremor, but Alec's sympathetic outrage undid me and my eyes filled with tears. 'Damned if you do and damned if you don't, eh?' I nodded and tried to resist sinking into self-pity; there was too much to tell.

We were sitting in the coffee room of the Royal Hotel, finally having the rendezvous we had planned. I gathered that Alec had spent quite some time battering against the doors of Aitkens' like a trapped bee, demanding to be let in and then pleading to be told what was happening by the witnesses as they began to emerge.

'And I can tell you this, Dandy,' he said, 'if I'd thought half of it were true I'd have launched myself through one of those bloody plate-glass windows like a human cannon ball and come to get you. Good luck to the police trying to get a straight story out of those damned ghouls.'

'You're swearing a lot, Alec dear,' I said, with a glance behind me where a hatch was open to the bar. I could just see the broad back of a barmaid, hovering nearby, discreetly listening.

'I'm sure all those damns and bloodies would be fine in the taproom but I think we might get chucked out if you keep it up through here.'

'You're right,' Alec said, 'but I've had a very frustrating afternoon, Dan. Only cursing or strong drink will dissipate it and strong drink gets in the way of detecting.'

'Speaking of which,' I said. I scraped my chair closer to his and lowered my voice. The broad-backed barmaid gave up and moved away. 'What did you find out from the Hepburns?'

'But you're not finished yet,' Alec said. 'Tell me how the family stood up to being questioned.' I sighed. Alec is the dearest man I have ever met in a life well-filled with men, but he could turn two flies crawling up a wall into a competition and no matter how mundane his discoveries might be and how dramatic mine, he was determined that his report would be the finale.

'Very well,' I said. 'Bella Aitken was quite simply stunned. Bewildered. Utterly unable to take in what had happened. Utterly without the first idea of why it could have happened. She kept saying it: but why, but why.'

'Nothing unusual there, surely,' Alec said.

'But that's the thing, darling,' I answered. 'No one except me and the police knows about Abigail. Jack asked where his wife was, of course, while we were all being held in the offices together, but only once and pretty late in the day – he wasn't about to fling himself through windows – and all the sergeant told him was that she was being taken care of. I honestly think he, Mary and Bella believed that she'd collapsed and a doctor had her.'

'Still?' said Alec. 'They'll have to let on sometime that she's been clapped in irons and taken away.'

'Hardly clapped in irons,' I said, remembering. 'Gently taken under the wing of one of her old Sunday school pupils. I wouldn't have thought an arrest could be a kindly thing until I saw that one.'

'Well, he'd handed her over by the time they got downstairs

then,' Alec said. 'She was marched out like Joan of Arc on her way to the stake.'

'How would you know how *she* was marched?' I asked, reasonably enough.

'In dramatic retellings,' said Alec with great dignity. 'I was that maid once, you know. In a school play. Anyway, she was marched out and bundled into the Black Maria with absolutely no kindliness whatsoever.'

'Huh,' I said. 'I thought a Black Maria was for plague victims. Or am I getting mixed up with Typhoid Mary?'

'You're wasting time on idle chat when we should be concentrating,' said Alec, and even though what he called idle chat was bringing me back to life after the suffocating effects of my horrible afternoon, I gathered my wits again and resumed reporting.

'So we must ask ourselves why Bella Aitken can't make herself believe that Mirren committed suicide.'

'You're sure she would have assumed it was suicide?'

'Completely. It's what I thought when I saw Mirren – I even rootled around for the gun. It was the obvious thing to think. Mirren was unhappy, she went missing and she killed herself. That's what everyone who wasn't up there must be thinking.'

'So Aunt Bella shouldn't really be so puzzled,' said Alec, with a nod. 'Yes, I see. And how did the Queen Bee take the news?' I felt some remorse that the way I had spoken of Mary Aitken had caused Alec to make his mind up about her so completely.

'She was very shocked, very surprised – horrified – and she—'

'Hang on,' said Alec. 'Horrified how? Wringing her hands and saying 'Oh, how horrifying,' or something that can't be faked, like going pale?'

It was a fair question, even a good question, but so blunt to one who had been there with them that I am sure I frowned at him even while I was answering.

'Oh, she was pale enough,' I said. 'And trembling and her

hands were cold. No doubt it was real shock; I'd take an oath on it.'

'Only, of course, I was thinking perhaps this was what you could scupper today.' Frankly, I had been thinking the same. '*This* was why Mary Aitken wanted you to turn up tomorrow. So that she could point at you as evidence that she knew nothing and was trying to find the girl.'

'Mary Aitken knew her granddaughter was going to be killed and yet still invited all those people to come along and be there when it happened? It's not very likely.'

'And finally, Jack,' Alec said, ignoring my quibbles. 'The father.'

I drew a deep sigh and tried not to sob as I let it go.

'It's as though a part of him has died too,' I said. 'When the inspector told him, he just . . . I was going to say crumpled, but that's not right. He turned to stone. Or clay, almost set, just able to move, but only just. It was one of the saddest things . . .'

'And quite a change from how he'd been before, from what you were saying on the telephone,' Alec said, tapping a little tune against his teeth and frowning at me.

'When he hears it was his wife I really do fear for him,' I said. 'When he hears she did it with his gun, I can't imagine what he'll do. Thank goodness the gun will be held as evidence, that's all. With any luck he only had the one or I wouldn't put a shilling on him making it through the night.'

'Service revolver, was it?' said Alec.

'I think so,' I said.

'That's most likely,' Alec said. 'If you smelled cordite yards and yards off after one shot it must have been pretty old and dirty. A service revolver from the back of a sock drawer sounds about the size of it.'

'Poor Jack,' I said.

'So you're pretty sure he didn't know what was coming?'

'Positive,' I said.

'Only I was thinking about your description of Abigail saying she "couldn't" and everyone else trying to persuade her that she had to. You thought she meant going out in public, but maybe . . .'

'What? They're all in it together? Impossible. Although, on the subject of alliances, I did get the distinct impression there was something going on between Mary and Lady Lawson.'

'What do you mean? What kind of something?'

'No idea,' I said. 'Or perhaps they're just very good friends and were succouring one another with affectionate glances.'

'Have you been reading Richardson again?' Alec said.

'One thing *is* troubling me about the idea that Abigail acted off her own bat.' I folded up my little napkin and tucked it under the edge of my plate. I had not touched the sandwiches and I knew I was not going to. 'I don't see how she would have had time to get there. She didn't go in the lift, and if she had raced up the stairs in time to shoot Mirren after the last time I saw her on the ground floor, she'd still have been panting when Bella and I got there. I'm sure of it.'

'Well, how long are we talking about?' said Alec. He took his fourth sandwich, folded it in two and put it in his mouth.

'I'm trying to think,' I said. 'Jack left first. To go and tell the staff to close the front door— Oh!'

'My God, Dandy,' said Alec, through a mouthful of sandwich. '*Jack left*? You might have said that before now. When did he come back again?'

'Not until after the gunshot,' I said, 'because his first words were to ask what the noise had been. But hush, Alec, something just struck me.'

'But that means it might have been *him*. If the problem with Abigail was lack of time.'

'Be quiet, you just distracted me when I'd almost remembered something.'

'Are you quite sure that he left before she did?' I gave up chasing the thought that had brushed against me and drifted off again.

'Absolutely certain,' I said. 'It was Jack leaving that made Abigail feel woozy – she had been holding on to him, you see. And when he went she said to her mother that she wanted to sit down or something and her mother told her to stay put. And that's when Bella went away to get her a glass of water.'

'Bella left too?' Alec was looking at me as though I were an idiot of some interesting kind.

'Yes, but Alec, it's not the way it sounded. There wasn't time. Jack went and then Bella went and we waited for the merest minute and then Mary got impatient and started things off and the Provost only spoke for a moment – that was long enough – and then he pulled the cord.'

'And how long after that was the shot?' said Alec. I had already told him every scrap of this, but he is not above treating me like a witness when he feels like it and so I told him again.

'Instantaneous,' I said. 'Almost. The tiniest delay. I did tell you, darling; I thought pulling the cord had *caused* the bang.'

'Maybe it did,' said Alec. 'No, listen. Maybe something was rigged. Maybe that's why Mary Aitken did what she did that was so odd.' I shook my head, not following. 'She started the proceedings when two, possibly three, of the principals weren't there. She deliberately went ahead when her sister-in-law and her son-in-law were nowhere to be seen and would be left having to account for themselves.'

'But she tried to keep her daughter on the scene,' I said, nodding. Then I tutted at him. 'How could it be anything like that? How could pulling a gold cord three floors below make a gun go off?'

'It could send a signal to an accomplice,' Alec said. We pondered this in silence for a moment or two. Then Alec puffed his cheeks out and patted his pockets in the manner I knew so well. I coughed and pointed to a discreet sign requesting gentlemen to retire to the lounge bar to enjoy their pipes. I laughed at his face and tossed him over a cigarette.

'Filthy habit,' Alec said, lighting it. 'Have you remembered your elusive titbit yet?'

'I haven't,' I said. 'But it's interesting that you assume it's a titbit and not a clue of great magnitude. Why don't you fill me in on your visit to the Capulets?'

'Montagues,' said Alec. 'Yes, I'm sure, before you shout me down *again*.' He stuck his tongue out at me. 'Because I always thought "Juliet Capulet" was proof that Shakespeare had a tin ear for poetry.' He took a deep puff of his cigarette then frowned at it and stubbed it out. 'There were two Hepburns in the directory, but I hit the mark first time.'

'You got to speak to the boy himself?'

'No,' said Alec. 'I mean, I hit his father. Also – briefly – his mother.'

'And?'

'Very interesting,' Alec said, slowly and annoyingly. I waited. 'The father was absolutely dead-set against the marriage.'

'I don't blame him,' I said. 'No one likes to push in where he's not wanted and the Aitkens cannot stand the Hepburns. I wouldn't have thought rivalry could be so fierce. I mean, companies are always amalgamating, aren't they? Especially these days.'

'I don't think it had anything to do with the business as far as Robert Hepburn is concerned,' Alec said. 'It was more heartfelt than that. He looked – what's that word – thoroughly scunnered when I made him talk about it.'

'How did you make him anyway?' I said. I could not imagine the scene: Alec rolling up at the man's house, a perfect stranger, and asking him to explain such a private matter.

'Easy,' Alec said. 'I told him Mirren was missing and he turned quite pale and rushed off to the telephone. It was while he was out of the room, incidentally, that I got a few words in with Mrs Hepburn. She came to see what the fuss was and she told me that Dugald was "away from home staying with friends".'

'Ah,' I said. 'So his father had shot off to telephone these friends and check that the boy hadn't disappeared too?'

'Exactly. Or that Mirren hadn't turned up there, I suppose.

And when he got back, he was so relieved that he spoke quite freely. He said he would never consent to his son marrying "such a girl", from "such a background", with "such relations". But here's an interesting thing. Hepburn said his wife agreed with him, but while he was out of the room, she seemed to suggest that the objection was all hers and she had had to talk her husband round. She seemed surprised that she'd managed it.'

'And was she any more forthcoming about what the problem was?'

'No,' said Alec, 'but she wasn't nearly as . . . visceral about it all. Ruefully amused, I'd say rather, as though the whole thing was a bit of a joke.'

'A bit of a joke . . .' I repeated, feeling a memory stir. 'Ha-hah! That's it. I remember. I remember why Jack Aitken was sent to close the doors. Mrs . . . I can't recall her name, but she's a senior member of staff at the Emporium . . . said she thought there had been an *entente cordiale* – except she made it sound fruit-flavoured – thought, and I quote, "them down by" were coming to the jubilee. Said it was just the sort of thing they might do and think it a great wheeze.'

'What are you talking about, Dandy?'

'Mrs Somebody who is a manager at Aitkens' said that the girls in the Household Department had reported seeing Mr Hepburn in the store.'

Alec stared.

'And where is the Household Department?' he said.

'It's split into two, but at least some of it's on the top floor.'

'The top floor,' Alec repeated. 'Close to the attics in other words then.'

'But Mr Hepburn was at home, Alec. You were there with him.'

'I was with *a* Mr Hepburn,' Alec said. 'There is young Mr Dugald Hepburn to be accounted for as well. And I was there briefly. Ten minutes at most.'

'We're getting carried away,' I said. 'Yes, people were running

49

around the store like mice and perhaps one of the girls did see an unexpected visitor, but Abigail Aitken killed her daughter. She had a smoking gun in her hand, almost literally. And she confessed. There's no reason to doubt what I saw.' On the last of these points, however, I was wrong.

Alec and I lingered over our coffee and then with no particular enthusiasm I stirred myself to go to the police station, find out whatever news I could and bear it back to the Aitkens. I hoped I could somehow soften the blow for them, I suppose, or at least tell them of Abigail's demeanour and pass on my heartfelt belief that she had lost her mind that afternoon and was more to be pitied than reviled. Just as we reached the police station, however, we almost had our heels clipped by a small black motorcar emerging from a side lane at some speed and roaring off along the Maygate.

'That was Abigail Aitken in the back seat,' I said, stepping out into the middle of the road and staring after it. It was setting a tremendous pace for a narrow street in a busy town.

'And it was definitely a bobby driving,' said Alec. 'Are you all right, Dandy? Did it brush you?' I shook my head.

'I wonder where they're taking her?' I said. 'Good God, surely a hospital. Surely. Not a prison. *Is* there a women's prison anywhere near here?'

'Let's go in and ask the sarge,' said Alec. 'I should think you can claim to be a representative of the family, don't you?'

The front office of the station was fairly buzzing with news; clumps of constables standing around with their uniform jackets off and their hats on the back of their heads, reliving their uncommon afternoon. It was with some difficulty that they managed to stop gossiping when Alec and I appeared amongst them.

'The sarge' however was immovable. I petitioned as a witness, as a family friend, as a prominent member of society who could command an audience with the Chief Constable at a click of the fingers, as a licensed private detective (the licence was fantasy,

50

of course; if such things exist I certainly did not possess one) and finally as a subject of His Majesty and citizen of what I believed to be a free democracy and not the kind of totalitarian state where he would clearly be more at home, but there was no budging him. I was just gathering myself to deliver a farewell tirade which I hoped would spoil his dinner and his night's sleep even if it got *me* nothing much, when Alec cleared his throat and tapped the side of my shoe with the side of his. I turned. Someone was signalling to me from the street door, a young man in grey flannel trousers and a knitted pullover whom it took me a moment to recognise as Constable McCann. I shut my mouth, tirade undelivered, and followed Alec outside to where McCann was waiting.

'I dinnae ken why they're being so close wi' it,' he said. 'Mrs Aitken is away hame. It's no' a secret.'

'Out on bail, eh?' said Alec. 'Perhaps they fear a mob descending if it's generally known.'

At that moment another pair of young officers in their civvies came out of the station and stared hard at us in passing.

'I cannae talk here,' said McCann. 'I'll meet youse roond at the park gates on Pittencrieff Street.' He pointed. 'None o' my brother officers stay oot that way.'

He took off at a good pace and Alec and I followed casually, after an interval. When we reconvened, Constable McCann asked us to walk along with him, saying that his mother would have his tea ready and the dog would get the lot if he was late again.

'It's no' bail she's got,' he said when we were under way. 'She's let go. She's innocent. Wee Mirren killt herself, so the doc said anyway.'

'But I saw her,' I said, stopping walking until Alec put a hand under my elbow to get me moving again. 'She was sitting there with the gun in her hand and the blood still dripping. Besides, she confessed.'

'Aye well,' said Constable McCann. 'The thing is, see, the police surgeon took – what d'ye cry them? – swabs. From Mrs Aitken's

51

hands and from Mirren's hands an' a' and it turns oot they can tell fae the gunpowder how Mirren had fired the gun and her mother hadnae. So there it is.'

'And the confession?' I said. We had arrived at McCann's house it seemed: a small grey cottage in a long terraced row. He stopped at the open front door. From behind a fringed fly curtain, there drifted the smell of bacon and the sound of a wireless.

'Dr Stott said it happens all the time,' he said. 'A suicide and the mammy pretending she did murder.' He touched his cap and disappeared behind the coloured beads of the curtain.

'Can you believe that?' Alec said, looking after him.

I nodded. 'Thinking back, you know, she practically told me. In subtle code, but all the same. She said she didn't have the courage to turn the gun upon herself, but she wanted to sit there holding it until the police came, because Mirren was dead and only if they hanged her could she be dead too.'

Alec heaved a sigh up from his boots.

'What a god-awful mess,' he said. 'Poor Aitkens. I wouldn't be in that house right now for a pension.'

'Ah,' I said. 'I was just going to suggest we paid them a visit.' Alec looked suitably horrified and I hastened to explain.

'I was supposed to find her, Alec. I was charged with finding her and bringing her home. As awkward as it's going to be socially—'

'Awkward!' Alec squawked and I grimaced, agreeing with him.

'—professionally, the least I can do is go and acknowledge . . . my complete failure.'

Abbey Park, however, was shut tight against all comers. The gate by which I had entered that morning was closed – locked and padlocked – and the tradesmen's gate the same. The little lodge had its door locked and windows shuttered, and the house itself was hidden behind its walls.

'I'll write to her, then,' I said, standing peering up at the chimneys, unable to help imagining what scenes of despair might be playing out in those rooms now. I hoped perhaps that Mary would be comforting Abigail, that Bella might have found it in herself to succour Jack, but when I remembered them all at the Emporium, stunned and crumpled by the shock of it, it was only too easy to think that each of the four would be curled up alone in some separate quiet corner, silently aching.

4

One could hardly believe it was the same town. The sun was shining as it had a week before and there was nothing the park-keepers could do about the beds of tulips and pansies but otherwise, when I emerged from the station on the day of Mirren Aitken's funeral, it was into a very different Dunfermline. Black ribbon wreaths were pinned to the doors of the Carnegie Library and, as far as I could tell all the civic buildings with which this tiny city is so lavishly endowed. All the shops in the High Street had their shades half-lowered and were displaying in their windows only the soberest and most blameless of wares: dark clothes, tartan carriage rugs and luggage; for some reason every shop which could muster it had filled its windows with luggage. The protocols and etiquettes of the merchant trade, I thought (not for the first time), were a mystery to me.

Needless to say, Aitkens' long row of plate glass was covered completely over with what looked like best black velvet. It must have cost them a pretty penny and I wondered idly if the bolts would be rewound and go back on the shelves to be sold after-wards or if the sunshine would have streaked it to uselessness. It was slightly out of my way but I could not resist walking down as far as Hepburns' to see how their window trimmers had responded to the tragedy. With a dignified restraint which was somehow more excruciating than respectful, was the answer: the sporting young couple and the backdrops of their leisured life had been removed and in their place was set a single dark hat on a milliner's stand just off centre in each window.

The investigation had been completed within days, the inquiry satisfied in a few days more and, although the procurator fiscal

54

had mouthed familiar words about the balance of her mind, he had also taken his chance of a swipe at her family for their part in the sad affair and thus had appeared to align himself with the newspapers and the gossips in the streets, where revulsion at the families' behaviour was the dominant note in the chord.

It was reported with the most bitter relish of all in the *News of the World* from which Grant had read it out to me. To be fair, though, the *Scotsman* had also 'let out quite a bit of line in its editorial, judging the rivalry of the Aitkens and Hepburns an indulgence for which the life of a pretty young girl was far too high a price to pay. *The Times* meanwhile had reported the matter with a disdainful loftiness which must have hurt more than the gossip in its way, and I hoped the families had not seen it and did not have the sorts of friends who would summarise the articles at future meetings, or indeed clip them and read them out, or even – as one of my great aunts used to do in the name of helpfulness, but really out of devilry – clip them and actually post them to the parties in question with biblical verses printed out on little cards.

All that was left now was the funeral and it was set for two o'clock in the afternoon. Yet here I was at just gone eleven in the morning, retracing my steps of a week before. I had an address written on a card in my hand (although it was my butler's own clear writing, since the message had come by telephone) and had been engaged by a lady I did not know to discuss the matter of Miss Aitken in a professional capacity.

I found the end of Pilmuir Street after a little effort and toiled up it, realising too late – once I had deserted the busy part of town where there might be taxis – that number one hundred and twenty could be a stiff hike away. Sure enough I was puffing like a tugboat by the time I arrived.

So perhaps it was shortness of breath that was making me dizzy and perhaps that contributed to the nasty prickling I could feel, but at least some of it was owing to the nightmarish sense that I was reliving a dark reflection of that cheerful day a week before. Once again the house for which I was bound surprised me;

Roseville was Georgian grey just like Abbey Park, but was very wide and low, and set back from the pavement behind white railings with two patches of tumbling cottage garden on either side of a flagged path. It had a coach house at one flank and a high orchard wall at the other and was as charming as it was unexpected: a village house, my mother would have called it (never suspecting that when she did so in those ringing tones of hers she always offended the owners, who heard the echo of 'a village child' for which read apple thief, 'a village family' where laundrymaids and jobbing gardeners might be found, and 'a village affair' by which she meant any feud or scandal she deemed beneath her notice which was nonetheless too significant to be ignored).

A maid who had clearly been told to expect me – 'advised of my arrival' as she put it – let me in and showed me into a morning room at the back of the house with a french window open onto the garden. I just had time to note the pale carpet and silk-covered walls, the elegant gilded furniture and delicate watercolours, but I had no chance for my customary snooping before the door opened again and someone strode into the room. A young woman, a woman, an elderly woman, I thought in quick succession as she came towards me and held out her hand, for the initial impression of vigour was seen off by the matronly cut of her coat and skirt and the confident rake of her hat (an angle like that only comes, if it comes at all, with maturity), and the coat and skirt and hat (and brooch and pearls) in their turn could not disguise the iron grey hair, lined skin and thickened wrists of quite advanced age. She wore startlingly red lipstick and had painted very thick black eyebrows onto her head; her nails too were red and black – red from paint and black from gardening. I knew the type. She was not, after all, an elderly woman: she was a game old girl.

'Mrs Gilver,' she said, giving me a wide grin and showing strong yellow teeth which were not flattered by the lipstick, neither the shade of it nor the fact that a great deal of it was on them. 'Fiona Haddo. Bella Aitken told me about you. Thank you for coming and do sit down.'

She rang for coffee and then eased herself into an armchair and regarded me.

'It's about Mirren.'

I nodded. The nightmare was going strong.

'I'm Googie's grandmother, you see.' I said nothing and my face must have been blank because she hurried to explain. 'Dugald. Googie was his little sister's best attempt and it stuck. Hilda – my daughter – hates it.'

I could not help my eyebrow rising at her daughter's name. Hilda Haddo was a dreadful curse to visit upon a child.

'Oh, I know,' said her mother, getting the point of the raised brow. She was clearly an old girl of great perception and I would need to disport myself more cautiously. 'But she *was* a Hilda. If you'd only seen her the day she was born – glaring up at me with that look on her face telling me the whole thing was an outrage. A Teutonic battle-maid if ever I'd seen one. Anyway, she's Hilda Hepburn now which isn't so bad. Unless one counts it as bad that I married off my daughter to a draper's boy. Sounds like a music-hall song, doesn't it?' She laughed again. 'But Robert Junior – Robin, as the family have always called him – is a dear man, with pots of money, and Hilda has been very happy. Until now, of course. Until now.'

'The boy must be distraught,' I said. 'I can quite imagine his mother suffering along with him.'

'Hm,' said Fiona Haddo, but did not elaborate.

'Was he terribly fond of her?'

'Googie adored her,' said Mrs Haddo. 'To see them together was almost enough to make one believe in love's young dream again. Even a cynical old trout like me could grow quite misty. So it's almost beyond belief that . . .' She gave me a shrewd look. 'How much do you know?'

'Well,' I said, carefully, 'I've heard a great deal but all from one source. Another perspective would perhaps be illuminating.' Fiona Haddo gave a twisted smile in acknowledgement of my carefully chosen words.

'I'll start at the beginning,' she said. 'Mirren and Googie had

57

many friends in common as you can imagine – Dunfermline is a small town – but they were never particular friends of one another. So it was a surprise to us all when Googie told us he was engaged. Just after St Valentine's Day. He must have proposed then – such a sweet boy. Twenty years old and he informed his father and mother about it as though he were the headmaster giving out extra prep.'

'Mirren wasn't quite so forceful with her parents,' I said.

'And the Aitkens were adamant in their refusal. Beyond adamant.'

'Not all of the Aitkens, surely. I can't imagine Abigail . . .'

She grinned at me. 'No, not all. Perhaps just one. But that one is very forceful indeed. You know, of course, that she was a shop-girl when Ninian married her?' I nodded. 'And of course, Aitkens' is the older of the two firms and they view the Hepburns as fearful usurpers. But it was her mother and father that Mirren spoke of when she came to me. Abigail and Jack had forbidden it too. Well, who can guess at that – they're an odd pair from all I hear. But what did seem odd was that Googie's parents thought the same. And actually, I suppose if one's being fair they were pretty adamant too. Especially Robin. "No son of mine" and all that.'

'Did he say why?'

'He talked about "poor stock" and "weak blood" which was ridiculous.'

'Well, Mirren's mother and father are cousins,' I said. Fiona Haddo shuddered.

'I know,' she said. 'Isn't it ghastly? When I think of my boy cousins, I could almost retch! But people in glass houses . . .'

I looked inquiringly at her.

'The Hepburns themselves are not exactly sturdy stock,' she said. 'Thank God Hilda seems to have brought a bit of vigour back to the line.' Then she moved on very crisply and in a manner which prevented any wheeling back again. 'So. Robin put his foot down about the marriage. Hilda put hers down like Rumpelstiltskin, which isn't like her. Robert Senior – he who established House of Hepburn – was no keener and he's a shrewd businessman that I'd have expected to be all for a merger. Dulcie, Robin's mother, was vehemently against the thing too. Most odd, because Dulcie – perfectly pleasant little woman as I'm always the first to say –' poor Dulcie, I thought – 'is very . . . *Home Chat*, don't you know. Knitting and recipes and what have you, and one would have thought that Mirren Aitken would be her dream of a daughter-in-law. Only I was in favour. And on the other side, as I say, Jack and Abby said no, ghastly Mary did the same and only good old Bella couldn't see the difficulty. We talked about it on the telephone, she and I. You've met Bella, of course?' I acknowledged that I had. 'She's splendid. Another old trout and one of the highest order. We're a force to be reckoned with, you know.' I smiled and waited.

'Anyway,' she said, resuming after stopping to give me a cigarette and light one for herself. I noticed that her hand shook slightly as she held it to her lips and I surmised that we were coming to the crux of the matter. 'The thing is, I wasn't prepared to sit idly by and let young love be snuffed out for no reason. I live here – have done for years – but I still have a dower house of my own. My husband left it to me and I kept it to annoy my daughter-in-law. I also kept a tiara and a couple more pieces I should really have sold if I wasn't going to pass them on. But it's always irked me the way that we old girls are expected to relinquish our jewels – we need them more than pretty young faces, don't we? Also – here's the nub of it – I have shares in House Of Robin gave them to me in a fit of . . . something or other, when he and Hilda were married. Sort of welcoming me to the clan kind of thing, I suppose. So all in all, I was just about able to toddle on and do my fairy godmother routine. They were going to elope and stay in the dower house – poor things: it's pretty crumbly – living off the proceeds of the tiara until I had used my shares like a mallet to din some sense into everyone.'

'I see,' I said.

'Good,' said Mrs Haddo, 'but I'll spell it out anyway.' She

stubbed out her cigarette, grinding it away to fragments in the ashtray. 'Mirren Aitken didn't kill herself. She had no reason to.'

I watched her through the ribbon of smoke which was drifting upwards from my own cigarette. She was very sure and very angry but I wondered if she had followed those angry thoughts through to their ends.

'Yes,' she said. The way she read my mind was beginning to unnerve me. 'I think someone killed her. And I didn't tell the police at any point during the last week because it was obvious who the suspects would be. The family of the boy.'

'So what's changed?' I asked her. 'Why are you speaking up now?'

She tried to light another cigarette, but her hands shook so much that she could not get the match to strike against the side of the box. When she had missed it three times I half-stood to help her, but she waved me away.

'I thought I'd be able to pull this off,' she said. 'Almost made it, eh?' She grinned again but there was no humour in it now. Her eyes were large and stark in her face. 'A week past Monday—'

'You mean after Mirren had run away?' The Scotch, with their next Friday and last Tuesday there, were always confusing me.

'Was it? Well around then anyway, it was suddenly decided to pack Googie off to our friends at Kelso – as though a few days' fishing were going to cheer him up again like a lollipop for skinned knees used to – and the thing is, they telephoned this morning. Googie disappeared from his room last night.'

'You think he might turn up at the funeral and make a scene?'

She shook her head. She was looking down at the floor, digging one elegant heel into the pile of the carpet.

'Well, do you think he might suspect someone in particular? That he might be intent on revenge?'

'That's the least of my worries,' she said. Her eyes filled and, compared to their shining, all of a sudden her face looked grey and papery, terribly old. 'The thing is, Googie is absolutely hope-less at keeping secrets. Always has been. So when it came to the elopement, I cooked it all up with Mirren behind his back, Bella helping. We were going to spring it on him.'

'And since Mirren died?' I said, very quietly.

'I didn't tell him. I thought it would be best if he could think of Mirren as . . . well, as not the sort to make a good wife, even if she did love him . . . doing that to herself. I thought I was helping him get over her.' Then she sniffed and put a tight, brave smile – terrible to behold – upon her face. 'And now he's gone missing – not angry and vengeful, Mrs Gilver, but wretched. And no one knows where he is and I keep thinking of Romeo and Juliet. Because I didn't tell him. He still doesn't know.'

I questioned her very closely, asking about Dugald's friends and habits and favourite places, and left her eventually well after one o'clock (when I was beginning to feel some concern about the length of Pilmuir Street and the nearness of the funeral hour) with a long list of telephoning to do. Quietly to myself, I remained convinced that the funeral was where Dugald would be bound after bunking off from Kelso and I was glad that Alec was going to be with me; between us we would be able to keep a sharp eye on all corners of the Abbey and might even be able to bundle the young man away before he caused a scene.

At least the return journey was downhill but even so I became rather flushed on the way and much more dishevelled than one ought to be when presenting oneself as a mourner, my hair flying out at the sides from under my hat, my coat unbuttoned and silk scarf flapping, gloves off and jammed in my bag which had seemed a good idea for a brisk trot on a warm day but now left me with the task of getting them back again onto hands swollen with heat and hurry. I was wrestling with them as I turned down the Kirkgate, assuring myself that at least I would be able to dodge into the Abbey at the other end from where the family party would be arriving, for Abbey Park lay beyond the far side of the church grounds with a gate very handy, when to my horror in the distance I saw the unmistakable sight of four nodding black plumes which could only be the head ornaments of horses pulling a hearse. They had gone right around the Abbey to arrive at the most impressive entrance – of course, they had! Had I forgotten the winding procession on the jubilee day? – and we were set to meet on the very steps unless I swerved and found another route quickly.

I swerved. Thankfully Dunfermline Abbey Church, plonked in the middle of the city that way, is well served with gates and I darted unseen into the nearest one.

I should have known really that the funeral arrangements for Mirren would be lavish to the last degree. Peeping between the gravestones I could see not only the four plumed horses pulling a glass-sided hearse carriage but feathermen too, pages with batons, and what might even be mutes, if such things really still existed. Behind all of that came the same two motorcars from last week, their hoods up and their side windows shaded with black netting. The strain of moving so slowly could be heard in the rumble of their engines, and the chauffeurs' faces were grim with tension as they tried to avoid the ignominy of stalling.

Alec was waving at me from the Abbey doors, hopping from foot to foot, and we slipped without a moment to spare into the great stone ante-room which leads on to the church proper. Hidden from view behind one of the mighty pillars there, I grabbed both his arms in mine and started talking very fast and low.

'Dugald's granny and Bella Aitken were hatching an elopement for them,' I said. 'Mirren knew. She had no reason to kill herself, Alec. It was murder. It had to be.'

'But what about the swabs?' Alec said. 'The police were sure.'

I had been thinking about the swabs and I had an answer. I folded one of my hands around one of his, guided it to his temple and squeezed his fingers.

After a moment, he nodded.

'But not Abigail,' he said. 'Unless she wore gloves.'

'Which she'd either have had on her or would have hidden somewhere,' I said.

'Did the police search the attics?'

'I don't know.'

62

Alec glanced round to the front doors where the sound of heavy tramping feet on the gravel announced the arrival of the coffin at the door.

'Should we try to stop this?' he asked. 'Make them take her body back to the doctor?' I am sure my face fell at the prospect and Alec was no keener.

'It's not a cremation,' I began and that was all he needed. He nodded energetically and together we hurried on tiptoe across the vast darkness and into the lighted nave.

We shuffled ourselves into a back pew, prayed briefly to avoid shocking our neighbours and then sat up and surveyed the sea of hatted heads stretching away in front of us to the distant altar. The Abbey was stuffed to bursting, even the side chapels filled with tight ranks of glum-faced townspeople. And I had forgotten, after years of village churches and house chapels, just how enormous Dunfermline Abbey was; my confidence that Alec and I could subdue Dugald Hepburn, should he suddenly appear, seemed like hollow hubris now.

'It would help if we knew what he looked like,' Alec whispered, clearly having similar thoughts to mine.

'He'll look like a twenty-year-old boy rushing up to hug the coffin,' I replied out of one corner of my mouth. The elderly couple who had squashed up to make room for us both swivelled their eyes and glared. They could not possibly hear what we were saying, but we were whispering in church and that was enough to earn black looks from them. I lowered my voice even further before I spoke again.

'Straight to the police after this?' The female half of the elderly couple gave a ringing tut which drew attention from all around, from members of the congregation who had not been troubled by Alec's and my soft whispering. He mouthed to me that we would talk later.

The organist was already in his seat and at that moment he pumped his feet up and down on the pedals and laid his hands against the keys, sending a miasma of doleful chords rolling over the bowed heads of the waiting mourners. I could hear muffled knocks and thumps from behind as the coffin was manhandled, and I shivered.

Perhaps it was just the cold, the chill of damp air pressing down and the chill of old stone creeping up, so cold that even though every side-table and pillar at the altar and every niche and alcove up the sides was filled with flowers none of their scent could reach us. That was possibly a blessing, for the arrangements – three feet across and cascading to the floor – were made up of enormous rhododendron heads in the palest pink and masses of white narcissus as well as the usual lilies; in a warm room they would have been suffocating.

Here came the coffin, white and glittering, with another heap of flowers resting on it. These narcissi were trembling, showing us that the pall-bearers, although they looked steady and strong, were not unaffected by the burden on their shoulders. Jack Aitken was one of them, Mr Muir the manager of the gentlemen's side another; I did not recognise the other four and saw no family resemblance although I was sure they were not professionals, being too individually dressed in their best dark suits and black shoes, not decked out with the uniformity of undertakers' men.

Behind the coffin the Aitken women made their way up the aisle as though it were a cliff-face and there were a howling gale blowing hard against them. Bella, towering over Mary and Abigail, spread her arms protectively behind them and ploughed unsteadily on, while the two smaller women tottered one faltering step and then with effort another and swaying a little yet another and the congregation held its breath, men in the aisle seats shifting, ready to help should the pitiful threesome flounder.

When they had made it to the front pew and sunk down out of view, the rest of us sat back and the gust of our collective sigh drowned out the low notes of the organ as it began an even more sepulchral lament than before.

Then the minister and two session clerks emerged from the vestry, bowed to the coffin, bowed to the family, and the minister mounted the altar to begin. I swept the edges of the pews with a gaze, checking the sides of every pillar to see if there were any trace of someone hiding there. I could see Alec doing the same. The minister was speaking, intoning, more mournful than the organ even, and he finished with the words: let us pray. I crossed my fingers and bent my head.

'We should have stayed standing up at the back,' Alec whispered.

'Well, we can't go skipping off now,' I whispered back.

'Ssh!' hissed our neighbour, managing to imbue the sound with all the indignation we deserved. I bent my head even further and tried to block out the words of the prayer, listening hard for movements where they should not be.

As it turned out, our vigilance was unneeded. The service wore on, ended, and the coffin and woebegone trio of Aitken ladies left again without any interruptions beyond the odd moment when one of the congregation, trying to weep silently, momentarily failed and had to apply a handkerchief to smother a sob or one of those great wuthering sighs. Alec and I had slipped out in advance of the family party of course, to keep an eye on potential trouble in the kirkyard, but the coffin was deposited back into the hearse, surrounded by wreaths, and the family deposited back into the motorcars, without incident. As the congregation filed out a procession formed behind the second motorcar and then at a snail's pace and with the engines growling, the chauffeurs as tense as before, they drew away from the Abbey doors and began the dreadful journey through the streets to the cemetery (The Abbey kirkyard had long been full, I concluded, looking around at the mossy old gravestones with their epitaphs worn away, and even if there were a plot remaining here and there into which a town worthy or church official might be squeezed, a suicide was never going to have rules bent and space found for her.)

Alec stood watching the procession snaking away. 'Police now or graveside first?' he said. He shivered slightly as he spoke, although one could not tell whether to blame the prospect facing him on the sudden chill in the air – the sun had retreated behind a bank of dark, determined-looking clouds as though it meant to stay there.

'Police for me and graveside for you,' I said. 'I'd stick out like a sore thumb anyway.' The old Scotch tradition of women staying away from the burial held strong in Dunfermline, it seemed. The procession was made up of men alone, and their wives idled at the Abbey door and among the graves, wiping their eyes and shaking their heads and beginning to talk of Mirren and the shame of it all and then slowly but inevitably of other things.

I kissed Alec's cheek and was watching him edge up the side of the procession with a perfect mixture of purpose and decorum so that he could be close to the hearse, when someone sidled up to me and passed me a folded note.

'From Mrs Ninian, dear,' she said. I recognised Aitkens' institution, Mrs . . .

'Mrs Lumsden,' she said, seeing me searching for her name. 'Mrs Ninian asked me to make sure you got this if you were here.'

I opened the note and began to read it.

Dear Mrs Gilver, it said.

'This isn't Mrs Ninian's writing,' I said to myself, frowning.

'No,' said Mrs Lumsden. 'She was very upset. She dictated to me.'

'Oh,' I said. 'Well, how kind you are. You must be such a help.' Mrs Lumsden looked a little uncomfortable, which was puzzling. I gave her an uncertain smile and returned to the note again.

I must beg your patience with regards to a meeting to settle your account. I will be detained at the funeral tea for Mirren today.

I stared, disbelieving, then, aware of Mrs Lumsden waiting for me to answer, I roused myself.

'There's a reception?' I said faintly. Her homely face puckered as she tried to combine her natural loyalty with her equally natural good common sense.

'At the Emporium. Just for the staff,' she said, at last. 'There are a hundred of us and we all loved the lass. Loved her dearly.

We want to give her a send-off no matter what the rights and wrongs of what she did to herself, the poor love.'

'You knew her well, then?' I said. Mrs Lumsden's face was formed for cheerfulness and it took some effort for her mouth to turn down and stay there, but she managed it.

'From as soon as she could walk, she toddled about the store,' she said. 'Up and down on that lift like it was a see-saw. The hours she spent sitting on the counters and she never once fell off. Well, it's every wee girl's dream, isn't it? Playing at shops in a real shop. Yes, we all loved her.'

'And did it seem . . . that is, were you surprised at what she did?'

'Surprised is hardly the word,' said Mrs Lumsden. She looked startled at my understatement and I tried to explain.

'Of course, I do beg your pardon. Of course, it was a horrid shock. It must always be so. But surely, I mean to say, I imagine there are people one could always see taking that way out of life's difficulties and then there are people one couldn't believe would ever do it, no matter what the provocations.'

Mrs Lumsden was frowning at me.

'Take my two—' I was going to say sons, but a flash of white panic at the thought stopped me from going further. 'Take my brother and sister,' I said instead. 'Mavis is a gloomy sort of girl, always was so. She used to have funerals for her dolls and she has a dreadful habit of adopting three-legged horses and one-eared mongrels and then weeping over them. I've told her time and again to get a healthy puppy from good stock and a clean home and she won't spend such hours nursing and mourning. But she's half in love with easeful death, Mrs Lumsden. I wouldn't drop from shock to hear that Mavis had killed herself, so long as it were beautiful enough. Floating off like Ophelia, you know, or something.'

Mrs Lumsden was staring aghast at me and just too late I remembered that Mirren's death had been anything but beautiful, slumped against brown distemper with blood matting her hair. I pressed on.

67

'Whereas my brother, Edward, is quite the opposite. He left his right hand and his right eye at the Somme and all he ever said about it was that it got him a prettier wife than he deserved because she felt the patriotic echo of Lord Nelson.'

Mrs Lumsden was blinking rather, but she did answer.

'Hard to say, Mrs Gilver, about our Mirren. Very hard to say. She was a cheery, sunny wee thing, right enough. More like Mr Jack than Miss Abigail in that respect although she doesn't favour either of them in looks. Didn't, I mean. Didn't favour. Oh my!' I patted her hand. 'And she wasn't a girl ever to make a fuss or throw a tantrum. She had wanted to go to school, you know, and then to college – she was as sharp as a tack, for all her sweet ways – but she didn't sulk and huff when her grandmother said no. Now you're asking about it, in fact, Mrs Gilver, it *is* out of character. Not that she didn't love the boy.'

'Her grandmother,' I said.

Mrs Lumsden started and put one of her plump little hands over her mouth. 'Her family, I should have said. I spoke quite out of turn. Mrs Ninian has been a good friend to me.'

The females left behind by the procession were beginning to disperse now and despite the many gates in and out of the Abbey grounds it seemed to me that it was the narrow way by the old Abbot House, past the library and on towards the Emporium, where Mrs Lumsden kept glancing.

'Does the reception begin soon?' I asked.

She nodded, shifting from foot to foot.

'Right away,' she said. 'Best way to keep the lads out of the public houses. Mrs Ninian isn't coming along until later, when she's got Miss Abigail home and settled, and I promised I'd keep an eye on everything.'

'Don't let me keep you,' I said and it was as though I had cut the string of a balloon. She sped off, throwing apologies and explanations over her shoulder. I heard 'temperamental tea urn' and 'far too much lipstick if I'm not there to stop them' and she was gone.

I stared after her and then at the note again, and began to wonder.

If I put on my most innocent face and roundest eyes, could I claim to think I had been invited? If, I debated to myself, I went straight to the police now as I had promised Alec I would, it would be cap in hand, knees knocking, to deliver a theory that would sound like criticism to the nasty inspector who already disliked me. If, on the other hand, I went to Aitkens', found the girl from Household who had seen Mr Hepburn in the store, slipped away to the attic rooms and found a pair of ladies' gloves hidden there, still bearing traces of cordite, I should be able to waft along to the police station trailing clouds of glory and a witness behind me. Besides, standing in the churchyard was getting too miserable to be borne.

So I hurried after Mrs Lumsden, with the note in my hand, threading my way through the narrow streets, watching the town come back to life again. The shops, which had closed while the funeral was going on, were beginning to raise their shutters and turn their signs back to *Open* ready to furnish all comers with luggage and rugs once more.

Aitkens', of course, was closed for the day, a discreet card in the lower left corner of every window announcing that business would resume on the following Friday morning, and Ferguson the doorman in deepest black was letting in staff members while deftly turning customers away with ambassadorial ease. He hesitated when he saw me but I waved the note and so he opened the door and held it for me; the revolving door with its whirling gaiety was, I gathered, unsuitable for such a sombre day.

'Welcome, Mrs Gilver,' he said, bowing. 'I hear the funeral passed off as well as could be expected.'

'Weren't you there?' I said. A spasm crossed the man's face.

'Someone had to mind the shop,' he answered. 'And they tell me Mr Muir carried out his task most competently.' His look discouraged further comment and so I contented myself with a sympathetic smile and made to move away.

'It's the second floor, madam,' he said, 'but the lift boy isnae on duty today. Do you think you could manage it?'

'No, no,' I said, remembering the slow creaking. 'I'll take the stairs, Ferguson, gladly.'

'Aye but the staff's all using the big stairs, today,' he said, 'since the store's closed anyway.' He frowned at me, calculating how the necessary distinctions might be maintained, how the prospect of a shopgirl sharing stair treads with me might best be avoided, until his attention was summoned by a banging on the door. He turned and his brow cleared at the sight of a young girl in a suit of rather flashy grey hound's-tooth check and, as Mrs Lumsden had feared, a great deal of red lipstick.

'Oh, here's Miss McWilliam,' he said, opening up again. 'She's a dab hand with that shipper rope, are you no', hen? Goan take Mrs Gilver up, will you?'

'Fine by me,' said the girl. 'Save my legs in these shoes.' And with that she swished off on her high heels, leaving me to follow her.

The lift seemed wheezier and more arthritic than ever when we entered and the girl pulled the rope which was supposed to set it rising. It gave some very alarming clanks, moved a foot or so and stopped.

'I don't mind the stairs, actually,' I said and the girl, heels or no heels, nodded in fervent agreement, but then before we could get out again the carriage started moving and we had missed our chance. I held my breath as it hauled us up two storeys and only let it go once we had arrived and the girl had jerked the rope to stop us and opened both doors. Even then, as though by way of farewell, it dropped an inch or so as I stepped forward and we both got out very hurriedly.

'I'll send it back for the missuses,' said the girl, leaning in and tugging the rope again while beginning to close the carriage door with her other hand. 'It's a knack,' she said, hauling shut the shaft doors too. 'Takes years, but it's Mrs Ninian's rules. If staff *must* use the lift when the boy's not on it – and only on urgent business for customers, mind – they send it back to wherever it was when they got on, so it's like we never used it at all.' She laughed and shook her head.

'This is not the day to be speaking lightly of any of the family, Lynne,' said a voice. The thin manageress of 'the ladies' side', whose name I had forgotten, had emerged from behind a display of curtain fabrics with a deep frown upon her face.

'I'm not, Miss Hutton,' Lynne said. 'I'm devoted to them all.' She turned and gave me a wink which showed that her fabulous black lashes had been applied at the same time as her red lips.

'Lynne?' I said, remembering. 'Were you one of the nymphs?'

Lynne laughed and Miss Hutton tried not to.

'I was supposed to be a water kelpie, madam,' Morna said. 'If my old dad heard you calling me a nymph I'd be pitten oot the hoose.'

'You'll be pitten oot the shoap, if you don't mend your ways, Lynne McWilliam,' said Miss Hutton, but she was smiling.

'Anyway,' Lynne said, 'I reckon the poor old lift wouldn't be giving up the ghost like it is if it didn't have to do so many double journeys, eh no, Miss Hutton?'

Miss Hutton only shook her head.

'Now,' she said, 'I'm very glad to see you, Mrs Gilver. I advised against this party, you know. Most unseemly, but at least if there are guests as well as the staff it will keep the youngsters in some kind of order.'

'I was touched to be asked,' I replied, feeling rather uncomfortable. 'I feel Mirren's death most dreadfully.' Miss Hutton raised a polite eyebrow. 'Oh, not the loss of her – I wouldn't presume to say so to those of you who've known her so long and loved her so well – but the sense of being asked to find her, bring her home safe and sound, and then such a thing happening before I had even got started. I wouldn't blame her poor parents if they never wanted to lay eyes on me again.'

'Her parents?' said Miss Hutton, as though only just remembering that there were such people. 'Oh well, I shouldn't think Mr and Mrs Jack will be here. But – forgive me, madam – when you say you were asked to find her . . . ?'

'Mrs Ninian engaged me,' I said. 'I'm a private detective. A staff member, after all, in a way.' I saw no reason to keep it from

Miss Hutton now but she reared backwards as though I had said I was a dancing girl.

'Mrs Ninian engaged you to *find* Miss Mirren?'

Now why, I thought to myself, should that be puzzling? Before I could ask her we were distracted by the machinery of the lift starting up again beside us as it heaved another load up from the ground floor.

'You're right, Lynne,' said Miss Hutton, absently. 'It sounds worse than ever today.'

Indeed, I was almost at the stage of crossing my fingers and holding my breath as we waited for it to arrive. When the doors opened, Bella and Mary Aitken stood there looking very tense and flustered under their veiled mourning hats, their mouths dropping open at the sight of me. They stared and stared until, once again, the lift dropped a sudden lurching inch and they practically jostled one another getting out of the contraption onto solid ground.

'Mrs Aitken,' I said, addressing Mary, 'thank you for asking me along. I'm very honoured to be included.'

'What—?' said Mary Aitken.

'Mary?' said Bella, turning to look at her. 'I didn't know you had invited other people.'

'I—' said Mary. For a long, skin-crawling moment we all stood there gawping at one another. My nerve cracked first. I fished in my pocket for the note and pretended to read it again.

'I'm terribly sorry if I misunderstood,' I said.

'Perhaps Mrs Lumsden didn't quite catch my drift,' said Mary coldly. I held the note out towards her, but she snapped her eyes away from it and looked hard at me. 'You are most welcome, of course,' she said, about as convincingly as a prisoner greeting the hangman.

'Did you come up on the lift?' said Bella. I turned to her with gratitude for the change of subject and nodded, grimacing. She looked behind herself at it and then back at me. 'And did you notice anything . . . odd about it?'

'I . . . um, well, it was a little hair-raising, yes,' I said.

Bella regarded me for a moment and then nodded. 'You might help me talk sense into my sister-in-law, then. I think we should ring up the mending man and get him to see to it this afternoon while the store's closed anyway.'

'Bella, we can't,' said Mary. 'What will people say?'

'Mary, for the Lord's sake,' Bella answered. 'No one will think ill of you. And how much worse if someone were to have a mishap.'

'But we can't order repairs and have men in overalls in the store today. What will Jack and Abby say?'

'Come along, Lynne,' said Miss Hutton, whisking the younger woman away from this scene of family discord. Lynne went with some reluctance and the tilt of her head suggested that she was listening all the way.

'Jack and Abby?' said Bella. 'No need for them to know. And I'd rather offend sensibilities – even theirs – than have blood on my hands if someone ends up injured in that thing. What do you say, Mrs Gilver?'

'Well,' I answered, 'no one need know if your repair man isn't a talker.'

'There you go, Mary,' Bella said. 'And I'll take full respons-ibility if tongues start a-wagging.'

Mary Aitken shook her head again but the fight was out of her and Bella sensed it. It was remarkable the way that the power seemed to have shifted between the two of them. Or perhaps it was just that Bella's stout practicality stood up better under strain than Mary's rigid, watchful ways.

'Right then,' Bella said, evidently finding agreement in her sister-in-law's silence. 'I'll take it upstairs out of harm's way and telephone to the chap, then. He'll be in our address book down in the office, is he?' She stepped into the lift, shut the carriage door and the shaft door and left us listening to the groans and squeaks of the old lift's uncertain ascension.

Presently, Mary turned to me and gave a ghost of the old on-and-off smile.

'I haven't had a chance yet to tell you how sorry I am,' I said as we made our way through the Curtain Department towards the sound of conversation and clinking china. 'Last week things were so very tumbled and confusing. But I truly am, Mrs Aitken, most sorry.'

'You who have nothing to be sorry for,' she said, looking straight ahead. 'Imagine the sorrow I feel.'

I took pity on her then. If she really believed that forbidding Mirren's engagement had led to the girl's suicide, she must be wretched now.

'You can't possibly have foreseen it,' I said. 'We can't shrink from guiding our children – and grandchildren – in case they . . .' And besides, that is not what happened, I wanted to say. But if Mirren *had* been murdered, Mary Aitken was a suspect and I could not show her my hand. She stopped walking and faced me, then she seemed to lose some of her courage and turned away a little again, smoothing a shelf of folded flannel sheets, tweaking the corners straight and lining up the ribbons which bound each one so that the stripe of blue satin rose up, dead straight, through the pile.

'I have done things in my life that make me scared of the day I'll meet my maker,' she said. I said nothing. '"And shall come forth; they that have done good unto the resurrection of life and they that have done evil unto the resurrection of damnation." I already know what damnation feels like, Mrs Gilver.'

Most assuredly, I said nothing in answer to that.

'Do you believe what the Bible says about suicides?' she went on.

'I'm not sure I know what the Bible says, Mrs Aitken,' I answered. 'I know what the churches say, but that's not the same thing at all.'

'"Know ye not that ye are not your own, for ye are bought with a price",' said Mary. 'So perhaps I've got more chance now of seeing Mirren in the hereafter than I ever did before.'

My childhood inculcation was not notably thorough – my mother had been more interested in Art and Beauty and Nanny Palmer cared only for shining hair and clean fingernails – and my long years in the land of John Knox had left me somewhat between two stools when it came to the details, but I was pretty sure that one could not expect to meet lost loved ones come what may, only the venue undecided until Judgement Day had dawned. Thankfully, Mary Aitken did not seem to notice the lack of an answer. She subjected the stack of sheets she had been tidying to one of her fiercest stares.

'Bella can say what she likes,' she said. 'I think it matters what folk think and it matters what folk say. And these sheets should have a pillowcase folded into a fan on top and a ribbon rosette too. Not just lying there in a heap like your linen press at home.' She looked around herself, her neck elongating and her spine straightening as she did so. 'In fact, this shouldn't be sheets at all. This should be eiderdowns, here on the aisle where they'll be seen by anyone going by. Sheets should be at the back. It's the only decent way and it's the Aitkens way. I'll need to get this seen to.' With that she stalked off leaving me to trot after her.

Aitkens' tearoom when we finally arrived was found to be a large square room off the back of the food hall, with an endless brown horsehair banquette undulating around its walls and tables to seat six pushed up against it at intervals. The walls were adorned with prints of lochs and mountains and around the top ran a painted frieze of clan shields. In the middle of the floor was a high and forbidding counter where large platters of fruitcake and sandwiches were laid out and where an elaborate and well-polished electric samovar spat and grumbled, drawing uncertain looks from the members of staff closest to it and even causing those standing in groups further away to stop talking and look round as it let out a particularly vehement hiss and rocked on its little chromium-plated legs.

'Oh Mrs Ninian!' said Mrs Lumsden, who had been peering at the samovar from a safe distance. 'Somebody's let this blessed urn empty to the very bottom and it's not happy.'

'I keep telling you, Mrs Lumsden,' said a hefty female who, although she was in a cloth coat and black straw hat with a brooch pinned to her lapel and a handbag looped over one elbow, nevertheless screamed 'cook' louder than any striped frock and white apron ever could, 'my girls would no more drain the water off the element than yours would . . .'

'Put flannel sheets on an aisle stand?' said Mary Aitken. Mrs Lumsden raised a hand to her mouth. 'Just this side of the mercerised madras,' she went on. 'You'll need to get it changed before tomorrow.'

'Yes, Mrs Ninian,' chorused a good few of the girls and women who were listening. The Household Department, one presumed.

'And just go ahead and pour the tea,' Mary said. 'If it's kippered it'll teach you for next time.'

'Yes, Mrs Ninian,' chorused another section of the choir, but when their voices faded I could hear a few grumbles too.

'Dinnae see how we should hae burnt tea. It wisnae us that drained the damn thing.' This was from a young man dressed in spiffing style, although perfectly properly in mourning. I took him to be from Gents' Tailoring and thought that he was an excellent advertisement for the store.

'Jist tell yersel' it's Lapsang Souchong,' said another young man.

'Aye, or ask yersel' whit's the use of a tea kettle that can burn the tea. My Annie's the worst cook that ever spiled a pun o' mince and even she cannae burn tea.' They all laughed at that and Mrs Ninian sent over one of her piercing glares.

'Shotty, shotty!' said the first young man. 'She can hear ye.'

Trying to be very casual, I edged away from them and towards the nearest of the young women who had piped up in response to the news of the eiderdowns. She watched me approach with a shy look and she bobbed a curtsey when I got to her.

'And where do you work, my dear?' I said.

'Here at Aitkens',' she answered. I looked sharply at her, suspecting cheek, but she returned a limpid blue gaze.

'In the tearoom?'

'Oh no, madam,' she said. 'I'm a sales assistant, not a waitress.' She sounded very proud of the fact and another girl standing nearby – a waitress, I guessed – snorted and threw a look of

76

disdain such as only pretty girls with slim ankles and waved hair can throw at shy girls in home-knitted jerseys and with hair scraped back into a ribbon.

'In which department?'

'Household, madam,' she said. 'Were you wanting something? Because we're really closed but I could lay it aside for you until tomorrow.'

'Here on the second floor?' I asked her. I smiled. 'I hope it wasn't you mixing up sheets and eiderdowns.'

'I never touched them!' she said. 'I work in the basement, in the bazaar.'

A pair of older girls, coming to stand close to us with cups of tea and plates of cake, giggled. One of them gave me a very pert look and joined in our conversation without invitation or apology.

'You'd be surprised the way things flit about in a place like this, madam,' she said. 'Mrs Ninian was worried about it on the jubilee day – worried that with all the crowds, we'd have trinkets away under coats and up jumpers – she had us all stationed round the scarves and notions, all the wee things that would be easy swiped.'

'But it's never the stuff you'd think, madam,' said her friend. 'You'd laugh if we told you what goes missing, wouldn't she, June?'

June nodded. 'Like that time we left the cash tube with a ball in its mouth carrying thon cretonne curtainings to the lift for Mrs Taylor – they weighed a wet ton and she's always the same – takes everything home in her wee car with her chauffeur no matter how much work it makes instead of getting a delivery like e'bdy else does.'

'And guess what went, madam?' said the other, dabbing up cake crumbs with her finger and licking them off. 'You never will.'

'I'd never leave my cash ball lying,' said the girl from the bazaar.

'You've no' got a key to the chute, you wee besom,' said June. 'You're only jist up to scuttles from buckets.' Her friend laughed and the shy girl scowled at them.

'But when I *do* get it, she said, 'I would never.'

'The bell,' I said, taking a wild guess. They all frowned at me. 'Scissors? Tape measure?' I had named three items I always coveted from the cutting counters of shops when I was buying cretonnes of my own.

'Stamps,' said June. 'A tube full of money, hanging wide open, and some funny wee buddy stole the stamps.'

I tried to look suitably diverted by this news but all I had really taken in was that these girls worked on the second floor, and I wanted to keep talking to them.

'One wonders that anyone had the nerve,' I said. 'Don't you girls have eyes in the back of your head for what's going on around you?' All three of them looked pleased with this compliment and ready to accept it as their due. 'I mean to say,' I went on, 'the idea that anyone could come skulking round and not be noticed – it's preposterous!' They were less certain now and who can blame them, poor things. I was no good at Giant Steps and Baby Steps when I was a child, always swaying and staggering when Grandma wheeled round and always out first. It was no different now. Try as I might to learn that stealthy detective's way of making conversations flow imperceptibly in my chosen direction, to lift my pet subject off the sand and carry it away, to insinuate all my little questions into the stream without a ripple, I did still tend to heave great lumps of suspicion into the middle of things like boulders into a pond, muddying the waters, killing little fish, and making everyone around back away, shaking themselves and planning, in future, to avoid me.

These three girls could not go that far; the boldest of them – June – spoke up gamely.

'Likes of who, madam?' she said.

'Well,' I said, nudging closer to them and dropping my voice, 'I heard that Mr Hepburn tried to gatecrash the jubilee. I heard he was up here on the household floor, hiding.'

'Mr Hepburn or young Mr Hepburn?' said the shy girl from the basement.

'I don't know,' I said.

'He was here when she——?' She bit her lip and her eyes filled.

'He was never,' said June. 'Was he, Poll?' Her friend shook her head. Both of them were staring at me as though they had found me under a rock and wanted to drop it back on top of me. 'I don't know who's been saying such things, madam, but you don't want to listen.'

'No one said *which* Mr Hepburn,' I told them. 'No one suggested for a minute that it was Dugald.'

'*Dugald*?' said Poll, her eyes just about popping out of their sockets. 'That's a story, madam, and a gey cruel one too.'

'Because she only did what she did because they were kept apart,' said June. 'If he'd come to get her she'd still be here now.'

'Stands to reason.'

'If he knew she was here.'

'And no one did.'

So whoever it was who had spied whichever Mr Hepburn it was, Poll and June it was not, but I could not stop them talking now. The ripples of my heaved boulder were sloshing around the banks as though they would never settle. Worse, Mary and Mrs Lumsden were walking towards us.

'Sssh!' I breathed, through still lips.

Thankfully, some sense of decorum or perhaps a healthy desire not to be sacked came to the fore and June piped up in quite a different voice:

'Miss Shields says it used to be tallow candles, madam, when they came in farthing boxes. She says she couldn't keep them on the shelves.'

'But everyone in Dunfermline's got the electric light now, so it's bulbs these days,' said Poll.

'And Miss Shields always says it was a whatchoocallit that pinched everything,' said the basement maiden.

'Wheesht, Addie,' hissed June.

'Miss Shields,' said Mary, drawing near, 'has too much imagination for her own good.' June and Poll dropped their eyes but poor Addie did not appear to have that talent which senses trouble and changes flight to dodge it.

'Right, Mrs Ninian,' she said. 'Because why would a whatch-oocallit need candles? What *do* you call it again? I cannae mind.'

'*Can't remember*, Adelaide,' said Mrs Lumsden. 'If you don't speak nice you'll be back in the stockroom.'

'And if you don't stop spreading tales you'll wish you were back in the stockroom because you'll be out on your stupid ear.' Mary delivered this in a cold, low monotone which made *me* tremble in my shoes, let alone the shopgirls. Then she turned and stalked away, so stiffly that she made me think of a clockwork soldier.

Adelaide's eyes were brimming.

'I didnae mean no harm, Mrs Lumsden,' she said. 'We were all talking about it. The poultry ghost. That's it! Poultry ghost. It was Miss Shields that told me.'

'Poltergeist, ye wee daftie,' said June. 'And it was never, anyway. Eh no, Mrs Lumsden?'

'It was donkey's years ago,' said Mrs Lumsden. 'And it was tramps. And if you don't have the sense to see that poor Mrs Ninian doesn't want to be thinking about ghosts in the attics today of all days, Adelaide McVitie, then you've even less sense than I've seen in you and that's saying something.' She shook her head at the poor girl, almost really angry, perhaps as near it as she ever was. 'Now get away into the kitchen and help the girls dry up the cake forks. Don't touch anything china and stop that petted lip before I skelp you.'

Adelaide fled.

'Mrs Ninian was just coming to speak to you, Mrs Gilver,' Mrs Lumsden went on. She shooed away the other two girls, who looked glad enough to go. Once they were out of earshot Mrs Lumsden gave something between a laugh and a sigh. 'I know I'm too soft with my girls. That Addie McVitie'll never make a sales assistant if she lives to be a hundred, but her father has no work and her mother's got a bad chest and five more of them at home.'

'Stockroom?' I said.

'The lassie can't add two and two and get four.' This time the sigh was a sigh, nothing more. 'Mrs Ninian has been good to me, keeping me on, and I try to do the same. Addie was getting a shilling a week in the council laundry when I found her.' I gave an understanding nod, but in truth I thought that Adelaide would be happier in a laundry where she understood what was required of her and then perhaps some bright girl could leave the laundry behind and flourish at Aitkens', rising from the basement buckets to the heights of the cutting counter on the curtain floor. And to be entirely honest, since sweet bright pretty Mirren Aitken had been snuffed out at twenty I had precious little sympathy left for laundry girls of any stamp who could still step out into the fresh air at the end of their shift and go dancing.

'What did Mrs Ninian want me for, Mrs Lumsden?' I asked 'Should I go after her?'

'No,' said Mrs Lumsden, putting out a hand to stay me. 'It was just to apologise, really. She meant to say a few words to the staff, you know. But she doesn't think she'll be able to, as it turns out. She's taken this so hard, just gone to pieces really. So Mrs John's going to take her home.'

'She certainly doesn't need to apologise to me,' I said, feeling very uncomfortable. What Mrs Lumsden said next hardly helped.

'Well, she knew you must be expecting an audience with her a wee bit later,' she said. 'You know – *to settle up* – but she'll have to ask you to wait for another time.' I could feel myself blushing. 'And to be honest, Mrs Gilver, Mrs Ninian was surprised to see you here – they both were, her and Mrs John. She said to me she didn't mean her note that way at all. And I can't think what I wrote because my mind was on ten other things and I just scribbled it. But there's proof of the state she's in right there, not saying exactly what she means. Not like her. Not like her at all and I've known her woman and girl.'

I was squirming by now, as can well be imagined, with a horrible wriggling guilt which crept in at my collar and scuttled up and down my spine, even though I told myself that it was *exactly* like Mary, for had she not written the wrong date on her first postcard to me? To salve my conscience, I told myself that the least

I could do was carry out the plan for which I had infiltrated this wake in the first place. I only hoped I had the chance before it ended.

'Are you going to switch off the urn and send them all home?' I asked.

'No, I don't think so,' said Mrs Lumsden. 'In fact between you, me and the gatepost, Mrs Gilver, I think I might just slip through to the food hall for a couple of bottles of sherry. They look like they need it.' Indeed, the few dozen men and women, the handfuls of boys and girls *were* looking pretty woebegone, standing around with their cups of tea. 'Anyway, we need to wait for Laming now.'

'Who?' I said.

'Mr Laming, the lift fixer. Well, locksmith and small engine and anything else he can turn his hand to. Oh my goodness, but Mrs Ninian wasn't pleased about that, madam, was she now? She'll not be sorry to be away out of it and missing him.' She nodded as she spoke and I turned to see Bella and Mary Aitken making a slow path to the head of the stairs which led out of the tearoom. When they had descended out of view, the first of the young men began to slide into seats on the long banquette and a few of the bolder girls – I noticed June and Poll among them – perched on the wooden chairs opposite and started giving out smiles.

'I'll need to judge this sherry carefully, eh?' said Mrs Lumsden with raised eyebrows. 'I don't want to be ringing the polis to help me clear the place later.'

Her words were prophetic, as we were soon to know.

5

Between the rise in spirits which Bella and Mary's departure could not help but cause, cats and mice being what they are, and the introduction into the party of two bottles of cream sherry and one of whisky, I was not lamented as I slipped away to the back stairs and crept up to the attics to search for clues.

I was hoping for gloves, even though gloves would suggest that Abigail Aitken had killed her child and had thought up a fiendishly devious way to get away with it, but the longer I considered of such a woman hatching such a plot the more convinced I was that it could not be. It would have taken such pluck to sit there, gun in hand, waiting for the police to come and see past the surface, as far as the trick beneath it but no further. Such a strong will would be required and I just did not believe that Abigail Aitken possessed one.

Still, I would search since here I was with a chance to do so and if I found nothing I would tell the police, better trained at such things than I, to search again.

The landing seemed darker today with the large hanging lights in the atrium unlit and those dark clouds massing, so I felt around the top of the stair head for a light switch. There did not seem to be one, however, and so I began to make my way along the wall towards the switch by the lift which Bella Aitken had used that earlier day.

Halfway there though I stopped. I had suddenly remembered what had been upon this wall I was touching; the stain bright and shocking, the thin trails of blood running down to the skirting and pooling there, the slight but unignorable *texture* to the stain because it was not blood alone that clung there to the brown distemper.

Shuddering, I scuttled sideways to the middle of the floor and walked forward blindly with my hands out in front to feel the far wall when I got there. How could it be so dark up here? Clouds or no, how could it be that I needed to feel my way?

My breath was quickening and it seemed that I could hear it inside my head, louder than it should be, as though the air around me had changed. It was thick and muffled and I could not understand, began to think that I was not where I had thought to be, that somehow I had come to a different place from that landing where Mirren died, because where was the ledge to the atrium and why could I hear my own breathing so loud and how *could* it be so dark at this time of day?

When my fingers touched something cold in front of me I squealed – that is the only word for it – but the darkness swallowed the sound at a gulp. Then, almost whimpering, I began to run my hands around the edge of the cold slab – it was the metal frame of the lift shaft, of course – looking for the light switch I knew was there. But where? I felt to my full arm's reach on both sides, higher than any switch could ever be, lower too, and could not find it, and all the while the darkness was pressing against my back and the sound of my ragged breathing was growing louder, joined now by the pounding beat of blood in my ears and throat, and over and over again I felt the edge of the lift-shaft door and the raised plate of the call-button panel; I even pushed it and heard the faint ping of the call inside the lift carriage. When the sound had faded I felt around again, the edge of the shaft door and the round polished handle there and nothing else. And now I could not imagine ever finding the light switch and I could not imagine letting go and walking back through that blackness behind me to find the stairs and then, just as I let that panicky thought engulf me, just as I began to see that the only way out was to give in to terror and scream for help, sweet reason returned and half-laughing from the flood of relief through my body I grabbed the lift-shaft door handle and opened it and wrenched the door of the carriage open too and light from the lift poured out onto the landing.

84

I turned and rested my back against the wall, heaving deep wonderful breaths down into my lungs and panting them out again. I looked to the one side and saw the light switch, right there, blamelessly there, as why would it not be, just beyond where my frantic hands had been scrabbling. I looked to the other side and laughed at myself in earnest now. The opening onto the atrium was gone indeed; it was covered over with Aitkens' best black velvet curtaining, tacked along the top and long enough to pool on the floor below. Of course, this dreadful place was blocked off from view – of course it was – or gawping ghouls would stand at the balcony one floor below and stare up here and point and wonder. I looked over to where Mirren had been. This time, I did not laugh and I was glad that I had stopped feeling my way along the wall before I got there. A wreath the size of a barrel was on the floor – I do not know how I missed the scent of it; lilies pumping out that choking reek like so many factory chimneys – and above, on the wall, where the stain had darkened the drab, was a patch of shining white paint, shaped like an arch so it almost looked as though a little shrine had been made there.

Suddenly I did not want to be here, grubbing around for clues on the strength of an invitation I knew I had imagined, while downstairs the girl was toasted and mourned. I stood up straight and had put one foot into the lift – I would take my chances with it on a downward journey – when I felt it start to rumble. I leapt backward, but my first panicked thought was wrong. It did not plummet; I had not witnessed its end. It was gathering itself with all its usual effort to descend with all its usual stately torpor. Mr Laming, the mending man, must be on the ground floor, and must have summoned it to him in some mysterious mechanic's way.

Realising that when it did leave me I should be in darkness again, I stepped over and threw the light switch and when I stepped back the carriage was just beginning to move. Its floor dropped away from the landing and its ceiling began to drop down towards me. I looked away; it is most disconcerting when

85

a part of one's surroundings suddenly begins to sink like that, and it had given me a mild swirl of vertigo.

When I looked back again, the carriage was halfway down the opening and for a moment I had a plain view of the top of it: the heavy bolts like great steel knuckles bent against the roof of the thing, holding fast the enormous plates as thick as the palm of my hand, through which the cables groaned and thrummed.

All of that and the boy, dead and broken, lying with his legs folded under him and his head twisted round, one cheek dark and raw where it had scraped against the ropes, one hand even now dragging against the side of the shaft, making his arm jolt as the lift moved him towards my feet, carrying him away from me.

I crouched, reached out and managed just to grasp that arm. He shifted slightly, but I could not lift him clear; I could not hope to stop him dropping away. For a moment, I was almost decided to step onto the roof of the lift beside him, because I was sure I could feel a faint warmth through his sleeve and his arm moved so freely that I tried to believe it was not too late for me to help him. But then, as my hold slipped and I felt his cold hand and his icy fingers, stiffened like twigs and cracking as I clutched at them, of course I let him go.

Instead, I pulled hard on one of the ropes, trying to bring the lift back up again, but I do not even know if it was the right one and however these matters were decided, wherever they were decided inside the machine, Mr Laming on the ground floor took precedence over me. I could only stand and watch the boy getting smaller, the outlines of his broken body hidden as the dark throat of the lift shaft swallowed him, even the knocking of his hand against the wall growing indistinct until I could no longer see the movement and could not pick out the sound of it from all the other notes in the tired old song of the lift on what must surely be its last journey now.

I swung so fast down the six flights of stairs, hanging on to the banisters and wheeling past the landings, that I was dizzy by the bottom and staggering a bit as I burst out into the back of the Haberdashery Department. Over at the lift shaft, a middle-aged man in overalls under his coat looked up from where he was kneeling at an impressive toolbox and lifted his cap to me. A gormless-looking boy stood by him, who too doffed his cap. I noticed that both men wore black armbands.

'Mr Laming?' I said, trying not to gasp but still far from having enough breath to speak clearly. 'Don't touch the lift. Don't do anything to it.'

Mr Laming had got to his feet and was scratching the dome of his head, his cap pushed back as he stared at me.

'Are you . . . ?' he said but came up short of sensible suggestions.

I took a good deep breath and spoke very calmly.

'There has been a terrible accident,' I said.

'Poor Miss Mirren,' said the gormless boy.

'Today,' I went on. 'Someone has fallen down the lift shaft and I'm sure he's dead.'

Mr Laming and the boy both turned to look at the floor of the lift and then back at me.

'Doon there?' said the elder man. 'For sure?'

'Onto the top of the carriage,' I said. 'I just saw him. He's on the roof. We need to get the police. I'll ring them if you stand guard here.'

His eyes narrowed a little at that.

'Madam, pardon me, but—' he said.

'My name is Mrs Gilver and I'm a private detective,' I said. 'I was trying to find Mirren when she died and just this morning I was given the job of finding Dugald Hepburn too. I hope to God I haven't.'

But of course there was not a particle of me that doubted it. Mr Laming rubbed his face hard with one large and oily hand, rasping his stubble and leaving a dark streak across one cheek.

'There's a hatch,' he said, pointing up at the roof of the lift carriage. 'I'll just take a wee keek.'

I nodded. I needed him as an ally and he would be the better for seeing it with his own eyes, for not half-wondering if this

87

were some kind of madwoman he was humouring. He closed up the enormous toolbox and lugged it into the lift, positioning it under a small, brass-edged panel I had not noticed before. Then he stepped up onto it and, reaching above his head, slid open a latch and very cautiously raised the trap-door. I think the fact that it rose at all set up doubts in him and I too suffered a pang of confused panic. Was not the body lying on that side of the roof, slightly curled around the rope where his cheek had grazed? Should not the hatch be weighted down, immovable?

Mr Laming grabbed the edges of the hole and, with a little bounce, hoisted himself off the top of his toolbox and popped his head up into the darkness. He swore, just once, quite loud and echoing, and dropped back down again, stumbling to the floor and leaning back against the wall of the carriage. He took his cap off and stared at me.

'Aye, that's Dougie Hepburn, right enough,' he said. 'I'll get this thing stopped and you away and ring the polis, hen.'

'Again,' I said, staring back at him. He bent and opened his toolbox once more.

'Hector,' he said, over his shoulder. 'You get away hame to your mammy. This is no place for you. Not today.'

After a few false starts into stock cupboards and one nasty moment at the head of a basement staircase which dropped down from right behind an inward opening door, at last I found the corridor into the back offices and, there, a telephone. Even then though I fumbled and wasted time, because it seemed that the instrument was attached to some internal exchange with more buttons and levers than an ordinary telephone. I pressed and pulled them all in turn, with mounting panic, and must at last have hit upon the right combination because eventually a voice came down the line asking me for the number.

'Police,' I said. 'As quick as you can.'

'Isn't that Aitkens'?' said the voice, with deep suspicion.

'Yes,' I said louder. 'We need the police here. And an ambulance too.'

'Aitkens' is shut today,' said the exchange. 'To whom am I speaking?'

'Put me through to the police station this instant,' I said and by now I was almost shouting.

'But who are you to be in there when it's closed?' the girl said, a plaintive and insistent note creeping into her voice. 'What's going on there?'

'Yes, all right, if you prefer it that way,' I said. 'I'm a burglar and I've broken into Aitkens' and that's not all. There's a dead body here too. Perhaps I murdered him. What do you say to that?'

'If I hear reports of a crime being committed while I'm properly carrying out my duties,' she said, with a kind of prim boastfulness which made me want to reach down the telephone line and shake her teeth from her head, 'I'm supposed to report it to the police straight away.'

'Hallelujah,' I said, and hung up hoping that the way I banged down the earpiece might have deafened her.

There were no whistles this time; the first Mr Laming and I knew of the police arriving was when we heard the front door handle being rattled and fists pounding upon the glass. I hurried across the haberdashery floor and through the foyer towards the three large silhouettes waiting there and with some struggle threw back the bolts.

I had been hoping for Constable McCann and dreading the inspector but I did not recognise any of these men I was letting in.

'Dugald Hepburn has thrown himself down the lift shaft,' I said. 'I think he's dead.'

For just a moment they all stared at me and then the most senior of them, a sergeant I thought, stuttered into action.

'Did you see it?' he said, striding away from me. 'This way, boys, back corner.'

'No,' I said, trotting after him. 'I found him.'

'Over here,' called Mr Laming's voice and, perhaps in response to some note they could hear in the way he said it or perhaps because they knew the man and knew he did not always sound that way, all three of them broke into a run. I sped up too but then from behind us I could hear thumping on the outside door again and I wheeled round.

It was Alec, standing peering in at the door with his hands around his eyes making a visor. When he saw me he mimed enormous relief, clapping his hand to his chest, but before I had got the door open he had had time to register my expression and was worried again.

'Dandy, what the hell?' he said. 'I've just come from the police station. I went to meet you, like we said, and you weren't there and hadn't been there and then three of them went pounding off and wouldn't say where they were going. I thought something had happened to you.'

'I'm sorry,' I said. 'I changed my mind. I came here – there's a wake going on and— Oh Alec! It happened again.'

'What—?' he said and then we both turned towards the door as the light darkened. The inspector was standing there flanked by a pair of constables. He moved forward very deliberately, nodding to one of the men to lock the door behind him.

'Your pal here was at the station looking for you,' he said to me.

'Inspector,' I said, 'I'm so sorry – I don't know your name. There's been a horrible accident. Another one.'

'Aye, and you reported it,' he said.

'Dugald Hepburn has thrown himself down the lift shaft. I saw him.'

'Good God,' said Alec. 'Are you all right?'

'No, no, I don't mean I saw him fall,' I said. 'I mean I found him.'

'Again,' said the inspector. 'And what are you doing here?'

'There's a reception going on upstairs,' I said. 'For Miss Aitken. Just the staff.'

The inspector nodded to his men and, apparently understanding, they made for the stairs.

'Just the staff and yet you were invited?' he said, returning his attention to me.

'Now steady on,' said Alec. I could tell that he was troubled but I could not follow what it was that was troubling him.

'Is there a doctor coming?' I said. 'I think he's dead, but I can't be sure.'

'You said you didn't see him fall,' said the inspector.

'I didn't see him fall, but I touched him and he was warm. I'm sure of it. Well, not cold.'

'And *were* you invited?' the inspector said.

'Don't answer, Dandy,' Alec said. I blinked at him. Suddenly he seemed to be very far away and rather smaller than he should be.

'Not exactly invited, Inspector,' I said.

'Mrs Aitken told me you weren't invited last week either. To the jubilee.'

'Again, not exactly,' I said, nodding.

'This is ridiculous,' said Alec's voice, sounding to me as though it were at the bottom of a well.

'But along you came and "found" Mirren Aitken. Then along you came again today and now you tell me you've "found" Dougie Hepburn.' He turned sharply away as someone came towards us through the archway.

'It's him all right, sir.' It was one of the first three constables, looking rather green and with his voice wobbling. I gave him an encouraging smile; I was feeling rather green and wobbly too. 'Dead as dead can be. About two hours I'd say, from the state of him.'

'And when did you slip off to take your medical degree?' said the inspector, spitting the words out. 'Get Dr Stott. And escort this gentleman back to the station. I'll want to speak to him.'

'I'll come with you, Alec,' I said, and I was aware that my lips felt rather peculiar as I formed the words.

'Don't you move, *lady*,' the inspector said, and with those brutal words, so harshly fired at me, finally I began to make sense of what he was saying and Alec's protests and the strange sensation of my lips and legs knowing better than my brain what was happening to me.

91

'Don't be a fool,' I said, faintly. Alec put out a hand of restraint, because of course this was no way to be speaking to the man. 'You can't seriously . . . what are you . . .'

As I saw the dim foyer grow even dimmer and felt the air around me begin to roll past with a rushing sound, the last thing I heard was that ugly voice, uglier than ever.

'Oh, that's right! Treat yourself to a wee swoon, why don't you?'

I came round with a dull headache and a feeling of nausea just short of making me check my surroundings for suitable containers. Then memory flooded in and I sat bolt upright, headache sharper, nausea gone. I was still in Aitkens' foyer, sitting on one of the taxi chairs just inside the door. Alec and the inspector were gone and one of the second lot of constables, the ones I had thought of as the inspector's henchmen, was standing firmly planted in front of me, his face quite impassive under his hat.

I made as if to stand but he stopped me with a practised gesture, formed I suppose to keep motorists out of busy street junctions but just as effective at keeping me in my chair.

'You're to stay put till the doctor gets here and has a wee look at you,' he informed me.

'Very well,' I said. 'It's perhaps not a bad idea. I don't make a habit of fainting, you know.' At that I remembered the inspector's last words and a surge of fury gave me back every bit of the vigour which had temporarily deserted me.

'Here he's now,' said the constable as a man let himself in the front door. 'Doctor!' The doctor hurried towards us, frowning. 'This . . . witness fainted and the boss wants you to give her the all-clear before we shift her.' I blinked at his choice of words but before I could answer the doctor was upon us. He was a harried-looking sort who held himself at a forty-five-degree forward angle as though using gravity to keep himself moving at the pace he had set. He peered at me.

'Fainted, eh?' he said. 'You saw the body?' I resented the implication but it seemed easier than trying to explain and so I nodded. 'And how are you feeling now?' he said.

'Quite well, thank you,' I said. This was the answer I had been brought up to give and it came out of me without prompting.

'Fine, then,' said the doctor and he turned and propelled himself towards his real business at the back of the store. The constable and I watched him go and then caught one another's eye.

'Right,' I said, tucking my feet under me in preparation to stand. 'Thank you for waiting with me, young man. And do pass on my thanks to the inspector. It was most thoughtful of him to ask the doctor to have a word. Now, can you tell me where Mr Osborne went when he left us so that I can . . . What is it?' The constable had begun shifting his feet and was darting glances at me as though not quite able to look me straight in the eye.

'I'm sorry about this, Mrs Gilver,' he said, fumbling at his pocket or his tunic belt; I could not quite see. 'But it's my orders and I cannae help it.'

'Help what?' I said, but then I saw what he had been fumbling for; they glinted as they swung free, the two solid rings bright with polish and the chain between them sparkling. I stood up and looked him straight in the eye, pleased to see that he cringed a little under my gaze. 'Your inspector,' I said, in a voice I will never cease to be proud of summoning at such a moment, 'is an oaf and a bully and since you choose to emulate him, I expect you will go far. But your mother will be ashamed of you for this and rightly so.' Then I turned, very slowly, and keeping my eyes locked on his as long as I could.

'It disnae have to be behind you,' he said, in a mournful voice.

'No, no!' I said, rubbing it in hard. 'I would hate the inspector to suspect you of chivalry.' And I thrust my hands upwards, wrenching my shoulders horribly. Silently, he clicked the hand-cuffs closed about my wrists and then guided me to the door and out onto the street, where a small knot of onlookers, attracted by the commotion, were well rewarded for their wait; a thrill which was almost a shriek ran through them at the sight of me. I kept my chin very level, resisting the temptation either to bow my head or to stick my nose in the air, and stepped into a waiting motorcar. It was no mean achievement, what with having no

93

hands to help and with my legs weak from rage and fear, but I made it and I slid onto the seat, crossing my legs at the ankles and letting my shoulders rest lightly against the seatback as the driver started the motor and we pulled away.

At the police station, minutes away down the High Street, I began to shake and I had to clench my jaw to keep my teeth from chattering for I half-suspected that I would be thrown into a cell and, trying to picture it, I could not decide which would be worse between the prospect of being all alone behind bars in a little cell of my own or of being cast into a crowd of the sort of women I thought might be there already.

In the end it was not so bad as all that; perhaps Dunfermline did not possess those sorts of women anyway. I was taken straight from the motorcar into the type of little room I had seen before in my few visits to police stations; a bleak enough place, furnished with three hard chairs, one very plain table and an empty waste basket, but at least it had an ordinary door with a handle, no bars, no shackles and no grilled window to the street through which my loved ones would have to feed me titbits to keep me alive. (My imagination had soared away from all controls during the short trip and had left me somewhere between Marie-Antoinette and the Pankhursts for pathos and hopeless damnation.)

I was given a disgusting cup of dark brown tea and was left alone to stare at it for almost an hour until the inspector opened the door, entered and sat down opposite me.

I pushed the cup towards him.

'I'm finished with this, thank you, Mr . . . ?' I said, but I did not succeed in making him angry. He was used to insolence from his captives, I supposed. 'Now,' I went on. 'You've been very clever and if this is the sort of nonsense the Fife Constabulary go in for, I'm sure you'll be due a medal at the end-of-year party, but it's gone on long enough. Ask me what you would like to know and then be kind enough to telephone a taxicab for me. I don't feel up to walking to the station, as I'm sure you can appreciate.'

94

'I'll give you this,' he said, 'you didn't go straight to the county.'
I frowned. 'Your pal's been dropping names like autumn leaves,
threatening me with every top brass that ever walked a golf course.'

'My good man,' I said, '– since you won't introduce yourself
properly to me – you are being so ridiculous that I begin to
suspect some political motivation. It wouldn't be the first time
I've discovered rabble-rousers where I'd least suspect them. But
let me say this as slowly and clearly as I can.'

'I have a few questions for you, Mrs Gilver,' he said, opening
a notebook and unscrewing the cap on his pen.

'I am a detective,' I went on, 'brought here last week by Mrs
Ninian Aitken to help find her missing granddaughter. Your
surgeon decided that the girl died by her own hand and I was
in full view of the Provost, Lady Lawson, and Mrs Aitken herself
when it happ—'

'What is your full name and address, first of all?'

'Today I was invited to an interview with Mrs Haddo—'

'And your next of kin?'

'—Dugald Hepburn's grandmother—'

'Or someone of good standing who might be persuaded to
vouch for you?'

'—who wanted my help in finding *him*.'

'That's right,' said the inspector. 'You were asked along by two
families who were having trouble with their youngsters and now,
it's safe to say, their youngsters will trouble them no more.'

I gaped at him.

'That's an extraordinary insinuation,' I said.

'Two young people dead, the same stranger present both times,
unexpected, uninvited. There's extraordinary for you.'

It was ludicrous, preposterous, as impertinent as it was baseless and actually, surely, not even coherent on its own terms when
one faced it squarely. What had he just said?

'Uninvited,' I repeated to him.

'Mrs Aitken told me last week that she didn't ask you to the
jubilee. She didn't know why you were there that day at all, she
said to me.'

'And today?'

'Nobody up in that tearoom could tell me what you were doing there.'

I nodded. 'Very well, let me see if I understand you, Inspector. After – one assumes – too many evenings in the cinema gallery, you are accusing me of killing two innocents and making it look like suicide?' He said nothing. 'And the central plank of my guilt is that I insinuated myself into the jubilee and the funeral tea without the families' blessing and perhaps even against their wishes.' Again he was silent. 'So, tell me, am I supposed to have been hired specifically to kill the children? Are the Aitkens denying inviting me to cover their guilt? Wouldn't they deny all know-ledge of me in that case? Would they have invited me to the house, for luncheon?' He frowned. 'Or did they engage me in good faith to find Mirren and Dugald? Do I just happen – most unfortunately for them – to be some kind of homicidal maniac who killed them for reasons of my own?'

'You were there,' he said, in very firm tones although his expres-sion was more troubled than I had yet seen it. 'Both times. Right there. And it's all just a bit too convenient for everybody, if you ask me.'

I took my time before answering. It was not clear to me whether this man were a fiend or a fool but I knew I had to tread carefully around him.

'Very many people were there when Mirren died,' I said at last. 'Most of us in the presence of most others. And who can say who was there when Dugald met his end, Inspector? We don't know when it— Hah! Your young constable said he thought an hour or two, didn't he?'

'He'd no business sticking his—'

'And I expect the doctor is making the same calculation right now if he hasn't already. Well, then, two hours before I found Dugald's body I was . . .' I looked at my wristwatch. '. . . I was at Roseville at number one hundred and twenty Pilmuir Street, talking to Mrs Haddo.'

'I'll be asking her about all of this too,' he said.

'Ah, back to your dramatic conspiracy again,' I said. The look that flashed across his face then startled me and at last I stopped thinking about my own plight and my outrage over it and began to think of it from the inspector's point of view. That is, I tried to do so, but there was a great gaping hole in the middle of his theory and I had nothing with which to fill it.

'What do you know?' I said. My tone must have been very different, all inquisitiveness and no annoyance now. Was I imagining that he shifted a little in his seat? Could that be a sheen of sweat suddenly on his brow? I sat forward and stared hard at him. 'You do know something, don't you?' I said. 'Two young lovers kept apart, both go missing, a detective is employed to find them, one kills herself – as far as we all know – and then the other, broken-hearted, does the same. That story sounds well rounded enough to me. What is it you know that's making you baulk at it?'

'I'm the one asking the questions,' he said, rather late in the day if anyone were keeping tally.

'Do you have children?' I said. 'I have two. I cannot imagine a state of affairs where the death of my child could be – as you said – "convenient for everyone".'

He hesitated, as though considering.

'Tell me,' I breathed. 'Perhaps I could help if you tell me.'

He got as far as taking a breath, readying himself to begin speaking, and then we both jumped as a sharp rap sounded on the door. The inspector barked out a short word I did not understand – it sounded like the code a shepherd might use to keep his dogs in order – but it must have been an invitation to enter for the handle turned and the doctor stuck his head around the door. His eyes flared at the sight of me.

'A minute of your time,' he said to the inspector.

'First reckonings?' the inspector said. The doctor nodded.

'You wait here, you,' said the inspector to me as he rose. Perhaps I had been imagining the wavering towards sharing what he knew, then. Perhaps he had been gathering breath for a fresh onslaught of insults.

97

They went outside and pulled the door closed behind them, but I was very gratified to see that the handle, perhaps exhausted by years of being wrenched and rattled by angry prisoners, had failed to latch. Silently, the door swung open about three inches and I could see the dark line of the inspector's shoulder in the gap.

'Broken neck, broken vertebrae, one leg, a wrist and minor abrasions,' the doctor said.

'Any sign of struggle before the fall?'

'If you're asking about handprints on his back,' said the doctor, 'there's nothing. I'd say he either fell or jumped, facing the way he was going, about sixty feet, which would easily take him from the top landing to the roof of the lift on the ground floor.'

'And can you tell me when?'

'From the temperature of the body, in that cold lift shaft, assuming he hadn't been taking any strenuous exercise just before he died, and before I've had a chance to look at his medical records,' said the doctor – the inspector gave an audible sigh – 'about half past two o'clock, I'd say.'

I am sure I saw the inspector's shoulder stiffen.

'Half two?'

'Between two and three, let's say.'

'Right,' said the inspector. He glanced behind him, saw the door sitting ajar and closed it. I could just hear the sound of his footsteps and the doctor's moving away.

I smoothed my hair and resettled my hat, jabbing the pin in very firmly. Then I opened my bag and took out my gloves. I was still working them on – Grant is very fussy about well-fitting gloves and it takes me an age when she is not there to help me – when a constable knocked and entered, looking up at me from under his brows.

'Can I get you a cup of tea?' he said. I stared pointedly at the cup on the table in front of me, which now had a disc of congealed milk floating on top and a dark orange tidemark round the edge.

'You can get me a taxi,' I said. He gave me a pained look and left again. I waited. Various footsteps passed along the corridor outside in either direction. I took my gloves off again. I put my bag back on the floor. Presently I moved the teacup down onto the floor too; the sight of it was beginning to repulse me and I was getting thirsty enough to wish I had drunk it while it was warm.

I was starting to imagine that I could see a difference in the quality of the light, and to assure myself that I would not, could not possibly, be spending the night there when the same soft knock came again. The same constable, still looking at the ground, entered the room.

'Inspector Smellie says you're free to go, Mrs Gilver.'

I let my breath go, picked up my bag and, standing, set the chair back tidily under the table. Then his words sank in.

'*Smellie?*' I almost shouted it. 'Oh, how splendid. How absolutely perfect for him. No wonder, then.'

Alec was waiting on the bench in the front office and he leapt to his feet when he saw me.

'Where have you *been*?' he said. 'I was hustled away and no one would tell a thing except that you were "helping with the inquiry". What happened to you?'

'Same as you, darling,' I said. 'Hustled away and grilled. And something very—'

'Until *now*?' said Alec, turning and glaring at the blameless desk sergeant. 'I only gave my name and address and they spat me out again. I've been going absolutely frantic with worry and . . .' He gave me a sheepish look.

'And what?' I said.

'Well, I'm afraid I rang Hugh. To see if you had rung him. See if he could tell me what was happening to you. He seemed a bit put out.'

'Oh dear,' I said and even as I said it, at that very moment, we heard the heavy front door of the police station being wrenched open and banging back on its hinges as it was flung wide. The same treatment was meted out to the inner door and Hugh, dressed in gumboots and britches, barrelled into the office as though he had been shot from a cannon. When he saw me he stopped dead. His nostrils were doing something I had never seen them do before today, turning white and thin as he dragged in every breath and flaring wide as he forced it out again.

'It's all right,' I said to him, willing myself not to take a step backwards. 'They've let me go.'

'They've just let you go now?' he said. He was wrestling with his coat buttons and trying to get shaking fingers into his watch pocket. 'Osborne rang me almost three hours ago. What the dickens is this about?'

'They wanted to ask me a few things,' I said. 'Really, Hugh, perhaps we should discuss this at home.' I had though, as I was soon to see, quite misread the nostrils and shaking fingers.

'*They* wanted? They who?' said Hugh, looking wildly around him. 'Who did this? What's the man's name and where is he?'

'Inspector Smellie,' I said.

'And where's he hiding himself?' Hugh's voice, naturally quite loud to begin with and then honed by years of bellowing across moorland to beaters and ghillies, not to mention years of bellowing up and down staircases to wife and servants, was shaking the very rafters of Dunfermline police station now.

In reply, a frosted glass door behind the counter opened and Inspector Smellie swept into the room, looking at Hugh with a measure of disdain similarly honed by the years *he* had spent despising ne'er-do-wells and cracking alibis.

'Smellie?' Hugh boomed. The inspector nodded. Then so fast that I hardly saw it happen, Hugh stepped up to the desk, drew back his right fist and drove it hard into the side of Inspector Smellie's face. There was a sharp crack, a short silence and the inspector dropped out of view.

Alec stepped forward to look over the countertop, Hugh swung round and left the way he had come, but the sergeant and I simply stood staring at one another.

'Aren't you going to arrest my husband for that?' I said.

A groan came from near the sergeant's feet. He glanced down

then looked back at me and mouthed his words almost without a sound.

'Had it coming,' he said.

The inspector rose, clambering up with both hands clutching the edge of the counter. He worked his jaw to one side and then the other. It gave a couple of blood-curdling clicks but came to rest somewhere near the middle. Now it was time for me to be brave.

'I won't make any formal complaints about my treatment this afternoon,' I said, 'if you agree to call that quits.'

'Get out and don't come back,' the inspector said. 'If I see you again or hear your name . . .' Then he turned on his heel and disappeared once more into the back regions. Stumbling a little, for this day's alarums were mounting up by now, I allowed Alec to usher me out onto the street.

Hugh was sitting bolt upright in the driving seat of his Rolls, staring straight ahead, looking like a chauffeur, but it was what I saw in the back seat that finally, after all that I had been through, brought tears to my eyes.

'I brought your dog, Dandy,' said Hugh. 'Thought you might like its company on the way home.'

'Oh Hugh!' I said. 'Oh Bunty! Oh!'

'You tuck up in the back and Osborne can keep me company in the front here,' Hugh said. 'You came on the train, didn't you, old man?'

I climbed in and put my arms around Bunty's neck, letting my tears fall on her and not even trying to stop the howling sobs that holding her wrenched out of me. Bunty started howling too; she is always a very gratifying companion to misery.

By the time we had cleared the suburbs of the town, though, I was feeling rather better and I sat forward and slid open the little window.

'Alec?' I said. 'I want to talk to you about a very strange hint I got from Smellie. Hugh, can you pull over and let Alec nip in the back, please?'

'No,' said Hugh. 'Not tonight. You are going to rest and think pleasant thoughts after your ordeal, Dandy. And, besides, I believe I need Osborne to take over the wheel. It might be staved, but I don't think so – I think that policeman's jaw broke my finger for me.'

6

Hugh had never seemed so much like Nanny Palmer in all the years I had known him, but he was right. I was taken home, only very blearily aware of having dropped Alec off at Dunelgar on the way, and was deposited straight into bed without so much as my face being washed, since the bathrooms at Gilverton are amongst the chilliest bits of that chilly house and June is always the coldest month of all; we give up on the groaning, clanking radiators after Easter whenever it falls and the servants have an unshakeable penchant for throwing windows wide as part of their big spring cleaning. I sometimes think, in a spirit of mutiny, that if we hoarded the hard-won warmth of the winter fires a little more jealously we might, in those odd years when the weather is kind, float all the way to summertime with the house snug about us like a tippet, instead of spending May and June noting that every day a little more comfort seeps out of the old stone walls until at last it is colder inside than out in the garden.

Mrs Tilling, briefed by Hugh one assumes although I cannot imagine the scene, sent up supper in the shape of egg and bread in a cup and a flask of cocoa and Grant, heaven be praised, left my clothes overnight on a chair. All in all, I do not think I have been so comprehensively coddled by the members of my household in the entire course of my life, and as the dire warnings always have it, it very quickly spoiled me: the next morning, lying stretching deliciously in my warm bed with Bunty rolling and moaning just as deliciously beside me, the thought crossed my mind that if only I had a telephone in my bedroom as they do in pictures from Hollywood I could ring Alec and begin to chew things over without the nasty preliminaries of cold floor, uncertain bath water, wet neck and draughty corridors. In my imagination, my bedroom was flooded with light, my bed jacket trimmed with swansdown and my bed itself was oval in shape and raised up on a platform like a sacrificial altar in a jungle clearing. I looked around and sighed. My bedroom faced due west and was as gloomy as a cave in the morning, my dressing gown hanging on the back of the door was best tartan felt with buttons from neck to ankle and my bed was one I rather suspected Hugh might have been born in; I had always been very careful not to find out for sure.

'Anyway,' I said to Bunty, who recognised my tone of voice and slithered onto the floor, stretched and shook herself all over, 'what possesses a person to sleep on a platform? And how does one tuck in the sheets on an oval bed?'

At my desk, after breakfast, safely back on the solid ground of real life – for Hugh had skipped off early to some distant part of the new estate which was his current pleasure ground, thus avoiding any unseemly affectionate gratitude the way that a small boy will avoid a grandmother's kiss or a mother's scrub with a wetted hanky, and Mrs Tilling had sent up only porridge because 'I wouldn't want another egg so soon after my late supper, surely' – I noticed two telegrams amongst my morning's budget and fell on them.

I read one – *Appreciate no mention of visit yesterday. No case now. Fiona Haddo* – and then the other – *Send bill at convenience. No further need for services. Mrs N.L. Aitken*, laid them side by side and stared hard at both for so long that Bunty had time to fall into the deep, snoring sleep for which she needs perfect silence. When finally I stirred myself to reach for the telephone, it rang just as my hand touched it, and I smiled.

'You woke Bunty,' I said.

'I left it until now so as not to wake *you*,' said Alec. 'How are you this morning, darling?'

'Itching,' I said. 'Listen to these telegrams and see if you don't start itching too.'

He was silent for a moment after I read them.

'Who's N.L. Aitken?' he asked at last.

'Mary. Mrs Ninian. Is that all you've got to say?'

'Sorry. I can't see whatever you're seeing, I'm afraid. Lay it out for me.'

Now this gave me a moment's pause, for it is more usually the case that Alec's thoughts and mine march in step, or at least stagger along in a three-legged race together. If he had not leapt to the same conclusion as had I, perhaps I had been wrong to.

'Very well,' I began. 'All right. Yesterday Fiona Haddo thought that Mirren had been murdered. Now that murder has cost her beloved Googie his life, wouldn't she be more keen than ever to get to the bottom of things?'

'No,' said Alec. 'She was spurred into action by worry about Googie – do we really have to call him that? – when he disappeared, in case harm came to him. Well, now harm has come and there's nothing to fight for.'

'What about justice?' I said. 'And why would she say there was no case? That's very different from saying she wanted the case dropped, isn't it?'

'It was a telegram, Dandy. She was trying to save words.'

'And as for the other one,' I went on, 'could anything read more like a satisfied customer whose object has been achieved?'

'Eh?'

'No further need for your services, please send your bill? Sounds like job well done, thank you and goodnight, to me.'

'What are you talking about, Dandy?' Alec said. 'You can't subject telegrams to literary criticism and hang people for them. I can easily imagine that both families want only to close the shutters and never speak to another soul about any of it ever again.'

'It's not a telegram alone I'm hanging them from,' I told him. 'And anyway, it's not both families; it's two grandmothers. There are another two grandmothers in the case, not to mention all the parents.'

'So what are the other strands in the rope then?' Alec said.

'Inspector Smellie is one.' Alec snorted. 'I know,' I said. 'Why could he not change the pronunciation to Smiley and then change the spelling and save people a lifetime of trying not to giggle? It's almost rude not to. But Inspector S. knows something. Something that made him haul me off to the clink. It took me a while to stop panicking and realise it was so, but I'm convinced now.'

'Clink!' said Alec.

'Yes, but think about it, Alec dear. What in heaven's name about the incidents of the last week would make the fragrant inspector decide that I had been engaged by the families to kill their little ones?'

'What?' said Alec, so loud that even Bunty raised her head and looked at me. 'Shush, down, good girl,' he went on, revealing that at the other end he had woken Millie too. 'Hang on a minute, Dan, while I let her out.' I waited, watching glumly as Bunty settled again. Alec's spaniel is so well trained as to be rather sickening and I knew that there was only one way to explain her being let out to romp off her high spirits while Bunty simply yawned and turned her head away. The fact was that my darling was almost twelve years old. I could not help a quick glance towards the bookshelf where Merriman's *Care and Training of the Dalmatian* sat as it had done since the day in 1915 when I had put it there after a quick read-through and an even quicker realisation that Colonel Merriman's regime was not for me. I knew that the last chapter concerned itself with the long list of diseases to be expected in old age, the stark facts of average life length, and the brutal advice – this was what had finally caused me to slam the book shut and shelve it – that the next puppy should be acquired before the end, to give the old dog an interest and teach the new one its place in the pack and save it from spoiling. In other words, I had thought, to force the old dog to spend its last days having its ears chewed and make one resent the usurping puppy so much that any chance of its relieving one's grief was dashed even in advance of the grieving. I roused myself as Alec returned to me.

'Did he actually say that, Dandy? Engaged to kill them?'

'Not in so many words,' I admitted. 'But he insinuated like anything. He said it was suspiciously "convenient" that I had been there.'

'The man's a fool,' Alec said.

'He would have to be,' I agreed, 'but since he's probably not, he must know something we don't in order for such a wicked thought even to occur. And I almost got it out of him, you know. He was just about ready to cough it up when the doctor nabbed him. Then he found out I was in the clear and he must have been so embarrassed about pinching me that he went to ground.'

'How did the doctor put you in the clear then?' said Alec.

'Timing,' I replied. 'Dugald died about half past two.'

'Ah, when you were in the Abbey with hundreds of witnesses.'

'Exactly. And then came Hugh.' I sighed a sigh that rattled and whistled and buzzed all the way down the many lines and exchanges. 'I can't exactly go back and resume the conversation now, can I?'

'Come on, Dan,' Alec said. 'Be fair. I won't listen to you moaning about what Hugh did yesterday.'

'I suppose not,' I said. 'It was quite something.'

'I'll cherish the memory all my days.'

'And he can't have guessed in advance that he wouldn't be had up for it.'

'Not a bit,' said Alec. 'He leapt to defend you without a thought of himself.' We were quiet for a minute. 'I felt a bit of an idiot, to be frank. Sitting there for hours, waiting, and then Hugh rolls up and . . .'

'Huffs and puffs and blows their house down.'

We were quiet again.

'So given that,' said Alec presently, 'and given the fact that the families want it left alone . . . *why* exactly are you itching?'

'Because something just doesn't add up,' I said. 'The inspector knows it. Listen: most members of both families, Aitkens and Hepburns the same, think that Mirren and Dugald killed themselves for love.'

'Right,' Alec said. 'I think I might too, actually. I know what we said about gloves and lurking strangers and everything, but after Dugald . . .'

'But it makes even less sense now, after Dugald. Mirren knew about the elopement plan. Why would a girl engaged, in love, with a wedding planned and friends helping – Fiona and Bella, this is – shoot herself?'

'The only engaged girls I've ever heard of harming themselves are jilted ones,' said Alec. 'He changed his mind?'

'That's all I can come up with.'

'Oh, I see,' Alec said. 'So why would a boy kill himself because a girl he jilted died?'

'Exactly. If he loved her he wouldn't jilt her, if he didn't love her he wouldn't kill himself over her. Either Mirren or Dugald has to have been murdered. If jilted Mirren killed herself then heartless Dugald was pushed. If expectant Mirren was murdered, then lovelorn Dugald jumped. And we'd have to think that an Aitken killed jilting Dugald or a Hepburn killed hopeful Mirren.'

'Unless he jilted her and then jumped out of guilt.'

'If he had such capacity for guilt, how could he bring himself to spurn her and break her little heart in the first place? And I've been asking about both of them, Alec. They weren't the type. Oh, I know Fiona Haddo was in a tizz about him – *that* was guilt, if you like, because she'd kept such secrets from the boy – but the way she described him to me . . . And no one who knew Mirren can credit it of her. Mrs Lumsden at the Emporium gave a very clear character reference and Mirren's parents and grand-mothers – in spite of everything that had happened, they were absolutely dumbfounded. Not a one of them could take it in.'

'Of course they couldn't. It's horrible.'

'But it shouldn't have been a shock. Horrible, yes. But they shouldn't have been so surprised by it, should they?'

'I can't say I'm convinced, Dandy,' said Alec.

I could not help tutting again. 'All right. *You* convince *me* then. If you think there are no puzzles here, you explain it so it all makes sense and stops worrying me.'

'I'm not saying there are no puzzles. Of course there are.

Muddles and trouble and everyone's feelings all upside down. I'm just saying that's inevitable in a mess like this one and I think you should leave it alone.'

'Well, I'm not going to,' I said. 'Fiona Haddo maybe doesn't want me any more and Mary Aitken was playing me like a trout from the off, if you ask me, but I'll bet Bella would welcome me back. And I bet that nice Constable McCann would help me.'

'No, Dandy, now I really must insist,' said Alec. 'I can't stop you going to Dunfermline if you're fixed on it, but stay away from the police. I mean it. You could get McCann into a great deal of trouble, not to mention that Hugh might end up breaking rocks in a striped suit.'

'Hm,' I said. 'I daresay Hugh's gallantry wouldn't go as far as that. Not for a case with no pay anyway.'

'Poor Hugh,' Alec said and we made our goodbyes.

Poor Hugh indeed, I huffed to myself as I went to fetch my coat and hat and leave word of my departure. Perhaps it was crude to speak so plainly of it, but it was true: Hugh had deplored and despised my 'racketing about' until he saw my pay-packet, at which he executed a smart one-hundred-and-eighty-degree turn and started spending it. The recently purchased new estate, doubling the size of his property and solving the problem of Teddy, our younger son, was thanks to me, having been got at a snip out of a bonus from a satisfied customer, and at a recent dinner, when I had overheard Hugh's gloss on it all, I had been sorely tempted to kick him. 'Yes, I've been rather lucky with this and that despite the times,' he said in an oleaginous drawl to his neighbour. 'And the fellow was glad to be shot of it. He wasn't a landowner – wasn't the sort. Gave me a good price and off back to Glasgow with a sigh of relief. Dandy?' I had leaned even further away from my own neighbour to make sure of hearing the next bit. 'Oh, I'm more than happy for her to amuse herself when I'm so busy. My mother must be turning in her grave, of course, but Dandy has always been *a free spirit*, you know.'

So when I passed him in the back hall when I was on my way to the stable yard where the motorcars stayed and he was on his way to his business room with a roll of plans under his arm, he was quite safe from any displays.

'Back already?' I said. 'Well, it's not much of a day.' Nothing annoys Hugh more than an accusation that he is an indoors sort, prone to the sucking of pipes and wearing of slippers, rather than a boots-until-bedtime countryman such as he most admires.

'Getting a bit of fresh air at last?' he countered, for my habit of answering letters and telephoning in the morning is taken by him to be tantamount to invalidism. He does not count my early walk with Bunty because we rarely go beyond the park these days and fresh air, for Hugh, starts at the railings.

'I'm going back to Dunfermline,' I said. His eyes flashed and I found that I had not quite recovered from my gratitude after all. 'Thank you, Hugh,' I said.

'Nonsense,' he replied.

We almost smiled at one another as we went our separate ways.

'Mrs John, Trusslove,' I said, when the Aitkens' butler opened the door to me. He stared. I am sure he was no more acquainted than was I with the protocols of condolence after the funeral of a suicide when there has been another at the funeral tea, but he was as sure as I was that unannounced visits by near strangers to the family home were beyond the pale. Add to that the fact that I had left my Cowley on the street, had come up the side drive and had presented myself at the servants' entrance and he was stumped beyond recovery. 'And I'd be grateful,' I went on, since he was standing there immobile and I had the chance to say it, 'if you could keep it under your hat.' He drew himself up a little; always a danger with butlers. Pallister is well short of six feet ordinarily, but can draw himself up, if affronted, to a veritable colossus. 'That is, not trouble Mrs Ninian or the Mr Jacks with news of my visit.' I had hoped that my easy use of the family names would help my cause, but they seemed to offend him. He narrowed his eyes slightly, and as he did so I noticed the red rims to them and the crumpled bags under them. He had been mourning his young mistress, it seemed, and I took a gamble that her loss would trump his other loyalties today. 'You do know who I am, Trusslove, don't you?' I said. His eyes narrowed further. 'I'm a sleuth.' Recognition broke over him like a dropped egg.

'*That* Gilver!' he said.

'That Gilver,' I agreed, nodding. 'And here's the thing: I don't believe Miss Mirren killed herself. Do you?'

He looked behind him before he answered, as cautious as could be, but when he spoke conviction rang out of him.

'Never.'

'I'm going to find out who killed her,' I told him. 'And whoever killed her is responsible, in my book anyway, for the boy too.'

He looked behind himself again then and a frown puckered at him.

'Mrs John . . . ?' he said.

'Not a suspect,' I assured him. 'Only a witness.'

At last he drew the door open wide and beckoned me in. At the first bend in the corridor, however, he stopped.

'I don't know just where to rightly put you, Mrs Gilver,' he said. 'Mrs Jack is walking the house like an unquiet spirit and she'd likely burst in on you wherever you go.'

'I could go to Mrs John's own room if there's a back way,' I said. He looked startled. 'Or where is she now? Take me to her and we can both of us hide in a broom cupboard.' He shook his head. 'Well, does she ever come down here?' I went on. 'Perhaps, if you would be so kind, we could borrow your pantry?' At this he positively took a step backwards. 'It's not a social call, Trusslove,' I said. 'I'm working. And I'm no stranger to a servants' hall, I assure you.'

'Really?' he said. 'Well, I must say, my dear, you've got that toff's way of speaking off to a tee. My little parlour – I prefer to call it a parlour, don't you know – is this way.'

Bella Aitken was a faint ghost of herself. I had seen it once or twice and heard of it many more times than that: a person keeping going up to and through a funeral and unravelling like a picked seam thereafter. She was without even her carpet slippers today, but instead shuffled into Trusslove's pantry in her stockinged soles, not a pair of stockings either: one pale silk one, rather gone at the heel, and one sturdy brown lisle article, which would never go at heel or toe but would live on and on, stretching and sagging and never giving one fair cause to chuck it. I counted it one of the blessings of adulthood that I could choose never to wear lisle stockings ever again, and Bella's pitiful mismatched ankles brought a lump to my throat and turned me yet more gentle.

'Mrs Gilver?' she said, peering through the low light at me.

'Mrs Aitken, please forgive me for this rather . . .' I waved my hands around the little room. 'And please sit down. You look . . .' I left this sentence hanging too, since both 'ten years older than yesterday' and 'about to fall over' were best left unsaid.

'Was it Mary you wanted?' she said, nevertheless sitting down with a great exhalation of breath. She leaned back in the chair, even her head dropping back as though she could not support its weight. 'Trusslove might be confused; he's not himself either.'

'No, no, it was you I asked him to fetch for me.' I paused, wondering how to go on. 'I went to see Fiona Haddo yesterday. She told me about your plan – yours and hers – for the young people.' Bella nodded dully. 'And it explained to me why you were so cheerful when I first came here and why you were so very shocked by Mirren dying.' She closed her eyes and was so still that I wondered if she had slipped into sleep, sitting there. 'Mrs Aitken, you know she had no reason to kill herself.'

'And yet,' she said, very quietly, 'that's just what she did.' I could see her eyes moving under their closed lids but they did not open.

'Your sister-in-law wants me to drop the case now,' I said. At that she gripped the arms of her chair and hauled herself upright, but what she said was not what I had been expecting.

'Yes. That's what to do. Nothing will bring her back.' Then she let go of the chair arms and dropped back again. 'Mary is right. Leave it now.'

I sat looking at her, exceedingly puzzled.

'But don't you *still* wonder why Mirren would have done such a thing?' I asked her.

She shook her head, or rather rolled it to one side and then the other along the back of the chair.

'No point,' she said. 'I did everything I could for her. Nothing will bring her back again. Please just leave us now.'

I rose and tiptoed out of the room, to find Trusslove hovering in the passage. A nearby door was open and there was something about the quivering stillness that made me suspect that a good few more servants were listening in.

'She's very tired, Trusslove,' I said. 'Perhaps more than tired. Has she been seen by a doctor?'

Trusslove gave a short laugh.

'Who's going to get one?' he said. 'There's nobody fit to look after anyone else in this house now. Walking wounded they are. The four of them.'

'As bad as Mrs John?' He hesitated then.

'She's maybe the worst, right enough,' he said. 'Surprised me, I'm telling you. She's always been so . . .' I nodded, remembering the loud laughter and the slightly coarse vitality of the woman I had met just over a week ago. 'And she kept them all going up to yesterday,' he went on, 'then pfft! Out like a wee candle when they came home from the funeral tea.'

I left by the servants' entrance again and trudged back down the side drive to the street but did not get all the way, stopped by the sound of hurrying footsteps behind me while I was still in sight of the house windows. I guessed who it would be even before I turned; for had not Trusslove told me about the unquiet spirit wandering?

'Mrs Gilver,' said Abigail Aitken. 'My mother isn't here.'

She had caught up with me on a particularly gloomy patch, with a spreading beech tree on one side and an even more spreading chestnut on the other, so that she was cast into green shade and as a result looked utterly ghastly.

'Actually,' I said, 'it was your mother-in-law I came to see but if I'm to be really thorough perhaps it's best that I happened to chance upon you too, Mrs Aitken.'

'Oh?'

'Your mother told me she wanted no further investigation, but I'd like to be sure she spoke for all of you.'

'More investigation?' Abigail Aitken's voice came out as a rough whisper, almost a croak. 'Of what?' She looked about herself in a distracted way and then seeing what she had sought she laid a hand on my arm and drew me off the drive towards a wire bench set up around the base of a large tree. 'I knew nothing of any "investigation",' she said, when we were sitting. 'I thought my mother had asked you simply to *find* Mirren.'

'Yes, yes she did,' I said.

'And she was hiding at the store all the while.'

'Yes,' I repeated. 'At least, we can assume so.'

'So what investigation could there be?'

'About what happened,' I said. 'The deaths. Whether we've got a clear picture.'

'Oh,' said Abigail and she sat back against the trunk of the tree. 'Yes, I see. I see what you mean. In case it wasn't suicide. Well, it was. My Mirren. It was.'

'You're very sure.'

'Who could be surer?' she said.

'And Dugald too?'

'Dear boy.'

I was intrigued to hear her say so since the family had spurned him as a suitor.

'Did you know Dugald Hepburn then?' I asked her.

She shook her head. 'Not at all. I only met him once and even that was not really a meeting. I just saw him with Mirren. They didn't even know they had been seen. But he must be – must have been – a dear boy, mustn't he? He couldn't live without her. Didn't want to. He must have been a very different sort from the rest of them.'

'The Hepburns?'

She put her hand up to her mouth as if trying too late to stop the words she had already spoken.

'I shouldn't have said that. They are a cruel family. Heartlessly cruel – it's easy to be heartless when you are so carefree – and

'I'm envious of them, but I shouldn't let myself turn cruel too, in my envy.'

'What is it you envy, Mrs Aitken?' I said.

'The children,' said Abby simply. 'Hilda Hepburn has three children. Three more, I mean; three still. And Mrs Hepburn had five when all's said and done and she had the four grandchildren too. Dugald and the girls. But I only had Mirren and if I hadn't had Mirren I would have had no one. And my mother as well, because I was an only child. Bella had two more sons – Lennox and Arthur – but they were killed in the war and so Mirren was all that any of us had.' Then she caught her lip in her teeth. 'I shouldn't be saying this. You shouldn't take any notice of what I'm saying, Mrs Gilver.'

With that she stood, picked her way over the roughish ground back to the drive and hurried away in the direction of the house. I followed her as far as the driveway and stood looking after her. She had her head down and her arms clutched about her body and was moving at a kind of harried trot – straight into the arms of her husband, who it seemed had come looking for her. As he had before, that day in the library, he caught her in a strong grip and pulled her close to him. I was too late to duck out of sight and he stood comforting his wife, staring at me with his head high like a sentry, a grim and unreadable look upon his face.

I could hardly wave goodbye and leave, nor could I approach the mournful little marital scene and join in, so I stood there, kicking at the beech cobs under my feet until, with a fond pat and a little pinch of the chin such as one would give to a child, Jack Aitken sent his wife back to the house and came to join me.

'What have you been saying to her?' he asked when he was close enough to talk without shouting. 'She's very, very upset about something.'

I stared at him. Of course a mother, a week after the death of her only child, was 'upset' and surely her husband, the child's father, should not wonder what about, should he? As though he read my thoughts, Jack Aitken cleared his throat and rubbed at his face with the side of his hand.

'I was just making quite sure that she didn't want me to carry on trying to piece together exactly what happened with Dugald and Mirren,' I said. His eyes flashed, black and sparkling, and for some reason the thought which popped into my head was that John Aitken must have been a handsome man, for Jack was quite unlike poor Bella. 'Would *you* like me to carry on, Mr Aitken?'

'I thought Mary . . .'

'Called me off?' I supplied. 'Yes, she did. Twice. *She* most certainly doesn't want any more meddling. But I thought it might be a comfort to a mother to know as much as possible. A father too.'

'And what did Abby say?' he asked, looking over his shoulder towards where she had gone.

'Plenty,' I replied. 'Mostly about the Hepburns.' He tried to look interested and unconcerned but failed rather spectacularly, a muscle dancing in one cheek and those black eyes wide open again.

'She barely knows them,' he said. 'Couple of committees, a few church bazaars, that kind of thing. We don't fraternise.' He bit this off rather and was right to do so, since the non-fraternising of the Aitkens and Hepburns intrigued me; birds of a feather being what they were when it came to flocking.

'Yes, your rivalry looks almost like a feud sometimes,' I said.

'Is that what Abby told you?'

'She said they were cruel people,' I replied. 'I think she meant callous. But that Dugald was a dear boy, quite unlike the rest of them. That he must have been to have loved her so.'

Jack Aitken smiled absently and then his face twisted into a sudden spasm of pain. I started forward, unable not to; no one would have been able not to, for at that moment there was no filmy curtain up between Jack Aitken and his audience, no performance going on. He was white with shock, as wretched as a man could be. He waved me away with one hand and put the other out to brace himself against the sturdy weight of the nearest tree.

'I keep forgetting,' he said. 'With everything so topsy-turvy and everyone upset and angry. I keep forgetting what it's all about and then I remember again. And it's like a knife.'

'I'm so very sorry,' I said.

'Mirren forgave me for forbidding the marriage, you know,' he went on. 'She was sweeter and more loving in the last two months than she had been since she was a child in ringlets. She seemed almost grateful to me – well, terribly kind and affectionate, anyway. That's why I was so sure she wouldn't elope. As for killing herself, I still can't believe it.'

'Nor can I,' I said. 'I'm so far from believing that she did it, Mr Aitken, that here I am, seeking permission to prove that she didn't. Dugald too.'

'What?' he said. He was staring at me then he blinked twice in quick succession and swallowed very hard. '*That*'s what you meant?' he said. 'When you said "piece things together"? You meant how they died? Whether they killed themselves or . . .'

'If someone murdered them.'

'Who would . . . who would ever dream of . . . what would ever have made you imagine . . . What are you accusing her of ? You think she would kill a child? You – you – *witch*. You – twisted . . . get away from here. Don't you ever, ever, dare to show your face here again or I will strangle you with these two *hands*.'

I could only imagine the gesture that went along with the last words, for I was off, sprinting down the drive towards the gates and my motorcar with my heart hammering.

What the hangment is going on, I asked myself, driving off rather jerkily – for my hands were far from steady. I rattled up to top gear and threaded my way through the streets to the other side of the town trying to sort it all through: Bella's collapse, Abigail's odd hints and Jack's extraordinary outburst. When at last I spotted a telephone kiosk at the side of the road I pulled over and hurried towards it, scrabbling for tuppences.

'Alec, listen,' I said. 'First of all, here is the number of the kiosk. Ring me back when this three minutes is up if I haven't convinced you by then. But listen. I've just been run off Abbey Park on pain of having my neck wrung for me.'

'Dear me,' said Alec. 'Dunfermline has been no friend to you, Dandy.'

'I wasn't exaggerating, darling,' I said. 'It wasn't a metaphor. I've collected the full set to go with Mary. Bella Aitken, who must know that Mirren had no motive for suicide, wants me to leave it alone. Abigail Aitken spoke a great deal about the Hepburns being callous and cruel but wants me to leave the whole thing alone. Jack Aitken was wringing his hands with guilt about having caused Mirren's suicide yet when I suggested that it might not have *been* suicide he reacted, as I say, by charging at me with bloodcurdling threats and accompanying gestures, which I took to be an indication that he wanted me to leave matters well alone.' I took a deep breath. 'What do you say to that then?'

'What do you think I say?' said Alec. 'Get back in that silly little car and come home. Get out of there, Dandy. You have been sacked by the entire family now, arrested, imprisoned, threatened and almost assaulted. Go for a nice quiet walk in the jungles of Borneo if you will, but for God's sake get out of Dunfermline.'

'But there's something *wrong*,' I said. 'There must be. What kind of people would rather have the stain of suicide upon their family than try to uncover their daughter's murderer and have him hanged?'

'Dangerous people,' Alec said. 'Really, Dandy, come home. Probably they all know exactly what happened and they have closed ranks to protect someone and there's an end of it.'

'To protect whom?' I said. 'Who do *you* think is behind it? Why didn't you tell me you had a suspect?'

'I don't,' Alec said.

'But if you had to make a guess?'

'Mary Aitken,' he said. 'I don't know what and why but she's the one pulling all the strings, isn't she?'

I was silent for a moment and then nodded, although he could not see me.

'She practically had kittens yesterday when Bella took over for once and steamrollered her into getting that man to look at the lift,' I said. Then I gasped. 'Alec! You don't think she knew about Dugald Hepburn too, do you? As well as Mirren. Knew he was there? His body. Killed him, even?'

'She can't have,' Alec said. 'She was in the Abbey with everyone else, remember. Dugald Hepburn killed himself in an empty building when anyone with reason to hate him was in view of a hundred strangers. And he killed himself because his sweetheart was dead. That seems very clear. But there is something rather fishy about how Mirren died. And why. That I'll give you.'

'I tell you what I'd dearly like to know,' I said. 'I'd dearly like to know whether there's the same unanimity chez Hepburn as I found chez Aitken this morning. Because there shouldn't be.'

'Dandy, you can't go barging in the day after the boy died when Mrs Haddo was so clear about not wanting you.'

'I must do something,' I said. 'I can't just leave things be. Alec, I'm more sure than I've ever been about anything that . . . Well, actually I'm not sure what I'm sure of but I am sure.'

'I believe you,' Alec said. 'But you have no authority, Dan. We have no client and you have no evidence. Come home.'

Alec had often laughed at me for the way I could think of something while saying it, and I did wish that I had come up with a different summary of the process, but it was about to happen again. I started up a defence of my position with nothing behind its robustness except my own conviction but while I was speaking the sense appeared that supported it.

'We have a huge heap of evidence,' I began hotly. 'We have a crowd of grieving relatives whose attitudes only make sense if we posit at least one murder if not two. Look at the facts. The Hepburns don't want their son to marry the Aitken girl and she conveniently dies. Then the Hepburn boy follows her. Both families want nothing said and nothing done, even those – like Bella and Fiona – who must suspect the truth. It's a stand-off, Alec. Tit-for-tat. An eye for an eye.'

'One of the Hepburns killed Mirren?'

'Fiona Haddo thought so. And one of them was seen in the store, remember?'

'And one of the Aitkens killed Dugald?'

'Mary, you said. She arranged it anyway.'

'That's monstrous.'

'Well,' I said slyly, 'the inspector certainly thought so.'

I heard Alec take a sharp breath.

'I'm going to Roseville to quiz the Hepburns,' I said. 'I'll speak to you later, Alec dear.'

Although the house was in the deepest mourning I gained entry without difficulty, recognised by the little maid from the day before. I asked for Mrs Haddo and was ushered into the same sitting room to wait for her there.

The woman who entered the room minutes later was quite simply Fiona Haddo thirty years ago. Hilda, Mrs Robin Hepburn, was her mother's double; the elegant limbs, the fine long neck, the strong lean features which managed to be feminine without any weakness about them and managed, which was more remarkable, to be handsome even today, when she was stricken with grief and pale from weeping.

'Mrs Gilver,' she said, sitting and taking a black-edged handkerchief from the belt of her black dress which she pressed against her eyes to soak up the tears that had sprung there. 'I must try hard not to cry,' she said. 'The girls are coming home from school and I don't want to upset them. Dulcie went to fetch them for me from the station. Wasn't that kind? Would you like some coffee? The house is in disarray – the servants were all so very fond – but I'm sure some coffee could be had.'

'Mrs Hepburn,' I said. 'It was your mother I asked for. Perhaps the servants— Oh, I feel wretched to be here on such a day.'

'My mother has sent me in her place,' said Mrs Hepburn, with a very odd note in her voice. 'She won't be joining us. She warned me that the telegram she sent this morning probably wouldn't do the job. She said if you arrived here, asking questions, I would have to answer them.'

'That seems very strange,' I said. 'One would have expected

your mother to be sparing you all possible burdens.' I frowned at her, very puzzled.

'My mother and I had a talk last night, in the middle of the night,' she said. 'She told me about the plan for the elopement. And I told her why it couldn't have happened.'

'Are you going to tell me?' I said. 'Why you disapproved of Mirren Aitken so?'

Hilda blinked. 'I didn't,' she said. 'Charming girl. Sweet little thing.'

'Well, why you disapproved of the family then?' I asked, trying to hide my exasperation.

'I didn't,' she said again. 'I don't. I mean Abigail is hard work, by all accounts. She wasn't always, you know, but she has turned heavy-hearted in her middle years, so they tell me. But I always liked Jack a great deal.' My eyebrows rose and she saw them; she was as noticing as her mother. 'Oh, I know. He's as tricky as a bag of monkeys, but entertaining – sometimes even deliberately so. Mind you, perhaps a lifetime of that sort of entertainment has made Abigail turn into the lump she is today. And then poor Jack grumbles and Abigail sinks a little more.'

Abigail Aitken was right, I thought, regarding her. This was a callous and rather cruel woman to be speaking that way today.

'Mrs Aitken is certainly heavy-hearted now,' I said. 'Her daughter gone. Her only child.'

'And she was lovely, wasn't she?' said Hilda. 'Poor thing. Poor Aitkens. She was perfect really. I'd have liked such a daughter.'

'So why not welcome her into your family?' I said. 'It seemed a perfect match to everyone looking on.'

'A perfect match!' said Hilda, and her eyebrows were as high as a clown's painted arcs, her forehead rippled above them. 'Well, not really. I liked the individual Aitkens, as I said, some more than others and I don't include Mary, but it was the family as a whole.' She dropped her voice and looked away to the side. 'Cousins,' she said. 'Full cousins. And Mirren the only child, simply years into the marriage too. Weak blood.'

'Ah, yes, weak blood,' I said, remembering Mary Aitken saying the same about the Hepburns while we were having luncheon in the garden room on jubilee day. 'On both sides?'

Hilda stared and a blot of colour somewhere between pink and purple – an angry, ugly colour – rose up out of her collar and crept over her jaw and her cheeks leaving just her eyes still pale.

'You know about Robin's sisters then?' she said. I inclined my head as if to suggest that I knew everything. The ploy worked. The angry colour deepened. '*I* didn't, when I married Robin. Mummy didn't. If either of us had known there was such a stain on the family . . . but one didn't expect it. Sturdy merchant stock, one would have thought. It's supposed to be the Haddos and their like who have relations not to be spoken of in polite company.' She was making an attempt at lightness but her voice was brittle.

'Well,' I said, rather at a loss and rather disgusted by the agricultural turn the conversation was taking, 'I suppose I can understand your anxiety. But on the other hand . . . Mirren was a bonny healthy girl and your husband and children are all hale and hearty, aren't they? I don't quite see the need for such excessive scruples, if I'm honest.'

Hilda Haddo blew out hard and gave me a considering look.

'Mother told me you wouldn't be put off,' she said. 'Very well. My scruples, as you put it, my anxiety, got the better of me twenty years ago. I was angry when I found out about Robin's sisters and I decided not to risk it.' Mrs Hepburn stuck her elegant chin in the air and spoke as though to the back of the balcony. 'Dugald was Jack Aitken's son, Mrs Gilver. Mirren was his half-sister.'

Her words seemed to reverberate in the following silence. I felt myself flush and waited until my blood had subsided again before I spoke.

'I didn't think you even knew one another.'

'Oh, we were very chummy for a while when Robert and Dulcie first dragged us all here,' she said.

'And does he know? Jack Aitken?' I said.

'Yes,' said Hilda. 'Apart from anything else, Dugald looked more and more like Bella with every passing year. Robin never noticed but when one was guiltily watching for it, it was plain enough to see.'

'So your husband doesn't know then?' I said. It was not quite a question.

'Good God, no!' said Hilda. 'Jack and I always kept scrupulously apart in public and, given the rift, there's never been any danger of us all coming upon one another.'

'So that's not what caused the rift?' I had thought at least to have got to the bottom of that little mystery.

'Heavens, no. That's ancient history. Shop business. Nothing to do with Jack and me, but it did mean that we couldn't sneak off at parties like ordinary people.' I raised my eyebrows, but Hilda sailed blithely on. 'We met in Aitkens'. After hours. It was like a game. Pinching a bottle of this or that from the food hall and a couple of glasses. We made a sort of little hidey-hole. Goodness knows what the floor staff used to think the next day.'

'They probably thought it was a poltergeist,' I said, and Hilda Hepburn laughed, carelessly. 'So if Mr Hepburn doesn't know . . . ?'

'Robin?' said Hilda.

'Why was *he* so against the marriage?'

'That probably *was* the thought of the cousins, as well as his sisters, you know.'

'But surely having daughters of his own has stopped his worries about his sisters now?'

'Exactly,' said Hilda stoutly. 'That's what I tell myself. What he doesn't know can't hurt him and as far as he does know I gave him four fine children.'

'As far as he knows?' I echoed.

'They *might* all be Jack's,' she said. 'Or a mixture. I could never decide about the girls since they take after me.'

'And did Abigail know? Did she tell Mirren? Is that why she was so sure Mirren wouldn't elope?'

'Jack swears she knows nothing,' Hilda Hepburn said. 'Actually,' – her voice shook – 'I couldn't bear it if Abby knew about Jack and me. The poor thing. Especially now.' Again she rallied, with a sniff.

123

'Not that I haven't paid for my sins. My oldest, my darling, my boy.' Her head had drooped but she lifted it again. 'But I still have the girls at least. And as I say they'll be here soon, so if you'll excuse me.' She stood and tucked her handkerchief back into her belt again. 'There. I've told you. My mother needn't send me to bed without supper.' She gave me a nod and looking, at last and very late, quite shame-faced she left me sitting there.

7

I departed Roseville in a daze. I am no prude, but she had been so blatant about it, so unrepentant, caring only about what was known and not a jot about what was done. I tried and failed to imagine the scene where Fiona had told her daughter about the planned elopement and Hilda had revealed to her mother what an abomination it would have been. Then with a shiver I put it out of my mind and turned instead to the question of what it meant for Mirren's death and Dugald's too, what light it cast on the mystery.

It all depended, I told myself, on who knew. Hilda had been sure that her secret was hers alone, hers and Jack's; but if Mirren knew, then she had a motive for suicide. And then any of her family had a motive for killing Dugald – if blind rage and senseless revenge could be said to be a motive anyway. But Jack Aitken had said Mirren was sweet and fond to him in her last weeks. Would she have been so to a father she had just found out was an adulterer? She would not. I let my motorcar slow down, struck by a sudden thought. If *Robin* knew, might he not kill the child of the man who had cuckolded him? Might he not kill either child, or both even? I had to find whoever had seen a Mr Hepburn in the Emporium that day.

A tooting horn behind me jolted me to sentient life again and I pressed my foot down as hard as it would go. Today, I told myself, was the perfect day to go searching for her. The Aitken family would no doubt be back at the store sometime or other, but on the day after the funeral I could be sure of a clear run.

I left my motorcar in a little parking yard behind the Kirkgate and walked towards Aitkens', planning my assault on its various members. As well as the elusive witness from Household, there was Miss Hutton to try to interview; I could not for the moment quite remember what it was she had said to me, or even when, which had led me mentally to turn down the corner of her card in this way, but I knew there was something I wanted to ask her. Then there was the doorman, the only individual, so far as I knew, who was inside Aitkens' when Dugald Hepburn died.

I was loitering now, pacing up and down outside the plate-glass windows. The bolts of black velvet were gone again, the riotous urns from the jubilee day too, and in each window was a large spray of lilies and narcissus. I kept squinting at the doorman, waiting for a moment when he was free to speak to me, but there was a steady stream of traffic out and in and he was much taken up with receiving condolences from the customers entering and saying a few respectful words of gratitude to those leaving. I had turned for the third time and paced all the way to the end window again, looking in most studiously – as though there were anything to see – when a pair of shopgirls emerging from a side alley saw me, took pity and stopped to explain.

'The store is open, madam,' said the younger of them; a pert little individual dressed in a black skirt and white shirt with a cardigan thrown over it and over the strap of a satchel. 'It's only that the displays aren't up because we're in the deepest mourning.' Her companion nodded, plucked at the armband on the coat she wore over her black serge dress and then folded her hands as though in prayer. 'On account of how Miss Aitken has just passed away.' She could not have spoken with more relish if she had been recounting victory in a sea battle and I wanted nothing more than to quell them with my severest nod, a talent closely related to that of cowing strange butlers which had worked so well on Trusslove a week ago. (Although I comfort myself that I have no effect at all on the servants at home. My goodness, the day I cow Grant will be the day I give up all pretence of youth and if I ever make a dent in Pallister I shall order my ear trumpet and bath chair.)

But the quashing down of my finer feelings is only one of the habits I have had to inculcate in the name of detection and one of these girls at least was clearly a gossip, and might be the very one I was seeking. I could not let either of them slip away.

'I heard,' I said. 'Well, actually I was here, you know, on the day of the jubilee. A dreadful thing.'

'Poor Mirren,' said the girl. 'Mr Jack's only child.'

'Twenty years old and all her life ahead of her.' The companion spoke up at last.

'Dear me,' I supplied, to keep things going. It was as though I had shovelled coke into a roaring boiler.

'Here today and gone tomorrow.'

'Snuffed out like a little candle in a storm.'

'Broken-hearted and couldn't go on.'

'Alone and unloved—'

'Well, Mima, not exactly unloved,' said the younger girl. Her friend caught her bottom lip in her teeth and blushed a little. 'She was engaged, you see, madam.' The girl hitched up the bulky satchel; she was wearing it across her body like a conductress's ticket machine and the strap was causing her some discomfort. 'To a lovely boy.'

'Lovely boy,' Mima echoed.

'Dugald Randall Hepburn. Doesn't he sound like a film star? Well, he looks like one too and—'

'*Looked*, Elsie,' her friend reminded her. Elsie shut her eyes as though a spasm of pain were sweeping over her and then went on in a voice even quieter and flushed with even more glee.

'Star-crossed they were, madam.'

'Forbidden love.'

'Struck asunder.'

'By cruel cold hearts who'd forgotten what it means to love.'

'If they ever knew.'

'And look where it's got th—'

'Elsie Dunn,' said a voice, making us all jump. Mary had done it again. There she was, tiny and furious, dressed in the same columnar black bombazine as the first two times I had met her, her widow's mourning impossible to deepen even after the recent dreadful loss, but today the spectacles on their black ribbon were joined by a measuring tape which she wore around her neck like a stole and a number of long pins in a sunburst pattern which stretched from the middle of her ribs all the way to one shoulder, wherever she had jabbed them during some task or other. 'What do you think you're playing at?' she spat at poor Elsie. 'And you should know better too, Jemima. Get in there right now, the pair of you.' She pointed up the alley with a stabbing finger.

'Mrs Ninian,' said Elsie in a tiny voice, all relish gone, 'we can't go in. We're on our way to the bank with the deposit.'

'On your way?' The black column spoke in a tone which should have cracked the tiles beneath her feet and caused the plate glass to fall to the pavement in shards like icicles. 'It would be bad enough loitering on the way back,' she said, 'but standing there goss—' She looked at me again and swallowed her words. 'Standing anywhere, doing anything with the deposit still on you.' She snapped her head round and looked along the street to the tolbooth clock which was showing twenty minutes past three. 'Get there now and get straight back again.'

Mima and Elsie bobbed and scuttled off like a pair of beetles, leaving Mary glaring after them.

'And I'll have their half-week's pay-packet made up for them,' she said, spitting the words through clenched teeth. I could not let this pass, in all conscience.

'Please don't blame the girls,' I said. 'I waylaid them. They were most anxious to be on their way but they could hardly cut and run, now could they?'

Mary said nothing.

'They'll make it,' I went on. 'How far away is the bank?' I could not help glancing across the street to where there was a branch of the British Linen into which Aitkens' cashiers could have shied their deposits from the Emporium windows. Mary caught my look and her eyes narrowed to slits.

'We have nothing to do with that place,' she hissed – I had

never seen such a blameless institution engender such venom – then she blinked.

'You waylaid them?' she said. 'Didn't you receive my telegram?'

'Certainly I did,' I said, thinking furiously. 'Yes, indeed.' What excuse could I possibly come up with for being here? Then inspiration dawned upon me. 'I'm here as a customer today, Mrs Aitken. I waylaid the girls, checking that the store was open.'

Her black eyes could narrow no further but her lips all but disappeared.

'Really?' she said.

'Of course, I feel quite dreadful now,' I said, truthfully enough as it happened. 'I never would have dreamed that any of the family would be here.' I was getting into my stride. 'In fact, I didn't suppose for the moment that any of the family actually worked in the store at all.' I gave the tape measure a little glance and let my gaze travel up the long arc of pins on her bosom.

'I only came in for Lady Lawson,' she said, forced into explanation. 'I take care of a *very* few, *very* special ladies myself.'

'But Lady Lawson surely can't have expected you to be here today,' I said. All the wisps of suspicion I had felt about the pair of them on the day of the jubilee were back, thicker than wisps now.

'I insisted,' she said. Was it my imagination that she shifted her feet a little? 'Lady Lawson herself has been nothing but gracious and kind.' She spoke in definite, or one might almost say, defiant, tones.

'Well, it's very kind of *you*,' I said, smiling.

'Not really,' Mary said. She turned and looked into the window behind her at the empty space and the wreath of flowers where the display of stock should be. 'They say life goes on, Mrs Gilver,' she said. 'And that time heals all ills. But I don't agree. Time unfilled is a burden. Work is the thing. Work goes on and work fills up time. I am seventy-four years old and I have filled my life with work. It has never failed me. My daughter has never worked, nor Jack, although he is a director, of course. A businessman, like his father. The devil makes work for idle hands.'

I started at that and regarded her very closely. *Did* she know about Jack and Hilda Hepburn?

'What I mean to say, Mrs Gilver, is that they have no duties to help them through difficult times. If they were kept busy in this place like I am . . .' She gestured towards the window, looking pained as she did so. I thought the wreaths and black velvet had suddenly reminded her of her loss, but when she spoke again she revealed the true source of her distress; a most surprising one. 'I let myself be talked into this but I'm not happy. They look too much like those clever-clever windows you see now.'

'Like Hep—' I bit it off just in time.

'One glove and a scrap of chiffon,' said Mary, with icy scorn. 'Frenchified. Aitkens' goes in for a good, honest, selling window, always has done. I like to see them decked out properly, not done up in that wheedling, arty way.'

I recalled the mannequins standing in the sand and although I could not agree with Mary, I did loathe Hilda Hepburn – if it were she behind them – for such teasing of a family she had secretly wronged.

'And speaking of good honest selling, madam,' she said, 'what is it you're looking for?' She folded her hands together at one side of her waist and inclined her head, looking every bit the perfect assistant, but the way her eyes glinted showed me that she did not believe for one minute that a shopping list had brought me here today.

I smiled confidently back at her; for I was getting good at this. Then my smile faltered. Actually I was hopeless at it. That is, I was very proud of having hit upon the strategy, thinking it a perfect way to start conversations in quiet shops and tearooms, but the only time I had put it into practice I had asked an antiques dealer if he had such a thing as a tip-top tea-table, while actually resting my elbow on one. I had to pretend I wanted it in oak and Alec had to walk out of the shop to hide his smirking. Surely, though, I could think of something beyond Aitkens'.

'Opera gloves,' I said, trying not to show too much of my triumph.

'Certainly,' said Mary, not bothering to hide any of hers. 'Let me show you to our glove department. Miss Torrance will be delighted to take care of you.' Who would have thought, I asked myself, following her, that one could buy opera gloves in Dunfermline?

I have always had a great affection and affinity for a gloves counter, from the days when I was taken to Liberty's twice a year to try on white kid and cotton in spring, brown leather and fur-lined velvet in autumn (gloves being the one garment which even my mother conceded could not be run up in the village or by nursemaids at home). I thrilled when the 'old lady' as I called her to myself, although she could not have been thirty-five in reality, stepped into the backroom and brought out the high chair for me to sit on during my fitting, and even though it was a sign of approaching maturity and these were usually welcome I was sorry the year I grew tall enough to sit on the ordinary chair like all the grown-up ladies. Only having had two sons of my own, of course, I could not say whether the chair still existed, with its dark green paint, its green and purple striped cushion and the scuff marks on the spars where generations of little girls had wound their feet for purchase as they struggled with those tiny pearl buttons, but I like to think so.

As we swept beyond the haberdashery, through one of the arches, I noticed a stout individual busy at the stationery drawers who had no fewer than three pencils sticking out of her bun and who had tucked a great many paper chits of some kind into the belt of her serge dress in the way a bookie's runner will stuff tickets into his hatband.

'Slips, Miss Armstrong,' Mary snapped as we drew close to her. The woman started, letting a handful of card samples burst out of her grasp and clatter to the floor. They must, I had time to think, be very good quality card to make that sound instead of fluttering. 'Slips belong in the order book,' Mary went on to the top of Miss Armstrong's head as she bent to retrieve them. 'Not about the person.'

'Of course, Mrs Ninian,' said the woman from her position on the floor. 'Sorry, Mrs Ninian.' Mary swept past and the woman shot her a look of such dislike that I was startled. I would make sure to talk to Miss Armstrong in the course of my day, I thought, as I hurried on.

'Madam requires *mousquetaires*, Miss Torrance,' Mary announced as she arrived at the gloves counter and ushered me into the chair beside the stretcher. Miss Torrance was a woman in her late forties with a pale oval face and a steel-grey bob which hung in long points almost meeting under her chin so that she looked a little like a crusading knight in his chain mail headgear. She looked very surprised to see Mary and glanced between her and me a few times, saying nothing. 'I'll leave you in Miss Torrance's capable hands,' Mary said. Then, very firmly: 'Goodbye, Mrs Gilver.'

'Now then,' said Miss Torrance. She took hold of my upper arm in both hands and gave it a squeeze as though she were wringing out a flannel. 'Yes, you have a very slender arm, madam.'

'Thank you,' I replied.

'A wise choice to start covering it now, though,' she went on, spoiling the compliment completely.

'Wasn't it kind of Mrs Ninian to take me under her wing like that,' I said, getting down to business. 'I mean, I can understand her not wanting to let Lady Lawson down even today, but she had no need to concern herself with me.'

'Mrs Ninian has no swank to her,' said Miss Torrance, 'I'll give her that. She runs a tight ship, and doesn't suffer fools, but I've seen her pick up a duster and wipe a display, ring up a purchase and pack it to clear a queue. And I'll tell you: there's more than Lady Lawson would like to have Mrs Ninian doing their alterations – well, you only have to look at her own costumes, don't you? She always says if it fits like a glove it looks like Paris couture.'

'Mm,' I said, thinking that Mary's bombazine fitted like a sausage-skin and did not remind me of Paris at all.

'And speaking of gloves,' said Miss Torrance. 'Do you know your size?'

'Seven,' I said. Miss Torrance, I thought to myself, was far too fond and loyal to be of use to me, and I put away all thoughts of detection until I could escape her for Miss Armstrong of the slips.

'Seven,' she repeated, pulling off one of my own gloves by pinching at the fingertips and tugging. She spread my hand on the counter and screwed up her nose. 'I'm sure you were once,' she said. 'Are you a horseback rider or is it tennis?' Thus having informed me that I had the thickened fingers of a hoyden to go with my scrawny arms she took a sizing board out of her counter drawer and got to work on me.

So it was with some satisfaction then that I found myself able to reject the gloves she showed me without a pang. They were elbow-length kid, had cuffs like gauntlets, and were rather yellowed along one edge; I supposed that there was not much turnover and this pair had been in their drawer for some years now with the light getting in through the glass front of it.

'Besides,' I said, 'I was thinking of black satin, actually. Or mauve.' Miss Torrance physically recoiled. Of course, I would no more wear black opera gloves than I would stick feathers in my hair and dance a can-can but Grant keeps me up to date with the fact that elsewhere, far from Dunfermline and even Perthshire, such shocking articles were being worn.

'I'm sorry, madam,' said Miss Torrance in low tones. 'But Aitkens' Emporium does not stock anything of *that* kind. We have a rose beige that is most becoming.'

'Not to worry,' I said cheerfully, standing up again. 'I'll keep looking.'

Miss Torrance hesitated and then lowered her voice even further before saying more.

'You might be able to find what you're looking for . . . down the street,' she finished, so quietly I was almost lip-reading.

'House of Hepburn?' I said, guessing. Miss Torrance made a hissing noise and looked around to see if anyone had heard me, but the gloves were modestly situated in a spot where no casual gentlemen passing by would be inflamed by the sight of a lady

133

with her wrist buttons in disarray and there was no one near us except for two girls in day-school uniforms giggling as they tried on the ready-to-wear hats at the next counter. Miss Torrance frowned at them and I decided to take myself off and let her go and intimidate them out of their fun.

'Miss Armstrong?' I said, back at the stationery desk moments later.

'Madam,' she replied, bobbing. 'How can I help you?' I noticed with amusement that already another 'slip' had found its way into her waistband.

'Is it just personal writing paper you provide?' I asked. 'Or do you do business cards too?'

'Oh no, we do gentlemen's business cards, madam, certainly,' said Miss Armstrong. 'There's a stationery counter up on first, beside Gents' Tailoring.'

'Ah,' I said. 'And what about ladies' business cards?'

Miss Armstrong blinked.

'What kind of . . . ladies' business would you be referring to?' she asked.

Her suspicions were so transparent and so outrageous that I burst out laughing.

'Miss Armstrong, really!' I said. 'It could be any number of things. A little dress shop, a little tearoom.' She was laughing too now, and blushing a bit.

'But they don't need cards, madam, do they?' she said.

'Actually . . .' I sidled closer and dropped my voice. 'It's a detective agency.'

She gave a very gratifying reaction, eyes wide, mouth open.

'Are you a detective?' she said. 'Truly?' Then she gave an out and out gasp. 'Here!' she said. 'You're not that "Mrs Gilver", are you?' I nodded. 'I wasn't here on jubilee day, madam. I was off sick. Well, I took a day's sick leave anyway. And then yesterday I just couldn't stomach it. But I'm glad to get a chance to meet you at long last, madam. And I'll do anything in my power to help you.'

I had, in a phrase Alec sometimes uses, struck oil.

'Why?' I asked, meaning it to encompass everything: the sick leave, the absence from the funeral and the willingness – nay, eagerness – to help. 'I should warn you that I'm not working for Mrs Ninian any more. I'm snooping now, not sleuthing. I'm doing what my fellow detective, Mr Osborne, calls my "servant of truth" turn.'

'Gilver and Osborne: servants of truth,' said Miss Armstrong. 'I can see the card now. Well, Mrs Gilver, madam, Mrs Gilver—'

'I know,' I said. 'It's a puzzler but either is fine by me.'

'Well, madam,' she said. 'I couldn't believe they were going ahead with it. That's all. With Miss Mirren missing.'

'So you all knew?'

'Well, those of a certain vintage,' Miss Armstrong said. 'Mrs John told Mrs Lumsden on the Saturday morning. And Miss Hutton knew. But the girls didn't and none of the menfolk – dear me no. No, no. But it wasn't just that, madam. It was all that trouble about the engagement too. There's always rivalry in business but Dugald was a lovely boy and he loved Miss Mirren and she him and if it hadn't been for Certain People, they could both have been happy. *Everyone* could have been happy. But then . . .' Miss Armstrong rubbed her thumb and fingers together in the age-old gesture. 'Miss Mirren was an only child of only children,' she said, 'seeing as how Master Lennox and young Master died in the war without so much as a sweetheart between them. Everything was to come to her. The whole of Aitkens'. If you ask me, Certain People couldn't stand to see the Hepburns walking into it all.'

'Well, Certain People must certainly be ruing their intransigence now,' I said.

'Her?' said Miss Armstrong. 'If she has a heart at all it's a cold black thing, Mrs Gilver.'

I thought about the searing words Mary Aitken had spoken about her own damnation on the day of the funeral.

'Oh, I think she has a heart, Miss Armstrong,' I said. 'A very troubled one, maybe.'

'Well, if a woman with a heart can care about slips the day after she's buried her only grandchild,' said Miss Armstrong, 'then maybe.'

'Is it difficult to work here when you hate her so?' I asked. Really what interested me was how a woman of such spirit as Miss Armstrong could serve at a counter at all, bowing and scraping and agreeing with the customer about everything, but since Mary Aitken was the embodiment of the Emporium, it came to the same thing. 'Wouldn't you be happier down the street?' I rather thought that the carefree mischievous Hepburns, light-hearted enough to seem callous to more sombre souls – and how on the button Abigail had been about that as it transpired! – would care less about a scrap of paper in the belt of a dress.

'Och, better the devil you know,' said Miss Armstrong. 'And I don't hate her, madam. I just think she's a silly old fool and she's suffering for it. And I think she's let this store take the place of her family, until she cares more about it than about them.'

'Yes, the slips,' I said, nodding. 'It is unseemly.'

'Well, that's Mistress Mary,' said Miss Armstrong. 'And it's not just the slips today, madam. Can you believe that she could care about a bit of muddle in my stock book the day after her only grandchild had disappeared? Can you believe she was checking up on my work last Monday, with Miss Mirren just gone and Miss Abigail out of her mind? Well, she was. No word of a lie.'

'Old habits,' I said. 'My father shocked the whole village by going off rabbit hunting the day my mother died. But it was Tuesday and it was November and he was a man with orderly ways.' I smiled, remembering. My aunts were gathered at the bedroom windows, chattering with prim disapproval like a flock of budgerigars as they watched my father striding across the park with his gun open over his arm and his rabbit bag slapping against his thigh. Only I noticed, I think, that instead of hopping over the ha-ha as he always did – as he was proud of still being able to do at almost seventy – he lowered himself down carefully holding onto a tussock and as he arose at the other side his shoulders were heaving.

'Dreadful man,' said my Aunt Rosalind.

'Oh, Rosa, stop clucking for heaven's sake,' I had said. We had been up all night around the deathbed and tempers were frayed to shreds now in the early morning. 'He was never going to sit around here to do his sobbing. It's not his way.'

'How can you, Di-di?' said my sister, lifting her head from where she had been resting it on my mother's counterpane, soaking it with her tears. 'How can you defend him?'

I did better; I joined him. I fetched a gun and tramped through the woods to his favourite rabbiting spot. He was sitting on a mossy stump, getting his britches soaked through, with his gun loaded and resting on his knee and with tears coursing down his face.

'I always said you were a witch,' he greeted me. 'Very well, then. I shall only shoot rabbits this morning after all.'

Of course, I did not tell my sister; Mavis would never have recovered from such melodrama and would have made his life utter hell with her prying. I did mention it to my brother, however, and he – practical soul – hit on a wonderful solution: a soldier's widow by the name of Gloria. My poor old father only survived his beloved wife by three years in the end, but I am sure that Gloria made them pleasant ones.

Miss Armstrong was looking at me in an inquiring way and I shook myself back to the present again.

'Sorry? Did you say something?'

'I was just asking about that card. Osborne and Gilver, or the other way?'

'Sorry,' I said again. 'Um . . . Gilver and Osborne is alphabetical. Now, Miss Armstrong, can I ask you about Miss Hutton? Would you say it's safe to go and speak to her?'

'Safe, madam? Well, Mrs Ninian is away home. I saw her go with her coat and hat on.'

'That wasn't what I was thinking of,' I said, blushing a little for myself, because of course I should have been. 'I meant, really, could I speak to Miss Hutton as freely as I have done to you? I need to ask her something but I don't know where her loyalties might lie.'

'Miss Hutton,' said Miss Armstrong, screwing up her face. 'Hard to say. If it were Mrs Lumsden now I'd say you should tread very carefully. Very carefully indeed. But Miss Hutton is a sensible soul.'

I thanked her and left her rummaging in her drawers for the stiffest possible vellum to guillotine down to size and fashion into a business card for me.

I had been in Aitkens' three times now but this was my first visit to Ladies' Gowns, usually an early stop in any department store. I took the wide sweeping staircase to the next floor and studied the large wooden plaque with the gilt names and arrows sending one to the various departments, Layette and Junior at the back, Gents' Tailoring down the windowless side, Gowns and Bespoke Millinery taking up all of the front and stretching down the windowed side of the building which faced out onto the lane. A proper disposition of resources, I thought, nodding, and entered by the nearest archway.

Grant would not have approved, I said to myself, as I looked around me – I usually hand down my judgements on frocks in Grant's name; it stops me feeling shallow although I fear that in fact it proves me shallower still – for Aitkens' ladies' gowns were much of a muchness with the yellowed elbow-length gloves and indeed the jubilee notions. Sturdy mannequins stood about on stout plinths wearing sturdy tweeds and stout shoes and, as one penetrated the depths of the department – again, I supposed, away from masculine gaze – they wore evening gowns hardly less robust, with much brocade and boning, over dancing shoes one would think were meant for dancing *girls* – eight shows a week, and no time for bunions.

'May I help, madam?' said a rather beautiful young assistant, who had used her bolt of serge to make a uniform dress more flowing than anything for sale. 'Mrs . . .' She registered a level of professional shock that she could not bring forth a name for a face she clearly found familiar.

'Gilver,' I said. 'I was here last week and yesterday.'

'Oh,' said the girl, relieved that she had not mislaid the name of a valued customer after all.

'I'm looking for Miss Hutton,' I said.

'Certainly, madam,' said the beautiful creature. 'Please come with me.' She turned and oozed across the floor, looking like something from a harem, and the swish of her slim hips triggered a memory in me.

'Were you the other kelpie?' I asked her. She looked at me and grinned.

'Yes, madam,' she said. 'Lynne told me you thought we were nymphs!'

'Sorry about that,' I said. 'And sorry about Miss Mirren too. Did you know her?'

'A bit,' said the nymph. 'She was closer to my older colleagues, really. She'd known them since she was wee, of course. But she was very nice. Not at all snooty. Shy, really, if anything. Very shy around Lynne and me.'

I could easily imagine that she had been rendered shy by this amazing creature, and she and Lynne together, if they were chums and went about in a twosome, would have flattened any ordinary girl to a wafer. I thought about Mirren Aitken's heart-shaped face and soft brown hair; she had not been ordinary, exactly, but all that I had heard about her left me with the impression of something far from a siren.

'If I'd had her pocket money and all her free time,' said the girl, 'I would have been like a star off the films. I used to feel jealous of her for that, Mrs Gilver.' She gave a laugh. 'And you should have heard Lynne when Miss Mirren got engaged. There was jealous for you!'

'Oh?' I said.

'Away!' said the girl. 'I don't mean like that. Only Lynne and her boy have got to wait till they're at the head of the housing list. Either that or take a spare room and share the kitchen at his mother's. But she wouldn't swap with Miss Mirren now.'

She had reached another of the many curtains with which Aitkens' was so liberally festooned, this one hiding a shut door. She knocked on it and called out.

139

'Visitor for you, Miss Hutton.' Then she opened the door and left me there.

Miss Hutton was sitting in a tiny office, a cubby-hole really, with just a desk and a rack stretching from floor to ceiling with quite a hundred little pigeonholes in it, all stuffed with bundles of yellowing tissue paper. She was opening letters and she looked up with great relief from them.

'Oh! Mrs Gilver,' she said. 'I'm answering condolence cards. Is there anything more draining?' She hauled herself to her feet and from behind the door she drew a folding chair, cracked it open and set it down at the side of the desk. There was just room to sweep the door closed again. I sat down – there was nowhere to stand – and Miss Hutton shoved the heap of unopened envelopes away from her.

'Is it really your job?' I said. 'Shouldn't one of the family . . . ?'

'In a family business,' Miss Hutton said, 'things do get a wee bit mixed in together sometimes. I offered, anyway. Just a first pass through them. I'll let Mrs Ninian see all the important ones.' She nodded towards a small pile, mostly letters, and then gave a rueful look at the much larger piles of letter and cards at its side. 'And don't you think it shocking, Mrs Gilver,' she said, her bony nose pinching with disapproval, 'how many of them . . .' She held up one card and another and a third, all of the same design – an improbable church on a hillside with an improbable sunset going on behind. 'These are ours,' she said. 'We sell them downstairs. You'd think people would have bought a different one to send us, wouldn't you?'

I could not imagine anything more vulgar than a condolence card of any sort, to be honest, and I could not resist taking one and opening it.

> *A golden Treasure in your heart*
> *The dear Lord loved it too*
> *And so has gathered it to Him,*
> *Sweet mem'ries left to you.*

I closed it again, thinking that I would have hit anyone who sent me such an article if a child of mine had died.

'I wanted to speak to you today, Miss Hutton,' I said, 'because I find myself still with a few loose ends to tie in. For my own satisfaction, you understand. Mrs Ninian has made it very clear that my formal engagement in the matter is over now.' I waited a bit, thinking that now was her chance to freeze me with a glare if she cared to.

Far from it; she continued regarding me with a calm, expectant look.

'Anything I can do to help,' she said. A singularly *un*helpful remark as it happened, since I still could not remember what it was that I wanted to ask her. Alec disparages what he calls my excessive note-taking – and to be frank, I have ended some cases with enough scribbled-over paper to support a bonfire while chestnuts are roasted upon it – but better that surely than this: sitting gazing blankly back at an important witness as she gazed at me. And looking at her, I remembered a very different expression of hers, puzzled and troubled, and that must have connected to the thing I wanted to ask her; it was tantalisingly close but still out of reach of me.

'Would you mind, Miss Hutton,' I said, 'if I just sat here for a moment and gathered my thoughts?' She glanced back at the piles of correspondence on her desk and I hurried to reassure her that I did not need her attention.

'Please do carry on with your work. So long as I won't distract you. I would even offer to help, but I wouldn't like to . . .' I made a fastidious expression and nodded to the letter she was even now slitting open. It was addressed to Mr and Mrs J.B. Aitken. Miss Hutton scanned it quickly and set it upon the pile to be passed along. The next envelope she glanced at and added to the same pile without opening. Then came a card which she opened, frowned at – it was the church at sunset – and placed on top of her stack. Then another unopened envelope onto the family pile.

'Do you recognise the handwriting?' I asked. A pained expression flashed over her.

'No,' she said. 'No, it's just that I wouldn't open anything addressed to Mrs Ninian herself, madam, until she's seen it. She wouldn't like that.' She held up the last envelope and I nodded, reading the name there. Miss Hutton sighed. 'I wish I'd broken my own rule last week, I can tell you.'

'Oh?'

'There was a letter for Mrs Ninian and it wasn't even sealed, just tucked over, you know, and maybe if I'd opened it I could have helped in some way.'

'Do you want to tell me about it?' I said.

'But then again maybe not,' said Miss Hutton. 'Most certainly not. Because you said Mrs Ninian asked you to find Miss Mirren, didn't you?'

'That's it,' I said, sitting upright in my chair. My voice had been far too loud for such a small room and Miss Hutton looked startled. 'That's what you said, that's been niggling at me,' I went on. 'You seemed surprised, the day of the funeral, when I told you what I had been asked to do.'

'I *was* surprised,' Miss Hutton said.

'Yes, but why?' I asked her. She hesitated, turning an envelope over and over in her hands. It was another condolatory church – I was beginning to recognise them. Then she began speaking in a great rush, like a dam bursting.

'I take Mrs Ninian's appointment list into her office at the start of every week,' she said. 'Just to help her. Everyone thinks she's such a tower of strength but I know what it takes out of her, what a toll. Anyway, when I went in on that Monday morning, I tripped over an envelope on the floor. It had been slipped under the door and it was addressed to Mrs Ninian and I was sure it was Miss Mirren's handwriting. She used to play at shops here when she was a little girl, you know. Writing out orders and receipts – she had her own little set of books and stamps and everything – and I know her writing. She never went to school to learn that same hand they teach them all, so I'd know her own writing anywhere. I'm sure it was hers. I know it was.'

'How did it get there?' I said. 'Surely the post isn't generally slipped under doors.'

'Oh no, madam, I don't mean a posted letter,' Miss Hutton said. 'I mean hand-delivered. It just said Mrs N.L. Aitken.'

'In Mirren's writing?' I said.

'Yes.'

'Revealing that Mirren had been here, in the store?'

'Yes,' said Miss Hutton, and she looked pained again. 'I even smiled when I saw it. We had all heard on the Saturday that Miss Mirren had run off and we were worried about her. Well, those of us who weren't cheering her on, you know. Quite a few of them thought she had eloped and all the best to her. But when I saw the letter, I thought: Ah! She's here. Hiding out in the store. And then I thought: Well, of course she is. Where else? Because whenever she wasn't playing at shops in the departments years ago, she was playing at houses up in those attics. So I put the letter on Mrs Ninian's desk with her other papers and thought we would soon all be back to normal again. So I couldn't understand why Mrs Ninian had engaged you. She knew where Miss Mirren was. I couldn't understand why she hadn't just gone to get her. Unless Miss Mirren left again.'

Not a natural detective, our Miss Hutton; no nasty habit of suspicion to stop her taking the facts at face value and trusting everyone. I had quite a different view. I thought nothing more likely than that, on finding the letter, Mary Aitken deduced where Mirren was hiding, perhaps even went to check, then decided to leave her there stewing in her own juices until after the jubilee, whereupon a detective summoned for the purpose would 'find' her. That, finally, explained the day's delay.

And certainly if Mary knew where the missing girl was and did nothing it would explain her self-flagellating guilt and her conviction that she was damned

'Miss Hutton,' I said, 'did you mention finding the letter? To Mrs Ninian, I mean. Or, I suppose, anyone.'

'No,' Miss Hutton said.

'Why not?'

Miss Hutton blinked again.

'I suppose,' she said slowly, 'I just sort of naturally didn't. I mean, I just sort of wouldn't, in case it was awkward for her.'

'Very discreet of you,' I said. 'Most admirable. I expect you must need a great deal of natural discretion to do what you do.' Miss Hutton looked uncomprehending. 'Madam looks lovely, and all that,' I went on. Her rather prim face broke into an unexpected smirk.

'Oh indeed,' she said. 'Ten years younger, perhaps even more slender without the stripes and we seem to have mislaid your measurements, madam, and beg your patience while we take them again.'

'If she's twice the size she was last time?' I guessed. Miss Hutton nodded. 'Well your discretion will stand you in good stead now.' She looked puzzled and I saw I would have to spell it out to her. 'About the letter: perhaps it would be best *not* to mention it to anyone.' She nodded again, reassured as easily as that, her innocence making me worry about her more than ever. Did she really not have enough healthy regard for her own safety to see that I was warning her?

'Do you think Mrs Ninian knows you found it and moved it?' I asked. The spectre had raised itself in me that if Mary Aitken guessed as much and if Mary Aitken had killed Mirren, she might even now be plotting to tie up a loose end of her own. But did I still suspect Mary Aitken? Was I not leaning towards Robin Hepburn now; an enraged cuckold hitting out at his rival's child? Miss Hutton was shaking her head.

'She probably just assumes Miss Mirren put it there herself, if she's thinking about it at all. And I hope she's not – brooding about it, making herself ill.'

'I wonder why Mirren didn't,' I said.

'Well, Mrs Ninian's door is kept locked usually. I have a key and a few other people too, but Miss Mirren wouldn't have had one.'

144

'A few others?' I said, relieved. At least if Mary Aitken had worked out that Mirren's letter had arrived on her desk via an intermediary, she would have a few from which to choose. She could not, surely, kill them all.

8

And so to the attics after all. Not to search for bloodstained gloves but to see what signs if any remained of Mirren's sojourn there. I was hoping for a note, or, if the gods were smiling, a diary although reason told me that the police must have found it if there were such a thing. I left Miss Hutton in her cubbyhole full of tissue-paper rolls – these, I now realised, were ladies' paper patterns, cut to fit regular customers and kept for them, until advancing years and an appetite for buns ended their usefulness; I remembered my own stalwart little dressmaker once telling me she had 'mislaid my numbers' and would have to beg my patience while she set about me with the tape measure again and I wondered now, after what Miss Hutton had told me. But I am more or less the same girth as when I ordered my trousseau, or at least I always tell myself so, since I can still fit into my wedding gown and into my oldest tweeds without much straining. A more Jesuitical soul (or do I mean less; Jesuitical seems to be one of those insults that two people can hurl at one another each believing stoutly in his own rightness to do so) would remark that elderly tweeds show their age in bagging more than anything and that my wedding gown, following the fashions of the day, was a sack – pouchy on top and with loops of satin hanging from its suggestion of a waist like great swirls of melting cream. Now that tastes have changed, it almost pains me to see my wedding portrait, the waste of my youth that it was to be got up in such an extraordinary way.

Upstairs I strode confidently across the darkened landing to the light switch and clicked it on. The wreath of lilies was still there and the black velvet curtaining but, perhaps from familiarity,

I found I could look upon them without my throat contracting. Now, where would one hole up here if one were . . . if one were what, though?

What *was* Mirren Aitken's state of mind when she had left her home and her family and come to the attics above the store to hide herself? It depended whether she knew about her father and Hilda Hepburn, about the impossibility of herself and Dugald marrying. Had she told Mary in the letter? Why would she tell her grandmother, though?

I tried the handle of the nearest door and it opened, but instead of a little attic room, which is what I had been expecting, I found on the other side a long corridor, quite dark, with at least six doors opening off it; this was not going to be a ten-minute job, it seemed, and I wished that I had had some luncheon before beginning, and had brought an electric torch with me, and a scarf to tie over my face against the dust I could smell in the quiet air. On the other hand, I knew that the store was free of Aitkens today – now that Lady Lawson had let poor Mary go home – and I could not miss the chance while I had it.

It was with some relief that behind the first of these new doors which I tried, in a kind of little ante-room, I found three paraffin lamps, full and clean, as well as a large sketching pad which appeared to serve as a stock-plan of the attics with coded notes about what was stored in each of them, and columns marked out to show what was brought in and taken away and when and by whom – initials I could not decipher – and to which department they were bound. Blessing Mary Aitken's tidy mind, I lit one of the lamps and began.

Soon enough, I was cursing Mary Aitken's mind, for it transpired that the plan with its columns was an aspiration rather than a reflection of reality and the attics themselves were a perfect chaos of objects and oddities, like a jumble sale after the passing of a tornado. There were crates – the rooms full of closed crates were not too bad, as a matter of fact, for crates must sit on one of their flat sides and the only way to add another one is on top of the first. The rooms where the crates had been plundered, however, were quite another matter. The lids lay about and packing straw covered the floor and miscellaneous items could be seen sticking out of the tops where they had been shoved to get to greater prizes below. Three vases perhaps would bar my way across the floor and a tottering heap of shirt boxes would threaten to fall as I edged past them to get to sets of saucepan lids tied together like castanets, the saucepans themselves nowhere to be seen, but an army of chimney pot nests – too small for any chimney I could imagine and perhaps that was why they languished here – would grab at my stockings as I left again.

There were still some signs that once upon a time these rooms had been staff quarters, as I had heard Bella tell me: fireplaces and dark-stained edges to the floors where linoleum or even rugs had once been put down. Now though there were only bales of mothy tablecloths rolled up like giant cocoons and propped in corners, a bouquet of nasty, shiny bed quilts all squashed together, each one a rosette, and stuffed in the space below a table, its legs wrapped in cardboard and tied with string and another one upside down on top. I glanced at the tables – pickled walnut, it looked to be, but not too successfully pickled because the worm had got into their underside, and little piles of orange dust revealed why they had been forgotten here. I found myself tutting. Those shiny quilts, nasty as they were, would be showered with woodworm dust, not to mention damp too, and they would have fetched – I glanced at one of the price tickets – ten shillings and ninepence apiece in their day, which seemed rather a lot and I assumed they had not been here as long as the yellowed tablecloths nor the millinery skeletons I found in the room next door, poor things, stiffened gauze mushrooms in grey and white and brown, waiting for the winding of silk, the ribbon band and the sprays of cher-ries which would never come now, since hats like mushrooms had gone the way of pouchy wedding gowns with loops of whipped cream hanging down.

And there was more of it, and more still; in the next room, the sudden macabre sight of plaster legs, arms and heads sticking all anyhow out of a heap of dismembered mannequins, looking like the fall of the rebel angels, and next door again countless drums of Dundee marmalade with ominously bulging tops and a sliding heap of India-rubber hot water bags with their stoppers swinging free and the ink on their labels all run into nonsense from wetting. But at least the smell was not too bad anywhere, just dust and a little damp, a smoky, almost bacony whiff in the room with the hot bottles and marmalade, burnt rubber probably, and the equally unmistakable pungent odour of lanolin hanging around a sizeable room where I found more woollen leggings than one could credit ever being purchased together at whatever wholesaler had supplied them; more woollen leggings, almost, than one might guess had ever been knitted up in the history of the northern hemisphere that had invented them; more, certainly, than I could have imagined in my childhood, when I was forced to wear the horrid itchy things from October to April, buttoned firmly to my vest and fastened under my instep with those woollen straps which somehow managed at once to be so tight they made my feet ache and too loose to stop the hated leggings creep up my legs so that the ankle cuff – the itchiest part of all – chafed at my plump calves and brought me many a tut and spank for scratching.

And another door and another room and I stopped on the threshold, disbelieving. This place was empty. A small room of perhaps eight feet square, with sloping ceilings and a tiny dormer window, a fireplace with an empty grate, a washbasin with a cold tap in one corner and nothing else at all. Not so much as a wisp of packing straw and it smelled of floor soap. I walked around it, wondering, and then understanding. If I had had to choose a little room to spend some days in, out of all these rooms up here, I should have chosen this one with the basin and the window. And if I had wanted to hide any signs of someone having been here, I would have emptied the room out completely and scrubbed it with soap until all traces of its occupation were gone.

I poked my head around the doors of the few remaining rooms for the sake of completeness and then began to retrace my steps to the landing. Having been so fixed upon the rooms' contents and not at all upon the labyrinthine layout of the accommodations, however, I took a wrong turn once or twice, confidently opening a door expecting a corridor and finding the dead-end of an inner chamber instead. When it happened for the third time, I stopped, stood quite still, squeezed my eyes shut and tried to *feel* the position of the building around me, the street and the alley, and the afternoon light from the west. Hugh, with his hands on his hips, used to stand and glare at me on foggy hilltops and in drizzly forests, back in the early days when he believed I would grow a passion matching his for sloshing about the countryside in the freezing rain. It doesn't matter if the sun isn't shining, he would say, shut your eyes and *feel* north. Feel it! I would shut my eyes tight and *feel* cold, wet, tired, hungry and sorry I had ever agreed to the outing, but north escaped me.

I opened my eyes and shuffled round so that I was facing into the corner of the room – I suppose I thought that since north was always drawn as a point there was more chance of *feeling* it with the help of a corner straight ahead. I closed my eyes again, but then snapped them open, overwhelmed suddenly by a wave of nostalgia. This room was full of old shoeboxes, rather good quality ones too: cardboard but covered over with that shiny coating of Rexine which makes cheap suitcases look a little like leather. I had forgotten that good shoeboxes used to be made that way and the sight of them took me straight back to childhood and the floor of my grandmother's clothes closet where I used to spend happy hours unhooking the catches on such boxes, lifting off the lids, working open the drawstring of the chamois bags and gloating over the fabulous objects inside them, patent, satin, velvet, silk and that stiffened lace which I loved best of all. Every year on our visit I would prise out the shoetrees – made to match and almost as richly bejewelled as the evening slippers themselves – and slide in my foot, thinking almost there, sometime soon, until the year when I looked at the slippers with a sinking feeling, removed the tree and worked my toes under the strap, knowing that I had missed my chance and would never wear one of these glorious little confections now. And actually, on closer inspection I could see that they were rather turned up at the toes – matching trees or no – and the paler ones showed the signs of clumsy dancing partners scuffing at them. I had closed the boxes for the last time and turned away, tramping back through the house in my sensible brogues, very much the ugly sister.

Perhaps, though, these boxes in Aitkens' attic were left over because they were unusual sizes; perhaps I might find a pair to fit me, or almost as good, find a pair miles too big and feel like a child again. The nearest box on the top of the pile was not even properly fastened, the little string hanging down and a corner of chamois peeping out. I stepped over and lifted the lid.

My first thought was that I would never again berate myself for being a shallow, silly woman concerned only with trivial fripperies and indifferent to the solid meat of life, for there in the shoebox, stuffed between the two chamois leather shoe bags, balled up and half inside out, clearly hastily removed and just as hastily hidden, was a pair of gloves; the gloves I had given up all thoughts of finding.

They were driving gauntlets, brand new and with their price ticket still pinned to one cuff. I held up the paraffin lamp and scrutinised them without touching, looking for a spot of anything that might be blood, but so far as I could tell the gloves were unmarked. They were that very pale mouse colour which driving gloves tend to be and there was no possibility that a drop of blood would not be seen if it had fallen there. I leaned in close and sniffed, but there was nothing to smell except, faintly, unused leather. Even if hands had worn these gloves to fire a revolver, though, would there be a trace of cordite more than a week later? Gingerly, I lifted out the right-hand glove and smoothed it back into shape for closer inspection. It was a man's glove, that was clear; not one woman in a hundred would need gloves this size, but that did not mean that Abigail had not worn it on her little hand while she shot her daughter, since the last thing she would have wanted was to be struggling with tight gloves in the few seconds she had to remove them, hide them and sit back down with the gun. Still, I could not believe that she had done all this, because even now I could not see so much as a pinprick of blood or a smudge of gunpowder anywhere on the article, front or back, cuff to fingertip, nowhere. I lifted the left glove out, smoothed it too and subjected it to the same close study, practically touching my nose against it. Again there were no bloodstains and no black marks, but this glove was not so pristine as its mate somehow; it seemed a little bedraggled here and there, with flat spots on the nap of the kidskin, watermarks I should have said if guessing. Might there have been tiny spots of blood which had been wiped away leaving water stains behind them? But Abigail Aitken would not have had time and if she had come back later to do it, would she not have simply taken the gloves away? Would not anyone?

Taking care to make a proper job of it, I crumpled the gloves back up and replaced them in the box then, resisting the temptation to look over my shoulder before I did so, I wiped the edge of the box with my coat sleeve where I had touched it and left the way I had come.

Going right instead of left this time, I found myself out on the landing very near the lift, but on the far side from the stairway – I had evidently come around in a loop from where I had begun. Quickly I re-entered the little ante-room, put the lamp back where I had found it and stole away down the stairs, listening at every bend in case I should hear someone coming. I managed to descend all the way and emerge into the back of the 'fancy notions' department at the ground floor without being spotted and I hurried towards the front foyer and the revolving door; the discovery of the gloves had put all else out of my mind.

'That you off then, madam?' said the doorman as I approached him and entered the revolving door. He gave it a nicely judged shove, allowing me to pass through without effort of my own but not causing me to rush to keep up with its revolution. While I was inside he popped out through the ordinary swinging door and was ready to meet me again on the pavement. 'Can I see if I can flag you down a taxi?'

'Thank you,' I said, giving him a half-crown tip, 'but my own little motorcar is round at the yard.' He frowned down at his hand, wondering perhaps what the half-crown was for in that case. The answer was that I had remembered my plan to grill him. One of many questions troubling me was how Dugald Hepburn had got into the store when it was closed. 'I felt for you most dreadfully about yesterday,' I said, with a nod at the coin, to explain it.

'Yesterday, madam?' he echoed. 'Me?'

'Being denied the funeral,' I said 'And then such a dreadful thing happening while you were here all on your own.'

'While I was alone here, madam?' he said. 'What would that be, then?'

'Of course, you won't have heard,' I answered, kicking myself a little.

'Heard what?' said the doorman. 'What's happened now? Where's it going to end?'

'No, not something new,' I said, laying a hand on his sleeve; he really was becoming quite agitated at the thought of fresh horrors, 'only that the police surgeon reckoned poor Dugald died at half past two.' The doorman frowned, calculating, and then his eyes opened wide.

'Dear God!' he said. 'Half past two? That's when the poor lad jumped?' He turned around and looked back into the store. 'I was right here, right in there, sitting on the chair there, waiting for the first of the staff to come back again after.'

'A dreadful thing,' I said.

'I was that close,' he said, and he took off his peaked cap and held it in both hands, newly struck by the fact of the death and needing to mark it once more.

'No one could have expected you to do anything,' I said. Of course, saying this to the man put exactly the opposite idea into his troubled mind, as I had hoped it would. (What a flinty soul a detective must have to be a successful one.) He began to talk nineteen to the dozen without a trace of artifice or self-regard.

'I didn't know a thing about it,' he said. 'I never heard a thing. You'd have thought I would, wouldn't you, madam? But I can assure you I never. Not a single sound. Or else I'd have been away seeing what it was.'

'You didn't hear any movement on the stairs or doors opening?' I asked. 'Only one does wonder how he got in if the place was locked up.'

'Maybe he came in the day before when we were open,' said the doorman. I nodded absently, but I knew that would not do. Fiona Haddo had been very clear about when Dugald had fled Kelso. 'I can tell you one thing – there was no jemmying locks or climbing in windows during the service, madam. It was as silent as the grave. I even thought that to myself, sitting there. As silent as the grave – and Miss Mirren going into hers and only twenty. On a Thursday afternoon too – that's usually our busiest day in the week barring Saturday because so many other folk in the town have half-day closing and come in to Aitkens'. I never heard so much as a pin drop. Much less— Of course my hearing's not as sharp as it was. I'm sixty-five this August and the wife's never done telling me to turn the wireless down before we getting next door complaining.' He turned again and looked in through the glass door. 'A younger man might have—'

'No,' I said. 'Absolutely not.' It was time for a measure of – belated – humanity. 'His neck was broken. He would have been dead instantly. There's nothing you could have done.' He looked somewhat mollified at this and I should have left it there. 'Besides, I daresay there was nothing to hear no matter how sharp one's ears. The lift shaft is a goodly way from the front door and there would only have been very dull sounds anyway. Muffled thumps at most, unless he screamed as he fell, which would resound right enough, so he can't have.' The poor doorman physically blanched at that. I pressed a further half-crown into his hand, squeezed his sleeve again and scuttled off with my head down, loathing myself and all my doings.

I was vaguely aware of a lounging figure pushing itself up from where it had been leaning against the window frame of the newspaper office across the way.

'For the third and last time,' said Alec's voice. 'I feel like your swain, Dandy, meeting you outside Aitkens' every few days this way.'

I turned to him with a great surge of relief, shading immediately into irritation.

'I didn't ask you to meet me outside,' I said. 'I could have done with you in there. I could have done with you all day, as it happens.'

'Why, what have you been doing?' he said. 'And where are we going at this brisk pace anyway?'

'To my motorcar,' I said. Alec tutted.

'I've driven down too,' he said. 'I was going to give you a lift back. We really must get ourselves a bit more organised, Dan.' I wondered whether now was the moment to tell him about the cards and deduced that it was not. Instead I answered his first question.

'Hilda Hepburn explained why Mirren and Dugald couldn't marry,' I told him. 'Accounted for her objection and Jack's – and what Jack's been hiding, by the way – and perhaps everyone else's objections too. If they knew. Which she says they didn't. And actually I believe her.'

'Dandy, for heaven's sake,' said Alec. 'What are you talking about?'

I told him and he gave a long, low whistle.

'So what were you doing in Aitkens'?' he said.

'I spoke – not quite deliberately – to Miss Torrance of Ladies' Gloves who told me nothing. Then to Miss Armstrong of Ladies' Stationery who told me plenty of little bits and bobs, Miss Hutton of Ladies' Gowns who told me one huge bit and bob which will knock you flat when I pass it on. Then I went rummaging around the attics—'

'I thought we'd decided against the Abigail in-gloves theory,' Alec chipped in. 'And why would Abigail kill her daughter because Jack had an illegitimate son?'

'—where I found the gloves,' I finished, with some triumph for which he would have to forgive me.

'You never,' said Alec. 'Have you got them? Did you bring them out with you?'

'I left them where they were for the police to find if it comes to that,' I said.

'Were they bloodstained? Gunpowder?' said Alec, but before I could answer, he went on. 'Hang on, though. Why would you think they'd be *left* there for the police to find in the sweet by-and-by if they ever get around to it? Won't she just spirit them away?' I opened my mouth to answer this and was interrupted again. 'But wait a minute, why on earth are they still there?' I drew breath. 'Where were they?'

'No,' I said. 'They weren't bloodstained. One of them looked a bit water-spotted but there was no blood or smell of cordite.'

'Wouldn't be by now, anyway, now I think of it,' Alec said.

'And would they have been bloodstained?' I asked him. 'I've been trying to work it out – gruesome business! – but I just don't know.'

Alec, as I had done, put two fingers up to one temple as though holding a gun then touched his other hand to the other temple where the bullet would have come out again.

'I don't know either,' he said.

'She was pretty close to the wall, I think,' I said. 'Judging by the stain there. So I was wondering if perhaps there would be a kind of backwards . . . even if her head blocked the immediate . . . dehiscence—'

'The what?'

'It's a botanical term. Hugh taught it me.'

'What does it mean?'

'The bursting open of a seedpod and scattering its—'.

'God Almighty, Dandy.'

'I know. But we have to consider these things. Would the blood and—'

'Let's leave it at blood.'

'Right. Would the blood come back off the wall with enough speed to hit the gloved gun hand once the head had dropped away?'

'If the head dropped away as fast as all that. People can take a surprising amount of time to fall, you know.' *He* knew; he had probably seen soldiers die on their feet at close range. He might even have caused a death that way. Of course, the last thing on his mind if he had would have been where a few drops of blood chose to fall. I decided to change the subject.

'As for where the gloves were,' I said, '– stuffed into a shoebox in a little room very near the lift. And there was just one pair, with their price ticket on, obviously plucked from the shop floor and taken up there. Most stuff – and there's a lot of it, I can tell you – can be counted in the dozens if not hundreds: vases, leggings, saucepan lids. And most of it has obviously gone straight from the wholesalers to the attics, unloved and unpriced. So the gloves stuck out most remarkably.'

'Which brings us back to the question of why she left them there.'

'Especially since the room where Mirren hid was cleared and scrubbed.'

'How do you know which room she hid in?' Alec said.

'Ah, now, yes. Miss Hutton's bombshell,' I replied. 'Mirren was there the whole time, Alec. She didn't just creep into the store and up the stairs on jubilee morning. She was staying there. In a little attic room with a fireplace and running water.'

'I suppose that makes sense,' Alec said. 'She had to have been somewhere. I can't agree about it being a bombshell, Dandy.'

'And between closing on Saturday and opening up on Monday morning she left a letter for her grandmother, a handwritten note, slipped under Mary's office door.'

'Boom!' Alec said. 'How do you know?'

'Because Miss Hutton trod on it when she unlocked the office door early in the morning to leave some papers in there.'

'Did she read it?' Alec's eyes were gleaming with the thrill of the chase. I shook my head. 'Damn,' he said. 'Sealed, eh? And she didn't even think of steaming it open over a kettle?'

'As a matter of fact, she said it was only folded in,' I said. 'But she didn't look at it anyway.' Alec snorted. 'I'm quite serious. She's as innocent as a flower. Worryingly innocent, if you ask me.'

'Meaning?' Alec said.

'She concluded that Mirren left the store after she dropped off the note for Mary, because if not, Mary would have gone looking for her and found her and Miss Mirren would be with us still.'

'Golly,' said Alec. 'Yes, that is an unusual amount of trusting innocence to find in a grown woman these days. What was your conclusion, in contrast, my darling?'

'That Mary Aitken decided to let Mirren stew up in the attics until her hired detective came to find the girl on a day and at a time of Mary's choosing. Once the jubilee was safely out of the way. And that after Mirren died, Mary got the attic cleared so that no one would know Mirren had been there.'

'But Mary didn't kill her?'

'I don't think so, or she'd have dealt with the gloves as part of the general tidy-up.'

'Back to Abigail,' Alec said. We went along in silence for a moment, trying hard to think with clarity about it all.

'I suppose . . . no,' said Alec.

'What?'

'I suppose they *were* women's gloves, were they? Sorry! Of course they were or you'd have said— Oh, Dandy!'

'Don't be so superior,' I said. 'It's all very well for you just waiting for my reports and then picking holes in them.' I blew upwards into my hair trying to cool my blushes.

'So. Not necessarily back to Abigail after all,' Alec said. 'Back perhaps to Mr Hepburn who snatched a pair of gents' gloves off the shop floor as he was passing, hid them after the dark deed was done so he couldn't be caught with them about his person and of course can't just waltz back into the shop to fetch them now, unlike Mary Aitken who needs no excuse to be there scrubbing and clearing away. Although, actually . . .'

'Any man who did that must have nerves of iron,' I said. 'I mean, he must have been there, hiding while the place was crawling with policemen.'

'Or have fled immediately and been out of the building before anyone worked out what the noise was.'

'Down a stair he was sure no one would use to come up.'

'Having hidden the gloves.'

'Unseen by Abigail.'

'Even though he put the revolver in Mirren's hands.' I kept walking without noticing that Alec had stopped. Then I turned and stared back at him. 'What?'

'We've got this all wrong,' he said. 'Even if we can bodge together a motive for Hepburn – something in the cuckold line, I suppose – how would he get into Aitkens'? How would he know Mirren was there? And worst of all for us, how could he have killed Mirren with Jack Aitken's service revolver?'

'He – he – she could have brought it with her and then . . . No. He could have come to see her not to kill her but she had planned to kill herself only . . . No, hang on. If she brought the gun . . .'

'He couldn't,' Alec said. 'It makes no sense at all.'

'But if he was *seen*,' I insisted. 'Alec, there are precious few hard facts to be grabbed hold of in this sorry mess. We can't afford to go discounting those we have.'

'You heard Mrs Lumsden say that she heard some unnamed girl say that she had seen one of the Mr Hepburns in the store. But it might have been Dugald Hepburn. It needn't have been Robin at all.'

'It couldn't be Dugald,' I said. 'He was in Kelso.'

'Still, until we find the girl and pin her down to it, it's not a hard fact as far as I can see.'

'So let's find her and pin her.'

'So why are we walking away from Aitkens', instead of scouring the Household Department?'

I looked at my wristwatch; it was almost five.

'We don't have time to do it today,' I said. 'The store will be closing. It's a pity we can't blockade the back door and quiz them all as they leave.'

'Or just ask Mrs Lumsden who it was,' said Alec, nodding.

'Well, we can't,' I said. 'I've been warned about Mrs Lumsden very specifically. She's squarely in Mary Aitken's corner, loyal to the core.'

'So let's join her there,' Alec said. 'Or pretend to anyway.' He grabbed me by the elbow, wheeled around and started back towards Aitkens' again almost at a trot, just as the town hall clock began to strike the hour.

Young men in pairs and threes, all with their black armbands on their overcoat sleeves, came strolling down the alley at the side of the Emporium and dispersed up and down the street, mounting their bicycles or hurrying for their buses and trams, then, when the stream of them had dried to a trickle, the girls began.

'Dawdlers,' said Alec. It would not have occurred to him, a bachelor still, how much longer it takes a woman to tidy herself for even the shortest and most everyday outing, but I could see in the newly brushed hair, the rouged lips and the straightened stockings – not just of the elegant creatures from Gowns tripping along on heels far too high for their homeward journeys, but of the plainer girls too in their plainer way – that they had all taken time at the end of their weary day to make sure they were ready for any adventures which might come along; adventures which might take the seat beside a girl on an omnibus and change her life for ever, adventures which might catch a girl's eye in the park and doff a hat with a smile and an unspoken promise to meet, doff and smile again tomorrow.

'I suppose you'd recognise Mrs Lumsden all right in her hat and coat, would you?' Alec said.

'Of course,' I replied. 'I expect the seniors have to stay behind to lock things and— Look, here she comes now.' Little Mrs Lumsden, in black straw hat, shiny black summer coat and very small and high-heeled black patent shoes, came bundling out – there is no other word for it – of the alley mouth like one of those very busy, bulbous little beetles. Alec had primed me with my lines while we hurried back to wait in the doorway and I stepped forward with an air of confidence I hoped was to be fulfilled.

'Mrs Gilver?' she said. 'Were you waiting for me?'

'I was, my dear Mrs Lumsden,' I said. 'I'm so glad I caught

you. I wanted to drop a word in your ear, very softly, if I may.' Mrs Lumsden, a born gossip, was almost quivering. 'It's about Mirren.'

'I'm afraid there's been idle talk,' Alec said. 'Of the most unpleasant kind.'

'And we rather think,' I put in, 'that it must have come from Aitkens' by some route or another.'

'I was just in the pub down the way there,' Alec said, 'and a chap at the bar was saying that Miss Mirren wasn't alone where she died. That she hadn't been alone, if you take my meaning.'

'She wasn't,' said Mrs Lumsden, who had not taken Alec's meaning, clearly. 'You know that, madam. Miss Abigail was close by. Mrs Jack, that is. If that's the talk it more likely came from the police, not from anyone here.'

'No, Mrs Lumsden,' said Alec. 'It was a man this chap was talking about. That a man had been up there before Miss Aitken took her life in that terrible way.'

'Well, that's a story!' said Mrs Lumsden. 'That's just nasty lies. And why you'd think it came from Aitkens' I don't know. And why you think it came from me! I would never spread such filth about the family and I know all the secre— I would never say such things about Miss Mirr— About anyone. Even if they were true and they're not true. Miss Mirren was as innocent as a newborn baby. It's not her fau—' With considerable effort, Mrs Lumsden managed to stop talking and just stood with her lips pressed shut glaring at us, her bosom heaving. I took a deep breath and pressed on.

'It was what you said about one of your girls from Kitchenwares saying she saw young Mr Hepburn upstairs on jubilee day.'

'What?' said Mrs Lumsden and the torrent of talk began again. 'No, no, no. It wasn't Housewares at all. It was Bessie Millar from Linens. And she's been here as long as I have and would never run about telling tales.' I cheered to myself. It had been Alec's brainwave to mention the wrong department and make a defin-ite accusation about Dugald in hopes that a rush of accurate information would pour out as Mrs Lumsden set the record

161

straight again. 'And it wasn't young Mr Hepburn. It was his father. And anyway, she didn't mean upstairs in the attics. She meant upstairs in the Linens Department, on the second floor. That was all. And besides, she must have been mistaken. Mrs Ninian said. It must have just been someone who looked a bit like him, for there had been no truce. Mrs Ninian told me so. So that can't be where the talk's coming from. It's tired old gossip that's forgotten. It's two things mixed up together and making five, madam. I don't want you thinking one of my girls is behind it. Why, it wasn't even jubilee day.'

'What?' I said, glancing at Alec and seeing him glancing at me.

'It wasn't the jubilee day Bessie Millar saw him,' she said. 'It was the day before, maybe even the day before that, the Monday. She just remarked to me that she had seen Mr Hepburn having a good look round the pillowcases. And it's not as if Bessie was up on a soapbox in the park. She just happened to say to me, in passing.' The tears were brimming now. 'And of course I knew it was unlikely. I knew about all the trouble, of course I did. That's what I said to Mrs Ninian, madam, and you were *there.*'

'I remember, Mrs Lumsden,' I said. 'You asked if there had been an *entente cordiale.* I remember it as clear as anything.'

'Now, you'll have to let me go,' Mrs Lumsden said. 'I'm that upset I hardly know what I'm saying. I don't understand this, madam. I don't see how anyone could have worked up old stories and got that out of them. I wouldn't have Mrs Ninian hurt and humiliated for the world. She's paid her debts twice over. She's made everything up to me that she ever— She's been very good to me. I wouldn't see her hurt for the world. I've got to go.'

'So,' I said, as we sat side by side in my motorcar, moments later. 'What do you make of all that then?'

'I feel as though I struck a single match and burned the house down. What was she talking about?'

'We definitely hit some kind of nerve. A story about a man up in the attics where he shouldn't be . . . an old story, old secrets. Do you think there was gossip about Jack and Hilda when they used to meet there?'

'That would be a woman where she shouldn't be,' Alec said. 'And Mrs Lumsden was talking about Mary, wasn't she? Not Jack at all.'

'Very odd,' I said. 'But did the struck match cast light on anything?'

'If "nothing at all" counts as anything,' Alec said. 'It was a case of mistaken identity and two days too early to be significant. Dugald's father wasn't seen in Aitkens' on the fateful day. There's no reason to think he wore the gloves to kill Mirren. Or that he killed Mirren, in fact.'

'And we agree that Abigail Aitken wouldn't have left the gloves in the shoebox to be found. If she'd killed Mirren, she would have gone back and removed them.'

'Same with Mary,' said Alec. 'She'd have taken them away along with everything else.'

'So the gloves are an irrelevance,' I said. 'My one discovery of the day.'

'Hardly,' said Alec. 'You found out about Jack and Hilda.'

'But it didn't lead anywhere. Hilda is adamant that no one knew about Dugald except Jack and her. Mirren didn't know. None of the Aitken women knew. Robin didn't know.'

'And you discovered Mirren's letter to her grandmother.'

'Again. Nowhere.' Suddenly, I seemed to have worked very hard for nothing.

'I don't like it that we suspect Mary of so much and yet can't suspect her of murder,' said Alec.

'Too bad,' I said. 'She was standing right next to me – not to mention the Provost – when the shot was fired.'

'She could have arranged it,' Alec said. 'She strikes me as an arranger. After all, she arranged for someone to clear the attic room. She didn't personally tie her hair up in a duster and set to.'

'Didn't she?' I said. 'Miss Torrance on the glove counter told me that Mary quite readily polishes counters and wraps up orders. "No swank to her" was what she said.'

'Only I was thinking,' Alec said, 'that it would be fine for her to tell one of her minions to tidy up, because the fact of Mirren's having been up there was out in the open after she died. But if Mary was implicated somehow in the murder, she could hardly tell said minion to go hunting for a single pair of gloves and burn them.'

'But she could have done it herself without any problem,' I said. 'She could have slipped into the shoebox room and got the gloves under cover of going to inspect the minion's work. I can't see the difficulty.'

'Only if she had the nerve to show her face in the store,' Alec said. 'And would she? Surely not. It would be worth rechecking those gloves after the first day Mary is back in Aitkens' for a visit, mark my words.'

Had I really not told him? In my recounting of my day had I really missed out the fact that I had met Mary Aitken? I said it all very quickly now, to get it – and whatever was coming after it – over with.

When I stopped talking, Alec shook his head like the affectionate owner of a puppy who has chewed yet another slipper but might still, one day, learn.

'I despair of you, Dandy,' he said. 'Why didn't that set off a hundred alarm bells in you? Hm? *Lady Lawson?* You said yourself you thought there was something going on between Mary Aitken and her. Some kind of understanding. And then today of all days they concoct a frankly pretty flimsy excuse to put their heads together and instead of haring off after it like a bloodhound you waste a whole afternoon on gloves that aren't even bloodstained and a mysterious visitor who wasn't even there on the right day!' He shook his head again. If I were a puppy I would bite him, I thought to myself; but I made an effort to speak calmly.

'Finding the gloves and discounting them, finding the visitor and the day of his visit and discarding him was a perfectly proper use of my time, Alec dear. One has to eliminate all extraneous features of the landscape in an orderly fashion and then what one is left with is the solution.' I could tell he was smirking even though I was not looking at him; I could practically hear his silent laughter. 'I don't care,' I said. 'It's the only reliable way and it should be the Gilver and Osborne way. Less plunging about hoping we trip over a clue and more concentrated, purposeful, focused— Oh shut up!'

'So let's concentrate on a purposeful visit to Lady Lawson,' Alec said. 'Where we shall focus on finding out what's going on between her and Mary.'

9

It was easy enough to find our way to Lady Lawson; the first person I asked – a working man on his way home, overalls black and expression weary – looked past me where I was hanging out of the driver's side window having hallooed to him and informed Alec that he should 'gang straicht oot b'yonder, ken Auchterarder wey, no twae mile and richt aff whaur ye're gaun. Their po-ists are crummelt awa', mind, but ye'll no miss it. Bu'ow, richt? Bu'ow. Aye, ye're grand.' He tipped his hat and resumed his journey.

'Got that?' I said, trying not to smile, as I got back into gear and pulled away.

'I bow to your greater experience, Dandy,' Alec said. 'I didn't think anyone could have a thicker Scotch burr than my head groom but this one has defeated me.'

'The house is called Buttell,' I translated for him. 'It lies two miles away, directly off the Auchterarder road, and we won't miss it, although the gateposts are somewhat tumbledown. And I think, in your defence, there was some Glaswegian in there, which no one would expect you to rise to after only five years of Perthshire for training.'

The gateposts of Buttell House were indeed 'crummelt awa' as was the wall into which they were set, the stone rotting away from around the railings, and the drive beyond was deeply potholed, so that I was prepared for the forlorn aspect of the house itself when it came into view: the tussocky grass, the rusty stains which blocked guttering and leaky downpipes had caused to spread over the pale grey stucco, the cracks in that stucco and worse than cracks – patches of bare brick where great damp lumps had fallen clean away. The windows were small-paned and many and so were dusty with neglect (it takes a good many hours or a good many servants to keep dozens of fiddly-paned windows gleaming) and the roof showed more than a dozen crooked slates beginning to slip out of place. It was at the roof that Alec sucked his breath in over his teeth and shook his head slowly.

'You're as bad as Hugh these days,' I told him.

'Hugh is a very sound chap when it comes to roofs,' said Alec.

'Always has been,' I said. 'When my mother and I paid our one and only visit to Gilverton during my engagement, he took us up into the attics and showed us the sarking. It was an omen.'

'He probably thought you'd be interested, coming from the Shires,' Alec said. 'Sarking is unknown in the south.'

'That's exactly what Hugh said,' I replied. 'As though he were showing off koala bears or something.'

'Anyway,' said Alec as we drew up close to the house, 'the Lawsons are either utterly feckless or pretty near broke to have let their roof get this way.'

'Broke,' I said. 'I thought so the day of the jubilee.' We stepped down and mounted the short flight of stairs to the front door.

'How do we play this then, Dandy?' said Alec when we were installed in a small sitting room and the maid-of-all-work who had let us in had gone to fetch her mistress.

'No idea,' I said. 'As it lies?'

Lady Lawson joined us in a matter of minutes and greeted us with that vague and fluttery manner of hers, no visible curiosity about what on earth we were doing there.

'Tea?' she said, sinking into a chair. 'A little late, perhaps. And a little early for sherry, but welcome to Buttell all the same. How nice of you to come and see me.'

Thus she managed the problem of refreshments for two un-expected strangers; I would have taken a bet that if we had rolled up bang on four o'clock 'tea' would still have been prevented somehow and if we had waited until seven 'sherry' would like-wise have met a handy obstacle. For the Lawsons were not just broke in the way that almost everyone is broke these days, I thought, looking round at the dark patches on the walls where pictures had been removed for sale – and not large patches either; not grand masterpieces gone to put a boy through Oxford or a girl through her season, but small patches of eighteen inches square, hinting that little prints and watercolours were being sold off now, for grocers' bills and servants' wages.

Lady Lawson was telling us that she had only a few minutes before the dressing bell and she hoped that we would forgive her, but she really could not ask us to stay for dinner because there was a small party of intimates gathering.

'And one of my chums – my dear old chum – is in mourning, strictly speaking. Quite all right to come over to us, you see, but she's not up to general company.'

Alec made a good selection of understanding noises and I let them go for both of us: I would have eaten my book and a half of pencilled notes if the Lawsons still dressed for dinner or invited friends to join them.

'We won't keep you long, Lady Lawson,' I said. 'It's just that I have a question to ask you.'

'Mrs Gilver, isn't it?' she said. 'A friend of the Aitkens, like me.' She simpered a little as she said this; as though she found it amusing that she chose such friends, as though it were a sign of her modernity instead of her desperation. But what was she getting out of it? I asked myself. There had to be something.

'Indeed,' I replied. 'Well, I'm more of an agent of the Aitkens, rather than a friend.' Lady Lawson would never do anything so vulgar as scowl, but her vague, amused expression grew a little pinched at this.

'An agent?' she said.

'I know you went to see Mary Aitken this morning,' I began, feeling my way.

'I kept my appointment,' said Lady Lawson. She rearranged the pleats of her tweed skirt over her knees in a gesture that was almost fidgety. 'I should not have dreamed of its standing but Mary bade me go and so I went.' Then she looked over my shoulder and spoke the next part very fast and high. 'I left her in no doubt as to my thoughts on her proposal and I cannot see why she has sent you. I must beg you to return to her and reiterate my refusal, my most definite refusal, in the firmest terms.'

I was quite at sea now and I could see from the way Alec was frowning that he was even more lost than I.

'Her proposal?' I said, and in repeating the word at last a faint idea began to stir in me.

'I am very sorry about what happened but it did happen and there is an end to our plans and nothing to be done about it.' Lady Lawson sat back in her chair.

All of a sudden it was clear to me. I had been unable to account for Lady Lawson's presence that day of the jubilee and I had certainly failed to see why the policeman who had grilled us all in the back offices at the store had leaned so heavily on the oldest Lawson son – what was his name? – Roger. And throughout the whole affair I had been lost as to why the Hepburn boy was not welcomed as a suitor for the Aitkens' heiress, why Mary Aitken felt she had scope to despise him so. Now, I saw that Mary Aitken had her sights set on a greater prize. Now, sagging wall paper and threadbare rugs before my eyes, I knew the nature of the understanding between the mother of one and the grand-mother of the other. Mary Aitken's aspirations had reached as high as this and impoverished Lady Lawson had stooped that low – rank given and a load of roof tiles got, along with a roll of banknotes to pay a man to fit them. And the police had guessed or had heard about the trading of the Lawson name for the Aitken money and asked themselves what the boy – one of the parcels of goods in the transaction – might do to break the deal.

'Roger was supposed to marry Mirren,' I said.

Never in Lady Lawson's long life of decorum must she have had to reach so deep inside herself to summon the light smile and airy wave of a hand that she bestowed upon us now. She shook as she did so.

'He was,' she said. 'Are you shocked, Mrs Gilver? My late husband would have been *horrified*.'

'But – forgive me, Lady Lawson.' Alec was speaking now, sliding forward in his seat and staring at her. 'What proposal of Mary Aitken's were you refusing just now? What new proposal, I mean. Now that poor Mirren is gone.'

'I thought she sent you here to press it upon me,' Lady Lawson said.

'Press what?' said Alec. 'The girl's dead.'

'She asked me this morning,' said Lady Lawson, 'and I was shaken to my core. She wanted Roger to say he hadn't thought much of the idea and that he probably wouldn't have gone through with it. She wants my son to accuse himself – in the eyes of the world – of breach of promise and – in the eyes of God – of ending the poor girl's life.' She sat back in her chair as though exhausted. 'I was not brought up to games of intrigue and I have no skill at them.' She sighed and there was a tuneful note in it which turned the sigh into a snatch of song. She had been brought up to games of flirtation, I thought to myself, and she was a master of *them*.

'Why would she think you'd go along with it?' I said.

'Well, the absolute plain bald fact of the matter,' said Lady Lawson, 'was that Roger *wasn't* terribly keen. And who could blame my poor boy? What man would want to marry such a shrinking, quaking girl? If she had smiled and batted her eyes a little he'd have been pleased enough to put her on his arm and show her off to people, department store or no.' Alec was looking quite revolted, but not me; I knew of old what underlay the wan and flowery surface of women like Lady Lawson and it was always pretty steely, every time. 'A courtship, a marriage, a son of his own, a bit of help for his brothers and then a pleasant life filled with his choice of pleasant things. It wasn't much to ask of him, was it? No more than we all owe our parents and our family name.' By now, Alec was far beyond revolted, a little sick in fact, and I hid my smiles.

'So Mary only wants Roger to be honest really,' I said. Lady Lawson sat bolt upright in her chair.

'Not a bit of it,' she said. 'Mirren Aitken didn't kill herself because Roger let her down. Oh, he groaned and grumbled, but he would have gone through with it in the end.'

'Even still,' I said, 'wouldn't you rather have him known as a heartbreaker than as . . .' She waited, giving me no choice but to go on: '. . . as a man a girl would kill herself to escape from?'

At this Lady Lawson burst out in an incoherent stream of denial, but then just as suddenly she stopped again. 'I never thought of it that way,' she said. 'Oh my goodness, you're right. But it's nonsense. Everyone knows Mirren wanted to marry the Hepburn boy and Mary wouldn't let her. No one will believe that her heart broke because of poor Roger. Oh, my poor boy! He'll be a laughing stock. What was it you said? A man a girl would kill herself to escape from? *Poor* Roger! Oh, I'm a such a silly woman to have got mixed up in the grubby business in the first place.'

'Why did you, if you don't mind my asking?' said Alec.

'Well . . .' Lady Lawson, I assumed, was seeking a euphemism for 'hard cash'. I thought I would help her by suggesting something even worse, which she could vigorously deny.

'She wasn't in a position to put any pressure on you, was she?'

'Hardly!' said Lady Lawson. 'It's I who know more than I ever wanted to about her, not she me.' This was interesting and both Alec and I tried to look alert but not so vulturous that we scared her. 'Mary Aitken has been my personal dressmaker since I was a girl. She knows all my numbers off by heart, carries them in her head, isn't that touching? We come from the same village, you know, on the other side of the river.' She waved a hand towards the windows, indicating the Forth, Edinburghshire and the Border country. 'My mother gave her work when she was trying to eke out her wages from her first job in town and stuck with her when she went to Aitkens' and so Mary stuck with my mother and me when she married and here we both are. My patronage of her has slowly become hers of me over the years until we found ourselves at the point when she could feel bold enough to look up, with a mouthful of pins, and put such a notion to me, woman to woman, like some kind of business dealing.' Lady Lawson blinked her pretty eyes very slowly two or three times to show us how overwhelming the thought of *business dealings* was to a flower of femininity such as she.

'But – once again, forgive me, Lady Lawson,' I said, 'but Mary makes no secret of her humble beginnings. Why should you call all that "knowing more than you want to"?'

'It's not her beginnings, Mrs Gilver,' Lady Lawson said. 'It was her route out of them. Such scheming, such naked ambition – most unseemly. She snared poor Mr Aitken like a rabbit in a trap, you know. And he wasn't the first one she had set her sights on either.'

'Dear me,' I said, thinking I could easily believe it of Mary.

'And then marrying off Abigail to her cousin that way? Too dreadful. I couldn't understand it. There was no reason for it. Abby was a lively pretty girl and could have had her pick of the young men. She had a fortune, you know.'

'It certainly does seem a little . . . careless,' I said.

'And then so scrupulous about a match with the Hepburn boy for Mirren.' Lady Lawson lowered her voice. 'You know about the Hepburn girls, I suppose?' Alec's shoes squeaked as he writhed in discomfort.

'A little. You think that was Mary's objection? I thought it was business rivalry.'

'Oh well, yes, that too. She certainly resented them. But if she ever got on to the subject of the sisters she was quite frightening. And to think I was going to marry my son into such a family. Cousin marriage, and suicide, and spite so bitter that it twisted her up into knots sometimes. What kind of mother must I be? Oh, my poor boy.'

And so on and so forth for quite some time, while Alec and I sat squirming. When at last she ran out of exclamations, or perhaps breath, she left us with a faint allusion to a headache and an ethereal farewell. We stayed behind in the little sitting room, puffed out a few good breaths between us and reviewed the interview.

'That's how I was supposed to be brought up,' I said. 'It's exhausting, isn't it?'

'Damned irritating,' said Alec. 'Makes me feel like Professor Higgins. Makes me want to throw things. How did you escape it, darling? Not that you never make me want to throw things, but not in the same way.'

'I'm not quite sure,' I said. I was always wont to sum up my mother as a dreamer, slightly to despise her aesthetic bent and her enthralment when it came to nature and freedom and even less slightly to scorn her passionate declarations on them, but when faced with the kind of fluttering *she* had despised I did begin to see how stoutly she had held against *her* mother's expectations and how valiant she been in her way. Then I remembered that the fresh air she so loved was the air of spring and that she kept to the fireside in her shawls at the slightest drizzle and disappeared under a parasol in the summer sun; that the nature she adored was the nature of rose petals and bluebell woods not the nature which will swell a turnip and feed a family on it; that a beautiful death had had so much more allure than precious life got by sullying herself with the ugly words doctors use and the ugly things they do. Besides, it should not be forgotten that my mother had produced my sister Mavis as well as me.

'Nanny Palmer,' I said to Alec, realising that of course this was the key. 'Nanny Palmer never would have any truck with the vapours – everything from squealing at mice to getting seasick was "the vapours" to her, you know – and then of course it would have been wasted on Hugh all these years anyway, and no daughters, and now the casework . . . who knows where it will end.'

A memory came back to me unbidden of Mavis, on her wedding day, sitting at her looking glass as my mother lowered the coronet of flowers onto her hair. They looked at one another in the glass and exchanged misty smiles. Then Mavis caught my eye and the smile died. 'What is it?' she had said. I replied truthfully that it was nothing, but she was not to be denied, not on her wedding day. 'Go on,' she had said. 'Tell me what you were thinking. I insist that you tell me.' I had assured her that I was thinking nothing at all, only how pretty she looked in her frock, which was very drooping and medieval with long points to the bell-sleeves and a low girdle of plaited silks with ends as long as her train, but the truth was that I had looked at those pointed sleeves and wondered if at the wedding breakfast she would be able to help them going in her soup.

'Alec,' I said, 'tell me something – and I'm serious, I assure you. Would you describe me as "hearty"?'

'Hearty?' said Alec. 'No. Why?'

'Because that's what lies at the other end of the line from Lady Lawson and the likes of her and much as I loathe one, I do dread the other. My sister called me hearty once and it still pricks me.'

'It wouldn't prick at you if you were hearty,' said Alec with great kindness.

'Thank you, darling.'

'Don't mention it. And let's get back to the case, for God's sake,' he said. 'Right. Lady Lawson has given us an embarrassment of reasons for Mary Aitken to deny Mirren the right to marry Dugald. Jack and Hilda we knew about anyway. And I suppose the business rivalry – feud, call it what you like – might just explain Robin and his father being against the match.'

'We haven't accounted for Abigail's misgivings yet. And we haven't got a motive for Mirren's suicide except jilting, in which case we haven't got a motive for Dugald's.'

'Mirren first,' said Alec. 'She didn't know about Jack and Hilda. Did she know about Roger Lawson? Did she care about the Aitken–Hepburn feud? Would she have resisted eloping because of it? I wonder what caused the feud, by the way. Mrs Lumsden seemed to hint that it wasn't always this way between them.'

'I wish we could just barge in like the police and demand that everyone answer our questions,' I said, dragging up another hefty sigh and letting it out. 'We can't even threaten them with the police!'

'Why not?' said Alec. He had been stretched out in his chair, practically horizontal in that way of his, but he hauled himself upright and his eyes were alight again. 'Why can't we?'

'Because if I go back to Inspector Stinky, Hugh will be clapped in irons.'

'But no one knows that,' said Alec. 'We can threaten ourselves blue, Dandy. Of course we can.' I clapped my hands together with glee.

'You're right,' I said. 'We really can! Of course we couldn't actually carry *out* the threat if it doesn't work, but let's cross our fingers we don't need to.'

'Who do we start with?' said Alec. 'Bright and early tomorrow morning, I think. And bring an overnight bag along too. I don't know about you but I'm getting heartily sick of that road here and back again.'

'Abigail Aitken,' I said. 'If we find out that she knew about Jack and Hilda and told Mirren, then we have a motive for Mirren's suicide and enough reasons for the marriage ban to go around everyone. Then we can assume Dugald killed himself out of grief and the case is closed. We won't need the overnight bag after all.'

'What about the inspector?' said Alec. 'Are we saying that he somehow knew about Jack and Hilda? Knew that Mirren and Dugald were siblings? How could he?' I said nothing. 'Put your toothbrush in a little bag and bring it with you, Dandy. We're not done yet awhile, if you ask me.'

It was bright and early indeed the following morning when Alec's motorcar swung into the front drive at Abbey Park and rolled up to the house. We stepped down, two of us all swagger and determination and one of us all wagging tail and snuffling with excitement at the new scents in this new place. Alec had raised a sardonic eyebrow when he saw Bunty on the end of her lead, but I had insisted.

'She can still put up a pretty chilling growl and quivering lip if someone shouts at me,' I said. 'And she's a good intimidating size, especially in a drawing room, and don't forget that time last year.' That had been my darling Bunty's finest hour; she had gone for a villain with her lips drawn back and her teeth gnashing, snarling like a wolf. If she did the same to Jack Aitken he would never chase me down the drive again.

'Well, thanks for the vote of confidence,' said Alec, but he had opened the door for her and whistled her in.

Down at Dunfermline, Trusslove greeted me like an old friend.

'Thank the Lord,' he said. 'Good news, is it? I've told all the staff you're helping, dear, and we're sending up prayers. I only wish we could do more, but nobody downstairs knows anything worth telling.' He looked at Alec. 'And are you another of them, my friend? Good. More power to your elbow.' He beckoned us in and made off ahead of us to the library. 'My friend?' Alec mouthed to me, behind his back.

'Right then,' Trusslove said. 'And who is it you're after today?'

'Mr Aitken,' I replied. 'Mr Jack, if he's here, Trusslove, please.'

For Alec and I had decided on the journey to give Jack Aitken a shot at chivalry, a chance to save his wife the humiliation of confirming to us that she knew of his affair.

Less than a minute after Trusslove left us we heard Jack Aitken coming from the other side of the marble hallway and he entered the room like a rocket, ready for a fight, fists bunched and chin stuck forward, but evidently Trusslove had announced only me because when Aitken caught sight of Alec he stopped so abruptly that he had to take a step to the side to get his balance back again.

'Mr Aitken,' said Alec smoothly. 'Let me introduce myself. My name is Osborne, I'm an associate of Mrs Gilver, and I've come along this morning to see if I can't help matters run a little more easily than I heard they did yesterday.' He had not rehearsed this speech in my hearing and I tried very hard to take it in my stride, but I was most deeply impressed and gratified by it and in danger of beaming, because I could not imagine anything more subtly menacing if I tried. 'First of all, though,' Alec was saying, 'I must give you my most heartfelt condolences on the death of your daughter, sir. I am very sorry to have heard of such a loss.' This only bewildered Jack Aitken even more. He came over to where we were at a much reduced pace and sat down in the chair Alec had placed for him, giving Bunty a perplexed look as he did so. 'Mrs Gilver?' Alec said, opening a courteous hand to me. 'If you would care to continue.'

'As I was saying yesterday, Mr Aitken,' I said, taking up – I hoped – Alec's smooth and unsettling tone, 'I have strong reason to doubt that Mirren took her own life. I have some reason too to doubt that Dugald Hepburn did so. I intend to get to the bottom of it. If I am wrong, all well and good. I'm no busybody, no gossip. But if I am thwarted, Mr Aitken, if I am denied answers and threatened the way I was yesterday, I shall go to the police and hand the case to them. And they – as I am sure you will agree – are considerably less discreet than Mr Osborne and me.'

'We were your clients,' Jack Aitken said, staring horrified at me. 'If this is how you treat your clients I'm surprised you ever have any.' I tried not to let my face show that his words had hit home. Indeed, if anyone were ever to find out that Alec and I had come along like a pair of gangsters' heavies and intimidated a grieving family this way after being told to leave them alone several times now, we would never work again and Gilver and Osborne's business cards would go straight from the printers to the fire.

'Now, when we spoke before, Mr Aitken,' I said, ignoring him, 'you told me your only misgiving about Mirren and Dugald marrying' – there was the look again, as though he had bitten down on a bad tooth – 'was that she was too young to marry at all. At twenty. You said you felt remorseful that your decision to forbid the match had led to Mirren's suicide. And of course you would; how could you not? But you see, what puzzled me was that when I suggested it could be murder you . . . took against me, shall we say? Almost it seemed you would rather have your daughter's death on your hands than on any other's.'

Jack Aitken made a valiant effort to look composed, but most unfortunately for him he had taken a seat in the window and was sitting in a patch of golden sunlight so that his tie pin twinkled as his chest rose and fell with a series of quickened, panicky breaths he could not control. His voice though, when he finally spoke, was the same old repertory company routine as ever; the juvenile lead lightly tossing off his lines with half a mind on supper after the show.

'I do apologise for yesterday, Mrs Gilver, I must ask you to forgive me.' He put a hand to his brow and pressed it there. 'I have never lost my temper that way in my life.' Alec and I exchanged a glance. He had come into the room like a bull into the ring not three minutes ago. 'I thought you were accusing me of killing her. My little Mirren. I saw red, I'm afraid.'

'Why would you think such a thing?' I asked him.

'Because it was me you were telling,' Jack Aitken said, with a sheepish shrug. 'I thought to myself, why else would you seek me out and tell me unless it's me you think did it?'

'But I was only talking to you because you happened to come looking for your wife,' I said. 'And I was only talking to her because she happened to meet me. It was your mother I came to see.' Before he could compose his next speech I came back at him. 'And, actually, Mr Aitken, after you had railed at me for the accusation you say you thought I made against you, you railed even more about the idea that – here I quote you – "she would kill a child".'

'Once again, Mrs Gilver, I apologise. Such strain, such unbearable strain and I have not held up under it at all well.' He paused as though for sympathy; receiving none, he continued. 'Well, it was just that my poor dear Abby was there, with the gun, and was questioned and so of course I did think for a moment it was her you suspected. Gosh, I feel wretched that I might have implicated my dear wife in some way.'

'You didn't,' I said. 'Not until just now, I mean. Reminding us about the gun that way. "She would never kill a child" doesn't sound at all like an accusation of a mother. Does it, Mr Osborne?'

Jack turned as Alec shook his head. '*A* child?' I said. Jack's head whipped back so he was once more facing me. 'One doesn't usually refer to a woman's own daughter that way.'

'I was very angry,' Jack said. 'Grief takes many forms.'

'Indeed,' I said. 'So you're sticking to your story, Mr Aitken, that you wouldn't have minded Dugald Hepburn as a son-in-law a year or two hence and you think Mirren killed herself because she wouldn't wait for him.'

He nodded, swallowing hard.

'And what did you make of your mother-in-law's hopes regarding Roger Lawson?'

Jack Aitken blinked and said nothing.

'You did know, I assume, that Mary and Lady Lawson were hoping for an engagement?'

'Roger Lawson?' said Jack Aitken, then he nodded. 'I see. Yes, I see. Well, that would have been a very satisfactory arrangement, I imagine.' Alec and I could not help turning a little towards another to exchange another glance then.

'Forgive me, Mr Aitken,' I said, 'but Mirren would have been the same age marrying Roger Lawson as marrying Dugald, wouldn't she?'

'Oh, yes, I suppose, in a sense,' Jack said. I could see Alec frowning deeper still. Jack Aitken saw it too and from deep within himself he dug out another of his endless little sketch routines. He threw one leg over the other – most unnaturally since his fists were still in his pockets – and chuckled. 'But you see if Mary organised it, the terms would be very different.'

'A long engagement, you mean?' Alec asked.

'Not a doubt,' Aiken said. 'She's a formidable woman of business as I'm sure you've noticed already. The financial arrangements would have been very secure.'

I could not begin to see what he meant; the financial repercussions of Mirren entering the Lawson family would have weighed very heavily on the Aitkens, surely.

'Mirren was only twenty,' Jack Aitken said. 'At twenty-one she was to come into her share of Aitkens'. And because of the fact that Abby and I are cousins and neither of us have siblings surviving, quite a lot of Aitkens' was coming to Mirren down a funnel, as it were. She would have had a controlling interest. Yes, after her birthday, she would have had outright control of us all. And if she were married her husband might have tried to influence her, but if she stayed unmarried until after she was twenty-one, she could dispose of her shares as she saw fit and *then* she could have married without her new husband . . .' He took one of his hands out of his pocket and waved it in the air.

'Scooping the lot,' I finished and something in my tone brought the wary look back into Jack Aitken's eyes. 'So really,' I said, 'when you talked about your poor little Mirren being too young for marriage and not wanting to lose her, what you really meant was something quite different.'

'Aitkens' was built up out of nothing by the sweat of my father's brow,' said Jack. 'And my uncle's too. We owed it to their hard work and dedication. Our stewardship. Our honouring of their vision.'

'Mirren did not owe it her life,' I said. 'No girl owes any institution *that.*'

Unbelievably, Jack Aitken gave Alec a man-to-man look then, as though to say that they two understood all about laying down one's life for glory but that a mere woman could not be expected to feel the swell of pride. Alec returned a blank, dead gaze which made me want to hug him.

'And besides,' I said, 'we know that wasn't what troubled you about Mirren and Dugald. That was a remarkable tale you dreamed up, Mr Aitken, and you told it well, but we know exactly why you were against the marriage.'

He stared hard at me, without answering, probably trying to work out if I were bluffing.

'Mrs Hepburn told us yesterday,' said Alec. Jack Aitken did not turn to him and did not answer. He simply deflated and his eyes dropped until he was staring at the floor.

'What we want to know, really, is if your wife found out.'

Again there was no answer. 'If perhaps she told Mirren.' Yet more silence. 'If that perhaps was why Mirren—'

'No!' said Jack, his head jerking back up. 'Abby doesn't know. And Mirren certainly didn't know. I told you, she was so kind to me the last weeks, she can't have known about my . . . lapse.'

'That's right,' I said. 'I'd forgotten. Well, in that case, can you explain why Abby was against the marriage?'

'She's a dutiful daughter.'

'And why she was so sure Mirren wouldn't elope?'

'So was Mirren,' he said. The look that crossed his face was the genuine one I had seen once or twice before. When all was said and done, he was not a monster and his child had died. Not his only child, since he had at least one (and possibly four) with Hilda, but his child, all the same.

'We won't detain you any longer,' I said, trying to speak kindly.

'Let me see you out,' Jack said, standing.

'Oh, we're not finished,' said Alec, who had clearly not been entertaining any such sentimental thoughts as mine. 'We'll ring the bell for Trusslove when we're ready to speak to your wife.'

'You won't tell her, will you?' said Aitken.

'Not if we can avoid it,' I said. 'I'm not in the business of doling out gratuitous pain.'

Jack Aitken crumpled at that – sagged anyway – he was no match for Alec and me. He nodded his head wearily and went on his way.

'Well,' I said when he was gone. 'He is the worst and yet the most dedicated liar I have ever seen. One almost wants to laugh. Does he think we can't see the joins, between one posture and the next? Are we supposed to forget the last mood when he clicks his fingers and moves on to the next one? Grieving father, man of the world, fierce protecting husband, loyal son . . .'

'You can't see whatever it is that Hilda Hepburn sees in him then?'

'Not a bit,' I said. 'She called him as tricky as a bag of monkeys. She finds it entertaining but it makes me sick.'

'I especially didn't swallow the act of protective husband,' said

Alec. 'Well done, Dandy, spotting the flaw. You're right of course. He would have said "her child" or "her own child". It was Hilda who was making him so fierce, not his poor wife.'

'And speaking of his poor wife,' I said, 'shall I ring for Trusslove to fetch her? I have to know why she banned the marriage. I'll never sleep again otherwise. And, besides, I'd like to ask her about what happened up on that landing. She was right there. If there's any chance a murderer was there too, surely she'd know.'

The butler's good, kind face clouded a little at our request but he went just the same.

'This is quite a place,' Alec said, looking around himself as we waited.

'The house, you mean? Or the library?'

'Well, both,' Alec said, 'but especially the library. If we can call it that. Where are the books?'

'In those glass cases,' I said. 'All five hundred years old and worth a fortune. They must keep the almanacs and three-volume novels elsewhere.'

The door opened and Abigail Aitken came in.

'Again?' she said. 'More questions? I've told you everything I know.'

Alec stood and guided her to a chair. Dear man, he could not help it; she looked even more frail today and she looked, too, as unkempt as Bella, her great mane of hair dull and greasy at the roots and the shawl which once more she hugged about herself giving off the kind of stale, sour odour I had only ever smelled in two-room cottages before.

'My dear Mrs Aitken,' I said to her, 'I am more sorry than I can tell you, but I have no choice but to come again. I wouldn't be able to live with myself if I didn't try to get to the bottom of what happened here.'

There was just one quick glint in her eyes then.

'You would be surprised, Mrs Gilver,' she said. 'You would be very surprised to find how able we are to live with ourselves. What choice do we have after all? Our eyes close at night and open the next day and we are still here. We breathe in and out and we drink water and eat food and our eyes blink and we shiver in the cold and squint in the sun and go on and on and on.' Her head had fallen as she spoke but now she looked up at me again. 'And after an eternity, we add up the days and it has been ten. Ten days since she died. Fifteen since I saw her alive. And we go on some more.'

I looked over at Alec. Despite everything I had said, I was willing to leave this house and this case and let this poor woman grieve in peace, if he gave me the slightest sign. He stared ahead stonily.

'I made a mistake, you see,' Abigail Aitken went on. 'I thought if I could just get through the funeral, everything would be better then. If I could make it through until after the funeral and come home . . . you won't believe what I thought if I could make it through the funeral and come home.'

'You thought she'd come back again,' Alec said.

'Yes!' said Abigail and it was almost a shout, she was so delighted that he had understood her. 'How did you know? Oh! I'm sorry. Who have you lost? That you should know.'

'My brother,' Alec said. 'It was his memorial, for me. If I got the memorial finished and installed in our little chapel at home, he'd come to see it and complain about the wording probably.'

'Your brother,' Abigail said. 'Jack's brothers died too, you know. But he doesn't understand how I feel.'

I tried to stop shock showing on my face. And not only his brothers, I thought. His daughter too. Did his wife not see what a monster she made him sound? In case it should occur to her and pain her, I hurried to fill the silence in the room.

'Mrs Aitken,' I said, 'I know the police have closed the case, but I also know that they have some misgivings. I would rather not go to them if I can avoid doing so. I would rather spare you all the pain.'

'I think I must be immune to further pain, Mrs Gilver,' said Abigail, 'but if you could spare us disgrace – my mother and Bella too who have done nothing to merit it – I would be thankful. I don't care what happens to me. Ask away.'

'Very well,' I said. 'First, if you can bear it, I'd like to ask about what happened up on the attic landing when Mirren died.'

Abigail nodded, but drew her shawl a little tighter around her. 'There would be no point in my confessing again,' she said. 'It didn't work the first time.'

'Can you tell me why you went up there?' I said.

'The police asked me that,' Abigail said. 'I was downstairs with Jack and Mother – but of course you were there, weren't you? – and then Jack went away – I don't know why.'

'He went to check that the doors were closed,' I said. 'Your mother was worried about gatecrashers.'

'All I knew was that he was gone and I thought I might fall down. I felt faint and there were so many people all watching. I wanted to hide. I just wanted to curl up somewhere until it was over. I didn't want to be there at all, really. But then I remembered Mirren's special little place, up in the attics – like a little play house really except that it was a proper room. She had begged all sorts of things out of her granny to furnish it and so I went there. Or that's where I was going. To curl up and put my hands over my head and feel close to her.'

'You didn't suspect that she was actually there, then?' I said. 'When you say you wanted to be close to her . . .'

'No,' said Abigail. 'I had no idea where she was. I'd have gone to her otherwise. I'd have comforted her and brought her home.' She fell silent.

Very gently, Alec tried to jog her into speech again. 'So you went off to the back stairs?'

Abigail blinked. 'Yes, I went up the back stairs and when I was near the top I heard a noise and I went out onto the landing and Mirren was there. On the floor. And her pretty hair.' Abigail Aitken put her hands up and stuck her fingers into her own hair, pulling them through its tangles. I winced, hearing it snapping and watching her tug her hands free again. 'She had the softest, most golden curls,' she said. 'As light as little feathers. When she was a baby she had a halo of gold all round her head and then little curls along her neck and then when she was three, finally enough curls to make a pigtail and she used to ask me "When will I have lady's hair like you, Mama?" and I would think how I hoped she would never have anything but those thistledown curls.'

After a pause, I took a turn at nudging her.

'And you took the gun out of her hand?'

'Yes,' said Abigail. 'No. She wasn't blinking, you see. So I put the lights out in case they were hurting her. Because she wasn't blinking and she used to get sore eyes sometimes and I would put drops in for her. *Then* I took the gun. And I walked away, because I didn't want to fall on top of her and hurt her, and I turned it on myself and shut my eyes and tried to squeeze the trigger but I couldn't do it. I couldn't make my finger move. And then I was sitting down and you came with Bella and then Bella went away and that's when I saw how I could make it work. If I said I *had* squeezed the trigger and I had killed her then they would hang me. And do you know what I wish now?'

I shook my head.

'I wish I hadn't walked away to the other wall. And do you know why? Because then when I sat down I would have been beside her and maybe even touching her and I didn't get to touch her after the police came. So that's what I wish now.'

Bunty stood up, took a few paces forward and looked up at Abigail's face, her tail waving very slightly. Then she turned and shuffled herself as close as possible in towards Abigail's legs, sat down and leaned. Abigail laid a hand on her broad smooth head and patted her.

'Good girl,' she said. 'Good dog.'

'Now, Mrs Aitken,' I resumed, feeling quite a lot better about questioning her now that she had darling Bunty as solace, 'in the time between hearing the shot and coming onto the landing, did you hear anything else? Footsteps, doors opening or closing, any kind of scuffling? Any indication that someone else might have been there?'

Abigail continued her steady stroking of Bunty's head. Bunty's eyes closed in bliss. Abigail was almost smiling.

'There was no one else there,' she said. 'My poor Mirren shot herself, Mrs Gilver. I wish you would believe me.'

'If you would tell me why you're so sure perhaps I could,' I said, but Abigail shook her head.

'I promised to be as open as I could without hurting another person,' she answered. 'If I told you why I was so sure I would be hurting someone who has done nothing to deserve it.'

'Then let us tell you something,' Alec said. 'It might change your mind about suicide. Your mother-in-law, Mrs John, along with Dugald's grandmother had formed a plan for the young people.'

'I know,' said Abigail. 'An elopement. Mirren told me.'

'She did?' This was surprising news. 'When?'

'The night before she ran away,' said Abigail. She withdrew her hand from Bunty and, winding both fists into her shawl, she stretched it tight across her body. 'The night before.'

'She told you about a planned elopement and the next day she was gone and yet you were sure she hadn't eloped?' Alec said. Abigail nodded her head.

'She would never have married him,' she said. 'Never.'

'That brings us very neatly to the next question,' I said. 'Why not? What was wrong with Dugald Hepburn? Why was the marriage forbidden so vehemently?'

Abigail said nothing for a moment or two. Then she spoke up with a harder note in her voice.

'You should ask my mother,' she said. 'She was the "vehement" one.'

'But you were against the notion too, Mrs Aitken, and so we are asking you. You liked the boy and Mirren – no matter what you say – seemed to love the boy. So what was wrong?'

'My mother didn't want it,' said Abigail. 'Nor my husband.'

'Yes, we've heard from your husband,' I said. Alec started, but I wiggled my eyebrows at him and went on. 'Do you know why he was against it? Is it the same reason for you?'

'No,' said Abby quietly. 'It can't be. He didn't know . . . Mirren's secret.'

'He told us it was money,' I said.

'What?' said Abigail.

'Mirren's shares,' Alec said. 'The future of Aitkens'.'

'Oh, yes, that,' she said, doing nothing to shore up any belief we might have had that the shares really were a part of the difficulty. 'My mother didn't want to see Aitkens' being . . . what was the word she used . . . consumed by Hepburns', you see.'

'Subsumed, I think you mean,' said Alec. 'She would rather have seen the business bled white by the Lawson estates?'

'What?' said Abigail.

'Your mother and Lady Lawson were hoping to broker an engagement between Mirren and Roger,' I said.

Abigail considered this for a moment or two, then she nodded.

'Yes,' she said. 'That might have done very nicely. I wish my mother had told Mirren about it. It might have given her something to look forward to.'

'You'd have gone along with it?' I asked. 'You'd have taken your mother's side in it?'

Abigail nodded, smiling.

'My mother likes to have the arrangement of things,' she said. 'She chose Jack for me, you know. My father was not in favour of it – Uncle John was already gone by then – but Mother won the day. My father never really forgave her, you know. And when he died, I think Mother berated herself. For displeasing him. Even though it was too late then to undo the harm. Poor Mother. She's the same now. About Mirren.'

She gave me a quick look, to see – I think – if I understood and I nodded to show that I did.

'She spoke most heartrendingly to me,' I said. 'She feels utterly wretched about Mirren. She blames herself.' I sat forward and fixed Abigail with my most serious stare. 'If you could take that burden off her shoulders, Mrs Aitken, you would be doing a very fine thing.'

Abigail stared back at me and then she flushed and tears sprang into her eyes.

'You mean tell my mother someone killed our girl?' she said.

'That wasn't what happened. Why don't you believe me?' Bunty, upset by her voice, turned round and put a paw up onto her lap. Abigail shook it and a ghost of a smile came back to her face. 'Good girl,' she said again. 'Good dog, aren't you? We should get a dog,' she said, looking up again. 'I might get a puppy for Mother. Anything to help her. Anything to stop her being ill.' She bent down and kissed Bunty's head. 'After my father died,' she said, sitting up again, 'my mother had to go away for a while. That's how bad it was. In her grief, she became quite . . . it sounds dreadful to say this, but quite peculiar. She spoke very oddly, saying some dreadful things. About Jack and me – our being cousins, you know. So long as she said them to me alone, I didn't mind, although it was very upsetting, but I was concerned when she started talking to the staff, you know.'

'The servants?' said Alec.

'No, at the store,' said Abigail. 'Mrs Lumsden, for one. Telling her things that no one should say outside the family and even inside the family really.'

'Yes, Mrs Lumsden and Miss Hutton both hinted to me that your mother was not so strong as she looks,' I said.

'They didn't tell you what she said, did they?' said Abigail.

'Do these secrets have any bearing on what's happening now?'

I had never seen any family resemblance between Abigail and Mary before. Both were small, but Abigail was a plump, sweet, little dumpling of a woman still, at nearly fifty, with a round rosy cheek and a full curve to her shoulder and hip, while Mary was like an iron poker, a tiny rigid pillar of black, tight-lipped, straight-haired, the skin stretched across her jaw and her neck as though no flesh cushioned it from the bones beneath. Now, though, for the first time, I saw the mother in the daughter. Abigail's eyes turned to chips of grey ice and her mouth was a lipless line.

'I apologise, Mrs Aitken,' I said, 'if I sounded flippant. I didn't mean to be.' The line softened and a little blood came back into her lips, although her eyes stayed just as hard when she answered me.

'The two things are not connected,' she said 'My mother felt that she had been a poor wife to my father, giving him only one child and a girl at that. And she regretted pushing me into marriage with Jack. We had been five years married when my father died and there were no grandchildren.' Alec was squirming so hard he might almost have worn his seat away. 'My mother thought that all her life was coming to nothing. She felt she had displeased God and was being punished for it.' I am sure that I boggled at that, and certainly my mouth dropped open. 'But I don't think she deserves scorn. I think she was right. About Jack and me.' A small sound escaped Alec's lips. Bunty wrinkled up her brows and gave him a puzzled look. 'We weren't blessed the way that other marriages had been. After five years we were still waiting and Mother became convinced that we weren't really married in the eyes of God. That we were' – she whispered – 'fornicators. She read her Bible day and night. Scoured it for guidance, I suppose you would say.'

'And then eventually she . . . went away?'

'For a while and when she came back she was her old self again. And I—' Abigail flicked a glance at Alec but went on, although her cheeks burned a little, 'I had happy news for her. Then when Mirren was born, we all doted on her. It was a wonderful time for us Aitkens.' There was a defiant note in her voice which I did not understand. 'We needed no one and nothing except ourselves. Bella and Mary had their granddaughter and Jack and I our daughter and all was well at home and what matter anything else.'

'Twenty years ago,' I said, thinking that perhaps I could, after all, guess the reason for such emphasis on the family circle and the new baby and the rest of the world go hang. Twenty years ago was when House of Hepburn arrived to end Aitkens' Emporium's uncontested rule of Dunfermline town.

'We had twenty very happy years,' said Abigail. 'Perhaps I should be grateful for that. It's more than some people have in a lifetime. My husband has never done anything I can berate him for and I had my lovely girl, even if I was not allowed to keep her.' Abigail pushed Bunty's head off her lap and stood. 'She was bought at a price,' said Abigail. 'That's a saying of my mother's.'

'I've heard her say it.' I spoke very gently. 'The other day.'

'I've been thinking about what you said, Mrs Gilver. I *can* lift a burden from her, you know. I think I can. I can tell her it was not her fault that Mirren died. Shall I do that? Even if it hurts her in a new way she could not possibly be ready for. Should I?'

'If you would tell me what you're speaking about, Mrs Aitken,' I said, 'I could better advise you. Or I could go away and you could tell Mr Osborne here. He is, as you said, a very understanding man. He could help you.' Waves of reluctance came off Alec like steam from a boiling kettle but he said nothing.

'No,' said Abigail. 'I shall tell my mother – I've decided – that Mirren knew she wasn't a fit wife for Dugald Hepburn, and why, and then my mother will know that she has nothing to be sorry for.'

'You are a very good daughter,' I said. 'But can I give you a piece of advice, please?' She said nothing, but waited. 'Not today. You're too tired today – for which I can only say sorry – and you will be better able to be kind and cushion bad news for your mother tomorrow.'

Abigail passed a hand over her brow, sweeping her hair back, and she let out a ragged sigh. 'You're right,' she said. 'I'm in no state right now to help anyone.'

'Rest, Mrs Aitken,' said Alec. He had not spoken for a long time.

'I shall rest, Mr Osborne,' she said. 'And perhaps I shall even sleep. And when I wake up she will still be dead. Every time I wake up, just the same.' She nodded to both of us and left the room.

'Well,' said Alec. 'That was fun, wasn't it?'

Bunty stood up, stretched her front legs far out in front of her, leaned back and moaned. Then she stood up and shook herself all over, ears and jowls flapping.

'Exactly, old girl,' Alec said and he shook himself too, shuddering.

I nodded absently, for I was thinking.

'Punishment from God,' I said. 'Not blessed. Not a fit wife for Dugald. Alec, I think I know what made Mirren kill herself. Roughly, anyway.'

'I'm not sure I want to hear,' said Alec.

'Too bad,' I retorted. 'Listen: Mary shoved her daughter into a cousin marriage. No children – punishment from God. Ninian died – punishment from God. Mary cracks up. Then Abigail suddenly out of nowhere has happy news for her mother. Years later, when Mirren is grown up, Mary doesn't want a connection with the hated Hepburns – because of the unfortunate sisters and the feud – but Mirren and Dugald are adamant. Then Abigail persuades Mirren she shouldn't marry into a callous, thoughtless, cruel family where she would not be cherished. On the other hand, it would have been all right to marry into a family who would have cherished her for her dowry and . . . looked the other way with regards to other matters.'

'What other matters?' Alec said.

'Children,' I said. 'Progeny. Roger Lawson has two younger brothers and Dugald Hepburn had only sisters. Dugald was the only hope of carrying on the Hepburn name and Mirren . . . I have an idea that Mirren wasn't the girl to help him.'

'Dandy, that is the most disgusting thing I've heard in my life. Where did you get such an idea?'

'I'm sure I'm right,' I said. 'There was something wrong with Mirren. Something no one except her mother knew. Something Mirren couldn't bear when she found it out.'

'And now Abigail is going to tell her mother this monstrous thing?' Alec said.

'After the rest that you so sweetly advised her to take,' I reminded him. 'You're a better man than I am, Gunga Din.'

'What?' said Alec. 'I was only adding my voice to yours.'

'Yes, but you meant it, didn't you? I was only trying to stop her getting to Mary before we had a crack at her. Because if she's really losing her marbles, one of them might just roll our way.'

IO

Mary Aitken looked to me like a woman who had all her marbles organised in order of size and weight, cross-referenced for colour, and spinning in time as she juggled them one-handed and kept the other hand free.

'Mrs Gilver,' she said. 'Did you find a pair of opera gloves that suited you?'

I bowed my head in acknowledgement.

'Yes, Mrs Aitken, you saw through me yesterday.'

'And you'll not be here today to collect your fee?' she said, stalking over to the chair opposite us and sitting down on its extreme edge. She sent a split-second, shrivelling glance towards Alec.

'Mrs Gilver and I will not be sending you an account, Mrs Aitken,' he said. 'All things considered.'

'And what is it you want?' Mary said.

I took a breath to answer and then closed my mouth again. We no longer wanted anything very much, as far as I could see. Between the Lawson boy, Jack and Hilda's secret, Mirren's un-fitness, if I were right about that, and Mary's hatred of the Hepburns, we had perhaps explained everyone's disapproval of the marriage and we had provided motives for two suicides. Was it only loose ends to be tied in now?

'We know that Mirren was hiding in the attics,' Alec said, grabbing hold of one loose end and pulling firmly. 'And we know about the note she left for you.' If he had been hoping to surprise her he was disappointed. She only nodded.

'It occurred to me yesterday when I went into the store again,' she said. 'I unlocked my office door and that's when I realised that Mirren couldn't have put the letter on my desk. Miss Hutton, was it?'

'We know about your hopes for Roger Lawson too,' I said, sweeping past the question; we would not be responsible for getting Miss Hutton into trouble if we could help it. There was a slight visible twinge at my words.

'You spoke to Lady Lawson?' she said.

'She is a good friend to you,' I said. 'An old friend, I believe, but you've tested that friendship to its limits now. Why did you do it?'

'Do what?' said Mary.

'Ask Lady Lawson to say her son jilted Mirren,' I supplied. 'The attachment between Mirren and Dugald is common knowledge. What could you hope to gain?' Mary's face had pinched up into a little frown and a little pursing of her mouth.

'I just wanted a better . . . story,' she said. 'All her life will be now is her youth and her death. I wanted it to be nicer.' Her eyes narrowed now and her voice grew cold over the next words. 'And I didn't want those Hepburns to be part of our memories of her.'

'Those Hepburns,' said Alec, wonderingly. 'Why do you hate them so?'

'I don't hate them,' said Mary loudly. 'I wouldn't waste hate on them. They are beneath my notice.'

'But why?' I said. 'They should be rivals at worst, surely. If not colleagues, in a way. Allies?' I was imagining the sharing of rolls of tuppences when change ran out; the careful timing of seasonal sales so that both lots could have a good go at the bargain hunters, but Mary's lip had curled and she actually shuddered at the suggestion.

'Johnny-come-latelys,' she said. 'Encroaching. Leeches – sucking away all the goodwill we worked so hard to build up in this town. They only came here for spite, you know. Why would Robert Hepburn open a store in a town that already had one, if not for spite? To do us down and laugh at us when we fell.'

'But no one does business that way,' I said. 'Surely Mr Hepburn wanted a store here because here was where he lived? Or because here was where he managed to get premises to suit his needs? Why would he be spiteful? Why would he care?'

'He's not a Dunfermline man,' said Mary Aitken. 'He had no need to come here. He . . .' She shuffled her feet a little and then carried on. 'He followed Ninian. Ninian and Robert Hepburn started together in Patrick Thompson's over in Edinburgh. I was there too and that's where I met my husband. Of course, Ninian was a tailor and Hepburn was never anything but a draper's clerk.'

'I see,' I said. 'They were friends at one time?'

'It was John Aitken who made the leap and opened Aitkens' Emporium,' said Mary, not quite answering me. Her eyes lit up as she said the words. Still, after all these years, she was thrilled, as proud as she must have been on its opening day. 'And Robert Hepburn never forgave Ninian for going off into the world and making his fortune, leaving him behind. Oh, he was a spiteful, nasty, conniving piece of work. Not a scrap of honour or goodness about him anywhere. And it took him thirty years to scrimp and scrape and go coiling round every Jew he could and sell his wife's lockets to the backstreet dealers for an extra shilling but he got his wish in the end. Came here and set up against us.'

'But – bear with me while I try to work this out, Mrs Aitken,' I said. 'Hepburns' has been open for nineteen years?' She nodded. 'Weren't Mr John and Mr Ninian both already dead by that time?' She nodded again. Alec and I looked at one another, puzzled. Mary Aitken showed no signs of having said anything peculiar.

'Ninian wasn't cold in his grave,' she said. 'John was years gone. And I was away from home on a trip.' I tried to look as though I knew nothing of this trip. 'Abigail and Jack were newly married and they didn't need me there, grieving, making the house sad for them,' she said. 'I went off alone.'

'Newly married?' said Alec. That did not chime with what Abigail had told us. 'Five years, wasn't it?' Mary Aitken gave him a frozen stare, then shook herself.

'Was it? I'd have said less, but five years is a new marriage to an old woman like me.' She sniffed and tossed her head, changing the subject. 'Anyway, you wouldn't believe those wheedling, encroaching Hepburns while I was gone. Sucking up to Abby and Jack, tennis parties and card parties and dropping in, as if they'd never heard of mourning.'

'But you just said you went away so that Abby and Jack could stop mourning and be happy,' I said.

'They'd have been happy enough at home,' said Mary, her voice rising.

'Certainly,' I said. 'Your daughter just said as much to us, Mrs Aitken. That the family was very happy to live in its own company. She made it sound most pleasant and cosy.'

'Once I'd got rid of those Hepburns,' said Mary, 'it was. We were fine.'

'And . . .' Alec was struggling to make sense of what she was saying. 'Did you think Mr Hepburn was spying? Trying to find out trade secrets and help himself to Aitkens' success?'

'No,' said Mary. 'It wasn't Robert at all. He wouldn't have dared. It was the son and that wife of his and her mother. Taking Abby and Jack away from us, trying to get them into the Hepburn "set".' She spat the word. 'The Haddo "set". All jolly fun and what a lark, darling. Lady Lawson had nothing to do with them, you know.'

'I see,' I said, wondering if I did actually. She did not know about Jack and Hilda and yet she sounded quite unhinged when she spoke of the Hepburns.

'I came back just in time to stop their heads being turned completely,' said Mary. Oh no you didn't, I thought, or not Jack's anyway. 'I sent them packing, I can tell you.' I sighed; even ignoring Jack, she was mistaken if she thought she landed some kind of stunning blow. One only had to hear Fiona Haddo talking in her amused voice or look at Hepburns' lavish window displays on the day of the Aitkens' jubilee to see that Mary had provided nothing but entertainment for the Hepburns with her jealous fury. I imagined that the Hepburns enjoyed the tease and did not think about the Aitkens much besides. Poor Mary, she had never learned that indifference is the best revenge and I felt very glad for her sake that she did not know how Hilda Hepburn had ill-used poor Abby, how completely one of her family had had his silly head turned.

'So no chance of a rapprochement through the third genera-tion then?' said Alec. 'Ninian snubbed Robert, Robin and Hilda patronised Abby and Jack and no one wanted Mirren and Dugald to heal the rift after all those years?' He was nodding to himself, almost talking to himself really until Mary brought him up short with her crispest voice and most flashing glare.

'You are remarkably free with my family's Christian names for someone who has never been introduced to me,' she said. Alec flushed.

'I apologise,' he said. 'I used their names for ease of recogni-tion only. What I mean is that Mr Ninian Aitken snubbed old Mr Hepburn, and then—'

'*Old* Mr Hepburn?' said Mary. Alec's flush deepened; of course, old Mr Hepburn was her contemporary. Before he could take a third run at it with Seniors and Juniors at the ready, she swept on. 'Besides, it wasn't just about ancient feuds. I would not have let Mirren marry into that family if they had landed here from the other end of the country, strangers to us all.' She smiled and it was not a pleasant smile.

'Oh?' I said, although I was sure I knew what unwelcome topic she was getting to.

'They don't know that I know,' she said, her voice coated in a kind of delighted scorn, 'but the fact is that Robert and Dulcie Hepburn had four daughters before Robert Junior came along.' She paused, her eyes glittering. 'And not one of them has ever seen the outside of a nursing home.'

I nodded, trying to look neutral. Abigail had told us that Mary herself was no stranger to a nursing home and there was some-thing about the way she passed on the gossip with such relish that sickened me.

'How unfortunate,' I said. 'Ill health in a family is a great strain on everyone.'

'I don't mean ill health,' said Mary. 'I was being quite literal,

Mrs Gilver. They never brought the babies home. Never announced their births after the first one or two. Four of them! And they tried to stop the world from knowing.'

'The world can certainly be very unkind,' I said.

'I found out in my lying-in hospital when I was confined with Abigail,' Mary said. She was absolutely livid now, drops of spittle forming at the corners of her mouth. 'One of the nurses told me. As if I would let my Mirren, my girl, have anything to do with a family like that. Once I knew. Once it was all out in the open and their secrets weren't their secrets any more. I went to Humbie to the nursing home and saw those Hepburn sisters, you know. Three of them are still alive. You could see them yourself if you care to. And they thought they could hide it!'

'Mrs Aitken, please,' said Alec. He spoke mildly but seemed only to incense her more.

'Oh! Oh!' she said. 'You'd rather not think about such things, I suppose. You find it "distasteful", eh?'

'I find it illuminating,' I said. I had given up on my neutral expression and supposed that I was now looking at her as though she were a white toad someone had told me to pick up and cradle. 'Tell me, Mrs Aitken, did you take Mirren to the nursing home to visit these unfortunate women? Did you go that far?'

'I would have,' said Mary. 'I didn't need to. I explained it to her.' All of a sudden all the fire went out of her as though someone had turned down the gas in a lantern. She sat back, the last peep of flame snuffed out. 'I explained. And she . . . she died. I did that. That was me.' She closed her eyes. 'Our sins will surely find us out. My sins . . .'

Alec, who has surprised me more times than I can list through the years of our friendship, delivered his greatest surprise then.

'What about "Her sins, which are many, are forgiven; for she loved much"?'

Mary opened her eyes and gazed at him.

'Don't be so quick to blame yourself, Mrs Aitken,' he said. 'Your daughter Abigail has just told us that Mirren didn't kill herself because of anything that came from you.'

'Abigail said that? What did she mean?'

'She wouldn't say,' said Alec, firmly. 'It's a family matter, I understand. Nothing to do with Mrs Gilver and me.'

'Well, I must go and ask her,' said Mary, rising up with some of her old vigour. 'I can't imagine what she means but I must ask her to tell me.' She left us without another word, without even a goodbye or an order not to bother them again.

I was glad that she had not waited to see us off the premises; I do not think I could have peeled myself off my chair for a king's ransom.

'My goodness,' said Alec, when the silence had had time to settle around us. 'Between the three of them, that was the most uncomfortable series of conversations I hope I will ever have to endure. You weren't very sympathetic, Dan. What got into you?'

'It's a particular dislike of mine,' I said. 'Grisly news sucked like bon-bons.' I shuddered.

'But have we solved the mystery?' said Alec. 'Tied in all the ends?'

'I think so,' I said. 'Hilda and Jack, obviously, knowing what they know. Abby, if my guess was right. Mary, without a shadow of a doubt. Even without the business rivalry – and my goodness, wasn't she fierce? – her avoidance of the Hepburn "bad blood" accounts for her misgivings.'

'Odd though, isn't it?' said Alec. 'A woman who could marry her daughter off to a cousin and then suddenly grow so squeamish the next generation down.'

'Oh, Alec, don't!' I said. 'You sound like those horrid German scientists. What is it called, the thing they get so excited about?'

'Eugenics,' said Alec.

'Well, it's vile. As though we were dogs. Revolting.'

'We don't need to concern ourselves with it, thankfully,' said Alec. 'The point is that it could be two suicides after all. Two broken hearts. Star-crossed lovers indeed.'

'But what about the inspector?' I said. 'And the gloves? And do we rely on the business rivalry to explain the Hepburn men's opposition? We have no explanation for that otherwise.'

Alec only shook his head.

'It's not a new set of Meccano, Dan; it's a boxful.' Then seeing that I did not understand, he went on. 'There are bits left over even once we've built the best model we can.'

Reluctantly, I nodded.

'Come on then, darling girl,' I said to Bunty. 'I'm going to take you a nice walk up the High Street and find you a big juicy butcher's bone.'

Bunty, despite the fact that I had used two of her favourite words in the same sentence, ignored me. She had her head cocked to one side, with her brow wrinkling.

'What's wrong with her?' said Alec.

'Ssh,' I said. I cocked my head up too and, from what seemed like a great distance, I heard a voice bellowing. Alec and I raced out into the hall. It was upstairs somewhere. It was a woman's voice and she was begging for help. We wheeled into the stair-well and took the steps three at a time with Bunty streaming up ahead of us. We paused on the first-floor landing but the sound was still above us, and so again up we surged to the second floor and out onto the gallery under the cupola where the voice boomed around the empty space above and all around.

'Help! Help! Help me!'

Bunty, scared now she was so close to the noise, whined and pressed herself into the wall behind her, but Alec and I charged around the gallery to an open door on the other side and burst in.

Abigail Aitken was kneeling on the floor, still bellowing, holding her mother's face to her bosom, shaking the woman like a rag doll. Mary's hands lay limp at her sides and her legs were splayed out, her stiff black bombazine skirts twisted up and one seam split open. Abigail turned to face us, her mouth gaping open and an ugly raw sob coming out of it, her hair hanging down in tangled oily clumps around her shoulders and one cheek bright pink and shining.

'Help me!' she wailed.

I rushed over and knelt down beside them, taking Abigail's hands and prising them gently away from Mary's shoulders.

Mary's body slumped back into my grasp and with a great rush of relief I heard a low groan and saw an eyelid flickering. Very carefully I laid her down flat on the floor and then grabbed Abigail's shawl from where it sat in a heap and bundled it into a pillow. I lifted Mary's neck and set the bundle underneath her.

'What happened?' said Alec. Abigail did not answer but only stared down at Mary's grey face. I stared too, horrified to see how it had slipped downwards at one side, her eye, cheek and mouth melting into a doughy and expressionless travesty.

'Something dreadful,' I said. 'We'd better get a doctor. Or an ambulance if there is one. Tell Trusslove. He'll know what to do.' Alec nodded and left. I pulled down one of my cuffs and wiped Mary's mouth. Abigail was rocking back and forward, whimpering. I looked around myself for the first time and saw bedroom furniture. I wondered if we could, between the two of us, lift Mary onto the bed and wished I'd sent Abigail to the telephone and kept Alec with me. I put my hands under her shoulders and lifted them. She was a small woman but I felt numb and she was all but unconscious, a dead weight in my arms. I laid her back down and wiped her mouth again.

'Get a pillow and blanket from the bed,' I said to Abigail. 'And a handkerchief for her.' Abigail shook her head.

'It's Mirren's room,' she said. 'I don't want to move her things.'

'Get a blanket!' I shouted at her. 'Mirren is dead and your mother is alive. Help her.' Abigail stumbled to her feet and dragged the coverlet off the bed, dropping it on top of Mary. I tucked it in around her, my heart sinking to feel the leaden slump of her body on the hard floor. Her breathing was growing laboured and once or twice there came a choking sound from her throat. I remembered a snippet of my training from the early months of volunteer work when it was thought that I might make a nurse one day, and steadying her with my knee I hauled her onto her side and bent one of her legs up in front of her. It was like moving a sack of grain, like setting sandbags in place.

'Pillows!' I said to Abigail and as she threw them down to me I used them to prop Mary, front and back, until she was balanced and I could take my knee away.

Again I wiped her mouth and then for a moment just watched her and listened. Abigail went over to a chest of drawers and opened the top one. She gazed into it and put her hand to her mouth, shaking her head, then she rummaged inside her own sleeve, drew out a handkerchief and came back to kneel beside her mother, holding it out to me. I stared at her and she bowed her head and began dabbing at her mother's mouth herself. Her cheek was still glowing and was beginning to swell.

Mary's breathing was worse than ever and so I set to and began unfastening the scores of tiny hooks and eyes holding shut her bodice down her back. By the time I had them undone and had loosened the stays she wore underneath them, there were two servant girls in the room and I could see Trusslove and Alec hovering outside.

'I've rung for help, Mrs Gilver,' Trusslove called in to me. 'Oh, my poor mistress. Is she holding on?'

I took Mary's wrist and found her pulse, slow and sluggish, but steady enough. I looked at my wristwatch, but truth be told I had never known what it was one was supposed to tell from a pulse and watch together and so I just sat there feeling the steady beat, trying to tell if it were slowing, weakening or growing perhaps just a little bit stronger.

'She's still with us, Mr Trusslove,' I said. 'How far away is the doctor?'

'It's the ambulance men I've sent for,' he said.

'Not the fever wagon,' said Abby, turning terrified eyes on him. 'She's not going to that place.'

'No, no, the St Andrew's men,' said Trusslove. 'The volunteers, Miss Abby. They'll take her to the cottage hospital.'

'And where is it?' I asked.

'Not even a mile,' said one of the servant girls.

'And is someone downstairs at the front door to tell the men where to come?' I said. 'Alec?' But he was already gone.

Abigail was shivering now, rocking back and forwards and hugging herself and it was then that Bunty came into the room. She whined at me, gave Mary a long hard stare and then shuffled up beside Abigail again. Abby put one arm round her neck.

'She's warm,' she said to me in a voice reduced to a croak from her yelling.

I frowned and felt Mary's head. It was clammy, if anything.

'The dog,' Abigail said.

I reached over and put my hand on one of hers, feeling the icy chill of deep shock.

'Hug her,' I said. 'She'll warm you up. And you, girl?' I looked at one of the servants. 'Get a blanket for Mrs Jack, please. And a cup of tea if there's a kettle hot. Plenty of sugar.'

'Very good, madam,' said one of the girls and they scattered.

'What happened?' I said to Abigail once they had gone. She was hanging onto Bunty's neck like a drowning woman and Bunty was shifting a little, paddling her front paws in mild protest at being squeezed so. I clicked my tongue to placate her.

'If she dies, I will have—'

'Never mind that,' I said, thinking that never was there such a family for claiming to have killed their loved ones. 'She slapped you, didn't she? Because of what you told her?'

Abigail put one hand up to her cheek and stroked it.

'And pulled my hair too,' she said. 'Pulled me round the room by my hair, just as she used to do last time. When she wasn't herself, before.'

Mary groaned, a dreadful aching sound, and shifted her body, hauling her shoulder over so that she could look up at us from one half-open eye.

'Ssh,' I said to her. 'Shush now, Mrs Aitken. Rest. Lie still.' I took one of her hands and held it. I flashed a look at Abigail and mouthed shushing her too. If Mary Aitken were conscious, and it seemed she was, we must not say anything to cause her further suffering as she lay there.

'Where's Bella?' I said. 'Has someone been to her?'

'Out,' said Abigail. 'She went to thank the staff for everything. The last week, you know, and the police questions. She said they should be rewarded for their conduct. A little something in their pay-packets. It's pay-day today.'

'And Jack?' I said. In truth, I had no interest in his where-abouts, but talking had calmed Abigail down and so I thought I should encourage more.

'Out too,' said Trusslove, reappearing in the hallway. 'He went off in one of the cars after he spoke to you. Ah, here's some hot tea for you, Miss Abby. This'll help you.'

As the servant girl aided Abigail up onto her feet and took her to sit on the dressing chair, sounds came to us of the front door far below, quick footsteps on the stairway and then two St Andrew's ambulance men were in the room in their blessed smart dark uniforms, looking mercifully calm and competent as they eased me out of the way. They lifted Mary effortlessly onto a stretcher, one tucking a red blanket around her and one measur-ing her pulse against his fob watch, then the first deftly removing her shoes, chafing her feet and talking all the while to her in a bright, kindly voice.

'Right then,' said the other, putting his fob away. 'Who laid her down then and loosened her dress?'

'That was me,' I said, hunching a little in case he were about to scold me.

'Well, there's a good sensible girl,' he said. 'Well done. Are you coming in the ambulance with us or following on?' He was looking at me, but I turned to Abigail. Unbelievably she was sipping at her cup of tea, staring straight ahead.

'Mrs Jack?' I said. 'Abby? Are you going with your mother or would you rather the chauffeur drove you?'

'Both cars are out, madam,' said Trusslove.

'Not in the ambulance,' said Abigail, shrinking into the back of her chair. 'What if she dies?'

'Alone?' I said.

The St Andrew's men had Mary out of the room and halfway down the first flight of stairs, not waiting on our decisions.

'I couldn't,' said Abigail.

'You go, Dan,' said Alec. 'I'll bring Mrs Jack along.'

I had never been terribly keen on hospitals even before the war years when day after day I willed myself to drive over to that godforsaken officers' convalescent home for another seven hours of severed limbs, oozing stitches and shot nerves, but I sent up prayers of thankfulness when the ambulance stilled its siren and drew up beside the large double doors of the emergency entrance at the Dunfermline Cottage Hospital, not least because the name was a misnomer if ever there were one; the hospital was as grand and imposing as every other of Dunfermline's many public buildings and it was a great comfort to be arriving there. Running like an automaton in Mirren's bedroom, I had without thinking done the right things and had perhaps helped a little, even if I could wish to have been less harsh to poor Abigail about the blanket and pillows, but crouched in the ambulance all competence deserted me and I turned fluttery and tearful, dreading that indeed Mary Aitken would die as we swung around the roads at top speed, for she had sunk into a deep torpor and the ambulance man who sat beside her was frowning hard and had stopped all his kindly banter.

At the hospital doors, we were met by a nurse in a blue dress with a clean white apron pinned on top and white cuffs holding her sleeves up above her elbows. She was impossibly young but looked very strong and certain, with that extra-clean look of nurses as though they washed their faces with Lysol and a stiff brush instead of soap and a flannel.

'Stroke,' said the man who had made the journey in the back with Mary and me.

'Name?' said the nurse. She was looking at Mary as we trotted along in step with the men carrying the stretcher, but I guessed that she was talking to me.

'Mrs Aitken,' I said.

'From Aitkens'?' said the nurse, peering with greater interest at Mary. Then she remembered herself. 'Age?' she snapped.

'Seventy . . . four . . . ish,' I said, hoping that I had remembered accurately.

'First stroke?'

'I think so.'

'And were you with her when it happened?'

'I wasn't, Sister,' I said, thinking that even if she were only a staff nurse she would not mind a sudden promotion and better that than the other way. 'Her daughter was though. She's following along behind. She should soon be here.'

'Her daughter?' The nurse stopped. 'Who are you?'

'A friend,' I began, but the nurse stopped me.

'Back to the waiting room with you,' she said. 'You can't be in here out of visiting time.' I knew there was no point in arguing; everything about her tone, her looks and her firmly folded elbows as she turned, physically barring my way, said that she would win her point. The stretcher had arrived at a curtained cubicle and the ambulance men set it down with groans of relief.

'I shall send Mrs Aitken back here when she comes, shall I?' I said.

'We'll take care of things from here,' said the nurse, not even willing to discuss that small matter with me now. She marched smartly up to the bedside, twitched the curtains shut behind her and left me standing there.

I took a deep breath to steady myself, and felt goose pimples spring up on my arms at the smell, that unforgettable cocktail of chlorine bleach, disinfectant and strong soap which is almost as much part of a hospital as the starched white sheets and starched blue nurses.

Alec and Abigail arrived just as I had got back to the large double doors and been told by a porter in a cubby-hole there that this was the emergency entrance and I should come and go – although it was not visiting time, not nearly – by the front door like everyone else managed to do.

'How is she?' said Abigail. 'Where have they taken her?'

I turned an inquiring face to the porter.

'Admissions,' he said, 'but you can't come in through here. You'll need to go round to the front.'

'She was asleep when they took her out of the ambulance,' I told Abigail, 'but they whisked her straight in, a very competent nurse—'

'No doctor?'

'And I'm sure a doctor will be with her now. Let's go round and see if we can't get you to her, Mrs Aitken, shall we?' I threw A Look at the porter who affected not to notice and we left, working our way around the complicated set of alleys and in-shoots to the front of the building where we mounted the stairs and entered the foyer.

It was quite impossible, it seemed, to add a bedside companion to an admission which was already under way; the uniformed volunteer who manned a desk at the door, a nurse we waylaid and any number of passing porters agreed. So the three of us milled around, wishing for a seat and some tea, but when I asked the volunteer if a folding chair might be found for Abigail, I was treated to Another Look which suggested that my effort to the emergency door porter would have made no impression (not if the current effort was hospital standard) and which told me that there was no point even mentioning the tea.

'What happened, Mrs Aitken?' I said, as I rejoined Alec and her. She was leaning up against the wall with her eyes closed.

'She collapsed,' said Abigail, without opening her eyes. 'We were quarrelling.'

'Yes,' I said. 'She struck you.'

Abigail opened her mouth wide as though to test the feeling in her cheek, and nodded.

'You had told her?' I asked. 'The thing you said you had decided to tell her?'

As I watched, the lines of Abigail's lashes started to glitter and a second later two tears had formed, detached and rolled down her cheeks. She felt up her sleeve for her handkerchief and then, remembering that she had given it away, she lifted a hand and roughly wiped the tears away with her fingers.

'I thought it would help,' she said. 'I don't understand why it upset her so.'

'If you would tell us what it was, Mrs Aitken,' said Alec in his lowest, most gentle voice; trying, I think, to sound like a lullaby. I nodded at him, encouraging the effort, for I was beginning to wonder why Mary would strike Abigail over such a thing.

'Was it just the fact that you'd kept it quiet?' I asked. 'Or was it the secret itself that was so upsetting?'

Abigail shook her head so forcefully that the newest tears flew off to either side.

'She wasn't herself,' she whispered. 'Just like the last time. She wasn't well. I should have known she couldn't be expected to bear confidences.'

Alec and I were gazing helplessly at one another when the front door banged open and Bella Aitken came in at speed, one of the Aitken chauffeurs in his mauve and gold livery trotting behind her. She had made some effort with her appearance today, to visit the Emporium and hand out the staff's favours, but she was still very dishevelled, coat buttoned crookedly and only one glove on, and her face was every bit as stricken as it had been during our interview in Trusslove's pantry the day before. She saw us and bustled over, putting out her hands to clasp Abigail to her.

'Is she dead?' she said. 'Please tell me she hasn't died. Abigail? Trusslove rang me up at the store. They said she had been taken away in an ambulance. She isn't dead, is she?'

'She had a stroke, Mrs Aitken,' I said. 'She was alive but unconscious when I last saw her.'

'You said asleep,' said Abigail, struggling out of her mother-in-law's embrace and turning fearful eyes to me.

'Her breathing was very steady,' I said. 'And she's in the best place, in very safe hands.'

'I don't know,' said Bella Aitken, looking around, 'None of us has ever been in this place before. Did someone ring up Dr Hill? Wasn't he there?'

'We thought it best to summon an ambulance,' Alec said. 'Get her here as soon as possible, you know.'

'A stroke,' said Bella Aitken, letting go of Abigail and rubbing her hands over her own face. 'A stroke? Mary? She has always had the best of health. Healthier than me – physically anyway.'

'She does live a little on her nerves, Aunt Bella,' Abigail said. 'It wouldn't be wrong to say she was "highly strung".'

'No, I won't hear that of her,' said Bella. 'I've known your mother forty-nine years, Abigail, and she is as strong as an ox. Always has been. It's Mirren dying that's done this to her. It's Mirren that's brought Mary this low.' There was a curious, triumphant note in her voice. 'Losing that girl of ours has broken us all to bits. I'll tell anyone the same and there's no shame in it, if you ask me.'

'Aunt Bella, please,' said Abigail. 'Please don't blame Mirren. Mother and I were quarrelling. She was very upset and I did nothing to help calm her. If anything I made it worse. Don't heap this on my poor child.'

So intent were they on jockeying for blame – and it struck me, and Alec too to judge from his expression, as a most peculiar way to be carrying on – that they did not notice the approach of a white-coated doctor who strode up to our little group with his stethoscope still attached to one ear and his spectacles pulled far down on his long nose so that he could look at us over the top of them.

'Are you with Mrs Aitken?' he said. Bella turned. 'Ah, Mrs John!'

'Dr Spencer!' she said. 'How is she? Please don't tell me she's gone.'

'She's resting,' said Dr Spencer, with a slight frown (at the histrionics, I assumed; I suppose it is not the done thing to mention death so gratuitously to a doctor, who spends his days pitted against it). 'We'll ring Dr Hill to come in and see her now, but you did the right thing sending her to us without delay.'

'Can I see her?' said Abigail.

'Certainly, Mrs Jack,' said Dr Spencer. 'If you would care to sit with her and hold her hand and talk gently.'

'I need to apologise for something,' said Abigail and the tears were beginning to flow again. 'I must speak to her. In case it's my only chance, you see.'

Dr Spencer frowned again. 'She's not to be upset though,' he said. 'And perhaps – after your recent . . . perhaps it would be better if Mrs John here were to step in. She will forgive me for saying it but she has lived longer than you and learned how to weather life's storms.' He gave Bella a tight smile.

'It's my mother,' said Abigail. 'I must go to her.'

'A brief visit,' said the doctor. 'A *quiet* word.' With some reluctance he tucked her arm under his and led her away.

'Weather life's storms!' said Bella Aitken when they had gone. 'I'm not so sure about that. It was ten years ago when my boys died. Three months apart, separate campaigns, separate battles, but three months apart. I couldn't have faced a deathbed the next week, my own mother or no. Sickbed, I mean. Oh Lord, sickbed, let's pray.' Then with that utter lack of self-consciousness that had been behind the carpet slippers, the pinned curls and the mismatched stockings, she slid her back down the wall until she was resting on her haunches.

At least this indecorous display had the result that the volunteer summoned a porter who brought a chair and Bella sat down, unclasped the large black handbag which swung from one elbow and drew out a commodious flask, battered silver in a leather case. The porter looked back and scowled at the sound of the stopper popping out but did not come back to remonstrate with her. Bella took a long swig, wiped her lips and offered the flask to me.

I took it. It was whisky, but still I took it, helped myself to a good mouthful, and handed it to Alec. He took a goodly glug too and returned it to its owner. One final swig and Bella stowed the thing back in her bag again.

Then we all three turned at the sound of heels clopping briskly along one of the corridors which led off this foyer. A little nurse, even younger than the first and with her sleeves buttoned to the wrist – perhaps for this trip to front of house – came up and spoke diffidently.

'Doctor sent me,' she said. 'Mrs Aitken is very distressed, trying to ask for someone, and Mrs Aitken wants Mrs Aitken,' she stumbled a little now, 'to come and calm her.'

'Poor Mary,' said Bella. She rose and followed the nurse.

'Sit down, Dandy,' said Alec and I was thankful to take the empty chair.

'Poor Mary indeed,' I said.

'And what measure of guilt do you think you and I must bear for this?'

'Oh, don't you start!' I said. 'I won't have this hysterical clamouring for responsibility.'

'But we encouraged Abigail to tell Mirren's secret to Mary. And we hinted to Mary that there was a secret to tell and sent her haring off to hear it.'

'Yes,' I said. 'Alec, you know I thought I was very clever and I worked out what the secret was?' Alec nodded. 'Well, can you believe that kind of news would have caused a collapse like Mary's? And can you understand why the news would have caused her to strike Abigail? Strike her hard too. Her cheek is still flaming.'

'It does seem a little odd,' Alec said.

'But we can hardly ask Abigail now, can we? I hope Mary can talk once she's feeling better. We might have more luck with her.'

'This case is changing you,' Alec said, staring at me. 'I thought as much this morning when you were talking to Jack. You sound as tough as buffalo hide.'

'I don't like all these secrets,' I said. 'Everyone playing games with everyone else, no one telling the whole plain truth. I have no patience with it. Do you realise, Alec, that silly little Lady Lawson is the only individual we have met in this case who wasn't trying to hide something from us? And that was only after she *was* trying to hide and gave up because she was failing. If you ask me, despite all the talk of "our poor Mirren" and "our darling girl" half the time they've all forgotten what started the trouble. I should like to go around with a great big photograph of her pretty face and shove it at them when they start their games again.'

Alec had let me get all of this off my chest, bless him (perhaps he even delivered the opening insult to get me started), but now, hearing footsteps again, he shushed me, pressing downwards with a flattened hand. It was the little nurse again.

'News?' he asked her.

'She's trying to make herself understood,' the nurse answered. 'She's not talking and she's a bit woozy from some medicine she's had, but she kept doing this.' The nurse put her hand out as if to measure a short distance from the floor. 'We thought she wanted to see a child – thought her mind had gone, because of course we know about poor Miss Aitken dying like that last week – and Mrs Aitken was saying who do you mean, Mother, and Sister said she might mean you, dear, if she's wandered, she might be asking for her own little girl and not know you all grown up as you are. And that started young Mrs Aitken crying like anything and then the patient shook her head and went like this.' The nurse put her hand down again but this time she moved it with a stroking motion. 'And the other Mrs Aitken was saying, a dog, Mary? A cat? What do you mean? And the patient got all excited and nodding her head and then young Mrs Aitken said maybe she means Mrs Gilver – because of the dog – and the patient said yes, yes – nodding – and so Doctor has sent me to fetch you.'

'Well, for heaven's sake, after all that, let's hurry,' I said and set off.

The nurse sped up, overtook me and led us through a bewildering maze of corridors at top speed.

'Where *is* Bunty, by the way?' I asked Alec, as we followed her.

'No idea,' Alec said. 'I left her in that bedroom. I expect the servants will take care of her.'

At last we stopped at one of the sets of enormous wood and glass doors which we had been rushing past and the nurse opened one side and ushered us through. 'Quietly now,' she said. 'Last cubicle on the end there. On the left. Doctor's in there.'

We moved as silently as we could along the broad corridor, past drawn curtains on either side. In here the bleach, disinfectant and soap were joined by the other hospital smell, the worst of all, illness and exhaustion and the unmistakable trace of death, nearby and waiting. At the end, I cleared my throat and drew the curtain open a little way.

Mary was lying propped up on a high, narrow bed looking almost as white as the snowy pillowcase behind her head. Her hair was undone into a plait and it lay along one shoulder. Her face, which had looked melted in Mirren's bedroom, had set in some intangible kind of way, but it had set with that downwards drag to it and even now Abigail dabbed at her mouth with a swab of cotton. Bella, still swallowing, was just clasping her bag shut again. Dr Spencer stood at the end of the bed, writing on a piece of paper clipped to a stiff board. He turned, unsmiling, towards us.

'She wanted to see you,' he said. 'Very agitated, but once she knew you were coming, she slipped off to sleep and I don't want you to waken her.'

'That's fine,' I said, and turned to Bella. 'Why don't you take Abigail home? Take her home to Jack, and Mr Osborne and I will sit with Mary.'

Alec raised his eyebrows but did not demur, and he and I settled ourselves into the Aitken women's vacated chairs.

'You could have a long wait on your hands,' said the doctor over his spectacle tops. 'Well, mind and call a nurse in when she does waken.' He gave us an appraising look, appeared to decide that we would do as interim hand-holders and strode off in his rather grand and busy way.

'I wish Bella had left her flask,' I said after a while.

Alec gave a short laugh. 'I could get you one of your own for your birthday,' he said.

'Heavens, no!' I said. 'There's hearty, if you like. Still, good to see Bella more like herself.' I glanced at Mary. 'The Aitken family is going to need at least one stout pillar.'

Alec too looked at Mary and gently shushed me.

'Do you think she can hear us?' I said. We both watched her for a while in silence and I noted with a pang the sharp protrusion of her breastbone under the thin cotton gown, with what a jerk it seemed to rise as though each breath was being fought for. I had seen my mother breathe in just that way over the last night while we all sat around her, her breaths slowing and slowing, growing so far apart and so ragged that we took to holding ours until another of hers was got in and let out again, until the last breath that was not let out at all. We waited on and on and then eventually we still living had to exhale, and inhale again and carry on. I had still not heard that last breath leave my mother's body by the time we all kissed her head and left her there and as I wandered numbly through the house to find my sister and tell her the news – for, of course, Mavis had not been up to sitting quietly by a deathbed but had stumbled off to weep noisily on her own somewhere – I was still listening.

'I keep thinking about my parents,' I said to Alec. 'And Edward and Mavis. I don't know why.'

Alec opened his eyes very wide. 'Me too,' he said. 'I even dreamt about my brother last night. I haven't dreamt about him for years.' He paused. 'At least this was one of the dreams where he's still alive in it.'

'As opposed to what?' I said.

'Don't ask,' said Alec. 'I expect it's just the thought of Jack's brothers bringing back thoughts of mine.'

'I don't know what it is with me,' I answered. 'Nothing about the Aitkens chimes with my early years.'

'It's probably just that they're such a tight little band. Family business, marrying their own relations, all still living together. Do they even *have* friends?'

'Lady Lawson and the Provost?' I said, laughing a little. 'And remember the days of gay abandon when Mary was away? Tennis parties and all sorts of debauchery until she came back and put her foot down.'

'It makes me think of Whatsisname in the book coming home from the Indies and stopping the theatricals,' Alec said. I thought for a moment.

'Sir Thomas Bertram?' I said. '*Mansfield Park*?'

'That's the one,' said Alec. 'My mother read it to me when I had measles and had to keep my eyes covered with a black scarf from the headaches.'

'Poor you!' I said. 'Not *Robinson Crusoe*? Not *Gulliver's Travels*?'

'It was Mother's only offer,' Alec said, 'and better than nothing.'

We had almost forgotten the figure on the bed between us; certainly, when she moved her head and made a little groan, we both started violently. I sat forward. Her eyes were shifting under her eyelids and she moved her head again, squeezed her eyes more tightly shut and then opened them. She blinked, staring straight ahead, and then her body jerked and she looked wildly from one side to the other until she saw me. The hand lying on top of the covers at the side nearest me did not move, could not move I imagine, but Mary twisted herself on the bed, paddling with her legs, then reached over and gripped me hard with her other hand, looking searchingly into my eyes.

'Yes, I'm here,' I said. 'Mrs Aitken, dear, please lie back and try to be calm. I'm here to help you but please lie back on your pillows again.'

The effort had exhausted her and she did as she was bidden. I stood and straightened the pillow behind her, lifting her long grey pigtail out of the way again.

'Shall I go for the nurse?' Alec asked me.

Mary made a low moaning sound and shook her head. With her good hand, she touched her mouth and felt her face, then she lifted her other lifeless hand by the wrist and stared at it as she let it drop back down onto the sheet again. She made the moaning sound again and a tear rolled out of her eye. I dabbed it with a piece of cotton from the little enamel tray on the bedside table and then dabbed at her mouth. She gave me a look so piercingly piteous that I felt my eyes start to fill too.

'Wait a bit, Alec,' I said, and Mary nodded.

She opened her mouth and made a series of inarticulate sounds and then shook her head again.

'Is it about Abigail?' I asked. She nodded and pointed with hard jabbing motions towards the opening in the curtains.

'You want us to go and get Abigail?' Alec said. Mary shook her head furiously and made a kind of fierce growling sound.

'Please!' I said, taking hold of her arm and bringing it back down to rest at her side. 'Gently does it, Mrs Aitken. Mr Osborne and I have all the time in the world for you. There's no need to be anxious about anything at all. Now. Abigail? Yes. Mirren?' A nod, but thankfully a milder one. 'She told you something about Mirren, didn't she?' Another nod, but her mouth opened in a soundless sob. 'Did she tell you why Mirren killed herself?' Nod. 'Do you want us to know?' A furious shake, but she caught it and turned it gentle before we could remonstrate with her again. 'Do you want us to do something?' Yes, yes, yes. Three definite nods and a searching look into my eyes. She pointed again at the curtains.

'Nurse?' Alec said. Mary and I ignored him.

'Go somewhere?' I asked. 'Right. The attics? No, all right. Don't worry. Just let me guess again. Is it to find something? To speak to someone? Ah! Right, then. You want us to speak to someone.' Mary held out her good hand for mine and when I gave it to her, she turned it up and traced a pattern on my palm. It was very ticklish but I managed not to squirm and when she did it for the second time, I recognised the three strokes as a letter H. 'Hepburn?' I said. 'Which one?' Mary shook her head and shrugged. 'All of them then,' I said, nodding along with her. 'But what about, Mrs Aitken?' Mary took a long time thinking before she responded and when she did, it was to make the shape one makes for shadow-puppet geese, fingers and thumb opening and snapping together again.

'Yes,' I said. 'I know. I'm to talk to them.'

Mary shook her head and frowned, putting her finger to her temple and tapping, shrugging the shoulder on that side.

'Ah!' I said. 'What do they know?'

Yes, yes, yes, from Mary.

Then she hauled herself up as much as she could in the bed, digging her one good hand down under her and pushing away from the heap of pillows. When she was upright, she pinched her fingers together as though to sprinkle salt, put them to one side of her mouth and drew them across hard, dragging at her lips and glaring at me, willing the message into me with every ounce of energy remaining.

'Understood,' I said. 'Rest now.'

But Mary was not quite done. She prodded herself in her chest and then drew her pinched fingers across her mouth again.

'Absolutely,' I said. 'I'll make sure they know.'

As she dropped back, utterly spent, the curtain suddenly rattled open on its rings and a dapper little man entered the cubicle.

'Mrs Aitken,' he said. 'What's to do with you, my dear?'

This evidently was Dr Hill, the family physician, summoned to the bedside and responding in very smart time. Mary only flapped a tired hand at him and turned her head away.

'Come now, Mrs Aitken,' he said, bustling up to her bedside and taking hold of her good hand. 'I'll have none of that from you.' He looked quickly between Alec and me and we made our goodbyes – a swift salute on the forehead from me and a wave from him – and hurried away.

'Well, I'm glad all that meant something to you, Dan,' Alec said.

'Not all of it,' I answered. 'The thing Abby told her can't have been what we thought. How could the Hepburns know about it?'

'But you understand what she wants you to do?'

'Yes. She's willing to strike a bargain with the Hepburns. Whatever they know, whatever they did, Mary is asking for silence from them, offering silence from the Aitkens and ready at that to call it quits.'

'More or less what the inspector insinuated to you then,' Alec said. He was looking very troubled.

'Yes, two dead children and best for everyone to leave it there.'

'Can I make one request?' Alec said. 'Let's not start tonight. I don't think I've got the energy for any more dramatic scenes today. Let's march in and demand the Hepburns' silence tomorrow.'

'Agreed,' I said.

'As to how we can command them to keep quiet, when we don't know what the secret is . . .'

'I have no earthly idea,' I said. 'But at least we go invested with some moral authority.'

'We do?'

'Yes, darling. We go to carry out the wishes of a – possibly – dying woman. That's a lot better than: "Answer our questions or we're telling on you".'

I I

Dinner at St Margaret's Hotel was thick oyster soup, stuffed and be-crumbed cutlets and a concoction going by the name of Empress Rice, which appeared to be rice pudding made fit for company by the addition of a lot of unnecessary eggs, sherry and jam. After it I could have spent a comfortable night on a park bench, stoked by inner fires and in no danger of coming to harm even without the lightest covering of newspaper. As it was, in a vast, hot, plushy bedroom I felt I did not so much sleep as lie stupefied until morning.

The room smelled of mothballs, which mystified me; an hotel is after all under continuous occupation (I have to will myself not to think of that fact whenever I get into bed in one on the first night of a stay and, should I ever find evidence of the *last* occupant, I have to summon all my early lessons not to run away shrieking). The bed was very large and soft and groaned under a generous budget of blankets, which had been so expertly tucked in – I imagined a crack team of brawny chambermaids with their teeth gritted – as to be immovable, so that one had to insert oneself like a handkerchief into a breast pocket and resign oneself to be pressed there like a flower until one slithered out again, for there was no give which might allow tossing and turning. Indeed, the only moving part of the whole apparatus – the pillows and bolster tended towards the solid too – was one of those shiny quilts, neither use nor ornament, which slipped off if one so much as breathed. It was hideous, brick-coloured and glistening, but it looked fairly new – clearly not the source of the camphor smell – and so I wondered again why that great heap of the things had been whisked off Aitkens' shop floor to languish unloved alongside the woollen leggings of yesteryear.

The next morning, hotel life seduced me with the lure of a bathroom through a private door, no need to scuttle along the corridor meeting travelling salesmen in their dressing gowns, and since it too was quite amazingly hot and had, apparently, an endless supply of even hotter water, I slopped around for quite half an hour, topping up the water twice, so that it was a quarter to ten when I finally joined Alec in the breakfast room. He did not comment on my frizzed hair and pink glow although I am sure he noticed them.

'Thoroughly recommend the hot dishes,' he said, pointing to the sideboard.

I took a plate and went to peer under the covers. Indeed, the devilled kidneys were plump and glossy, the kedgeree bright gold and heavy with fish, not the salty porridge one always dreads and often finds, and there was a natty little toasting machine into which one could slip triangles of thin bread and out of which, moments later, popped crisp slices of practically melba toast.

'What a waste,' I said, bringing a piece of the toast and a cup of chocolate back to the table. 'If I'd known last night, I'd have hung fire with scrambled eggs and stoked up this morning.'

'You might have lost your appetite anyway,' Alec said. He had opened a Sunday paper and now folded it and showed it to me.

A **CURSE** ON BOTH THEIR HOUSES
DOUBLE **TRAGEDY** FOR MOURNING MERCHANTS

the headline read and below it were two photographs; one of Mirren Aitken, under a banner, smiling, with orchids in her hair, and a suggestion of a dark shoulder to one side where a companion in his dinner jacket had been excised. The other picture was of a serious young man, looking straight into the camera from under a campaign hat with a glimpse of striped neckerchief at his throat. I felt a prickle of unwelcome memory; the last time – the only time – I had seen that face it had been sinking slowly past me on the roof of the lift, blank-eyed and dreadful in death.

'Very clever,' Alec said, tapping both photographs with the tines of his fork. 'She's at a party and this is obviously a scout troop portrait so no one will ever pin down which so-called friend provided them.'

'Pass it over,' I said.

'It's muck,' said Alec, keeping a tight hold.

'I'm not going to read it,' I assured him, 'I just want to look more closely at them.' With some reluctance, Alec handed me the paper. The article began, *Prominent Dunfermline merchants, strangers to scandal, living under a cloak of respectability until now, today we bring shocking news to our readers of . . .* 'Hmph,' I said. 'If they can't even sort out their participles who would take their word on anything?' Then I sipped my cocoa and stared at the two photographs, Dugald first with his large, round, slightly bottom-heavy eyes and shadowed, sallow skin. I thought I could see just a trace of Bella Aitken there, a family resemblance anyway, if one knew the connection and were looking.

'His father – Robin Hepburn, I mean – has snow white hair and a white moustache,' said Alec. 'Pure white before fifty. I wonder if he'd have been suspicious in a few years if Duglad had stayed dark.'

I shook my head. 'There are always so many forebears to blame a child's looks on,' I said. 'It would only have been those who knew, or suddenly saw Dugald and Bella standing together. And even then, one is an elderly lady and the other a boy.' I sighed and turned to the picture of Mirren. Again there was an unpleasant flash of remembering.

'*She* was a lovely little thing,' Alec said. 'Like a flower.'

I had forgotten that he had never seen her before.

'I thought that about her mother the first time I met her,' I said. 'Like a little flower in the rain with its head bowed. But Mirren, to me, is more like a bird.'

'Yes,' said Alec. 'At least it's hard to tell from one photograph but she has a sharper look than Abigail. A bit of Mary in there?'

'Nothing like so sharp as all that!'

'Mind you, we've only seen Abby very cowed,' Alec said. I nodded and started carefully tearing around the picture of Mirren. 'Are you really going to take that and wave it under the Hepburn noses?' he asked me.

'We'll see,' I answered. 'Well, no, of course not. I was only going to wave when I wanted answers. Now we're extracting promises – like gangsters – I don't suppose we'll need it.'

'And do we really need to go round all of them?' Alec said.

I thought for a minute and then shook my head. 'Hilda and Fiona hardly need to have promises extracted. They have secrets of their own to keep. If they even know Mirren's secret – which I doubt, don't you? – they can be trusted with it. But we certainly need to speak to the menfolk and I suppose for the sake of completeness the other grandmother, Dulcie. It might be that no one knows anything anyway. Let's hope so.'

'Shall we start at Roseville, with Robin?' said Alec. I was still staring at Mirren's picture.

'I'll keep this with me,' I said. 'I'll wave it in front of my own eyes if my resolve falters. Look at her, Alec!'

But looking at her turned him so glum that I folded the picture away into my notebook to let him finish his breakfast without feeling like a monster for being able to do so.

Since it was a Sabbath morning between a death and a funeral we knew better than just to roll up and expect to find the master at home. Instead, we rang after breakfast and inquired of the parlourmaid who answered the telephone what time Mr Hepburn would be back after church.

'Mr Hepburn won't be coming here, madam,' said the maid in that refined shriek with which servants mistrustful of the new contraption conduct all telephone conversations. 'He'll be going to number eighty-six.'

'Number eighty-six?' I said.

'High Street,' said the maid. 'The old house. Mistress Dulcie's.'

'Ah, of course,' I said, bluffing. 'Thank you. We'll catch him there.'

'I'm glad we saved ourselves Pilmuir Street anyway,' Alec said, as we puffed up the hill from the hotel. 'The High Street's bad enough after that breakfast.'

'Easily,' I said, panting.

'So where's eighty-six then?' said Alec. We had emerged at the mouth of Guildhall Street and stood looking up and down the quiet stretch of shuttered shops and empty pavements.

'Close by,' I said, nodding at the other side. 'Those are the high seventies.'

'Which way does it go?' said Alec, strolling a little way down towards the tolbooth. 'No, this is wrong. Uphill, Dandy.'

'But can that be right?' I said, trailing after him and looking around myself with some puzzlement. 'It's all shops and we're practically at Aitkens'.'

'Eighty,' said Alec. 'Eighty-two, eighty-four is the bank.' Here he crossed the end of a narrow lane which led away up the hill beyond the High Street. 'So this must be . . . hmph. Eighty-eight.' He stopped, and looked back down the street with his hands on his hips.

'Could there be another High Street?' I said. 'It seems odd that the Hepburn house would be right here in the hurly-burly.' Alec had gone up the narrow lane and now he beckoned to me.

'Here it is,' he said. The number, burnished brass, was attached to an iron gate on the side of the bank building and the same number was painted in gold on the fanlight above an imposing door, just inside.

'A manager's flat?' said Alec.

I walked back around the corner, crossed the road, stopped outside Aitkens' plate-glass window – still bearing only some flowers – and simply stared.

'My God,' I said, looking up at the three floors of house windows above the branch of the British Linen Bank.

'That's spite, surely,' said Alec. 'Or something very peculiar anyway.'

For number eighty-six High Street was directly opposite Aitkens' Emporium and looked across the narrow stretch right into its upper windows.

'Actually,' I said, 'I remember Mary Aitken being most odd – even for her – when I queried her sending a pair of girls off down the street with the deposit. I couldn't imagine what such a blameless institution could have done to upset her so.'

'So Robert and Dulcie Hepburn live right opposite their arch-enemy,' said Alec. 'And in a flat? While Robin and Hilda swan around in Roseville.'

'Well, as to that,' I said, 'I've been in a manager's house above a bank branch once before. Upstairs here might surprise you.'

We recrossed the road, tried the iron gate and, finding it open, entered and pulled on the bright polished handle of the door-bell. A maid with a black cap and a red nose answered and nodded, sniffing, when we said we had come to see Mr Hepburn if he was there. She led us up the stairs, which were exactly as prosperous and substantial as I had expected, easily as broad and shallow as our back stairs at home, and into the upstairs hall which was quite twelve feet square and lit by a cupola, spangles of red and blue scattering down from its panes and dotting the good plain carpet and gleaming mahogany.

We waited in an equally plain but gleaming morning room, I on the edge of my seat although Alec managed to look as though he were not thrumming with nerves at the thought of the coming interview.

Mr Hepburn did not keep us waiting long. He entered the room slowly, looking rather stooped, and closed the door behind him before he turned to us.

'Yes?' he said, looking at Alec and me without recognition. I glanced at Alec, shocked. This was Hilda Hepburn's husband? He looked seventy. Had grief done this to the man?

'Mr Hepburn,' said Alec. 'Excuse us, sir, there has been a mix-up. We were hoping to speak to your son.'

'Robin?' said the old man. I could see now that he was an old man, not just tired and sad, but truly old. Robin Hepburn might well have white hair but this man's hair and his moustache too were thinning, his chin hanging in a wattle and his eyes creased and pouchy behind his pince-nez. It was only because I had expected Robin that I had assumed this was he. 'Robin is at home, young man. And perhaps as well you didn't find him. Today is a very bad day to seek out my son. He has had a dreadful thing just happen to him.'

'We know about Dugald,' I said, and my voice shook from fear of my own temerity. 'It was on that subject we wanted to speak to him.' I swallowed. 'That subject' sounded horribly cold when I heard it. Mr Hepburn Senior frowned but it was with puzzlement, not displeasure. He came over slowly and eased himself into a chair, looking at Alec and me thoughtfully.

'And what's your interest in my grandson's death?' he said.

'We have been trying to puzzle out what happened,' I said. 'There are some things that don't make sense, you see. We've even gone as far as to think, in fact, that Dugald might have been killed. By another person, I mean.' In fact, of course, we no longer thought any such thing, but it had been our opening to every interview and I could not drum up another one on the spot while he sat there looking at me that way.

Unlike Bella, unlike Abigail and most certainly unlike Jack, Mr Hepburn did not start up in violence or moan in agony at my words. He just nodded slowly again and waited for me to continue.

'We understand you were against the match between Dugald and Mirren,' I went on. He frowned very sharply at my words, but surely he did not know that Jack Aitken was Dugald's father as well as Mirren's? Surely such a paterfamilias would not have suffered Hilda for a moment if he knew. So did he know Mirren's secret, whatever it was? Or was it only the bitter rivalry with the Aitkens that had set him against the alliance with them? 'Can you tell us why?' I said.

'On what authority do you ask?' he said. It was a very proper response and delivered calmly.

'Mrs Ninian Aitken wanted us to,' said Alec, and at the mention of her name all the measured calmness was gone.

'Oh, she did, did she?' said the old man with the energy of someone half his age. 'Did she really? Well, you can go and tell her that she's had all the favours out of me she'll ever see in this life or the next.' I stared at him. 'And as to your question: I wouldn't stain my grandson by letting him marry into a family like *that*.'

'Like what?' said Alec and he sounded, as I felt, genuinely lost in the face of such sudden fury.

'Cousin marriage,' said Mr Hepburn, as though the words soiled his tongue. 'Weak blood. Poor stock. Quite apart from anything else, the cousin marriage meant it would never have done.'

'But there *is* something else?' Alec said.

'Of course there is,' barked the old man. 'I would no more let my grandson get mixed up with one of those Aitken floozies than I'd have let him pick up a tart at the docks of Leith.'

'Please, Mr Hepburn sir,' said Alec, protecting my modesty.

'I mean it,' he thundered. 'She was reaching, getting to the shop floor of PTs,' he said. 'But scum rises, and look where she ended up, eh?'

'But you were there too,' I said. 'I thought you all started out in the same place together and rose.'

'I rose by the sweat of my brow,' he said. It was exactly the expression Mary had used, eulogising the departed Ninian and John Aitken. 'Ninian just hung on to his big brother's coat tails, and as for her! All she did was follow her scheming, greedy, grasping nose to wherever the money was. Off with Ninian, off to the new store and then wheedling into his affections until she got in with him. And him supposed to be my friend!'

I was momentarily puzzled; he had not accused Ninian of any breach of friendship as far as I could see. Then suddenly an idea came to me.

'I see,' I said. 'Ninian was your friend and Mary . . .' I wondered if he would say it for me.

'Mary was my girl,' said Mr Hepburn. 'It should have been her and me, and Ninian was going to work for us. It was all my ideas, hers and mine, that she took to Aitkens' and gave to Ninian. It was my ideas that bought her her gold ring and her name. As soon as John Aitken got his hands on the money and opened his store, the pair of them were off.' I nodded. I could believe it even of the Mary Aitken I knew, in her seventies, her place in the world secure. As a young woman, desperate to rise, of course she would have done as Mr Hepburn accused her: following the money, in his brutal and undeniable phrase.

'Believing that Ninian Aitken was my friend was not the first mistake I made in my life nor the last, but it was the one and only time I ever made *that* one, I can tell you.' He sounded very proud. 'I've never made another friend since. I have my wife, my son and my granddaughters.'

'And daughters,' I said, for I felt it most unfair that he maligned the 'weak, bad blood' of a cousin marriage in the Aitken family when he had unfortunate family history of his own. And as for Mary's treachery, he had paid that back ten times over, surely, living here opposite her pride and joy, opening up in competition with her.

'My daughters?' said Mr Hepburn, and he blinked and frowned as though he were trying to recollect who such people might be, as though the knowledge of their existence had to come from a long way off or a great depth down. Slowly his face began to flush with colour in great mottled blotches and he sat forward and fixed me with a stare which it took all my courage to meet. 'What do you know about my daughters?' he said in a low voice, far more frightening than a raised one.

'Nothing,' I said. 'Only that there's weakness on both sides, isn't there?'

'Both sides?' he said, the livid patches spreading and darkening. 'Who the blazes are you to come here and rake up my mistakes? Who told you anyway?'

'Mary,' I said, with a cold fury in my voice which I hoped matched his own. How could he call his daughters 'mistakes' in that heartless way?

'She knows?' he said. 'How did she find out? Well, you tell her from me—' He was so angry now that he choked over the words and when he began speaking again, he made no sense at all. 'Jezebel, harlot, common, wanton slut. All of them. Aitken whores.'

'Mr Hepburn, really!' said Alec, but I was not offended; I was incensed. Fumbling a little, I got my bag open and my notebook out. I held the picture of Mirren out to him.

'How dare you,' I said. 'Look at the girl.' He had fixed his eyes on the picture before he could stop himself. 'An innocent child,' I went on. He was staring at the photograph with some kind of horrified fascination, tears forming in his eyes.

'Foul creature,' he said. 'They're all the same.'

'Yes,' I hissed at him. 'They are. Her mother is a poor, sweet, broken-hearted woman who deserves all our pity. Her grand-mother is nothing worse than a ruthless businesswoman and I daresay if she had joined forces with you you'd have been grateful for the very things you're reviling in her now. Not a single one of them is any of the things you called them, and this child,' – I shook the photograph – 'whatever the history between her family and yours, deserves to be spoken of with respect.'

At last, he had managed to tear his eyes away from the picture. He looked up at me.

'A ruthless businesswoman,' he repeated. 'And much good it did her in the end, eh? Look what she's come to now for all her scrabbling.' His words dripped icily from his mouth and I put a hand out to stop him speaking. He would surely hate himself for it when he heard about poor Mary now. 'Have you seen that so-called library of hers?' he said, with a note of real glee. I wanted to ignore him, but in fact the gleaming honey-coloured library with no books in it had intrigued me. It had puzzled Alec too and it was he who answered.

'What about it?' he said.

'All very fancy and no books,' said Mr Hepburn, and he was laughing to himself at some private joke.

'Beautiful books, actually,' I said. 'Incunabula worthy of a museum.'

'Incu-what?' said Robert Hepburn.

'The illustrated manuscripts,' I said.

'Aye, that's right.' He was smiling again. 'Books with pretty pictures. That would do Mary Lance down to the ground.' He was teasing us and loving every minute of it too. 'She can't read,' he said. 'She can't read or write. Acting like the Queen of Sheba.'

I stared at him. 'Of course, she can,' I said. 'She sent me a postcard.'

'Aye, that'll have taken her a night's work with a pencil,' he said. 'Any mistakes on it?' I couldn't help glancing at Alec. This did explain the mistake in the date on that first postcard. And the second time she communicated with me it was a telegram. And also I thought of Miss Hutton, loyally dealing with the post that way.

'Lady Lawson,' said Mr Hepburn, 'came to us once and she was full of how "wonderful Mary" never just left a note and fobbed her off onto an assistant. How she dealt with her person-ally and kept all her measurements in her head. Aye well, she would, wouldn't she? Keeping her wee secret and passing it off as a favour!' Again I tried to stop the man; he was pitiless and would rue it once he knew.

'Don't say such things,' I said. 'Yesterday, Mary—'

'I know,' he said. 'I heard at the kirk.' Unbelievably he smiled. 'Her sins have found her out.'

'You haven't accused her of any sins,' Alec said. His voice was trembling with fury. 'You've simply spoken of her in the foulest and most unwarranted terms, and gloated over her weaknesses, sounding – if you'll forgive me – like a sore loser.'

'Oh, she sinned,' said Mr Hepburn. 'She sinned all right. She left her husband once when times were hard. Did you know that? She came back to me.' He stopped for a moment, enjoying the effect he had had on us, then his eyes clouded. 'And like a fool I let her. I blamed Ninian for it all and thought he'd turned her head. I took her back, shop-soiled, you might say. Then I met a real lady. A proper, modest, respectable woman and I made her my wife and with her I've enjoyed the kind of decent, honourable life that hussy could only dream of.' He sat back, folded his arms and nodded, smiling with satisfaction at the effect of his words.

'Can I ask you one thing?' I said. 'And then we'll leave you.'

He inclined his head. 'Could you just forget all the old history now? Just say nothing about it to anyone and let it die?'

'I've no interest in any of that family or their doings,' he said – all very lofty and completely untrue; his cheeks were only now returning to their usual hue after his near apoplexy – but I believed that he would say nothing.

'And can *I* ask something?' said Alec. 'Why, in the name of heaven, after all that had passed, did you ever come here to set up your store? Why choose this town of all places?'

Mr Hepburn smiled again. 'To pay her back,' he said, and his voice sent goose bumps down my spine. 'To ruin it all for them.'

'My God,' said Alec. We were downstairs, in the cool darkness of the alley at the side of the bank, leaning back against the wall. 'What an absolute horror of an old man. Wouldn't you hope to be past such passions at his age?'

I nodded, but distasteful as the recent scene had been, something else was troubling me.

'That mix-up is very odd,' I said. 'Did I say *old* Mr Hepburn on the telephone earlier, Alec? Why would the maid at Roseville think "Mr Hepburn" meant the grandfather rather than her own master?'

Alec shrugged. 'It was lucky she did,' he said. 'We've added another big chunk to the story of the great feud, haven't we?'

'I suppose so,' I said. 'And I can quite believe there was enough bitterness to explain why Robert and Mary didn't want an alliance between their grandchildren. I think the cousin marriage and the unfortunate sisters are just a nasty red herring, don't you? An excuse for each lot to sneer at the others.'

'God, if he knew that Jack Aitken had cuckolded his son!' said Alec. 'If he knew that Dugald had Aitken blood in him, he would . . .'

'Explode,' I said. 'Burst with fury and ruin all those good Turkey carpets. He went absolutely purple at one point up there.'

Alec gave a short laugh. 'I haven't seen that since my brother was small. He had a talent for tantrums that had to be seen to be believed.' He laughed again. 'And my colouring. He used to go so black in the face that his freckles looked yellow. Very unnerving.'

'Which brother was that?'

'Ed,' said Alec, and the abruptness of that one syllable told me not to say any more. I tried not to mind how much more he had said to Abigail in the hospital yesterday than he ever had to me in the five years I had known him, but instead turned my mind back to the case again.

'I wish I knew *why* the mix-up was bothering me,' I said. 'This feeling is usually a sign that I've forgotten something. Is it bothering you too?'

Alec only shrugged again. 'Roseville now?' he said. 'Get to work on Robin? I'd like to be able to go back to Mary and tell her that the Hepburns, to a man, either don't know or have their lips buttoned.'

'On whatever it is,' I said. 'The thing Abby told her mother yesterday can't have anything to do with Mary and Robert's ancient history.'

'Yes, it's very frustrating, isn't it, to keep uncovering secrets and yet be sure that none of them is the secret we're after. The one at the bottom of it all. Oh, let's at least get out of here, Dandy. Let's go.'

When the door of Roseville opened on us twenty minutes later it was not a servant who stood silhouetted against the light there, but an old woman dressed in black who peered up at us and cleared her throat with a fussy little sound. Without understanding why, I found myself clutching Alec's arm, my heart suddenly hammering. Then in a moment the odd panic passed as she moved forward into the light of day.

She was a very small woman, neat and precise in her movements, and she fixed us with a bright, shrewd gaze that made me think of a robin, her head slightly on one side and the effect completed by a pronounced cupid's bow in her mouth, so pronounced that when it was pursed, as it was now, it really did look like a beak, like the beak of a budgerigar or perhaps a canary.

'Who are you?' I said. Alec glanced at me, puzzled by my tone.

'I beg your pardon?' she said, rather clipped but not angry. 'Can I ask the same of you? I'm afraid this isn't a good day for visiting.'

'Mrs Hepburn?' I said, guessing. 'We're not visiting, exactly. We've just been to see your husband.' Her head inclined even more to one side as she heard this and her bright eye glinted. 'I'm Mrs Gilver and this is Mr Osborne. I wonder if we might have a word with you.'

'Ah, the detectives,' she said. 'I heard about you. Come away in, then.' She swept the door wide and we entered the hallway.

'Please accept our condolences,' I said.

Little Dulcie Hepburn nodded her head thoughtfully and her eyes brightened further as tears sprang into them.

'It's a sad finish,' she said, 'the two of them so young. They'd have got over it as well – that's the worst thing. Nothing hurts more than first love, but live as long as me and you'll surprise yourself what you can get over.'

'You're quite sure that it was suicide then?' said Alec. 'In both cases?' His voice was low but Mrs Hepburn still shushed him.

'Of course,' she said. 'Of course it was.' Then she looked at Alec with a new, wary expression. 'But why is it you need to see me?'

'Mary Aitken sent us,' Alec said and I did not miss the quick puckering frown that hearing the name caused.

'She thinks you know something,' I went on, 'and she wants you to keep it—'

Again she shushed, peering at the doors around the hallway and up the stairs, her head making little pecking movements as she checked the corners and shadows.

'Not here,' she said, 'but I will talk to you.' She stepped very lightly across the floor and poked her head around a door, then, finding the room empty, she beckoned us and closed the door very softly behind us with one careful hand on the plate, shutting us all in.

It was another room very like the first I had seen at Roseville, with satiny little settees and gilt and white chairs and writing tables. Dulcie Hepburn rubbed the arm of her chair as she sat down and she smiled.

'Fiona has a right way with a room,' she said. 'But it would never do Bob and me.' She looked up at us again. 'Now,' she said. 'No one will disturb us here. Bob would like burst in to see what was to do if I closed a door on him in his own house. He's not a trusting man. Not easy in his own mind and it makes him restless. He always has to know what's to do.'

'We don't want to pry, Mrs Hepburn,' I said. 'I just want to be able to assure Mary—'

'Poor Mary,' said Dulcie. 'She was more sinned against than sinning, if you ask me. And if I can say it I don't see who in the world should disagree.'

'We know about her affair with your husband,' I told her gently.

'I don't begrudge my husband any comforts,' she said, and a swift look of pain flitted across her face and disappeared again. 'We've not had our troubles to seek and he's been very good to me. Stood by me and we have our son and our grandchildren. Still got our granddaughters even with Dougie gone. You can tell Mary Aitken her secret's safe with me.'

'I don't think she meant that secret,' I said.

'No, I'm sure she didn't,' said Mrs Hepburn and she gave a small, knowing smile. I could not help myself. In fact, I did not even try.

'I wish you would talk a little less obliquely, Mrs Hepburn,' I said. 'More straightforwardly. Tell us what the secret is.' She only smiled again.

'Aye, you say you're not prying,' she said, 'but I'll bet you'd like to know.'

'We might have to insist,' I went on. 'There's something not right here. Something I just can't put my finger on. And when that happens, I can't rest until I've straightened the whole thing out. Or until I hand it over to the police and they do. So if you won't tell us what it is we might have to turn to the police to carry on the interview.'

'The police?' said Dulcie. 'Away! You can't go to the police.

You know you can't, Mrs Gilver. Especially not when Mary's begging you to make sure things stay "under wraps". Now can you? Besides,' she said, and once again she rubbed her sleeve on the gilt arm of her chair making it shine, 'it's not a police matter.' She sniffed. 'See my good oak and mahogany isn't as fancy as this here, but it takes a better polishing. Or maybe just gets it. Fiona and Hilda are more caring about flowers changed every day than the likes of dusting. Do you know Fiona's maid has a wee comb to comb out the cushion tassels? Did you ever hear of such a thing?'

'What's not a police matter?' I said, hardening my heart. Perhaps Alec was right about this case toughening me.

'Very well,' said Dulcie. 'On the understanding of your complete discretion?' Alec and I nodded. 'You'll have heard about my daughters?' she said. She twinkled at Alec and me as we nodded again. 'My girls. They were bonny happy babies, but as soft as rag dolls and we'd to feed them milk off a spoon they were so weak. Notice I call them *my* girls. Robin is our son, but the girls are mine.' She gave a pretty, chirping little laugh at the looks on our faces. 'I don't mean what you think,' she said. 'Dear me, no. I call them mine because I know whatever it is that ails them came through me. And how do I know that?' She gave us that bright, robin-like look again and waited. Something was shifting deep inside my mind and perhaps I would have got there in the end, but she told us before all the pieces were joined together.

'I know that because Mary had Abigail and Abigail was a fine girl and is a fine woman still.'

I could not help a little gasp escaping me.

'Abigail is your husband's child?'

'She tricked him,' Dulcie said. 'Desperate for a baby, she was. She said she loved him, said she had made a mistake going off with Ninian Aitken that way.'

'Your husband implied that his affair with Mary was before he met you,' said Alec.

'My husband is good at that sort of thing,' said Dulcie. 'No, we were years wed when Mary snapped her fingers and got him

234

sitting up begging again. We had our girls already. Not that she knew that, I daresay.'

'She didn't,' I said, remembering this. 'She said she found out about them when she was lying in for her confinement. I wondered why it had incensed her so.'

'And so you see the problem with the two bairns,' said Dulcie. 'Mirren was Dougie's cousin and with such weak blood in the family, that marriage could never be, no matter how much they loved each other. And if it had ever come out why we banned it, we'd have been the scandal of the decade, wouldn't we? Poor Mary, me and my girls.'

'I suppose so,' I said slowly. Dulcie Hepburn did not know the worst of it. Dugald and Mirren were not cousins at all. Through Jack Aitken, they were brother and sister. The trouble with their marriage was nothing to do with Dulcie and her poor girls. What I could not decide was whether to tell her. No more could I decide whether anything about Mary and Robert's old affair could possibly be what Abby had suddenly revealed to her mother yesterday.

'You don't think so?' said Dulcie. 'You think we should have let them marry?' I could not help a shudder at the thought and Dulcie nodded, almost triumphantly. 'You do agree,' she said. 'I know it was the right thing to do. I knew in my heart and someone I trust completely told me so too.'

'Oh? Who was that?' said Alec.

'My milliner,' said Dulcie. 'Margaret-Ann for Hats. You'll have seen her shop in Bridge Street. Well, she does the special work at House of Hepburn too. And at Aitkens'.'

'Aitkens' and Hepburns' share a milliner?' I said. 'That's surprising.'

'Oh, she's an artist with hats,' said Dulcie. 'We wouldn't give her up and neither would they. She's a treasure and a friend. She knows about Robert and Mary, about Abigail being Robert's child, and when I told her about Dougie asking to marry Mirren she grabbed my hands in hers and shook them. I'll never forget it, for it wasn't like her to be so fierce. She grabbed me and shook me and said: It can't happen, Dulcie-bella – that's what she calls me – promise me you won't let them.'

'She sounds like a gypsy fortune-teller,' I said, thinking that somehow Margaret-Ann for Hats must know about Jack Aitken being the father of both children. That grabbing and shaking was not over the prospect of cousin marrying cousin, I was sure. And I still failed to see how Abigail could announce her own parentage to her own mother and shock her mother into collapsing by doing so.

We left Dulcie then, thanking her for her candour and promising to convey her good wishes to Mary.

'Which of course we shall not,' said Alec, once we were out of the house. 'She'd choke on them.'

'You sound rather fierce, darling,' I said. 'I rather took to little Dulcie. Brave in her own way and, as she said herself, she hasn't had her troubles to seek.'

'Hm,' said Alec. 'I can't get rid of the idea that she was laughing at us, just a little. For instance, when she said she knew we couldn't go to the police. She was twinkling away like anything. What was that about, Dandy?'

'She saw through my bluster,' I said. 'She knew I didn't mean it. Because of Mary.'

'But she said *especially* given Mary. *Especially*, do you see?'

'Not really,' I said. 'And speaking of Mary, shall we go and see how she is? We can tell her Fiona, Hilda, Robert and Dulcie are ticked off the list. That should give her some peace of mind.'

'If we wait until after Robin that's the whole boiling,' Alec said.

'But Robin can't possibly know anything,' I said. 'He's hardly going to know about his father's infidelity, and he certainly doesn't know about his wife's.'

'But are either of those two matters the thing Mary is desperate to keep secret? And he knows something. I told you about the way he galloped off to the telephone to make sure Dugald hadn't run off with Mirren. He was all of a twitter when he got back again.'

'All right then,' I said. 'But after lunch. And let's find somewhere other than St Margaver's Hotel to have it. And then pick up Bunty. She can't stay with the Aitkens for ever.'

Bunty, however, was lying on a folded blanket in front of the range in the Abbey Park kitchen and showed no signs of wanting to shift from it. When she rolled onto her back and waggled herself in greeting I saw that her stomach was as round as a beach ball.

'What have you been feeding her?' I asked of the cook who was smiling fondly down and now kicked off her clog and rubbed her stockinged toe up and down Bunty's breastbone.

'Oh, she's just had a wee bite of chicken and rice,' said the cook. 'And some broken meringue.'

'Lucky Bunty,' said Alec, with feeling. He and I had made do with sandwiches cut from very tough, day-old bread (it was Sunday, I suppose) and filled with bright orange cheese and thick slices of Spanish onion, washed down with bottled coffee.

'And how is Mrs Ninian today?' I asked the cook. 'Has there been news from the infirmary?'

'Mrs John said she slept right through and when she woke up this morning she wasn't so dribbly,' the cook said. It was to the point, if rather indelicate as bulletins go. 'Mrs John had stayed all night, madam. She only come home when Mrs Jack went in after breakfast to relieve her.'

'A good sister-in-law indeed,' I said.

'This last day or two,' said the cook, and a kitchenmaid engaged with pastry at the work-table murmured her agreement. 'I never knew how fond Mrs John was of Mrs Ninian before now.'

'Never knew how fond we all were,' said the kitchenmaid. 'Not that— I mean to say—'

'Wheesht your cheeky tongue, Elizabeth Rose!' said the cook.

'Oh my,' the maid said, quite unaffected. 'I get Lizzie usually, you know. It's only the full whack o' Elizabeth Rose when some-body's angry.'

The cook tutted good-naturedly and smiled.

'It'll come in handy if you ever start a little teashop,' I said. 'Like Margaret-Ann for Hats. We've just been talking about her.'

The kitchenmaid snorted and the cook tittered with one hand over her mouth.

'Well, you know why that is, don't you?' she said. 'Her right name's Mrs Smellie and nobody would buy a fancy new hat from that.'

'Smellie as in Inspector Smellie?' said Alec. He was staring at me and I was staring back at him.

'That's her husband,' said the kitchenmaid. 'He's a big man at the tolbooth but it's Maggie that's in charge when he gets home. Or so they say.'

'And he tells her everything,' said the cook. 'Confidential police business or no. I know that for a fact because she – well, she let my friend Nannie off with a big bill when Nannie's man was up to his neck in bad debts and in a load of bother with pawning stuff he shouldn't have, and the only way she knew was the inspector telling her. But she's a good woman. Knows it all and says nothing.'

Alec and I had risen, he shrugging himself back into his overcoat and I pulling on my gloves.

'If you really don't mind the dog trespassing on your hospitality a little longer then,' I said, making for the door with as much casual ease as I could muster. Alec was on my heels.

'Not a bit of it,' said the cook. 'I like a dog about the place, me.'

She was still saying goodbye when the servants' door banged shut behind us.

'At last!' Alec said. 'Whatever Margaret-Ann knows is what the inspector knows. The thing that made the inspector believe in murder, in the teeth of all the evidence. I *told* you Dulcie was laughing at us.'

'What do you mean?'

'You threatened her with the police and she said, "Oh, come now, Mrs Gilver, you can't go to the police, can you?" She knows about Hugh. Inspector Smellie told his wife and she told Dulcie. He tells her everything. He certainly told her something that made her go off like a rocket at the thought of Dugald and Mirren marrying, didn't he?'

'And it's not something we've heard already, is it?' I said, with a sickly feeling spreading through me.

'As dreadful as the things we've heard already are,' said Alec. 'I'm very much afraid not, no.'

12

'I think we're out of luck,' said Alec. Our sprinted exit from the Abbey Park kitchen the previous day had of course led to the scuffing of feet and clearing of throats, because Sunday is not a day for shopping and we could hardly beard her at home, where the fierce inspector would be ensconced in his carpet slippers, so here we were at ten o'clock on the following morning, Alec cupping his hands around his eyes and peering in through the window of Margaret-Ann for Hats, his breath fogging a growing ring on the glass, and both of us losing heart since the blind was drawn down on the door and the shop was in darkness. I squinted at a card propped up on a miniature gilt easel which set out the opening hours in copperplate script so decorative as to be almost illegible.

'We are,' I said. 'She's not open on a Monday. Not open until tomorrow afternoon.' I put my hands on my hips and puffed out a sigh of annoyance. Just then the bell of the newsagent's shop next door pealed as a man in a brown apron stuck his head out.

'If ye're after Maggie Smellie,' he said, effortlessly sweeping away all the sophistication of the copperplate script, the smart bottle-green and tawny paintwork and the artful swathes of chiffon hiding the interior from view, 'she does her stint at Hepburn's on a Monday. Ye'll catch her there.'

I was glad in a way, although a quiet word would have been easier managed in a quiet shop than in the bustle of a department store, but it was Monday morning after all and Monday-morning bustle tends more towards the butcher and greengrocer surely than towards purveyors of elegant hats. The truth was that I had been longing for an excuse to enter the House of Hepburn and see for myself the results of Old Bob's great spiteful retort to Mary Aitken, see for myself what Fiona and Hilda Haddo, who had filled their home with spindly gilded furniture and had tassel combs for their cushions, might have made of three floors of glass cases and mannequins, see for myself what other wonders there might be in a place where one could perhaps find mauve *mousquetaires*.

I was not disappointed: where Aitkens' was all dark oak and flannel sheets, Hepburns' was like an enormous boudoir, like the inside of a jewellery box, and it made me half-want to twirl with delight like the clockwork ballerina. The floors were pale – they must take a lot of washing, I thought, before I caught myself and banished such dreary practicality – and as for the counters, there were not many to be had. The perfumery, where we found ourselves upon entering, was set up instead with numerous little tables dotted around, white or dove-grey wrought-iron affairs such as one would find on a hotel balcony on the Mediterranean, and there were bottles of scent and tins of powder arranged on these tables and the assistants, dressed in pale lilac and more of the dove grey, simply drifted around amongst the customers, like hostesses at a cocktail party.

I scanned the far edges of the room and saw fountains of silk scarves and the glitter of costume jewels but not a single hat stand anywhere, so I beckoned to a nearby drifting sales assistant and asked her for directions.

'I'm not sure whether it's ready-to-wear or bespoke millinery we're after,' I began.

'We don't make a difference, madam,' said the girl. 'Millinery is on the first floor because we here at House of Hepburn value every lady just the same and we give our every lady the same devoted attention whether she is shopping for a bridal gown or a handkerchief-case. It's the House of Hepburn way, madam.'

And designed, I thought, to lure every woman of taste and fashion away from Aitkens' for ever.

'Right, well then,' said Alec. 'I'm certainly not going to penetrate the upper regions with you, Dandy. I'll go and skulk about in the Gents' Department and meet you afterwards.'

'Oh no, sir, sorry, sir,' said the assistant, who seemed well schooled, not to say indoctrinated. 'We don't have a Gents' Department, I'm afraid. We have Toys and Gifts in the basement if you have any, um . . .' – she gave him a swift once-over – 'nephews or godchildren with birthdays coming.'

'I'm allowed to wait in the cellars?' said Alec. 'Very well.' His mouth was rather tight as he smiled. I have often noticed how gentlemen who sense no danger of their own sex being overindulged by the existence of the many exclusive spike bars, pavilions and clubhouses in the sporting world, supper and pudding clubs at our universities and billiards rooms, libraries, gun rooms, estate offices and smoking rooms in our very *houses*, for goodness' sake, can suddenly get that lemon-sucking look if they ever encounter a ladies' carriage on a train or, as here, a few square yards of scarves and bracelets undiluted by cufflinks for a change.

'Or there's the café, on second,' the girl said. 'Gentlemen are perfectly welcome to wait there.' She gave a smile, blithely ignorant of the offence she had caused him, and turned, with a swish of her bias-cut lilac panels, and drifted away again.

'Coffee it is then,' said Alec. 'I'll see you up there when you're done.'

I tore myself away from the perfumery and scarves and padded up the broad staircase (it was carpeted – *carpeted*!) to the first floor. Here, although there was no scent for sale, the enveloping fragrance went on and I saw one of the assistants puffing clouds of it out of a scent spray into the air. She was dressed in a very pale eau-de-nil as all the girls were, no more dove grey and lilac, and I was enchanted to see that the tape measures some of them wore around their necks were that colour too. How was that possible? Had they dyed them? Even the pins, the very pins, had bobbles on the ends like little pale green pearls. Altogether, I thought that if the gowns were anything like as soigné as the fittings I should really send Grant down here for a treat one day.

I squinted around again looking for hat stands. There was one curtained archway clearly leading into a bridal gown salon, for boughs of orange blossom were hung around the entrance, with a great cluster of gilded horseshoes and slippers as a centrepiece. Another arch promised a lingerie salon, and in the most provocative way: by means of a mannequin halfway through the entrance dressed in a satin nightgown and trailing a matching satin and lace wrap – I supposed one might call it a negligee if one could bring oneself to – along the floor behind her. I turned around to look in the other direction, towards the front of the store, and gave a happy sigh.

The gowns – there were no frocks here – were simply blissful. I supposed Hepburns' had to sell some coat and skirt suits, some jerseys and warm coats, might even be able to provide one with fair isle and corduroy for bicycling, but on the shop floor, draped over the impossible mannequins – all six feet tall and with figures like pythons – the gowns were silk, lace, a little silk velvet here and there but only with lots of satin ribbon and only in sugared-almond colours, a great deal of chiffon, and some very daring cloth of gold, almost backless and, when one imagined it on a woman not six feet tall, pretty nearly frontless too.

'We have it in tinsel as well as the pongee, madam,' said a voice beside me as I stood staring.

'I beg your pardon?'

'Tinsel, madam. Cloth-of-silver. With madam's olive complexion, a tinsel would be much more dashing.'

No one had ever called my complexion olive before, It had been dubbed sallow by my mother and been sallow ever since except that an artist friend had once referred – not kindly, in my opinion – to its green tones, and Grant has a quelling habit of holding up prospective frocks under my chin and then whisking them away again saying: 'Beige'.

'Dashing,' I echoed, wondering if I had ever attempted to look dashing in my life.

'Does madam have any emeralds?' said the girl. I nodded 'And emerald eye-paint?' I shook my head, trying not to look too startled. 'We carry it downstairs in the perfumery,' she went on. 'So long as madam isn't against the notion of a good dark lipstick,

243

tinsel, emeralds and matching eye-paint with a peacock-feather headdress would be most becoming.'

I could feel myself physically swaying towards the mannequin, entranced by the mental vision of this silver and peacock-green creature, this dashing stranger I could apparently so easily become, and then I shook myself and asked the girl to direct me to Millinery.

'Just past tea-gowns on the left, madam,' she said. 'Then round the corner opposite our new cocktail range. You can't miss it.' Tea, cocktails and evening gowns: did none of Hepburns' customers ever get up in the morning? Did they have breakfast and luncheon in bed in one of those satin negligees and only descend at half past three in florals?

'And I'll look out a model in silver for madam meantime,' the girl said. 'If we have one in a small enough size.' I wish I could report that I rolled my eyes and tutted at the 'small enough size' for it was a ploy of no great subtlety and I was old enough not to be reeled in that way, but I must admit I felt a burst of pleasure and bestowed a flattered smile.

'So . . . these are ready-to-wear?' I said. Taking one home in a box tonight might prove irresistible.

'No, madam,' said the girl. 'Not this particular style, but House of Hepburn likes to keep some trying-on models if we can. It's more fun trying-on than just looking.'

I nodded as I walked away; this whole place was like a glorified playroom, I thought, dressing-up box and Wendy house combined; no wonder poor Aitkens' had to do what it could with sensible tweeds. For a moment I pitied Mirren as a child, playing at shops in the Emporium instead of here, and then, remembering why I had come, I hurried my pace, ignoring the floral tea-gowns and the fringed and sequined cocktail range, and rounding the corner with earnest purpose back at the helm.

The Millinery Department took the whole escapade one stage further into the realms of fantasy: it was pink. The floor was carpeted in pink, the little chairs in front of the looking-glasses were cushioned in pink and unless I was greatly mistaken the bulbs around these looking-glasses cast a decidedly pinkish light too. I was reminded of a Fragonard – or do I mean a Boucher? – well, of tumbling cherubs on blush-coloured clouds, and I slightly began to lose patience with the Hepburn way. What woman wouldn't look better by the light of pink electric bulbs? And what woman would not regret the hat she had bought by the light of these bulbs when she got it home and saw it in her own bedroom? Except that probably they sell the pink light bulbs somewhere too, I thought, beside the green eye-paint probably.

From a back room a tall and willowy woman in her middle years emerged, carrying a lavender and grey straw hat, ribbons trailing.

'I do apologise, madam,' she said. 'I didn't hear you arriving. How can I help?' She set the lavender and grey hat down upon the nearest pink velvet hat stand and smiled at me. She was the right sort of age and despite the searing refinement of her vowels I thought she was probably the right level of social standing to be a policeman's wife but I could not imagine this wand-like creature with her silver shingle and her long tapering fingers going home and mashing turnips for the inspector's tea. She gestured me to sit down on one of the little pink chairs set before a glass, with hand mirrors and hairbrushes laid out. It made me think of mermaids.

'Mrs . . .' I stopped myself. Hepburns' pink powder-puff of a Millinery Department should not be tarnished by the uttering of such a name. The shock might blow a bulb. 'Are you the milliner?' I substituted. 'Margaret-Ann for Hats?'

'I am, madam,' she said, bridling a little with pleasure to think that her fame had gone before her. 'How can I help you?'

'Mrs Hepburn recommended that I come to you,' I said. 'Mrs Hepburn Senior. Dulcie.' The woman's eyes clouded and she caught her lip in her teeth, nodding. 'And so I'm glad I've caught you today,' I said. 'Here, I mean. At House of Hepburn. You are the milliner at Aitkens' too, I believe?'

'There's a place in this world for spinach as well as ice-cream,' she said, with an unexpectedly wicked grin. 'There comes a time when we all have to get our hats from Aitkens', madam, when our Hepburn days are gone. But you're a long way from there yet. What can I show you this morning?'

'Well, mourning,' I said, spreading my hands. 'Do you carry mourning hats?'

'I do,' said the milliner. 'Lord knows, Aitkens' does and I'm trying to see what I can put together for House of Hepburn this very morning.' She gestured to the lavender and grey. 'This had red ribbons and silk poppies on it half an hour ago. But if it's black you're looking for, madam, you'd better go up the road. Is it a close bereavement?'

'Dugald,' I said. 'Something for his funeral.'

Mrs Smellie's eyes dimmed and she shook her head.

'You'll be fine in the lilac then,' she said. 'Mrs Haddo and young Mrs Hepburn themselves won't be in black. Pearl grey for the one and burgundy with ivory touches for the other.'

'And Dulcie?'

'Black, I'm sure, madam, but she's used to their ways. This place is all Mrs Haddo and her daughter, you know.' She looked around and sniffed. 'It'll give young Mrs Hepburn an interest. Help her get back on her feet, come the time, I daresay.'

'Very sad,' I said, agreeing. I could not quite see how I was going to propel this interview forward in a useful way. I took another nibble at the edge of it. 'Very sad for you to be busy with pearl grey and burgundy when you were expecting a wedding.'

'I wasn—' She bit her lip again. 'Indeed, madam.'

'You weren't?' I said, correctly interpreting what she had just managed not to utter. To my surprise, the woman sank down onto another of the pink chairs and put her hand, which was shaking, to her temple, rubbing the skin there in circles. I could not possibly just dive in, I told myself. This woman was the horrid inspector's wife. If she told him I had been here pestering her he would be after Hugh with leg irons before sundown. On the other hand, she knew something, was bursting with it while it gnawed away at her like a migraine.

'My dear,' I said to her, 'tell me what's wrong. Dulcie has, you know. Dulcie has told me everything.' She looked up, ragged and weary.

'She can't have,' she said. 'Dulcie doesn't know. Oh, she knows about Bob and Mary all right. She knew they were sweethearts years ago and she knows about when they took up again for that wee while. She told me that much and I'm guessing that's what she told you too.' Then she started rubbing her temples again, not looking at me as she went on. 'Yes, Dulcie knew that Mary and Robert's wee fling resulted in Abigail. That's why she thinks Mirren and Dugald were cousins.'

'*Thinks*?' I said. 'So you know different. You know about Jack and Hilda.'

Her hand froze and she looked up at me. 'Jack?'

'Aitken,' I said. 'I know too.'

'What about Jack Aitken?'

'He fathered Dugald,' I said. 'Isn't that what you know? That Dugald and Mirren were siblings?'

Mrs Smellie was staring hard at me now, her face growing pale.

'Dugald's father was Jack Aitken?' she said. 'So they weren't brother and sister after all?'

'I don't understand,' I said. 'They were. They were both Jack Aitken's children.' I frowned at her. 'If you didn't know about Jack and Hilda then why weren't you looking forward to the wedding?'

'I thought Dugald was Robin's child,' she said. 'And so there would never have been a wedding. I would have had to stop it. Or I'd have got my husband to stop it anyway. Quietly, I mean. Not standing up in the kirk and objecting. My husband is a policeman, you see.'

'How could it have been a police matter?' I said. She only shook her head as if she could not begin to explain what kind of matter it might be. 'I heard,' I said, very carefully, 'that the police knew something. Something that made them suspect the children were murdered. I couldn't begin to imagine what it might be.'

'It's not "the police",' said Mrs Smellie. 'It's just my husband. I told him what I worked out, you see.'

'Worked out,' I repeated. My thoughts went skittering over all the ground I had trod in the last two weeks. What could she have worked out that I had missed?

'I've got to tell someone,' she said. 'If you promise not to breathe a word to another soul. My husband won't let me talk about it. He's forbidden it even between the two of us. But if I don't say something I'll burst. My head is pounding with it. Can I trust you?' I nodded, not daring to breathe.

'I'm a good milliner,' she said. I blinked. 'I don't just make hats and decorate them. I study my ladies, madam. I get to know their heads, their faces, the turn of their neck, the line of their jaw, the way their hair grows up from the nape or over the ears, how high the forehead, how much space they need in the crown for a heavy head of long hair, whether a close brim will lift their cheekbones or press them down into jowls, what way to curl a brim to follow the line of their brow instead of clashing with it.' She was tracing imaginary shapes in the air as she spoke and I was mesmerised by her long white fingers fluttering. Then she stopped and let her hands fall into her lap. She looked at me. 'Can you guess?' I shook my head 'I started my apprenticeship at fourteen and I'm forty-seven now. I've made bridal-party hats for great-grandmother, grandmother, mother, aunts, bride, brides-maids and little flower girls, but I've never seen as close a match – the head, jaw, setting of the ears, hairline at the brow and the nape, the tilt of the neck, everything . . . as Dulcie and Mirren. Never.'

I stared at her for a moment in silence. And then I remembered something.

'Yes,' I said. 'Yesterday. Dulcie came out of the shadows and I thought for a minute I'd seen a ghost. Soft hair and that little face like a bird.'

'All of that too,' said Mrs Smellie. 'I wondered why no one else ever saw it, but then no one ever saw them together, not with the feud.'

'So . . .' I said. 'Well, it had to happen at least once, that someone took strongly after their real forebears instead of conveniently after their official family members.'

'You're not thinking straight, madam,' said Mrs Smellie. 'To speak in that easy way.'

I frowned. 'You mean that because Mirren took after her grand-mother everyone would guess about Mary and Bob?' I was being particularly dense, failing to see what she had just shown me.

'Think, madam,' she said. 'Think it through. How could Mirren Aitken look like Dulcie Hepburn? There's only one way.'

All of a sudden I saw it.

'Of course,' I said. 'Robin was her father.' Mrs Smellie nodded. 'But that means . . .' I said. 'That means Dugald and Mirren were no relation to one another at all! Dugald was the child of Jack and Hilda and Mirren was the child of Abby and Robin.' A vague feeling of unease brushed past me as I said this, but I ignored it. 'They could have married after all. They weren't related and Mirren wasn't even the child of two cousins!'

'No, she wasn't,' said Margaret-Ann. 'There's no word for what Mirren was. And she was no relation to Dugald, it's true. But would he have wanted to marry her if he'd known? Would anyone? Think about it, madam. You haven't seen the whole picture yet even though it's right there in front of you.'

I frowned at her and then it fell into my mind like a great cold boulder. All the strings uncoiled and straightened in my mind and on their ends bloomed the most disgusting little flourishes, like toadstools.

'The thing they were all so scared would happen if Dugald married Mirren,' I said. 'What Jack and Hilda thought it would be. Brother and . . . What Abby and Robin thought it would be. Brother and sister. It had happened already. That's how Mirren came to be.'

Margaret-Ann nodded again and at last a little of the dazed, pained look cleared from her eyes. I imagine that it set up home instead in mine. I put my hand over my mouth. 'And that's why your husband thought someone might kill her?'

249

'Put her away like a pup that's come out wrong,' said Mrs Smellie and her turn of phrase made my stomach lurch.

'And then even if Dugald was killed for revenge, both families might just keep quiet for ever?' Mrs Smellie was still nodding

'So the thing that Abigail told her mother was that she had an affair with Robin,' I said. 'And it almost killed Mary.'

'Well, it would,' said Mrs Smellie. 'But tell me this, madam: do you think Miss Abigail knows who her father is?'

I shook my head. 'No,' I said. 'Definitely not. She thought she was helping Mary when she told her about Robin yesterday.'

'What a mess,' said Margaret-Ann, almost groaning.

'I hope getting it off your chest will bring you some comfort,' I said. I noticed that despite the pink light bulb my face in the glass, and hers too, was rather grey. 'And you know the inspector was right in a way. It *is* perhaps best that Mirren at least is beyond the suffering that the knowledge must have brought to her. Oh, the poor child! I could never imagine what would make someone turn to suicide but I can see how she might not be able to *bear* herself once she knew.'

'The inspector?' said Mrs Smellie. I blinked at her. 'I never mentioned my husband's rank, madam.'

'I think you did, you know,' I replied.

'I know I didn't,' she said. 'I never do. Because my sister is married to an inspector. She always gets it in somewhere and it always grates on me.'

'Well then, I can't account for it,' I said. I stood and pushed the little pink chair tidily in under the looking-glass table. 'A lucky guess? Or maybe Dulcie said so. Yes, that's it. Dulcie told me.' A faint ghost of that mischievous grin was back on Mrs Smellie's face although her complexion was still waxy.

'Mrs Gilver?' she said. I froze. 'Oh!' she exclaimed. 'I was so angry with George when he told me what he had done to you. I didn't scold him because he had a steak clapped to his face and he couldn't answer me back, but for two pins I'd have socked him one on the other side and balanced it out for him.' I let my breath go in a huge rush.

'You were angry with *your* husband?' I said. 'Not mine? Not me?'

'Certainly not you, Mrs Gilver,' she said. 'My gracious heavens, if we all had to take the blame for what our husbands do! And as for Mr Gilver – he was sticking up for you; he sounds a fine man if you don't mind me saying. Besides,' she dropped her voice, 'policemen can get too used to tramping about in their size elevens telling everybody else what's what and how come. Don't you think so?'

'I wouldn't like to say, Mrs Smellie,' I said.

'Smiley,' she said, rolling her eyes. 'He's the stubborn one, madam, not me.'

Alec was tucked up in a club armchair in what I perceived to be the gentlemen's corner of Hepburns' tearoom. Most of its area was covered with more of the little Continental-looking tables and chairs where pairs of ladies perched and nibbled at pastries, but in one corner, furthest away from the doorway into the hair-dressing salon (from which unmistakable traces of Marcelling lotion were emanating to mingle with the aroma of good fresh coffee and warm buns), there was an oasis of armchairs, where daily newspapers were folded on the tables and where husbands and chauffeurs might wait in relative masculinity.

I waved to Alec and beckoned him to join me at a wrought-iron perch, rather an out-of-the-way one where I might speak freely.

'Well?' he said. 'Mystery solved?' I nodded. 'Coffee? Cake?'

I shook my head. 'You'll wish you hadn't had any either when I tell you.' He raised one eyebrow and sat back with his arms folded to hear the tale. Now, I know Alec thinks I veer too much towards the dramatic for no reason, so I should really have tried to make sure he braced himself for what was coming. As it was, his face drained and he gulped and one of the waitresses – Hepburns' staff were really quite stupendously attentive – came over to ask if he felt quite well and did he perhaps require a drink of water or a taxi. He accepted the offer of water with grateful thanks.

251

'No wonder Mary went off like a rocket years ago when she returned home to find things so chummy with the young Hepburns and Aitkens,' he said.

I shook my head; it was so awful that one almost had to laugh: almost.

'But what she didn't see and what Robert Hepburn didn't see either was that they made the other family forbidden fruit with their stupid feud. Jack and Hilda got an extra frisson from trysting with one another, and in Aitkens' too. Robin probably thought he was being very daring with Abigail.'

'And what was Abby up to?'

'Following her mother's hints,' I said. 'Finding an obliging lover so that she could carry on the Aitken name, even if not the bloodline.'

'Well, Abby doesn't have any Aitken blood, does she?' Alec said. 'No wonder Mary wasn't worried about her marrying her so-called cousin Jack.' He blew out hard. 'And so the secret of Mirren's parentage was what Abby told Mary yesterday.'

'And for all Mary knew, Mirren might have told Dugald and so Mary couldn't rest until she found out if any of the surviving Hepburns knew about it and, if so, whether they could be trusted never to say.'

'And do they?'

'I think Robert does,' I said. 'I'm sure he recognised Dulcie's likeness in Mirren and worked out what it means. Remember, he couldn't bring himself to look at her picture and when he saw it in spite of trying not to he was horrified. He saw his wife there.'

'How long do you think he's known? How did he find out?'

'No idea,' I said. 'Mary told Mirren that she was Dugald's cousin some time ago, trying to put a stop to the marriage plans. Abby told Mirren that Robin was her father, to make Mirren believe that she was Dugald's sister, to stop Mirren eloping. Of course, what that revealed to Mirren is . . . the thing I can't seem to say.'

'Her mother and father were brother and . . . Yes, I see what you mean, Dan. It doesn't trip. If the tongue.' 'And that's why Mirren ran away. She couldn't face her mother once she knew.'

'Poor child,' said Alec.

'Poor everyone,' I agreed. 'One can't really blame Robert or Robin, if the women were really out to ensnare them. And one can't blame the women. They each of them wanted a child. Mary gave it years and years with Ninian and Abby gave it five years with Jack.'

'Dandy, don't be so disgusting. You sound like a farmer. What about Jack and Hilda? Is it poor them too?'

'If, during that time of tennis and card parties when Mary was away, when Abigail was trying to seduce Robin—'

'Doesn't sound like any tennis party I've ever been to,' Alec said.

'—if, as I say, Jack and Hilda got a whiff of what their spouses were up to, why shouldn't they have thought that what was sauce for the goose and gander was sauce for the gander and goose?'

'Neatly put,' Alec said. 'And then of course Hilda had been kept in the dark about the four sisters until she was up the aisle and it was too late. I must say, I blame whoever brought about that piece of diplomacy.'

'Except, look around,' I said, waving a hand towards the hair salon. 'Hilda has been pretty lavishly indulged in her life, hasn't she? And anyway she found a way around the worry of Robin's poor sisters.'

'I feel for Abby most,' said Alec. 'Poor, heavy-hearted Abby doing her mother's bidding. I don't say Jack doesn't feel guilty, but he's guilty like a little boy, half-sheepish and half-pleased with himself and hugging his naughty secret.'

'But still I can't help thinking that Abby should have been more careful about parties and chance meetings in such a small town,' I said. 'I mean to say, we ourselves thought it was the most eligible match imaginable, didn't we? How could Dugald and Mirren have failed to meet? Either the Hepburns or the Aitkens should have cut their losses and left town. There are no innocents, Alec. Not a one.'

Alec thought for a moment and slapped his hand on his thigh. 'Bella,' he said. I cocked my head at him. 'She's innocent.'

'And Fiona?' I said.

'Less so if you ask me,' said Alec. 'Fiona sold off her daughter to the highest bidder and was so keen not to see his social background too clearly that she entirely missed the problems in the line.'

'Who's being agricultural now?'

For a moment we sat in silence, thinking about the secrets, the betrayals, the desperate schemes, the stubbornness, all the misunderstandings. Jack and Hilda's secret, Robin and Abby's secret, Robert and Mary's secret too. If only Mirren had never met Dugald all the secrets would have been kept for another twenty years and twenty more and both of them would have married and made lives and never suffered a day's torment.

'Talk about the sins of the fathers,' I said at last. 'And now back to Mary. If she's well enough to see us today.'

'Us?' Alec said. 'Do you think I'll add anything to the encounter?' And then seeing my expression he relented. 'Oh, all right then, I'll come too.'

An inquiry at the cottage hospital brought the news that Mrs Aitken had been moved home under the close supervision of Dr Hill, with two private nurses in attendance night and day, and so we took ourselves once more to Abbey Park, hoping not to see Abigail if I am honest, or Jack, and half-hoping we would not be given an audience with Mary either. In fact, Alec was probably right because only Bella of the entire household did not give me a shuddery feeling when I thought of her.

Fortunately, for the swift conclusion of the case if not for the comfort of the detectives, Dr Hill when summoned said that Mary had been asking for me and he was delighted that I had come. We were taken upstairs to the drawing-room floor and ushered into a large room facing the garden and for that reason flooded with fresh afternoon sunlight. It was not, I thought, Mary's usual bedroom, unless it had been hastily stripped of most of its appurtenances to bring it to the peak of sparse cleanliness hospital nurses demand, for there was nothing in it besides a high narrow bed – not quite a hospital bed but along the same lines – a side-table for measuring out medicines and some hard chairs for visitors. There was a second table in the bay window, where several florists' bouquets were arranged, too far away for the patient to derive any pleasure from them but probably still too close for the nurses' hygienic ways.

Mary, on the high bed, appeared to be asleep. At the bedside, Bella sat with her hands clasped and her eyes fixed on her sister-in-law.

'Have you come for the dog?' she said in a low voice. 'Pity. Abigail has taken a great liking to her. Poor Abigail, she tries to sit with Mary but she keeps weeping and then . . .' She nodded to one of the nurses and rolled her eyes. Indeed, this nurse was a fearsome-looking creature, with a complicated cap which came right down over her shoulders like folded wings and a dazzling white uniform so severely starched that it cracked like sails in a high wind whenever she moved. Her face was ruddy and stern and her chin, perhaps from years of her drawing it in to show disapproval, was almost non-existent, her face disappearing into her neck which disappeared under her collar and continued without any suggestion of a swell at her bosom or a dip at her waist.

'Are you family?' she said.

'Dr Hill was very pleased we'd come,' I replied. I knew a thing or two about nurses after my war years and a doctor was the only thing one could brandish before them which would ever make them falter.

'I might go and stretch my legs,' Bella said. 'Come and fetch me if she wakes and asks where I am.' She stood with a bit of creaking and groaning, looked down into Mary's face for a moment and then with a tear in her eye she turned and stumped off out of the room.

The nurse tutted when she was gone.

'Mooning around like that is no good to us,' she said, glaring at Alec and me. 'We need cheerful distraction and jollying along, not weeping and wringing hands.' Alec and I nodded and mumbled and all but curtseyed and the nurse, satisfied, left us with Mary while she went off to some mysterious task in a side-room where there seemed to be a sink with running water.

As soon as she was gone. Mary opened her eyes and lifted a hand.

'Mrs Aitken, I'm surprised at you,' I said, taking her hand and squeezing it. 'You were playing possum!' Mary rewarded me with a very faint smile and a suggestion of a laugh. Her face still had the slipped-down look on one side and the rings around her eyes were darker, if anything, the line between her brows deeper than yesterday, but then the move from hospital to home must have been draining for her and the forced cheeriness of the nurse along with Bella's doleful looks could not be helping.

'We've spoken to the Hepburns,' I said. 'They're not going to tell anyone anything. You have no worries there. I don't actually think that many of them, if any at all, know the thing that's troubling you.' She turned her head on the pillow and regarded me with a hunted look that made me want to take her in my arms and hug her. 'We worked it out,' I said and she closed her eyes and moaned. 'The one person we think might know the whole story is Robert Hepburn himself.' Another moan. 'But he won't speak up. How could he? He and his son would be as shamed in the eyes of the world as any shame he could hope to bring down upon you and your daughter.' Mary Aitken gave a short, harsh sound that might have been a laugh and rolled her head from side to side upon the pillow. 'Well, yes, probably not, the world being what it is,' I conceded, 'but there would still be enough opprobrium to make sure he never tells. So, there it is. You can put it out of your mind and direct all your efforts to getting better again.'

Mary shook her head with her eyes closed.

'But Mrs Aitken, you must,' I said. 'For Abigail. She blames herself for Mirren dying and she blames herself for you being ill now and if you don't get better she will be wretched. She doesn't deserve that. No matter what—' I bit off the prim censure and started again. 'And you don't either. You didn't know, Mrs Aitken. You knew half the story and Abigail knew the other half.' Actually, they each knew one third; the last third was Jack and Hilda's secret. Alec and I were the only ones who knew everything, except for a few very small little puzzles, one or two embers still glowing amongst the ashes.

'Can I ask you something?' I said. Mary opened her eyes and looked at me, rather wary. 'I know you didn't read Mirren's letter. Never mind how I know, I'm right, aren't I? But you must have realised that a hand-delivered note meant she was hidden in the attics. What I still don't really understand is why you didn't just go and search for her? Why get me involved?'

Mary had a most peculiar look in her eye now. She put the fingers of her one good hand up to her lips and rolled her eyes in a show of terror.

'You were frightened to go?' Alec said. Mary nodded and then she mimed a gesture that neither one of us needed to translate into words to make clear. She pointed one finger, cocked her thumb, put her hand to her head and made a popping sound with her lips.

Alec and I stared at one another.

'Did you know she had Jack's gun?' I said. I remembered the stock lists in the attic ante-room and what everyone had told me about Mary Aitken's grasp on what was where, and I felt pretty sure that she would have known exactly where Jack Aitken's old service revolver was kept and would have checked to see if it was missing. I felt a moment's umbrage that she had been happy to send me off looking for a girl who had a revolver and was in a troubled state of mind, but there was no point in making a fuss about what might have been and so I said nothing.

'You'd think if she was angry enough to shoot anyone, it would have been Hepburn,' Alec said. 'Old Mr Hepburn, I mean. She didn't know him and she'd been brought up with you, by you, and loved you. I'd have thought she'd have gone after the old man.'

'She did!' I said. I sat up very straight and said it rather loudly, loud enough to attract the attention of the nurse in the room next door. She came stalking back and with one look at Mary's pale and tear-stained face she bundled us unceremoniously out of the room, Dr Hill or no. Out on the landing, I grabbed Alec by the arm and hissed at him.

'She did go after the grandfather, Alec,' I said. 'Oh, glory be! This is like finally getting rid of a raspberry seed that's been stuck in one's teeth for a month. She wrote to Mr Hepburn. She must have and that's why he came to the store. On the Monday. To meet her.'

'Old Mr Hepburn?' said Alec. 'Her grandfather?'

'There's no such person as *old Mr Hepburn*,' I said. 'This had been niggling at me like nothing on earth. "Mr Hepburn" is Robert. Robin is "young Mr Hepburn". Dugald was "Master Hepburn". That's why the maid at Roseville sent us to the other house when we asked for Mr Hepburn. And I thought the Emporium girls were talking about Dugald when they mentioned young Mr Hepburn and accused them of changing their story when they denied it a moment later.'

'So Robert came to Aitkens' to see Mirren,' said Alec.

'Thinking he was coming to see the daughter of his daughter. And I'll bet that's when he recognised her. And that's when he realised that she was also the daughter of his son. I'll bet you something else too. I'll bet you it was Robert who suddenly hustled Dugald off to Kelso. Once he had seen Mirren and realised what it meant. I wonder what he said to her while they were together. Rather, I wonder if what he said to her was what made her kill herself.'

'You think she *did* kill herself then?' Alec said.

'Oh, she must have, poor little thing,' I said. 'And Dugald didn't know about the planned elopement and he killed himself too. All alone, both of them. Dammit!' I turned round and looked at the closed door of Mary's sickroom. 'I'm sure Dugald killed himself but I wish I had asked Mary while I had the chance if she knew anything about it. Remember I told you how agitated she was about the lift man coming.' Alec nodded and then put his fingers to his lips and a hand behind his ear. I listened too and could hear water running in the little side-room. Very quietly, I opened the bedroom door again and crept back to Mary's bedside. I could see the nurse's back, as she filled a hot water bottle from a kettle and topped it up with cold water from the tap. I turned to Mary.

'Mrs Aitken,' I said in a low voice. 'The day of Mirren's funeral, did you know or even suspect that Dugald was in the store?' She shook her head and looked so surprised at the question that I had no hesitation in believing her. 'You didn't guess what was wrong when the lift went wonky that way?' Another shake of the head. I patted her hand and smiled, then glanced at the nurse again. Evidently she had made the bottle too hot or too cold and was emptying it out again to refill it. She had wrapped a cloth around its neck to catch the drips. What a fusspot, I thought, but however fussily she carried out the task, it was almost complete and I did not want to get caught by her. I bent and kissed Mary Aitken's forehead, then stole out again and rejoined Alec on the landing.

'Nothing,' I said. 'And I believe her.'

'And so we leave them to what comfort they can bring one another,' said Alec. I nodded slowly. 'Bella seems to have come up trumps, doesn't she?' I nodded again and we descended the stairs in silence. 'Come on then,' he sighed when we got to the bottom and were standing in the hall. 'Out with it, Dandy.'

'Out with what?'

'I know that faraway look. Something's bothering you.'

'But what could it be?' I said. 'Everything's tied up. No loose ends at all. Unless it's the gloves.'

'Gloves?' said Alec, rather blankly, racking his brain.

'The one pair of gloves with the price ticket, slightly stained, in the shoebox.'

'The price ticket slightly stained or the gloves?' said Alec.

'One glove,' I said. 'I only mentioned the price ticket because it made them unusual amongst all the stuff in the attic. Almost all. But stained price tickets . . . What am I remembering?'

'Nothing much apparently,' Alec said.

'I wonder if they're still there,' I said. 'Let's go and see.'

'What for?' said Alec, like a whining child who does not want to go shopping.

'I'll tell you when we get there,' I said. 'I know! It annoys me too, but I can't help it. This case isn't over yet, Alec. I feel it in my bones.'

13

Ferguson the doorman gave me his everyday cheerful smile but it died on his lips a bit when he fully recognised who I was and remembered all the matters he would rather forget that seeing me brought back to his mind.

'I feel like the bad fairy at the christening in here now,' I said. 'I've just ruined that poor man's day.'

'How?' said Alec. 'You passed him without a word.'

'The very sight of me brings back painful memories,' I said. 'I quizzed him about what he might have heard during Mirren's funeral when Dugald fell down the lift shaft and somehow made him feel that he should have stepped in and saved the boy.'

'That's ridiculous,' Alec said. 'He'd never have heard noises from the lift shaft from out on the street with the doors closed behind him.'

'He wasn't outside,' I said. 'The store was closed, remember. He was sitting in the foyer, on one of those seats where I sat down after almost swooning.'

Alec stopped walking abruptly.

'You never told me that,' he said. He looked back the way we had come and then moved around one of the Haberdashery counters so that both the front door with its row of seats and the lift, cordoned off with a black rope now, were in view.

'What is it?'

'He was sitting there?' Alec said, pointing. 'And he didn't hear a lad falling down the lift shaft *there*? I don't believe it.'

'Really?' I said, but indeed standing here at the halfway point it did not seem like much of a distance at all. 'He is slightly hard of hearing,' I offered, looking over at the doorman who was ushering a customer out of the store with her parcels and tipping his hat at her.

'You mean actually deaf or just "not so young as once he was"?' asked Alec.

'Well, certainly he didn't have any difficulty hearing me when we spoke,' I said. 'Out on the street, with carts and trams going by. But there surely wouldn't be much to hear so long as Dugald didn't yell or make any loud noises of that sort—'

'Didn't yell?' said Alec. 'Are you mad, Dandy? He'd scream his lungs out of his chest. He'd howl like a banshee.'

'Are you sure?'

Alec gave me that very hard look that says I should not inquire any further. 'Yes,' he said. 'I'm sure.'

'Even if he had chosen to jump?' I said. 'Wouldn't that be different from being shoved or falling?' Alec was shaking his head as vehemently as he possibly could and his lips were pressed firmly together.

'Makes not a blind bit of difference,' he said. 'It's a reflex. It's an animal instinct. Horses are just the same.'

'So Dugald would definitely have been heard,' I said. I looked back at the doorman again. 'What does that mean? Is Ferguson lying?'

'Either that or the time's wrong, and the old boy *wasn't* in the store when it happened after all.'

'The doctor seemed pretty sure about the timing.'

'It always bothered me, actually,' Alec said. 'It seemed off, somehow, that Dugald should jump during Mirren's funeral. I'd have thought he'd either do it straight away, as soon as he knew she was dead, or he'd wait until afterwards, visit her grave, do it there, even. Why would he so conveniently jump during the ceremony and why here?'

'Because she died here, obviously,' I said.

'And how did he get in?'

'I don't know. Actually, now that you mention it, that bothered me too. Off and on anyway. Only there was so much else to think about.'

'Such as when was he told about Mirren's death and who told him and where he went when he left Kelso and . . . we've rather neglected him, haven't we?' Alec was giving me one of his stern looks.

'You thought the case was tied up in a bow half an hour ago,' I pointed out.

'Before I knew you'd let such a clanger of a discrepancy go past you,' he retorted.

'So let's interview Ferguson again,' I said, giving a sigh I hoped would express my admirable forbearance when he was being so tiresome. 'See if perhaps he stepped away for a moment.'

'Or the doctor,' Alec said. 'See if he worked backwards instead of forwards.'

'What do you mean?'

'Ask if he thought to himself: well, he died before everyone came back to the store and no one heard anything so it must have been when the store was empty. Quick look at the body; yes, that'll do. Two thirty and Bob's your uncle.' I was shaking my head at him.

'Granted, darling, I missed a tiny little trick about the doorman because I didn't know that people instinctively shout out while they're falling, but I'm sure the doctor is much more scrupulous than me. I overheard the first report, remember. He had done a proper examination, listed all the injuries, and he was working from the temperature of the body in its surroundings.'

'Doorman it is then,' Alec said.

'Lying for someone?' I asked. 'Bought off by a murderer? Because if the doorman's covering something up it's got to be murder, hasn't it? He's hardly likely to have taken a fiver from Dugald to let him in and ignore his dying screams.' I turned and looked at the revolving door. Only the man's uniform sleeve was visible as he spun the contraption from outside on the pavement. I could not believe that that man, who turned down his wireless when his wife asked him to, could be party to a murder. 'And I'm sure it's not Mary he's lying for. She was completely taken by surprise when I asked about Dugald. It was the furthest thing from her mind.'

263

'It might take care of your gloves,' said Alec. 'We're sure Mirren killed herself, aren't we? So hidden gloves are nothing to do with her death. They might just have something to do with Dugald's.'

'They might be something to do with someone having to move a dead pigeon six months ago,' I said. Alec said nothing. 'How about this?' I went on. 'Let's go up to the attics and if those gloves are gone, I'll take that as evidence of someone mucking around up there and trying to hide the fact that they'd done so. And I'll accept that it might have been when Dugald died and then I'll consent to grilling the doorman.'

'Agreed,' said Alec. 'Lead the way.'

We made for the back stairs, passing Miss Armstrong of Stationery on the way, who hallooed when she saw me and called out that she had a mock-up ready for my inspection.

'Not today, Miss Armstrong,' I said, sailing past.

Miss Torrance of Gloves gave me a mournful wave; the news of Mary's collapse must have gone around the staff already.

'Aitkens' will never survive without Mrs Ninian,' she said.

'Don't say that, Miss Torrance,' I protested – although, privately, I agreed. 'There's Mr Jack to take up the reins.'

'We need a woman's touch,' Miss Torrance said. 'Did you go "down the street" for your *mousquetaires*?' She had lowered her voice. 'Then you'd see what I mean. A woman's touch.'

'Well, perhaps Mrs Jack when she gets back on her feet again,' I said with no conviction. 'Or Mrs John even.' This last suggestion met with a look of such frank incredulity that I felt a pang for poor Bella. Right enough, though, a woman who could not be sure of two matching stockings on her own legs could hardly arrange three floors of merchandise into a tempting array.

We loitered at the back corner, pretending to inspect a coloured catalogue of headbands and tiaras which stood on an oak and brass lectern in a kind of little bower with a brown horsehair chair and a brass cheval-glass.

'What is this?' Alec said.

'I think one's supposed to choose a model and then sit here

264

and admire it,' I replied, thinking with fondness of the pink and white Millinery Department at Hepburns'.

'You know what, Dandy,' Alec said, looking around. 'I do disapprove of the way they treat menfolk but otherwise I think House Of might have the edge.'

'Just possibly,' I said, drily. 'Right, no one's looking. Let's go.'

Inside the stairwell all was quiet, all was dim, and we crept right up to the attic floor without interruptions or meetings. It was not a good sign, to my mind. The lift was *hors de combat* and by rights this stairway should have been bustling. I did not give Aitkens' much chance after all the scandals and with its rightful queen laid low.

'So which way are the shoeboxes?' Alec said, when we were out on the landing. The lily wreath was gone and only the patch of new white paint marked the spot where Mirren had died now.

'Let's go and get a lantern,' I said. 'I'm sure I'll find them quite easily.'

My words jinxed our chances, of course, as they always do. Lantern in hand, I set off on a backwards route through the attics, expecting to find the room of shoeboxes right away, but somehow I came upon Mirren's hidey-hole first. Alec looked around, shaking his head.

'I wonder if this is the same room Jack and Hilda used to meet in,' he said. 'Come on, Dandy. It must be somewhere: concentrate, darling.'

I opened another door, looked in and shook my head.

'This is the wormy tables and— Hello! Someone's been up and tidied the quilts.'

'What?' said Alec, distractedly. I had entered the room properly now. The heap of shiny eiderdowns which had been stuffed all anyhow in and around the card-wrapped table legs was now a neatish pile stacked in an orderly way with the corners of the quilts poking out from under the table-top.

'And the price tickets are gone too,' I said.

'The stained ones you mentioned?' said Alec. 'Do you think that's significant?'

'No, these tickets weren't stained,' I said. I went over and traced my hand up and down the pile, feeling the slippery satin of the covers and the slightly damp and clumped feeling of the feathers inside. 'Mary didn't make this pile of quilts. I can tell you that much.'

'How?'

'Because if she had the edges would be facing the other way and the folds would be to the front. I watched her tidying sheets when she was upset and close to tears and the pile she produced was perfect. It was second nature.'

'Someone else then,' Alec said. 'Perhaps they always stuff things up here and then take the tickets off when they get around to tidying.' I nodded. There was something moving in the back of my mind. These quilts and Mary tidying the pile and the nurse in the side-room. I shook my head and turned away.

'Gloves!' I said and strode off, hoping that an air of purpose would bring the room to me like Mohammed's mountain. Sure enough, not much later we found it.

'I'll bet they've gone,' I said from the door. 'They were in that top box here.' I walked towards it. 'This one. And it wasn't properly closed.' I unwound the little string from the cleat and prised off the shoebox lid. Inside were the two chamois bags and no sign of the gloves at all. 'Better check a few more but I'm sure it was this one.'

As Alec fiddled with the lids I stood thinking, chasing that wisp of an idea round the back regions of my memory like a housewife going after a mouse with her broom.

'Shame about these shoes,' Alec said. He was holding one up – a high-heeled evening slipper of plum-coloured kid with a glittering gilt buckle. The buckle was rusty and there was bloom of mould on the kid too. 'Shame the boxes aren't sturdier, I mean. There's water been getting in here. Or damp, anyway.'

'Water,' I said.

'Or damp.'

'Water bottles. Hot water bottles, Alec, let's find them.'

I could not remember where in the exuberant chaos of Aitkens' attics the hot water bottles had been and so we just circled around, opening door after door until my head at least – Alec kept his own counsel – was whirling.

'Ah!' I said, when we opened a door and saw a profusion of plaster limbs. 'I think they might be near here. With marmalade.' Alec had gone on ahead.

'Twenty-five tins, dangerously blown, masochists, for the use of,' he called back. 'Here's marmalade anyway. And, yes – eureka! – water bottles. Quite a lot of them.'

'With the price tickets gone,' I said, joining him and crouching down beside the heap of India-rubber water bags. Their stoppers were in now, but I unscrewed one and tipped it up. Some drops of brownish water fell out onto the floor.

'Something wrong with their insides to turn the water that colour,' Alec said. I sniffed the open neck of the bottle and then gave it to him to do the same.

'It's not water,' I said. 'It's tea.'

Alec stared, sniffed again, and nodded.

'India tea,' I said. 'If you don't interrupt me and I concentrate very hard I think I might be able to explain everything.' I sat back on my heels, took a deep breath and began. 'On the day of Mirren's funeral but well before it, when the store was empty, Dugald Hepburn came here to meet someone, to see the place where Mirren died. And that someone took gloves from the shop floor to guard against fingerprints and shoved him down the lift shaft. Then that same someone took a whole display of eider-downs from the Household Department and covered the body. Then took a load of bottles and filled them with the only ready supply of hot liquid – the contents of the tea urn – draining it to the bottom and burning the element. The bottles were put around the body too so that after the funeral it was still nice and warm for the doctor coming.'

'Mary after all,' Alec said. 'You said she was in a spin about the lift man coming.'

'No, Alec, you've got it completely upside down,' I said. 'The lift man *had* to come and find the body quickly so that the doctor could be here before it had cooled down. *Mary* was the one being normal. *Mary* thought it was hideous to have the lift mended on such a day. And besides, Mary complained about the sheets being where the eiderdowns belonged, with not a thought about drawing my attention that way. And Mary is competent to the core. The person who did this is clumsy and haphazard and was very keen to get the lift man here.'

'Bella,' Alec said.

'Bella,' I agreed. 'I remember thinking at the time how odd it was that they seemed to have swapped roles. One sister-in-law all gone to pieces and the other suddenly taking charge and getting things done. She said she'd get the lift up to the top floor and jam it there. She was the one who had the chance to take the quilts and hot bottles off and get them away out of sight.' Alec was beginning to nod. 'And she did a pretty shoddy job of it. Spilled tea all over the labels and stuffed the quilts away in a mess. Even when she came to tidy up, she couldn't make the neat job of it that Mary would have. And Mary wouldn't have burnt out the urn.'

'That woman downstairs just said as much, didn't she? There's no one to take the place of Mrs Ninian.'

'Bella stepping in was a special event,' I said. 'A one-day-only offer.'

'When did she come back then?' Alec said.

I thought for a minute or two. 'The day Mary collapsed,' I said. 'She was out, remember. She was at the store, ostensibly thanking the staff, actually up here kicking over her traces.'

'No wonder she's gone so badly to pieces about Mary then,' Alec said. 'Guilt. Because of course she must think it's the deaths that overwhelmed Mary. She can't possibly know about the rest of it.'

I put the stopper back into the bottle I had been holding and placed it carefully on the top of the slippery pile of them.

'That's right,' I said. 'She doesn't know about all the . . . bed-hopping, I suppose is the only word . . . the labyrinthine family trees of the Aitkens and Hepburns. Bella doesn't know any of the secrets.' We looked at one another, an uneasy glance.

'So why did she do it?' Alec said.

'I don't know,' I answered. 'And unless we come up with a motive, no one will believe she did. Who's going to listen to hot water bottles and eiderdowns and gloves?'

'But she *did* do it, didn't she? She must have. She was the one who summoned the lift-mending man.'

'But even that could be argued away,' I said. 'The lift was in a very bad state. Everyone agreed. No one was taking Bella's word for it.'

'Maybe she nobbled it then,' Alec said. 'Maybe she was surprised it was working at all. She meant it to be broken down completely when everyone got back. In fact, maybe she left it up at the attics and she was horrified to arrive and find it trundling up and down with the body all wrapped up in quilts and hot bottles just above people's heads. Imagine if someone had opened the hatch to see what the funny noise was and found him there?'

'If it was nobbled surely there would have been signs of mischief,' I said

'Let's go and ask Mr Laming,' said Alec. 'See if he noticed anything strange.'

Laming's Engineering: heavy machinery repair and maintenance and small engine specialists – which seemed to cover everything – was housed in a yard up a rough lane behind Mr Laming's house, which was out of town beyond the linen works. Mr Laming and the gormless boy were both there, bending with great concentration over a large lump of oily black metal – an engine, I supposed – laid on their work bench like a patient on a surgeon's table.

'May we interrupt you?' Alec said. 'Just a question or two.'

'Again!' said Mr Laming, straightening up and resettling his cap. 'I've just tellt the lad all I ken and I cannae do more.'

'Which lad?' I said. 'All you know about what? It's Aitkens' we're interested in.'

'Aye, that's right,' said Mr Laming. 'Hector, away you in and get a piece and cuppy. I'll shout you back oot when I need you.'

269

'I've had an extra piece already, Paw,' said Hector, 'when thon polis wis here. I'll no be fit for ma dinner.'

'Well, you can go and run aboot till yer appetite's back after this yin,' said his father. 'Gawn!'

'The police,' I said when the boy was gone. 'The lad? Let me guess: Constable McCann?' Mr Laming nodded. 'I *knew* he was a bright boy,' I said. 'Well, well. So he's been digging around too.'

'What did he ask you, Mr Laming?' Alec said.

'He tellt me to keep it to myself,' said the man. 'He was on his ain time.'

'Let me put it another way,' Alec said. 'What we'd like to ask you is what was wrong with Aitkens' lift. Did you ever get to find out? Did you go back to it once the police had been and gone?'

'Because,' I chipped in, 'we suspect it might have been tampered with. Nobbled, you know.' Mr Laming gave me a grin, his false teeth dazzling in his grimy face.

'You're no' so dusty either, missus,' he said. 'The boy McCann was just asking; he'd not guessed it for himself.' I kept my beam of pride down to a reasonable wattage, and he went on. 'Porridge oats,' he said. 'Fine oatmeal in the pulley wheel. I've seen bran before now.'

'Presumably,' I said, 'Aitkens' food hall doesn't carry bran.'

'Bran would like have made a better job,' said Mr Laming. 'Stopped the pulley deid, or made the rope jump.'

'My God,' I said. 'The rope might have jumped?' I remembered Lynne and me going up in the lift that day, listening to the creaks, and how it lurched an inch down once she had stopped it.

'And she left it in that state when all the staff were coming along to the party.' Alec's face was pale

'Aye, but there's clamps that stop it dropping if the ropes go,' Laming said. 'It's a grand bit o' engineering that lift, for all it's an auld cuddy noo.'

He failed, though, to comfort us and a rising tide of anger helped to carry us back through the town to Abbey Park Place and would perhaps have seen us storm in, find Bella and shake her by the shoulders until she confessed, but on the pavement outside the garden wall, our onward charge was interrupted by young Constable McCann. He was in his uniform now, evidently working on his own time no more, but had none of his brother officers with him. His eyes opened very wide when he saw us and then his rather stricken-looking face broke into a grin.

'Grand!' he said. 'I came on my own instead of tipping the wink to the boss cos I was thinkin' how come should I hand it all over and watch him get the glory. But I'll tell you this for nothin', I'm glad to have a wee bit at my back just the same.'

'You're going to arrest her?' said Alec.

'My first arrest,' said McCann, squaring his shoulders. 'Unless you count market night drinkin' and fightin' after dances anyway.'

I felt rather splendid as we set off up the drive, Alec and I flanking young McCann, but had begun to feel ridiculous and more than a little twitchy before we had climbed the steps and pulled the doorbell, not to mention the mounting feeling of unease at what we were about to visit upon an elderly lady whom I had never seen being anything but amusing and friendly. I tried to remind myself of Dugald Hepburn's face disappearing down into the darkness out of view that day.

Trusslove's smile of welcome died on his face as he looked around the three of us.

'Not suicide then,' he said. I shook my head and he half-turned towards the interior of the house, his grip on the door tightening as though he meant to bar our way. Then he let go and pushed the door wide.

'Who?' he said. 'Surely not Mrs Ninian. Not as she is now. You couldn't.'

'It's Bella, Trusslove,' said Alec. 'Mrs John – if you wouldn't mind fetching her.'

'She's sitting at the bedside,' Trusslove said. 'She's never away from it.'

'Tryin' to atone,' said McCann.

Trusslove shook his head and ushered us into the library to wait.

271

'And are you quite sure?' he said, as we walked. Alec and McCann had gone ahead and Trusslove and I fell in naturally together. 'How could she do such a thing?'

'I don't know,' I said. 'And I don't know why either. That's one of the things I want to ask her. Trusslove, you will just tell her that someone wants to see her, won't you? You're not going to warn her?'

He certainly did not warn her; Bella Aitken, when she swept into the room minutes later to see the three of us standing there, was almost her old self again, shoulders back, arms swinging, large feet turned out. She stopped and put her hands on her hips, frowning. Trusslove slipped in behind her and closed the door.

'I'm sorry aboot this, Mrs Aitken,' said Constable McCann. 'But I need to ask you to come along with me.'

Bella took a couple of deep breaths in and out, with her lips pressed hard together. Then she nodded.

'It was always going to be a risk,' she said. 'I knew that. What was it that undid me?'

'The oats,' said Alec.

'Oats?' said Trusslove, wonderingly.

'And the gloves,' I said. 'The hot bottles and quilts and the tea urn.'

'Lord, you really have seen through me,' Bella said. 'I thought I was being so clever.'

'What have quilts and tea got to do with shooting Miss Mirren?' said Trusslove.

Bella rounded on him. 'How dare you!' she said. 'How could you think such a thing? It was the boy, you fool. Only the boy. I could never have harmed a hair on Mirren's head. She was my grandchild. What kind of monster do you think I am?'

Of course, Mirren was not Bella's grandchild and she had indeed murdered her own flesh and blood when she pushed Dugald Hepburn down the lift shaft. But if she did not know that, then what part of the web of secrets was it that led her to murder at all?

'Mrs Aitken,' I said, 'can I ask you why you did it?'

'What?' said Bella. 'What do you mean, why?'

Constable McCann was frowning at me too. I glanced at Alec, but he only shrugged.

'We cannae really stand around chatting,' said McCann. 'Mrs Aitken, if you'll come quietly I'd be greatly obliged. I dinnae want a scene and a load of trouble.'

'Of course,' Bella said. 'I don't want trouble either. Mary's sleeping.'

Alec and I left quietly too, McCann asking us in a whisper if we would meet him after his shift so he could say a proper thank you. And so we were parked at the end of his street, at five o'clock as waves of men and boys in their overalls and caps, women and girls in their rough aprons and headscarves, returned soiled and weary from the works to the long rows of little terraced houses, their boots and clogs on the dry packed road making one think a beaten infantry was retreating. There was no sign of young McCann among them for the longest time, until at almost six, when I had sunk into a torporous near doze, Alec sat up suddenly waking both me and Bunty.

'Hello, hello!' he said. 'Here he comes, Dandy.'

Down the street, still in his uniform, came Constable McCann, looking like a man who had just won fifty pounds on the derby. I leapt out of the motorcar and hurried to meet them.

'All done and dusted,' he said. 'Away you come in and get some tea then, and I'll tell you the finish o' it.'

Mrs McCann, a born hostess, took only a minute to greet us, survey her pots and pans and quickly reconfigure tea into a meal for seven instead of five. There were ten sausages frying in a pan – three each for the men, two for mother and one apiece for the small sisters already at the table which she quickly chopped into pieces with a bread knife. She added the boiled potatoes to them, turned up the gas to brown the edges, shredded a spare half-cabbage and started frying bread. By the time the constable had been upstairs to shed his tunic and returned again, seven brimming plates and seven brimming tea mugs were waiting. Mrs McCann banged a wooden spoon on the kitchen wall, which

273

brought her husband from the parlour in his slippers with his newspaper tucked under one arm.

'Company, Faither,' she said and her husband discarded the newspaper and took off his cap before sitting.

The smaller sister said grace and all eight of us – I include Bunty, to whom I fed a piece of sausage until I had tasted another and found out how delicious they were (after which she had to get by with bread) – tucked in.

'So what's the occasion?' said Mr McCann with a glance at Alec and me.

'I've made an arrest,' said his son. 'A big one.'

'What's a rest?' said the smaller of the two sisters. Her mother swiftly made two fried bread sandwiches out of her daughters' remaining dinners, handed one to each of them and sent them outside.

'And nae fightin' and finish yer greens and I'll check the midden,' she called after them.

'Bella Aitken,' said McCann when his sisters were well gone. 'For murder, Mammy. She killt the Hepburn boy.'

'She nivver did,' said his father, struck to stone with a forkful of potato halfway between plate and mouth.

'She did,' McCann said. 'She got him on the phone and lured him back to toon here, said she had something to tell him. Oh, it all came pouring oot when I got her started. She met him in Aitkens' the day o' the lass's funeral and she shoved him doon the lift shaft where they found him.'

'That doctor one wants a skelp then,' said Mrs McCann. 'I thocht you said it all happened when folk were in the Abbey. How did she get away to do all that without anybody seeing?'

'I can take up the tale for this bit, Mrs McCann,' I said, and I recounted the details of the hot water bottles, the quilts, the tea, the gloves and the call to Laming.

'Porridge oats, she had worked into the lift doings,' McCann finished up.

'In the pulley or in the engine?' said his father. 'I hope in the pulley just, or that's a waste of a guid machine.' I met his wife's eye and we shared the same thought: with a boy dead the lift hardly mattered.

'See that's where you've got the spurt on me,' said young McCann. 'I couldnae go in and out of Aitkens' Emporium and slip roond the back like that.' I smiled and forbore to point out that he could, however, march into Abbey Park, arrest Bella Aitken and take her to jail.

'But you did better than us with the motive,' I said. 'We know she did it but we haven't been able to guess why.'

'I couldnae credit you asking her why,' said McCann, shaking his head. '*Why* wis the easy bit.' Alec and I shared a glance.

'Well?' Alec said.

'For sure?' said McCann. 'You cannae guess, really?' I shot a look towards the door to check that the little girls were out of earshot. Their tender innocence should not hear any of what was coming. 'She and Dougie Hepburn's granny had a wee secret wedding all cooked up atween them, and when Mirren ran away and shot hersel', Bella knew Dougie had backed oot. Jiltit the lass. So she killt him.'

For what seemed like an age, Alec and I sat in absolute silence, simply staring. All those secrets, all those shameful hidden minglings and reminglings of blood, and the murderer knew none of it, knew nothing. Eventually, I cleared my throat and managed to speak.

'So what put you on to her?'

'My, eh, my girl works at Aitkens',' he said, blushing a little to admit it. 'She kent there was something fishy aboot Auld Bella that day, steaming in and ordering folk aboot. And then she went back another day and gave them all a wee tip and a wee speech and Lynne said it jist stuck in her craw and she couldnae swallow it.'

'Lynne?' I said. 'She's your girl? Oh, I *am* pleased. Lynne's lovely. She was one of the nymphs, Alec.' Mr McCann's eyebrows joined together in the middle about an eighth of an inch above his eyes.

'One o' the whit?' he said. His son gave me a disbelieving look.

'Sprites!' I said, hastily and rather too loud. 'She said you're almost ready to set a date, if you're lucky with a house anyway.'

'Nae problem noo,' said Mr McCann. 'Sweet-pea said I would make sergeant for sure after this.'

'Sweet-pea!' Alec and I said in chorus and I clapped my hands, delighted.

'You'll have to learn a wee tate more respect to make sergeant, young Brucie,' said his father, but at least he was smiling again.

'Not at all, sir,' Alec said. 'This is a fine boy you have here. He shouldn't change a thing.'

14

It was some months later – almost a year – when I stopped off at Dunfermline on my way to pay a visit, long arranged and impossible to postpone any more. Alec refused point-blank to go with me but I could not rest until the trip was made. They had all been in my mind again, the Aitkens and the Hepburns, the House and the Emporium, the two dead children and the adults left behind them, all hiding something and all mourning.

Bella had been tried and convicted but thankfully the sentence passed down to her was a clement one. The jury had not pressed for hanging and the judge had no desire to send a woman in her seventies to the gallows for a crime – as he called it – of grief and of love. I had held my breath opening the newspapers every morning, expecting any day to see that some of the family secrets had started to seep out from around the edges of the ordered testimony; one drop of the poison would have led to a trickle and a torrent and a great thundering deluge – like Niagara – as everyone told the other's sins, and all were swept away.

As it happened, though, Bella knew none of it and no one else uttered a word. Of course, what that *did* mean was that when the shuffling began it hit Dunfermline like a tidal wave and the scandal was still rippling now. First up, Hilda Haddo had left her husband's protection and had gone to live with Jack Aitken at Abbey Park, whereupon Robin had promptly divorced her for desertion. He had not, however, to the bewilderment of the horrified onlookers, tried to prevent her continuing to have close motherly relations with the three surviving children, the girls. If anything, he was happy to see them living with Jack and Hilda, and Fiona Haddo of course, who had joined them in that great empty house and started making her mark there.

'His mother killed her son,' a fellow passenger on the train explained to me as we rattled down through Fife. It had only taken my saying I was going to Dunfermline to do a little shopping and there was no stopping her. 'Do you understand? *His* mother murdered *her* son and should have hanged for it if there were any backbone left in this country at all, and yet now she has gone to live in his house – she dropped her voice – 'as man and wife, one can only presume' – and returned to normal volume – 'and they say that his sisters spent their Easter holiday there.' She sat back, absolutely thrilled; nothing would have given her more pleasure if she could have ordered off a menu.

I could not see the attraction of Jack Aitken, speaking personally, but I would have felt sorry for him, rattling around that house all alone. Mary and Abigail, of course, were long gone even before the trial. Dulcie was gone too (I felt a flip of anxiety about the afternoon, like a seal turning over in deep water) but it was not until news washed back to Dunfermline's shore about *where* they were all gone that the second explosion of gossip occurred. Thankfully, my carriage companion did not seem to know about this part of the story, or did want to dwell upon it anyway.

As to the third revelation: I was reminded again of my father and Gloria and how he did not care what the world had to say, or rather what the world whispered behind its hand as he passed with Gloria's arm tucked under his in the village or up in town. Mrs Lumsden, little Mrs Lumsden, Mary's loyal friend, had spotted an opening, taken a running jump and landed with both her dainty feet firmly planted in the Hepburn home. The flat above the Linen Bank, that is to say; Robin remained at Roseville quite alone. So, I thought, little Mrs Lumsden all those years ago was pining for Bob, while Bob pined for Mary and Mary set her

278

sights at Ninian Lennox Aitken and his lavish plans. Now, fifty years later, at least one of them was happy.

I disembarked and strolled the familiar way through the town to the tolbooth. The House of Hepburn was open for business and customers entered it and left again. It was only April and far too early for a beach scene with real sand; in its place were stiff fans of handkerchiefs hanging from wires and pyramids of painted tea trays with, here and there, a small card announcing easy terms, ten weeks, nothing to pay until August. I looked in at the door. It was dove grey and lilac still (as how could it not be?) and the assistants drifted about in their matching frocks but there was a stand of leather belts in the middle of the floor. Black belts and brown ones, navy and racing green, like a solitary toad on a pool of water lilies, and I knew that someone without Fiona Haddo's eye was at the helm here now. Mrs Lumsden perhaps, after years of Household, and one could only imagine what she would wreak if it were true.

Along the street again my steps faltered. Aitkens' Emporium was no more. The plate glass and revolving door were the same but the mauve and gold livery was gone, the paintwork now picked out in smart black, white and scarlet, with lettering between the ground- and first-floor windows that read: *Fair Ladies*. The doorman was my friend of old, and he tipped his hat to me: a new, pale grey top hat, to match his morning coat, all very natty with the red and black striped waistcoat and the bright red spats over his black patent shoes.

Inside, the oak floor had been rubbed down to a golden gleam, the wood-panelling had been painted a rich cream colour like buttermilk and everything else of good solid oak which had stood in Aitkens' Haberdashery for fifty years was gone. The counters were floating tablets of glass with chromium legs and there were no glove drawers, no scarf racks, no bulging shelves of trim anywhere.

'Mrs Gilver!' It was Miss Armstrong, in a dress she had clearly not run up herself in her free evenings, but I smiled to see that she still wore a corsage of paper chits in her belt.

'Where is everything?' I asked.

'In the basement,' she replied. 'We're all worn out with running up and down to fetch and carry, but Madam said nothing could be done with the basement to make it fit for our ladies so there you have it. No more Kitchenwares and all the assistants with legs like racehorses from the stairs.' Miss Armstrong's legs – I could not help glancing at them – rose from her sturdy brogues to the fashionably asymmetric hem of her frock like two oatmeal puddings.

'Madam being Mrs Haddo, I presume.'

Miss Armstrong clicked her teeth and shook her head. 'I still can't believe what happened to us all since you were here before,' she said. 'Well, I know it started when you were here, but you know what I mean.'

'I do. Is Mr Muir still here? Miss Hutton?'

'Mr Muir couldn't get his notice in quick enough but Miss Hutton's here, still in charge upstairs. When Madam lets her be. You should go up and have a wee look, Mrs Gilver. It's all change up there, I can tell you.'

'But how can they afford to do it all?' I said.

'I cannot tell you for I do not know,' said Miss Armstrong. 'There was no life insurance for Miss Mirren what with it being suicide. And although her shares came back to her father,' Miss Armstrong's voice faltered, and I could not help raising my eyebrows, 'that is Mr Jack, I mean, and Mrs John signed hers away to him too, shares of nothing are nothing. And then it can't be cheap to keep Mrs Ninian in that fancy place – Miss Hutton's been to see her and says it's very comfy.'

'And how do you like the new regime?' I said.

Miss Armstrong screwed up her nose. 'Madam and Miss Hilda – that's what we call her; it doesn't seem right to say Mrs Hepburn now – are more fun to work for than Mrs Ninian ever was. And even Mr Jack's more . . .' She stopped and dropped her voice. 'But can you believe it? How she can even look at him, knowing his mother, his own flesh and blood, did what she did to *her* own flesh and blood . . .'

So Miss Armstrong did not know everything. She did not know that the same blood ran in Bella Aitken's and Hilda Hepburn's son's veins and she did not know what the Hepburn men had done to the Aitken women, that there was a great deal of forgetting required on both sides.

I did go upstairs and was unsurprised to see more pale paint, little tables, elegant gowns and pink light bulbs all over the first floor where Gents' Tailoring, Layette and Junior used to be. I did not need to stop off on the second floor to know that there would be no more eiderdowns on the aisle shelves and flannel sheets behind. I could hear the hiss of a tea urn – a new tea urn, a very clean hiss and no clanking at all – and could smell frangipani as I passed on the stairs.

The attics were worse than ever, jammed to the door with discarded Aitkens' stock so that one could no longer wander through the maze of little rooms and up and down the dark back corridors. I only really wanted to see the landing, but I could not find my way. I could have sworn that I was standing in the attic which had been the ante-room with the stock sheets and lanterns before – I recognised the shelves around the walls and the old ledgers mouldering there, but there was no sign of the door leading out to the top of the stairs and the lift. I played my electric torch all around (I had come prepared for this little pilgrimage) and that is when I saw that the door had been boarded up and the boards papered over. A shiver passed through me. I retraced my steps, descended to the first floor, skirted around the back of the Gowns Department and tried the other stair. It should have opened right onto the landing but at the top, above the tearoom, again it ended in a blank plastered wall. It was bricked up; the landing where Mirren had died and from where Dugald had fallen was simply gone.

From the first-floor balcony below looking up, there was no more to be seen. No ledge, no opening with black curtains, just blank wall painted in the same cream colour and dappled by the sun through the stained-glass window. An assistant, one I did not recognise, saw me standing there staring, and frowned at me.

I flushed, dropped my head and left Aitkens' – Fair Ladies, as it was now – knowing I would never return.

It took quite some time on the rattling little motorbus out from Waverley station into the rolling hills of East Lothian. I had never been here before, except for whisking past on a London-bound train, but at first glance it appealed to me. The sky was larger than in Perthshire, making me think of Suffolk and those roiling clouds which take up half Constable's canvas sometimes. This spring day the sky was a gentle blue, almost white at the horizon but pale even high above my head, and the drive, long and straight, passed between two rows of birches, just putting on their fresh green coats for the year.

The main house stood foursquare at the top of the drive but behind and around it I could see numerous little white bungalows with red roofs and blue paint. There were white fences around tiny gardens and only the slopes instead of steps at every door hinted that this village was unusual in any way.

The big front door stood open and I stepped in, quite diffidently but not wanting to take someone from a more important task to come and welcome me. A corridor led away towards sunlight at the back of the house and I ventured along it, coming out eventually into a kind of solarium or orangery. It was very warm, but still most of the ladies were tucked up under knee-blankets and with shawls around their shoulders. I looked around them, nodding in answer to their smiles and waves, for they were all pleased to see a visitor, even a strange one, and then at last I heard a cry of greeting.

Mary Aitken, sitting upright and smiling in her bath-chair, beckoned to me.

'Mrs Gilver,' she said, and my heart leapt with pleasure. It was not distinct. 'Mezzz Gilluh' would be the best approximation, but she was speaking and my greeting to her was not diplomacy.

'Mrs Aitken. My, you look *well*!' I bent and kissed her cheek. 'I didn't expect to see you looking so well. How are you?'

'Peace,' she said and she breathed out, long and slow, smiling even wider. She had cut her hair, I saw, a remarkable development for any woman her age and especially so for the Mrs Aitken I remembered. It fell around her face in soft white waves and, as though it had been that scraped bun keeping all the tension there, her face seemed to have softened too. Of course on one side the muscles were almost dead, but that is not what one noticed about her. Rather one saw the clear eyes, and pink glow to her skin, and then noted too the way she sat with her hands folded calmly. I gathered that Mrs Ninian of Aitkens' was pretty much gone.

'Peace,' I repeated, thinking that she had been due some, always worrying and scrabbling and fearful that the price she had paid was too high for whatever she had won.

'Poor Bella,' murmured Mary. 'Prison.' She looked around herself at the sunny room and the view of the gardens with the little white cottages dotted all around. Then she sat forward and gave me a closer look, a faint echo of Mrs Ninian from the old days. 'Jack?' I wondered what she knew and wondered even more what to tell her. As if reading my thoughts, she thumped herself on the chest. 'Strong,' she said. 'Brave. Now.'

'You always were brave,' I answered. 'And strong. Very well. Jack is living with Hilda Haddo at Abbey Park. And Fiona too. They seem to be running Aitkens' together. Lots of changes.'

'Pretty,' said Mrs Aitken, and it was halfway to a question.

I nodded. 'Pretty as a sugarplum,' I said. 'Does it upset you?'

'A shop,' she said. 'Building. Money. Pff!' She batted it away from herself with a backwards flap of her hand. Then she looked beyond me and her smile widened again. I turned. Abigail Aitken was there, dressed in starched blue cotton with her heavy hair plaited and pinned to her head.

'Mrs—' I bit my tongue. 'Abby,' I said and stood to embrace her. Then I held her at arm's length. 'You look like a nurse.'

'I am a nurse,' she said, laughing a little. 'Well, a nurse's help, anyway. I'll never forget how hopeless I was that day when Mother was first ill and how splendid you were. I was determined to make improvements!' She beamed at me. 'Besides, it's the only way we can afford to stay here.'

'I don't blame you for wanting to,' I said, looking around again. 'It's lovely.'

'The sisters,' said Abigail and the seal flipped inside me again, but I had misunderstood her. 'The sisters are very devout but really quite jolly. Most of them are a lot jollier than me!'

'Get there,' said Mary, and Abigail patted her shoulder and bestowed a smile on her that had as much devout devotion as filial devotion in it. I could see Abigail Aitken going from nurse's help to nun, if Mary lived long enough to give her the chance of it.

'So, Mrs Gilver,' she said, 'shall we go over now and then come back and have luncheon with Mother?' I nodded and, although I had thought my steeling myself was subtly done, Mary leaned over and took my hand again.

'All right,' she told me and squeezed hard.

We made for a cottage quite a way from the main house beyond a stand of spreading oaks, in a little green dip of land with a view of a pond. Abigail opened the gate in the white fence and ushered me ahead of her.

'Just go in,' she said. 'They're expecting you.'

My heart was hammering as I lifted the latch and opened the front door into a tiny hallway.

'In here, Mrs Gilver,' a voice called. I turned to the left and entered the sitting room.

'Oh my!' I said and before I could stop them my eyes filled with tears and spilled over.

They must have been in their fifties by now, but their faces were unlined by any worries and unmarked by troubles overcome, so that they looked like children still. Soft brown hair growing in feathery wisps and bright eyes in their three little heart-shaped faces, soft, slight little figures in their cotton dresses.

'This is Dora, my eldest,' Dulcie said, resting a hand on her daughter's shoulder. 'And Lucy. And this is Winifred. Smile for Mrs Gilver, girls.' All three of them gave me wide smiles of utter innocence and the vision flashed before my eyes of that photograph of Mirren at the party in her lacy dress with orchids in her hair. Then one of them – Lucy – put up her arms to me and I stepped forward to hug her.

'They don't speak, Mrs Gilver,' said Dulcie. 'Ruth was the only one of my girls who ever spoke. Mama, she would say.' Dulcie pointed to the chimneypiece where a photograph of another of these girls sat in a wooden frame.

'She had a heart attack,' Dulcie said. Absent-mindedly she lifted the little frame and polished it on her sleeve as I had seen her do with the arm of her chair at Roseville that day. 'And please don't look sideways at the frame. I would have solid gold and rubies, but someone' – she turned back to the room and put her hands on her hips – 'likes shiny things a little too much. Doesn't she, Winifred Hepburn, eh?' Winifred giggled but I rather thought she was responding to the smile and the sound of her name than the joke. She slipped down a bit in her chair with the laughing and Abigail hurried over to lift her up and pack her cushions around tightly again. Winifred, guilty as charged, it seemed, reached out and grasped the gold cross which swung free from Abby's neck as she bent forward. With infinite patience, Abigail tickled the girl's wrist until she let go again and then tucked the cross back inside her collar.

'Abigail is a born nurse,' said Dulcie, still smiling.

'I don't know about that,' said Abby. 'I like taking care of my sisters,' she said this a little shyly, 'but as for some of the ladies who come to recuperate for a month! I smile and do as I'm bidden but I say plenty under my breath in the sluice room, I can tell you.'

'I was a nurse in the war,' I said. It seemed to be what was expected, to sit and talk as though in any sitting room, in any company, while the three Hepburn sisters looked around and smiled and slowly lost interest in the new arrivals and returned to their inner calm. 'Soldiers. It was pretty horrid, sometimes.'

'Yes,' said Dulcie. 'We do very well here without men.'

'My sisters have hardly ever seen a man,' Abigail said. She used the word more boldly this time. 'I don't pity them.'

'They seem to be doing very nicely on it,' I agreed. 'And do you live here in the cottage as well, Mrs Hepburn?'

Dulcie nodded. 'Every third night one of the sisters comes instead and I go and sleep in the main house. Night-times can be difficult, you see. I used to have my own room, for when I visited, but now I share with my . . .' She stopped and both she and Abigail gave uneasy little laughs. 'We've been trying to decide,' she said. 'Something to say to stop questions from new staff, you know. God-daughter, I think we settled on, didn't we, Abby?'

I nodded, but inside I was beginning to shudder. Anything less godly than the relation between these two women was hard to imagine, one the by-blow of the other's husband and her son's mistress too. Thankfully I managed to think my thoughts while showing none of them. At least, perhaps Fiona Haddo would have said, 'Oh, I know,' and raised that arched eyebrow, but Dulcie and Abigail had half their attention on the three girls.

I left them soon afterwards, making my way alone back to Mary in the sunroom. Which path would I have taken if life had worked that way? If one could choose one's fate from a display on a shop floor and had it made up to fit one? Would I be Hilda Haddo playing at shops again in another store with another man in charge of me, or would I be Abigail Aitken, back in her mother's heart and with Dulcie as a second mother should Mary's frail health fail, here playing at houses in that little white cottage with three rosy-cheeked dolls?

Neither, I decided, and I would not be Jack nor Robin nor Fiona nor Bob nor, God knows, Bella. I rummaged in my pocket. Miss Armstrong had been keeping these tucked away on her private shelf in the staff cloakroom all through the closing, refitting and reopening of the Emporium. I rubbed my thumb over the black letters, feeling the good deep engraving and reading the words again with a swell of pride. *Gilver and Osborne. Servants of Truth.*

I would not even swap places with Alec. I was very glad indeed that, out of everyone around, I was me.

Postscript

15th May 1927

Darling,

I wish you would tell me what is wrong. I cannot imagine what it is I have done to make you angry with me or what someone might have said to turn you against me so. If you refuse to meet me or speak to me when I ring you up how can I make it right again? I know that you love me as I love you and I am going to trust that whatever has happened to upset you it will pass and you will be my same old darling again soon.

Your Dearest xxx

17th May 1927

Dearest,

We have had more happy times this spring than some people get in their lifetimes and must count ourselves fortunate for them. I will treasure the memory of your love as long as I live. I am not what you thought I was and not what I myself thought I was either. I cannot explain and I must not see you again but you surely know that my heart is yours for ever.

Your Darling xxx

Facts and Fictions

Abbey Park at 15 Abbey Park Place is a real house in Dunfermline. Once a bank, later the headquarters of the Carnegie Trust, in 1927 it was owned by an American by the name of Bishop. I have evicted Dr Bishop and moved the Aitkens in.

Aitkens' Emporium and the House of Hepburn are imaginary. Hepburns' is imagined to be diagonally oppposite the tolbooth and Aitkens' is next door to the Guildhall.

Bank House and Roseville are based on two real houses in Dumfries and Galloway which I have hauled north and plopped down in Dunfermline where I needed them, opposite the Guildhall and in place of Broomfield Drive respectively.

Needless to say, none of the Aitkens or Hepburns (or others in the book) are based on real people, except for Lynne McWilliam of the Gowns Department at Aitkens', who got her name courtesy of Mrs Lynne McWilliam of New Abbey, the winner of a character name competition. My good luck with suitable winning names continues.